The thought emerged from the shadowy recesses of her mind, a thrill of fiery excitement uncoiled within Joanna. She was alive—truly alive—and being given the chance to taste this fruit of heaven before reaching her life's end.

With a surge of rapturous delight, she tightened her arms around his neck, matching and returning the pressure of Gavin's demanding mouth.

"I think the devil has possessed my soul," he said hoarsely in her ear. Pressing her against the wall, Gavin took hold of her wrists and brought them down to her sides. His voice was ragged with desire. "Tell me to stop, Joanna, before I carry you to my bed." His powerful hands gently cradled her face as he tipped her head back and stared into her eyes. "You *are* flesh and blood. And for too long I have looked at you, fancied you, dreamed of making love to you."

Joanna stared into his chiseled face, his black burning eyes. "Then do with me what you desire. . . ."

Flame

by

May McGoldrick

A TOPAZ BOOK

TOPAZ
Published by the Penguin Group
Penguin Putnam Inc., 375 Hudson Street,
New York, New York 10014, U.S.A.
Penguin Books Ltd, 27 Wrights Lane,
London W8 5TZ, England
Penguin Books Australia Ltd, Ringwood,
Victoria, Australia
Penguin Books Canada Ltd, 10 Alcorn Avenue,
Toronto, Ontario, Canada M4V 3B2
Penguin Books (N.Z.) Ltd, 182–190 Wairau Road,
Auckland 10, New Zealand

Penguin Books Ltd, Registered Offices:
Harmondsworth, Middlesex, England

First published by Topaz, an imprint of Dutton NAL,
a member of Penguin Putnam Inc.

First Printing, November, 1998
10 9 8 7 6 5 4 3 2 1

 REGISTERED TRADEMARK—MARCA REGISTRADA

Printed in the United States of America

To Selma E. McDonnell,
and to
Colleen Admirand, Jody Allen, Edith Bron Chiong,
Sharon Hendricks, and Carol Palermo
for having faith in us every step of the way.

Prologue

Ironcross Castle
The Northern Highlands

MAY 1527

As the full moon began to rise from behind the distant brae, the shadows stretched up like gnarled, grasping fingers on the pale walls of the castle.

The shadow makers, on a nearer hill, began to descend from the summit, forming a line and moving toward the fortress. The sound of low chanting that had come in whispers on the ragged breeze died as the last of the dark figures disappeared amid the tumbled piles of slablike rock in the gorge beneath the castle walls. At the bottom of the gorge, the waters of the loch shimmered in the moonlight.

Moments later, far beneath the castle's massive walls, a heavy iron lock clicked, and a squat, thick, oaken door swung open.

In through the entryway the cloaked figures filed, silent as death. One after another they took unlit candles from a stone recess just inside the door. No light illuminated the darkness, but the line of figures continued relentlessly along the stone arched passageway.

A hundred paces further, the leader turned and proceeded down a half dozen steps into a vast, almost circular room. The open space of the vault was broken with pillars that rose into branchlike arches, supporting a low ceiling blackened with smoke and ash. On the far side of the room, beyond an unlit pyre of reeds and sticks, a stone table stood, an ornate cup and an oil lamp upon it.

One by one, the cloaked figures approached the table and lit their candles at the lamp. Then, moving to the crypts that lay along the perimeter of the vault, they all touched their foreheads to the stone before returning and forming a wide circle.

Hidden in the deep shadows of a niche not a half dozen steps from the stone table, a ghostly figure peered out at the ritual. The leader of the cult picked up the cup and then moved to her place beside the pyre. The onlooker pressed back further into the blackness as the leader's eyes swept around the circle.

"Sisters!" the woman called, waiting until she had the group's rapt attention. "For the souls of these dead who lie here entombed, we invoke the Power."

"Mater!" the women's voices proclaimed in response. "We invoke the Power."

"Sisters! For ourselves, in memory of their pain, we invoke the Power."

"Mater! We invoke the Power."

"Sisters! On the evildoers, with justice for a crime unrepented. We invoke the Power!"

"Mater! We invoke the Power."

As the woman continued, the gathering chanted their responses to her incantation, and the spectator looked on in horror. Minutes passed. Higher and higher their voices climbed, their bodies beginning to sway and jerk like branches bending to an unseen wind.

Finally with a wild shriek, one knelt by the pyre and lit the brush. With a crackling roar, the reeds ignited and the blaze lit up the crypt in an orgy of shadows and light. The circle broke down into a dancing, spinning frenzy of moans and howls.

"Sisters," Mater cried out above their voices as their wild pace began to slow. "Generations pass, my sisters, but once again, at the turning of the moon, we have fulfilled our vow to remember."

"We remember," the throng answered.

"We remember," Mater repeated, raising the cup high over her head before pouring the crimson liquid into the flames. Around her, the women fell to the stone floor, as if senseless, and the only sound was the crackling hiss of the fire.

Moments later, the women rose as one, and Mater addressed them once more.

"Tonight, my sisters, I have tidings to convey to you, for I have learned that a new laird is coming."

A murmur swept through the gathering, and the figure hidden in the niche edged forward as far as possible without being discovered.

"As we have seen in the past, evil stamps the souls of men." Mater's voice sank into a harsh whisper. "We all remember the reason for our vow, the reason for our gathering. We all remember, my sisters!"

The throng shifted excitedly.

"Once again, as we have since that night, we must carry on our tradition."

Mater raised her candle, and the onlooker saw its flame reflected in the eyes of the followers. A chill swept through the ghostly watcher.

"Let the curse fall where it may . . . we will remember!"

Chapter 1

Stirling, Scotland

"'Tis a wish for death to go there, Gavin, and you know it!"

Gavin Kerr pretended to ignore his friend's angry concern. Moving from one painting to the next, the black-haired giant continued to study the splendid canvases adorning the walls of Ambrose Macpherson's study.

"At least a dozen deaths in the past half year!" Ambrose growled. "Think, man! The last laird and his family died miserable deaths in that hideous pile of rock. By the saints, Gavin, no laird of Ironcross Castle has died of old age for centuries!"

"Ambrose, your wife has an astonishing gift—"

"We are discussing your foolishness in going to Ironcross just now," Ambrose interrupted.

"Aye, but these faces touch me nearer to the heart." Gavin reached up as if to run his fingers over the swirling colors of the canvas. In the portrait, a young child's face glowed as she looked lovingly at an infant in her arms. "Bonnie Jaime! She has grown so much since I saw her last. And Michael, already a strapping lad . . ."

Ambrose leaned on the table that separated the two of them. "Gavin, we are not discussing Elizabeth and my children. We are here to talk you out of accepting this curse of a gift that the Earl of Angus has bestowed upon you. Can't you see the Lord Chancellor is trying to be rid of you?"

"Nay, Angus would have no trouble thinking of easier ways of disposing of me than by making me laird of a Highland castle." Gavin ran a hand over his chin before moving to the next painting. "Though I should consider this reward more of a dishonor, considering the natural dislike I have for all Highlanders—with the exception of your family, of course," he added, grinning over his shoulder at Ambrose.

As the Highlander opened his mouth to speak, the door of the study opened and Elizabeth Macpherson walked quietly into the room. Like a full moon rising through the night sky, the young woman's entrance brightened the dark features of her husband's face.

"I see my prayer that you two might have settled this dreadful affair by now was for naught," she scolded with a smile. With a slap to Gavin's arm, Elizabeth moved around the table and nestled comfortably against her husband's side.

The news of his preferment had spread quickly through the court, so Gavin was hardly surprised at Elizabeth's sudden entrance. His friends clearly intended to overpower him with this show of force.

"To suit you, Gavin Kerr," Elizabeth said, "I've already had black cloths drawn across the windows at this end of the house—to shut out all light—and had the children moved to the west wing of the house—to eliminate any other signs of life."

"To suit me, Elizabeth?" Gavin repeated. "I cannot stay."

"But you *are* staying," the young woman said matter-of-factly. "I assume the only reason for you to abandon your own lands and go to Ironcross Castle is that you are once again seeking to withdraw from the world."

"You mean, my love," Ambrose put in, "that this pig-headed Lowlander is once again beset by those dark and melancholy thoughts in which he retreats from all decent folk, hating one and all . . . and himself!"

Elizabeth smiled. "Aye. So I thought to myself, handsome as he is in his new kilt, there certainly can be no need for him to travel so far into the wild and dangerous northern Highlands. After all, *we* could provide him with the same misery—I mean, the same hermit's retreat—right here with us!"

"You will not be swaying me from my decision to go."

Gavin looked gently at the two before him. Elizabeth's swelling stomach spoke of the imminent arrival of their third child. "You've enough to be thinking about, as 'tis. And my men are ready. A message has been sent to Ironcross Castle and to my neighbor, the Earl of Athol. I am expected there a fortnight from now, so whatever you two say will make no difference." He paused before continuing. "Besides, 'tis not any wish to become a hermit nor any desire to die, either, that compels me to go. But there is something."

Gavin hesitated, considering his next words, knowing that the truth would hardly make them worry less. After the devastating losses he'd suffered at Flodden Field, he had been left with no family, and there was no one closer to him than these two people. And he also knew that their concern for his well-being ran much deeper than his own.

Gavin started again. "A noblewoman came to me a fortnight ago. At the time I was still considering the Lord Chancellor's offer of Ironcross Castle. This woman who came to see me was old and infirm. She said you would remember her, Elizabeth. Lady MacInnes." Gavin paused as her expression softened, and Ambrose put a comforting arm around her. "Even before meeting her, I knew that Ironcross Castle was a MacInnes holding, that it had been in her family for years, but she told me that, after the latest tragedy, Ironcross could crumble to dust."

Elizabeth slowly eased herself into a nearby chair. "Last summer she told me a horrible tale of losing a husband and two sons in a number of strange accidents on castle lands."

"Aye. All her menfolk but one," Ambrose added grimly. "And she lost the third son in that fire, too, since then. Along with his wife and daughter."

Gavin nodded gravely in acknowledgment. "Aye. She told me that her granddaughter had been very fond of you."

"I shall always remember Joanna," Elizabeth whispered. "She was so full of life. A truly lovely young woman. And strong. Ready for whatever life might bring. She was to wed this spring—to the Earl of Huntly's nephew, James Gordon. But that is finished now. A life's dreams gone in an instant.''

"The reason for Lady MacInnes's visit, my friends, was not so much to retell those tragedies, but to ask a favor of me." Gavin Kerr turned and looked again at the paintings hanging on the wall. "She said that her granddaughter came to you to sit for a portrait last summer." He turned and found Elizabeth's gaze upon him.

"Aye, that she did," she answered. "And they took the portrait to Ironcross, I understand."

Gavin looked steadily at his two friends. "The old woman wants the painting. She is too old, she says, to make the journey to Ironcross Castle . . . even to visit their tomb. She cares nothing for what's left of the castle. She has no concern for what I do with it. The only thing she asks is that if the painting of her granddaughter escaped the flames, she'd like me to have it conveyed to her."

Ambrose looked at the Lowlander intently. "If that's the sole reason for you to go, then you can send a messenger and a group of your men to see to the task. There is no reason for you—"

"But there *is* a reason for me to go," Gavin interrupted. "There was something else she said that made me decide to go there myself."

He paused. The two before him stared in silence, awaiting his next words. "Lady MacInnes says that although 'tis unnatural how many of her kin have died there, she still believes that the curse of Ironcross Castle lies not in the realm of ghosts and goblins. There is evil there, she says, 'tis true. But the evil is human."

Gavin let out a long breath. " 'Tis time someone sought the truth."

Chapter 2

The charred shutter, high in the ruined tower, suddenly banged open as the afternoon breeze moved around to the west, and the golden rays of sunlight tumbled into the scorched chamber.

Huddled in the corner of a pile of straw, a startled figure pulled her ragged cloak more tightly around her. Even though it was late spring, she found it more and more difficult to shake off the chill that had crept into her bones. Perhaps it was because she so rarely saw the sun, she thought. For she was now a creature of the night, a mere shadow.

She shivered slightly, acknowledging the gnawing pangs of hunger in her belly. She shook her head, trying to dispel the feeling. There would be no food until tonight, when the steward and the servants that had remained since the fire all slept. Then she would partake of her nightly haunt. Then she would search the kitchens for some scrap that might sustain her.

Those remaining in the castle thought her a ghost. What fools they would think themselves if they only knew how human her needs were.

The wood plank continued to bang against the blackened sill, and she glared at it. This was her rest time, she silently scolded the troublesome shutter. Like the bats and the owls, Joanna thought. For it was only under cover of darkness that she could move about freely in this burned-out prison she had once called home.

Pulling herself to her feet, the ragged creature moved silently across the floor. As she neared the offending shutter, she was suddenly aware of the sound of horses in the distance. Shouts came from the courtyard below, and as she listened, the yard below seemed to explode in a frenzy of activity.

Taking hold of the shutter with her swathed hands, Joanna eased it shut without peering below.

The doomed man, she thought. The cursed laird had arrived.

The pawing hooves of the tired horses against the soft ground raised a gray cloud that swirled about the riders' heads. Gavin Kerr lifted his eyes from the approaching grooms and stared at the huge iron cross fastened to the rough stone wall above the archway of the great oak entry doors. From the blood-red rust stains on the stone beneath the cross, the new laird judged that it must have hung there for ages. Tearing his eyes away, Gavin glanced around at the buildings facing the open courtyard.

The castle itself was far larger than he'd expected. Stretching out in angles of sharp stone, the series of huge structures wrapped around the courtyard like a hand ready to close. Far above, small slits of windows pierced the walls of the main building as well as the north wing. The south wing's upper windows were larger. A newer addition, he thought. Gavin let his eyes travel slowly over what he could see. There was no sign of the fire that had claimed the life of the previous laird, his family, and their servants. The winter sleet and rains had scoured the stone of any trace of smoke, no doubt.

He caught the movement from the corner of his eye— the slow closing of a shutter in the tower at the top of the south wing.

Men approaching, however, drew Gavin's attention earthward again. The tall one scolding the running grooms had to be Allan, steward to the last four MacInnes lairds. The man's graying hair and beard bespoke his advanced years, while his powerful frame—slightly bent though it was—told of a strength necessary for the position he had held for so long.

Dismounting from his horse, Gavin nodded to a groom and handed off his reins as he exchanged greetings with the bowing steward.

"You did indeed arrive just as we had expected, m'lord. Not a day too soon nor a day too late." The old man's hands spread in invitation toward the entrance of the castle. "I took the liberty a day or so ago to have Gibby, the cook, begin preparing a feast for your arrival."

He paused as a dozen household servants, along with a dwarfish, sickly looking priest, came out to welcome the new laird.

"Your neighbor, the Earl of Athol," Allan continued, "has been quite anxious for you to arrive, m'lord. If you wish, I can send a man over now and invite—"

"Nay, Allan. That can wait for a day or two." Gavin's gaze took in once again the towers at either end of the courtyard. "While my men settle themselves in, I want you to take me through this keep."

The older man nodded his compliance as he fell in step with the new laird, who was striding toward the south tower. "You might, m'lord, wish to start in the main part of the house—what we call the Old Keep— and work toward the kitchens and the stables in the north wing. There is very little to see in the south wing."

Gavin halted abruptly, glanced up at the south tower, and then looked directly at the steward.

"Much of this wing was ruined by the fire, m'lord," Allan explained quickly. "From the courtyard, it looks sound, but inside, especially where the wing joins the Old Keep, the damage was extensive. The roof is gone in some places, and I've had the outside entrances to the building barred to keep—"

"Barred?" Gavin interrupted, staring at the tower.

"Aye. The worst of the damage is on the far side, though, where the tower looks over the loch. That's where they were all sleeping when the fire started, God rest their souls. By the time the rest of us in the Old Keep and the north wing smelled the smoke, the whole south wing was ablaze."

Gavin strode to the stone wall and peered through the slits of the lower windows. He could see shafts of light coming through the rafters of the floors above.

"Why do you allow servants into this wing?" Gavin

asked shortly, making the old man's face suddenly flush red. "Those upper floors look dangerous, even from here."

"No living person, m'lord, has stepped foot in this wing since the fire. I myself had all the doors barred and the inside corridors walled up. With the exception of some badger . . . or a fox, perhaps . . ." His voice trailed off.

Gavin stepped back from the building and looked upward at the windows in the tower, his eyes finally coming to rest on the last one in the top floor. "I saw the shutter in that chamber move."

The steward stared briefly at the tower windows, then looked at his new master.

"Aye, m'lord. We see the same thing from time to time, but 'tis just the wind." As the new laird moved along the front of the edifice, Allan followed along. "The smoke was everywhere, and the stairwells leading up to it are ruined. Of that I'm certain. The roof there may be sound, though, and a bird or two may have taken up lodging there. And wings are what you'd be needing to make your way into the tower."

Gavin peered up again at the looming tower. A number of shutters were banging against stone in the rising breeze. Nature, it appeared, had the upper hand in every window . . . but one. The window that he had seen open before, now stood closed against the north wind.

So the birds of the Highlands can latch a shutter, Gavin thought to himself. Turning without another word, he started for the main entrance of the Old Keep, his steward in tow.

No one ever dared step into her domain.

The crumbling, fire-damaged roofs, the gaping holes in the walls overlooking the sheer cliffs of Loch Moray, and the scorched, unsteady floors all combined to make the south wing of Ironcross Castle a forbidding place to enter. But as Joanna made her way quietly through a blasted room toward the wooden panel and the secret passageway that would take her down to the subterranean tunnels and caverns, she suddenly sensed that someone had been through there, and quite recently.

She paused and looked about her in the encroaching dusk. There was little to be seen. Dropping softly to her hands and knees on a plank by the doorway, she peered closely at the ash-covered floor of the passage beyond the door. She herself always avoided those corridors for fear of being discovered by some intrepid soul snooping in this wing.

Squinting in the growing gloom, she saw them clearly—the faint imprints left behind by someone coming from the Old Keep. Whoever it was had gone in the direction of her father's study—or what was left of it. Quietly, Joanna rose and, hugging the wall, followed the passage toward the study.

Standing rigidly beside the door, she peeked inside the charred room. The chamber was empty. She peered into the murky light of the corridor again. Since she had just come from the top floor, whoever had come in here must have continued on and descended the nearly impassable stairwell to the main floor.

Relieved, she wrapped her cloak tightly about her and glanced inside the study again. Her chest tightened with that familiar sorrow as she stepped inside the fire-ravaged chamber. Nothing had changed here since that terrible night. All lay in ruin. Hanging from one wall were the scraps of burned rag that had once been a tapestry. Elsewhere a scorched table and the broken sticks of a chair. Everything ruined.

Everything but the foolish portrait hanging over the mantel of the fireplace. She stared loathingly at the face that smiled faintly back at her. Her throat knotted at the sight of herself, of the picture of perfection she had once been. What vanity, she thought angrily.

She wanted to cross the room and take hold of the fire-blackened frame. She wanted to pull it down, smash it, destroy it as it should have been destroyed long ago. But the unsteady floor stopped her approach. From experience, she knew every loose board, every dangerous plank. Nay, she hadn't survived this ordeal so long just to break her neck falling through the floor. But those

eyes dared her. Challenged her to come ahead. She
hated that painting. Why should this blasted thing survive when no one else had? No one, including herself.

As a tear welled up, Joanna dashed at the glistening
bead. Turning away from that vain and beautiful face,
she pulled her hood forward and headed for the darkness of the passages that would take her deep into the
earth, where no one would see what she had become—
a ghostly shadow of the past, a creature of the night,
burned and ugly, miserable. Dead.

Disappearing into the dark, Joanna MacInnes thought
once again of her poor mother and father, of all the
innocent ones who had perished in the blaze with them.

Well, it was her destiny, now, to hide and await her
chance for justice.

As the fire's embers burned out beneath, a huge log
crashed down, sending cackling flames and sparks flying
in the Great Hall's huge fireplace.

The new laird's face was in shadow as he looked
around at the young features of the three men sitting
with him. Scattered about the Great Hall, servants and
warriors slept on benches and tables, and a number of
dogs lay curled up amid the rushes covering the stone
floor. Most of the household was already asleep, either
here or in the stables and outbuildings, but Gavin had
kept these three trusted warriors with him. In the short
time since they had all arrived, these men had been
tasked with determining what needed to be done to secure the castle. Each man had gone about his business,
and now the Lowlander leaned forward to hear them.

Edmund began. "I heard with my own ears the steward passing on your wish to have the south wing opened
for you to view in the morning—"

"Aye," Peter broke in, gruff and impatient. "And a
couple of the grooms and the old smith hopped to the
task of pulling down one of the blocking walls."

"The steward has fine control of the castle folk," Edmund added admiringly.

"That he does," Peter agreed. "Though a body would
think barring a door might have been plenty good

enough. Building a wall to stop trespassing!'' The thick-set warrior spat critically into the rushes on the floor. "Why, most of the servants are too old even to lift a latch unaided!''

Gavin interrupted the two men. "I can see Allan's concern. He told me that after the fire, he wanted to be sure that no one would go in that wing, not until such time as Lady MacInnes or the next laird came along to go through what was left.'' The Lowlander sat back and lifted a cup as he looked about the silent hall. "With so many accidents plaguing the lairds over the years, I am certain it shows good judgment to leave everything untouched. What did you find, Andrew?''

Andrew cleared his throat and spoke. "In my ride over to the abbey, m'lord, I ran into some of the Earl of Athol's men heading north. They all spoke of how strange it was here after the fire. None of the last laird's warriors stayed behind, they said. It seems that they all fled into the mountains as if they had the devil himself on their tails.''

Gavin drained his cup and put it back on the table as he turned to Andrew. "What can you tell us of the abbey?''

"'Tis an odd place, that abbey. Nary a league from here, following the shore of the loch, but 'tis nothing but a heap of stones and ruined wall in the shelter of the high hills. The place is surrounded by pasture and farmland and some crofters' cottages, though there is an odd lack of farm folk about the place.''

"But they are religious there, we were told.''

"That I don't know, m'lord,'' Andrew replied. "Those who remain live in the center of the ruined cloister, in stone cottages they've patched together from the old buildings.''

"Is there an abbot, or someone in charge?'' Gavin pressed.

"Aye, a woman they call Mater.''

"A woman?'' Peter blurted out.

"Aye,'' Andrew responded slowly. "They're all women there. All that I saw before they disappeared, at any rate." He paused. "And that abbey, m'lord, seems quite unprotected, sitting there in open as 'tis!"

"And isn't that like these Highlanders," Peter huffed, "leaving a pack of women . . ."

Gavin felt the hackles on his neck rise as his attention was drawn to the far end of the Great Hall. In a dark corner by the passage into the kitchens and the north wing, something had moved. A shadow . . . something . . . he was certain of it. Peering into the darkness, the firelight at his back, Gavin studied the sleeping figures on the benches as he continued to listen to his men. The servants had been dismissed hours ago. Other than the three men sitting with him, it was unlikely that anyone else in the keep would be roaming about.

"I took it upon myself, m'lord, to tell Mater that you would be stopping by yourself in a day or two. To pay them a visit."

"That's fine," Gavin answered. He shook his head slightly at his fanciful imaginings and filled his cup with more ale. He was tired, he decided, dismissing the notion with a last glance at the far end of the Hall. His first night in Ironcross Castle, and already he was falling prey to the strangeness of the place. Suddenly, he realized one of the dogs had come slowly to his feet. The gray cur trotted toward the kitchens. Pushing the mug away, the laird came to his feet as well.

"Also, the Earl of Athol's men mentioned that he'd be giving you a visit before the week's end." Andrew's eyes followed his leader as Gavin rounded the table where they sat. " 'Tis only a day's ride, they said, and if that's unsuitable—"

"That's fine," Gavin answered absently without turning around. "All three of you, get your rest. There is a great deal to be done tomorrow."

The three men watched in silence as their master walked quietly toward the darkened kitchens.

These newcomers were going to be more than a nuisance, she thought. They were going to be downright dangerous. And there were so many of them.

Coming out of the passages after the sounds of feasting had died away, Joanna had been surprised by the number of people remaining in the Great Hall. From past experience she knew that she would have more chance of finding food there than in the kitchens, but clearly that plan would no longer work. She only hoped the usually tightfisted Gibby had not locked everything away, as was her custom.

Entering the kitchens, Joanna peered into the corners for stray sleepers, but with the warmer weather, not a body was in evidence. The embers in the huge fireplace flickered, and she could see the rows of bread dough rising into loaves on a long table.

Moving to a sideboard, she found a large bowl with broken scraps of hard bread. Scooping out a handful, Joanna placed the bread carefully in the deep pocket of her cloak, then cocked her head to listen. With more people around, she would have to be far more careful than she had been in the past. Being discovered would mean the end of her plans. It would be the death of her only wish—the one that had been driving her to hang on to her threadbare existence. If she were discovered, there would surely be no dispensing of justice to those who had murdered her parents. Of that she was certain.

Joanna glided silently down through the kitchen, and then paused with a sigh by a locked larder. The gentle nudge of the dog's nose against her hip made the young woman's heart leap in her chest. Shaking her head as the corners of her mouth lifted in a wry smile, she crouched down to pet the gentle beast. All the dogs in the castle were quite accustomed to her, but shaggy Max was the only one that ever came to her. Accepting a wet kiss on the chin, Joanna gave the dog's head an affectionate pat. Wordlessly, she straightened and continued her search for more food.

The heavenly smells of bannocks and roasted mutton still hung in the air, making her mouth water, but to her dismay there was nothing else left over that she could find. High in the rafters, she could see the dark shapes of smoked meat, but she didn't dare be so bold as to steal anything that would raise a hue and cry. Hearing Max sniffing in a dark corner, Joanna spotted two balls

of cheese hanging from strings on a high pegboard, just
out of the dog's reach. Gratified at the chance to add
something different to her spare diet, she reached for
them.

"I am certainly sorry you'll have to shoulder the
blame for both of these," she whispered with a smile to
the happy dog. "But you can only have one." Rolling
his share playfully along the stone floor, Joanna placed
the other in the pocket of her cloak.

The dog leapt across the kitchen after it, but suddenly
stopped short, and the deep growl emanating from his
throat sent Joanna scurrying for cover. Quietly, she
moved into the deep shadows behind the giant fireplace,
to the narrow door that led down into the root cellars.
From there she could get into the labyrinth of passages
beneath the castle, but she paused for a moment, her
hand on the panel, ready to run if the need arose.

"What are you hiding there, you mangy cur?" The
man's voice was deep and strangely gentle. "Just you
and the hearth fairy, eh?"

Joanna pressed her face against the warm stone of the
chimney as she listened. From the dog's friendly panting
and the man's deep-throated chuckle, she could tell the
newcomer had already won over the animal's affection.

"Och, I can see already you are in for trouble. A thief
you are, is that it? A piece of cheese. A capital crime,
if that cook finds out, lad. Hmm. I'll not throw it for
you, you slobbering beast."

Joanna knew she should go, but she couldn't. Curiosity was pulling at her, driving her with a desire to put a
face to that voice.

"So, you want to play! You want me to chase you, is
that it?"

He had to be one of the new laird's men. She could
imagine him leaning against the edge of the long heavy
table in the center of the kitchen.

" 'Tis too late in the night, you beast. Very well. Bring
it here, and I'll throw it for you. But once only, do you
hear me?"

The dog's low-pitched growl was now playful, and

again the man's deep chuckle brought a smile to her face.

"Smart, too. For a Highland cur!"

So they're Lowlanders, she thought. Scowling now, Joanna edged forward slightly and peeked at the man in the dim light of the dying fire. Just as she had imagined it, he was sitting on the edge of the table with his back to her. At the moment, he was preoccupied with wrenching the ball of cheese out of Max's mouth.

"Now, don't force me to get rough with you!"

She studied his broad shoulders. The warrior was larger, by far, than any of the men her father had kept in his service. The red of his tartan was muted and dark. As he stood up for a moment, she drew back, but he only crouched over the dog again. He was certainly a giant, and not just for a Lowlander. His long dark hair was tied with a thong at the nape of a strong neck. In wrestling with the dog, he turned his face, and she got a quick glimpse of his handsome profile. Suddenly, she was aware of a strange tightening in her chest. Drawing back further, she felt her face flush with heat. What was wrong with her? she thought, fighting for a breath.

What did it matter that the man was handsome, she thought with annoyance. What difference did that make to her, a ghost! In the dark of the kitchens, it was easy to let imagination control reality. In the light of day, he might be the ugliest man in Scotland, though she would never see it. Darkness. Perhaps it was the place for both of them, she thought angrily. Who knows, in the gloom of this chamber, he might not even see her deformities. Bringing a shaking hand up before her eyes, she gazed at it momentarily, and then pulled her hood forward over her face.

Nay, no one was that blind.

"As your laird, I order you to share that cheese. Och, you are a pig. You've eaten it all."

Laird! Quickly, Joanna drew back behind the hearth. Her face grim, she slipped through the panel and into the blackness of the passageway. Feeling her way down the stone steps, she continued past the wooden door that led into the root cellars. Silently, she made her way through the winding, narrow passages, down more carved stone steps, and through wide, cavernous openings until she was far from the kitchens. Climbing to the top of another set of steps, Joanna stopped, trying to catch her breath, and leaned back heavily against a rough-hewn wall.

Laird! She wished she had never laid eyes on him. It would be ever so much easier to mourn his death if she'd never seen him. The poor soul, she thought, starting to move quickly along the tunnel again. He wouldn't have a chance against the evil that surrounded him.

Chapter 3

The smell of fire and rot hung in the air like death.

" 'Tis a grievous thing for me to see Ironcross Castle like this, m'lord." Allan's voice was tight. "It looks sound enough from the outside, but in here . . ." The steward looked back at Gavin and shook his head.

Gavin said nothing, but motioned for Allan to continue up the circular stairwell. They had almost reached the second-floor landing, which was as far as they would be going. Gavin gazed upward through the twisted and charred timbers that had once been steps, into the steel-gray sky.

"Aye," Allan said, following his master's gaze. "Nothing to keep the rain out here."

The new laird grunted and climbed over a burnt beam. Reaching the landing, he pushed past the steward into the corridor.

"This part of the castle seems much newer than the rest," Gavin said gruffly. The destruction was extensive, though he was beginning to think the building might be saved. He would need to get his men in here clearing out the debris before they could make a good judgment about the soundness of the walls.

"Aye, m'lord," Allan responded. "This wing was built by Sir Duncan MacInnes, father of the last three lairds. God rest their souls."

Gavin looked at the splintered sections of the beams above. The ceilings were high in the south wing. On this floor, at least, the corridor faced out on the courtyard, and the long, narrow windows let in light and air. Some of the chamber doors to the right hung open at rakish angles, and cobwebs and filth were everywhere. "How did Duncan die?"

"Duncan?" the steward repeated, surprise evident in his voice. "Why, the poor soul." He paused. "That was so long ago. More than twenty years has passed since—"

"You were steward of Ironcross then, were you not, Allan?"

"Aye, m'lord!"

Gavin turned a critical stare on the man next to him. "You do not remember how your master died?"

"Aye, m'lord! Of course I do," Allan said quickly. "'Twas just a surprise, your asking! The poor soul cracked his skull in a fall from his horse. 'Twas a sad and mournful day for Ironcross Castle." The older man looked down at his feet. "Hunting, he was."

"Who was hunting with him?" Gavin moved slowly down the passage, testing the floors as he went, and Allan followed behind.

"Hunting with . . . ?" The steward scratched his head. "Well, we had a great deal more folk about the castle in those days. Let me see. I believe Alexander, the eldest lad, was with him. And the hunters and grooms, of course. Lady MacInnes was back at Stirling then. She spent very little time at Ironcross during those years. Now, I'm thinking . . . aye, Lord Athol, the father of the present earl, was with the party as well."

Gavin held up his hand. Farther down the corridor, from one of the last rooms, the sound of scraping could be heard. As Allan stared, Gavin quietly drew his dirk from his belt and pushed his tartan back over his shoulder. Before he had gone two steps, however, a rat moved out into the corridor, spotted them, and disappeared back into the room.

The new laird sheathed his dirk, and turned to the steward. "I want you to have the grooms and any lads you can gather do a wee bit of rat hunting. I don't care to be sharing my dinner or my bed with vermin. I want the castle kept clear of them."

"Aye, m'lord." Allan clearly was trying to hide his surprise at such eccentricity, but nodded in response. "As you wish."

Gavin hated rats. He knew they were everywhere, in every castle and hut in Europe. In Florence, Paris, and even the newly rebuilt Edinburgh, but he hated them, and he'd not have them in his keep, if he could help it.

Turning his back on the steward, Gavin looked into the chamber that they stood before. It, too, had been badly burned, and pieces of broken, charred furniture littered the room.

"This was the laird's study, m'lord," Allan offered. "Sir John, the previous master of Ironcross Castle, spent a great deal of time in this room. He was a great scholar—more so than his father or the two brothers who preceded him."

As Gavin turned to continue down the corridor, his eyes were drawn to a partially open door in the carved wood paneling just inside the study. Stepping into the chamber, the new laird moved casually over to the panel and pulled open the door. A small cabinet had been recessed into the wall, and several books lay on a shelf, completely undamaged by fire. Surprised, Gavin took them out of the cabinet.

"Ah, m'lord," Allan said apologetically, taking the books from the new laird's hand. "I should have taken them to the Old Keep after the fire. I am afraid I have been negligent in leaving off the care of this wing. But now that you are here, I shall . . ."

Gavin no longer heard the old steward. His gaze was fixed on the portrait hanging above the small fireplace, and everything else in the world suddenly ceased to exist. Locked on the object across the room, his eyes drank in the vision of the young lass's golden hair and ivory skin, the straight nose and the delicate mouth that showed only the hint of a smile. But it was the eyes, the deep blue eyes, that enraptured him. In spite of the dark smudges of soot that covered almost half of the painting, her nearly violet eyes twinkled, laughing, shining with the joy of life, with the pure radiance of youthful innocence.

" 'Twas Mistress Joanna, m'lord! Sir John's daughter."

Gavin started at the steward's voice, and turned to him.

"God rest her soul," Allan continued reverently. "She was a bonny lass, inside and out. 'Twas a waste for her to be taken so young."

Gavin turned his gaze back to the portrait. Joanna MacInnes.

"We only knew her here a short time, since the laird never allowed her to stay at Ironcross for too long. I know she was schooled in Paris—raised as a court lady. Though the lass liked her visits to the north country, Sir John was fixed on having her stay with his mother, Lady MacInnes, at Stirling." The steward shook his head. "Meeting her, m'lord, you'd have thought you were meeting an angel. All kindness and compassion, she was. Nothing like those ladies that Thomas, Sir Duncan's second son, would bring up here."

Gavin gazed again at her eyes. There was an openness in them, no hint of coyness.

" 'Twas very sad," Allan continued. "The loss of such a young woman as this."

Gavin took another step toward her, toward the painting.

"She was the first of the MacInnes ladies to show any interest in the women of the abbey."

Gavin took another step and then turned back to look at the steward.

"Tell me," the laird began, "did she and Mater—"

But he did not finish. Without warning, the floor opened and fell away beneath him.

Joanna sat bolt upright from beneath her covering of straw.

The bone-chilling crack gave way to a shuddering crash, and the entire south wing shook violently. With her heart pounding in her chest, she sat frozen, unable to move. It had to be the new laird. He was dead! Another life wasted . . . and for what?

Damn you, Joanna MacInnes, she swore under her breath. When will you find enough courage to put an end to this curse? How many more must die before you act?

* * *

"M'lord!"

Dangling high in the air, with his fingers barely holding on to the edge of a projecting beam, Gavin ignored the steward's shout and tried to swing his legs over the edge. On the second attempt, using another charred beam, he pulled himself onto the narrow remains of the burned flooring in the corner of the chamber.

"These floors, m'lord!" the steward called out from across the way, the distress evident in his voice. "Who could know what is sound? There was a good—"

"Enough, Allan!" Gavin ordered, pushing himself gingerly to his feet as he eyed the gaping hole in the middle of the room. "Go after some help. Edmund should be inspecting the curtain wall. At least bring back some rope with you." Upon seeing the older man hesitate, he ordered again. "Go, man, before the rest of this floor gives way!"

With a quick nod, the steward scurried off down the corridor toward the burned-out stairwell.

Alone, Gavin leaned back against the carved wood paneling and looked about the room. The thunderous hammering of his heart at last seemed to slow its pace. He had been very close to falling. Too close, he thought, peering at the wide gap and the considerable drop to the wreckage below.

Then he heard it clearly. The creak of a board above his head. Looking up, he surveyed the soot-covered ceiling. Another rat? It moved again. He tried to gauge the weight. If it was another of the vermin, it was a big one. And it was moving toward the wall he had his back to.

He listened intently. Silence. He waited, but only silence encompassed him.

The panel stuck slightly before giving way to the pressure of her hand. Joanna pushed it open hesitantly, listened for a moment, and then slipped into the darkness of the passageway between the walls.

The narrow tunnel was dimly lit, the only light coming from a small hole in the roof. Stealthily, Joanna moved to a ladder that led to the passageway below and eventu-

ally to the tunnels beneath the castle. Slowly and carefully, she made her way down, rung by rung, until she
reached the next level.

Standing on the narrow ledge, Gavin glanced along
the wall at the portrait hanging above the open hearth.
It was some distance from the corner where he stood.
For a moment he considered trying to get to it, but the
ledge was narrow and unstable.

A sound—a faint squeak of wood against wood—came
from the panel behind him, and, whirling around to face
it, the warrior chief nearly went over the edge.

Quickly regaining his balance, Gavin pressed himself
into the corner and started inspecting the panels. One
clearly appeared to warp a bit beneath a carved edge
piece.

Joanna listened carefully for some sound from the
other side of the panel. She was fairly certain that the
crashing noise and the shouts had come from this chamber, but there was nothing to be heard now.

With her hand on the latch, she toyed with the idea
of waiting in the tunnels beneath the castle until dark
before venturing out. If the new laird was dead, there
was no use in exposing herself just to find out what
happened.

Something gnawed at her, though, and she could wait
no longer. Pushing at the warped edge, she released the
latch silently and started to pull the panel open.

Chapter 4

"**M**'*lord!*"
    The shout from the far side of the panel stunned Joanna with its nearness. What was worse, however, was the sight of the new laird's profile through the narrow opening, only a breath away. His face was turned toward the study, as the shout came again, clearly but from below.

Gaping at his profile, Joanna quickly shut the panel as quietly as she could. Sliding the latch, she pressed her palms against the wood and let out a soft, strangled breath. For the first time in months, she'd almost given herself away; she'd come face-to-face with the man. Pressing her forehead on her knuckles, she closed her eyes. She had to gather her strength. She had to run away. That was far too close! Her body shivered, and she was shocked to feel her knees about to buckle as she tried to rise.

Gavin turned back to the panel—his fingers traveling across the rough, scorched wood, checking every seam. He could have sworn a moment ago he'd felt it move.

"M'lord!" This time Edmund's breathless voice came from across the room. "The damn floor . . . By the Virg . . . what a mess . . . Gavin, are you hurt?"

There was something on the inside of this wall. Gavin could feel it. Could it be someone, he wondered. He knew of other castles that had secret passageways. And if there was one, it would allow someone to travel through this wing. Gavin pulled back a hand and smashed it hard against the wall. He felt it move—not as part of the whole wall—but only the section. Pushing at a seam by the edge piece, a crack appeared. Beneath him the floor groaned ominously, and he eased the pressure. There was a shuffling noise on the other side of the panel. Pressing an ear to it, he could clearly hear movement. The sound of hurried steps.

"M'lord?"

Gavin ignored the man as he pressed his ear tighter against the wood.

"What's behind here, Allan?"

The old man paused a moment before blurting, "The wall?"

"You think me daft?" Gavin growled, turning a menacing glare on the man. "You were here when this wing was built. Are you telling me—"

"There *were* passageways built at the time," the old steward broke in quickly. "But only the laird knew . . . the passageways lead down to the caverns that honeycomb these hills, and down to the loch. But no one has used those caverns since Duncan's time, m'lord."

"How do you open this?" Gavin asked shortly. "This panel is an entry, is it not?"

When Allan paused, Edmund spoke. "M'lord, if you'll allow me at least to secure this rope, in case that floor—"

"How does this damn thing open?"

His angry roar got the old man talking. "In the cabinet . . . there at the corner by the outside wall . . . aye, that one . . . a wee iron ring . . ."

Gavin crouched carefully and reached inside. Running his fingers along the wood, he found the metal circle. Pulling it, he watched with satisfaction as the panel that he had been standing before only a moment earlier snapped open a crack.

"M'lord. You don't plan to go in there alone," Edmund said with alarm.

"Once you are beneath the castle, there is no rhyme or reason to the paths," Allan agreed. "In fact, one of the builder's apprentices disappeared in those tunnels. 'Tis dangerous, even for those who know the passages. There are chasms that have no bottom. The lad was never found, m'lord, and he was not the only one!"

Gavin moved toward the panel and pushed it open wide.

"Pray, m'lord," Edmund's voice was the more persistent. "Allow me, at least, to come with you. I've never seen a—"

"Find a way to get your rump up to the hearth." The Lowlander glanced over his shoulder at the redheaded warrior. With his eyes he motioned toward the portrait of Joanna MacInnes above the fireplace. "Take the painting to the Old Keep. Put it in my chamber."

Without another word, Gavin squeezed through the panel and disappeared into the darkness of the passage.

The slender back of the old woman bowed under the weight of the heavy satchels she carried. Dragging her feet another few steps through the mud, she spotted more herbs by a protruding boulder. Leaning one gnarled hand on the rock, she grasped the top of the plant and pulled. The stubborn root wouldn't let go.

Though the sun had broken through the heavy clouds, the air was thick with moisture from the rains. Tugging at the plant again, the woman wiped the dripping sweat from her eyes with the other hand, leaving a smudge of dirt on the fan of wrinkles by the exposed white hair at her temple. She gave a sigh of relief when the root let go at last. Wiping the dirt from the greens with one callused hand, she placed it carefully in one of the satchels before painfully straightening under their weight.

"Och, Mater," the low voice scolded from behind. "Why must you carry both bags in this sun. Let me give you a hand."

The old woman waved a hand dismissively in the air while continuing with her search. But she didn't fight when, a moment later, the younger woman reached her and silently took one of the satchels, swinging it over her shoulder.

"The rest of us could do more of this. There is no reason for you, at your age, to always do so much to take care of so many."

"There is," Mater said plainly as she bent down to tug at another root. "What news have you from the castle?"

"Molly has come to visit her sisters. She brought word. There was an . . . accident . . . this morning in the south wing. The laird insisted that Allan show him the fire damage in the south wing."

"I knew he wouldn't be able to stay away from there. What happened?"

"One of the floors collapsed beneath him. But he was not hurt."

Mater paused for a moment, nodded, and turned her steps down the valley toward the ruined abbey. "Anything else?"

The younger woman fell in step. "Just as his man told you yesterday, Molly says that the laird plans to pay the abbey a visit." The woman stared at the aging leader. "Will you see him, Mater?"

Mater stopped and looked up at the sky. "I have no choice. I will see him . . . if he still lives!"

The chapel perched, squat and ancient, on the edge of the cliff in the southeastern corner of the castle, with the gray waters of the loch below. Except for a low archway that had been built to give access to the small kirkyard, the construction of the south wing had completely cut off the little church from the castle's courtyard.

" 'Tis a miserable place," the pasty-faced little priest spat out, glaring at the building. "Hotter than hell in the summer, and windier than Luther's arse in the winter. 'Tis no wonder the peasants of the holding want nothing to do with it."

Aye, Gavin thought, glancing at the man's sour expression. No wonder.

"They have little faith in these hills, you know. 'Tis comfort they crave. Sir John MacInnes, the last laird, promised me that he'd rebuild the chapel, but he did no such thing."

"Show me the inside, Father William," Gavin ordered, striding toward the building.

"Aye, of course," the scrawny cleric replied, running to keep up. "Though I'll be hanged if you find anything to interest you there."

Gavin let that comment pass, though the priest's attitude was curious, to say the least. Father William pulled open the thick oak door.

"Not the way it once was. No faith. No sense of duty. Since the death of Sir John, I have watched as nearly all of his peasants . . . your peasants . . . packed up their wee ones and moved onto the Earl of Athol's land to the north."

But not all of them had left, Gavin thought. Not all. One of them, he was quite certain, was the "ghost" who was haunting the south wing.

Earlier, when Gavin had stepped into the narrow passageway in the study wall, he had easily found the ladder leading up to the top floor. The chambers above had obviously been comfortably designed and furnished, but now they were in shambles. Working his way through the rooms, the warrior had been quite careful to avoid any repeat of his near disaster in the study. Finally, he'd made his way up to the tower room where he had seen the shutter close.

There, the bed of straw, a scrap of burnt blanket, some rags, a wooden bowl told him that he had been correct. Someone had been taking shelter in the tower, and he had probably found his way into the castle and its passageways from the caverns below.

If what the priest had just said was true, then Gavin knew this stranger had to be a peasant. The Lowlander had investigated what passages he could in the burnt-out wing, but he had reluctantly put off exploring the tunnels leading below. He would need a torch, and preferably a guide, for that little expedition.

In fact, he thought, he could use a torch now. The chapel, dark and musty, offered little to refute the cleric's words. The few long, thin windows provided hardly any light or air in the sanctuary. No ornaments of value adorned the altar. Only a cross of wood, studded with iron nails, hung on the wall above it. That was all.

Surveying the rest of the interior, Gavin nodded toward the steps leading down into a dark alcove. "The crypt?"

"Aye, m'lord." The note of contempt in the man's response was obvious, and, though Gavin was unsure what it was directed toward, he was tiring quickly of the little man.

"Get a candle."

As the priest returned with a light, Gavin started down the steps into the crypt. It was a low, square chamber, with stone tombs lining the walls. Some were adorned with the effigies of knights, their carved stone swords beside them. As William kept up a running commentary on the relative superiority of past generations, Gavin discovered the low doorway into another area, and, taking the candle, led the way into the newer part of the musty chamber.

"Sir Duncan had this part built before my time here. That is his tomb, with the stone carving. His sons never had much opportunity to plan for their own burials."

"Where are Sir John and his wife and daughter?"

William's face looked yellow and quite unhealthy in the flickering light of the candle, and he seemed to hesitate before answering. He gestured with a toss of his head.

"In the kirkyard, m'lord."

Gavin stared at the man a moment. "I want to see where you've put them."

"Aye. This way."

As he and the priest retraced their steps, Gavin considered what would be involved in reinterring the previous lairds and their families in the crypt.

The sun that had broken through briefly in the early afternoon had once again been swallowed up by the clouds. As Gavin gazed out over the low wall that separated the kirkyard from the sheer cliffs above the loch, he could see the storm to the west sweeping in over Cairn Liath and Cairn Ellick, hiding their summits in a cloud. The wind had picked up considerably, and Loch Moray's waters were now a churning mass of whitecaps.

Gavin followed the little priest to a large slab by the cliff.

"Here, m'lord," Father William said brusquely. "We put them here. Close enough to Sir John's brothers. They lie over there." The man pointed at two other slabs not far away. "Sir John meant to have his brothers moved inside the crypt. As you can see, the good Lord didn't see fit to give him time for that."

Gavin looked back to the large slab before his feet. "You say all three lie here?"

The awkward pause in the priest's response was obvious, and the new laird turned his gaze on the man.

"Do they lie here?" he repeated.

"Aye, for all that we could tell."

"The bodies were burned?" Gavin asked.

"Aye," the priest replied with disgust. "Like hell's own demons, they were. All burnt. All lost . . ." The man's voice choked. "There were so many of them. The wing was filled with Sir John's servants and the ladies' maids . . ."

Father William faltered and came to a stop. Gavin crouched before the slab and placed a hand on the tomb. It felt strangely warm to his touch. In a moment the priest continued.

"We couldn't tell one from the other. We found no one in the laird's chambers nor in Mistress Joanna's room. Most of the bodies lay in a heap at the stairwell. Some of the maids, we think, may have tried to leap into the loch." The priest looked away at the turbulent waters. Drops of rain began to spatter the stones around them. "We found traces of blood and torn linen on the cliffs, but no bodies. It seems the rest all ran into the corridors. That's where we found them. All charred and heaped together."

"Were you able to recognize them?" Gavin came to his feet.

The man slowly shook his head. "Nay. The laird was a goodly sized man, though, so we could be fairly certain of him, and his body lay apart, with two women by him. So we wrapped those three and placed them here. The rest . . . the rest we buried there."

Gavin looked in the direction that the priest pointed. A dozen or so graves with new grass sprouting on the dirt mounds could be seen in the corner of the kirkyard. The little man walked unsteadily toward the graves and stared down at one set slightly apart from the others.

The rain was starting to fall harder now, but neither man took notice of it.

"Who is buried in that grave?" Gavin asked, following the other man's gaze. "The one away from the others?"

"Who?" The priest's head snapped around toward the other graves, his eyes avoiding the laird's gaze. "Why, one of the servants."

"Why is it separated? If they all died together, why bury this one apart?"

"Because she did not burn like the others," William answered irritably. "She was one of Lady MacInnes's serving lasses, and she broke her neck leaping from a window in the tower."

"Perhaps a better way to die," Gavin said quietly, looking intently at the carefully tended grave. "What was her name?"

"Her name?" The priest ran his hand over his eyes. "I cannot remember."

A bolt of lightning lit the sky.

"Iris!" he blurted quickly. "That's it. Iris, I believe 'twas."

Thunder rumbled after the earlier flash. A movement by the chapel drew Gavin's attention. A woman stood holding folded linens in her hands. Gavin recognized her as Margaret, the mute sister of the steward.

The little man mumbled something Gavin thought must have been an apology and hurried over to the woman.

The Lowlander turned his attention back to the graves at his feet. Death was something that he was no stranger to. As the laird gazed at the earthen mounds, it occurred to him that losing those he loved was something he'd been facing all his life. Strange, he thought, that some pain never ends.

He never knew his mother. She'd died bringing him into this life. His father and two older brothers had been rough tutors—they'd showed him a kind of love, one based on loyalty and strength and courage. But then, all three of them had been cut down in one day—fighting against the English at Flodden Field. He himself had been injured that day. He himself had faced death's raw visage. And if it hadn't been for Ambrose Macpherson saving his life, he would assuredly have had his throat cut by the battlefield scavengers.

Though that had not been his destiny that day, he wondered now—as he had wondered often since that day—if death held the only end to pain.

Gavin strode back to the slab, now nearly black with the falling rain. Small wisps of steam, like souls released, rose from the surface.

Staring at them, he thought of another grave. In his mind's eye he saw Mary, her dark hair swirling around her pale skin in the summer wind. She had been the only woman he'd ever allowed to get close to him. Odd, he thought, he had spent almost all of his life in the service of his king. A man of action, a man of war. He had seen the world, and he had known the beds of many women. But with Mary, he had known something else. He had learned about the yearning of two souls, about the opening of hearts. But then she had died as well. Her life snuffed out before his eyes. Taken from him—like all the others he had ever loved.

The rain suddenly began to fall in earnest. Driven by the wind, it lashed at his face.

Again, looking down at the dark stone covering the grave, Gavin felt the dying fire in his heart and knew the cold misery of his life.

For death awaited anyone ill fated enough to be loved by Gavin Kerr.

Chapter 5

S he was cold. She was miserable. He was a hateful man. He had taken away her shelter.

Cursing him, Joanna stepped out of the dark water of the underground lake. Shivering, she climbed the odd, stairlike rock formation onto the flat, stone slab where she had left her "new" clothes. Slipping into the shift, she quickly put on the dress she had also managed to steal from Gibby, the cook, earlier tonight.

Joanna glanced again at the dark stains on the rock, close to where she had laid her dress, and peered up into the darkness of the cavern ceiling far above her, wondering what could have produced such a mark on the rock. Shrugging, she turned her steps toward the small fire on the other side of the cavern, where she had made up a bed of rushes and straw stolen from the kitchens.

Picking up her old shift from the bed, Joanna tore a strip from it and tied it around her waist to gather in some of the oversized dress. Throwing her ragged cloak over her shoulders, she felt the warmth spread slowly through her, and a moment later, she pushed her long, golden hair to one side, wringing the water out and combing her fingers through her tresses. Then, with a deep sigh, she crouched as close as she dared to the small fire.

Absently watching as the light of the flame danced against the roof and walls of the cavern, Joanna's eye was suddenly drawn to what looked like markings on the cavern wall not far from where she sat. Taking a burning stick from the fire, she walked toward the wall and held the makeshift torch high. She could just make out figures—a cross and beneath it, the prone sticklike figure of a woman. Not far away, on a level with the woman, another stick figure could be seen clutching what looked like a head by the hair and, in the other hand, a large knife. Odd drawings, she thought, feeling a chill prickle along her neck and scalp.

Walking back to the fire, she seriously pondered who might have painted the figures. They looked like the work of a child. There were so few children anymore.

Seating herself again beside the small blaze, Joanna used more strips from her shift to wrap up her scarred hands. Then she let her mind drift back over all that had happened.

Late in the day, as she had crept as close as she dared in the concealing darkness of the tunnels, she had heard the sound of men in the south wing of the castle. The new laird seemed to have put every available hand in Ironcross Castle to work tearing away the wreckage. But in doing so, the damned Lowlander was taking away what little safety and comfort she had. The sound of axes chopping through burned wood and the ripping sound of plaster had filtered down to her. But then, at last, when it all had fallen silent for the night, Joanna had stolen back through the passages to her room in the tower in search of what she could salvage. All her meager possessions, even the rag she wore as a dress, had been cleared out.

Nothing had gone right since he'd arrived. Nothing. Joanna tried to ignore the rumbling growl of her stomach. Even her foray into the kitchen tonight had been a failure. Well, not a total failure. Gliding through the pitch-black chamber, she had been lucky enough to stumble on this old dress, folded on a bench in the corner. At least she wouldn't have to haunt the castle wearing only her shift.

Not a comforting image, she thought, gathering her knees to her chest. Her face clouded over. She had a bit more than a fortnight before the full moon. So few days to build her courage and finally go through with her plan of revenge. But until then, she wouldn't sit back and let this Lowland usurper ruin her existence. Not one bit, she thought, brightening.

From the time she was a bairn, she'd been hearing about the Ironcross curse. She'd heard the women talk of its ghosts. Aye, she knew the truth of it now.

But as for the ghosts, this Lowlander must be hearing some of the same tales.

A mischievous glint crept into her eyes. Let the shadows rise, she thought. Let the ghosts of Ironcross teach this laird a lesson about disturbing a spirit.

Still clothed in his wet garments, Gavin gazed out through one of the small open windows into the pitch black of the moonless night. During the day, one could see the loch from this chamber, as well as the trail of hills leading southward toward the abbey. On a night such as this, one could not even see the boulder-dotted gorge below, and the only sound was the pattering of the rain and the occasional echoing rumble of far-off thunder.

He was not to be disturbed, he'd said before retiring to the master's chamber of the Old Keep. In the morning, Andrew would ride north to Elgin and collect enough carpenters to rebuild the south wing of the castle—and a stonemason to build the tombs for the family of his predecessors.

Aye, for you, he thought, turning to the portrait of Joanna MacInnes, propped up on a chest by the fire.

Gavin tore his gaze away from her alert, vibrant eyes and stared at his dinner, untouched on the small table beside the fire. Of all that had happened that day, his visit to the kirkyard had been the most troubling of all. So many fresh graves. And so many who had died so young. He couldn't shake off the melancholy that had descended on his soul as he had stood in the wind-driven rain.

Stripping off his wet tartan, shirt, and kilt, the laird heaped the clothes on the hearth. He gazed into the fire for a moment, but as he sat down and kicked off his boots, Gavin's eyes were again drawn to the face of Joanna MacInnes. What was it about this woman that haunted him so?

Gavin drew back the blanket from his bed and climbed in between its linens. Lying back with a hand propped behind his head, he stared across the room at her face. He was glad, now, that he had told his men to have the painting brought here, rather than having it immediately wrapped in preparation for the journey back to Lady MacInnes. It was selfish, he knew, to delay the old woman's request. But staring at the portrait, he realized how dazzling a creature Joanna MacInnes had been.

And he realized how easy it would have been to fall under her spell.

There was something much more powerful than her beauty that captivated him. Nay, he had known many bonny women. There was mystery in the violet-blue depths of her eyes, in the hint of a question that hung on the edges of her full lips. Of a secret locked in her heart.

And then there were the alluring ivory shades of her skin. He caressed with his eyes the gentle swell of firm, young breasts that rose above her brocaded dress. Suddenly, Gavin felt the stirring in his loins as he imagined the feel of his lips on her . . .

"Are you mad?" He started, tearing his eyes from the portrait and rolling away from the light. He must be out of his mind, indeed, he decided, clenching his teeth. Aroused by a woman long dead.

Joanna paused quietly in the wedge of open panel and listened carefully to the sound of his breathing. He was asleep—she was sure of it—lying on his stomach on the great bed, the curtains drawn back on the summer night. His face was turned toward her. Even knowing exactly what she wanted to do, she still could not bring herself to move. Not yet.

Wisps of black hair had fallen across his eyes. His handsome, chiseled face was stern and troubled, even in sleep. Joanna's lips parted and her breath caught in her chest as her eyes roamed over the rest of him. The blanket only managed to cover the lower part of his back

and one of his legs. She felt the heat rising in her face
at the sight of the sinewy muscles on his broad back and
thick, scarred arms. Deep in her belly, another heat
began to emerge, a wild, molten heat that frightened her
with its suddenness and with its power. Joanna quickly
tore her eyes away.

Stunned that she should respond this way to the mere
sight of a man, Joanna found herself growing angry and
chided herself silently. That's just what you need now,
she thought reproachfully. Some momentary lapse of
sanity. Shaking her head, she looked across the chamber.

The painting was there. Somehow, she knew it would
be. Stepping quietly onto the woven rush mat that covered the floor, she paused after each step. Deliberately,
she put out of her mind any thought of the consequences
of being discovered. As she moved toward the fire, she
thrilled at the sense of danger that now gripped her.
Playing the ghost, for some reason, seemed worth the
peril of capture.

As she reached the hearth, she spotted the full platter
of food and cringed at the sudden growl emanating from
her empty stomach. Throwing a nervous glance over her
shoulder, she stared, waiting. But he didn't move.

Well, first things first, she thought, wrapping the bread
and beef in the linen cloth from the tray. The smell of
the food made her mouth water, but she fought off the
urge to eat it immediately. She had a task to accomplish,
and the cook's dress was clearly designed for practicality
rather than fashion, so Joanna tucked the dinner, as well
as the empty goblet, into the huge pocket.

Her two hands free, she reached for the painting and
quietly tucked it under one arm. Glancing cautiously in
his direction again, she started to back up, but nearly
tripped over a pile of wet clothing.

Balancing the portrait against her leg, she picked up
the articles of clothing and spread them, one by one,
over the table and chair to dry. Amazing, she thought
wryly, how living without the comforts of a home for
half a year can change one's perspective on the privi-
leges of day-to-day living.

And besides, she mused, picking up the painting and

starting again across the room toward the panel, in the morning he wouldn't think entirely ill of his ghostly visitor. True, she had taken the painting and his dinner. But she had, at least, done one good deed.

As she reached for the panel, she froze in her tracks as the black-haired giant rolled onto his back. Joanna was only a step away from the panel, but she didn't dare to move. The smell of warm, wet wool wafted across the chamber, and she watched, petrified, as the man's hand started slowly moving over the linens. From the rhythmic rise and fall of his chest, Joanna knew he was still sleeping, and she prayed that her stomach would not growl now.

But before she could slip through the panel, the sleeping giant kicked restlessly at the blankets, and Joanna's heart stopped.

She looked. She blushed. She fled.

At the sound of the angry laird's roar, the long benches of the trestle tables cleared in an instant.

Motionless on the dais, the three warriors watched Gavin Kerr stomp into the Great Hall. His blazing, black eyes locked on them.

"Cowards," Peter whispered under his breath as the men who had been at their morning meal moved *en masse* toward the door—and out of striking distance of their raging warrior chief.

"What have you done now, Peter?" Edmund asked quietly, frowning at the burly man beside him. "Tell us now so we can think of an answer."

"Nothing!" he replied, with a quick glance of entreaty at Edmund and Andrew. "Nothing that should get him so riled. I only—"

"So you three have decided to play the fools!" Gavin roared, lifting one of the long heavy benches as if it were a twig, and charging toward the stunned trio.

Holding the bench across his body, the laird drove the warriors over the food-laden table with the force of an enraged bull, sending food and drink in every direction and pinning all three on their backs on the far side.

"So you think I am in the mood for jesting!" None

of the three dared even to breathe, but only stared at the man sitting on their chests. "So you blackguards have nothing better to do than trifle with me!"

"Trifle, m'lord?" Edmund flinched as Gavin suddenly turned on him.

"Aye, trifle! And I will twist those thick necks of yours with my own two hands unless one of you returns it to me this instant."

The three Lowlanders stared in confusion at their master, and Gavin's piercing gaze moved from one to the next.

"*It*, m'lord?" Peter asked finally.

"So, 'twas you!" the laird shouted, reaching down and grabbing Peter by the neck. "Nimble of mind and as quick to start trouble. I should have known. Bored already, no doubt. Any excitement to liven things up, I expect. I'll liven things up for you. We'll draw and quarter you and nail your tongue to the castle gate."

Gavin shifted his full weight onto Peter and tightened his grip on the warrior's neck as the other two scrambled from beneath the bench.

"I'll give you one last chance, you thieving bulldog. Where the devil have you put it?"

Andrew, of the three the closest to Gavin in size, was the one who was able to pry the warrior chief's grip from Peter's throat.

"M'lord," he rumbled, leaping back as his master's head whipped in his direction.

Gavin glared at him for a moment.

"I believe," Andrew continued. "I believe that not one of us has any idea what you are missing."

The three men nodded in unison.

"No idea, m'lord," Peter added quickly. "I am guilty of no wrongdoing!"

"*No* wrong?" Gavin drawled, suspicion etched in his features as he looked down at his man.

"Well, in jest I might have said . . ." Peter flushed crimson. "Well, m'lord, I . . . I did . . . well, my tongue did flap a wee bit last night about the fact that . . . that you were spending a night in Mistress Joanna's company—"

"Only a jest about the portrait. 'Twas just the ale talking," Edmund put in. "And everyone . . . I mean, no one laughed, m'lord."

"Aye, almost no one," Andrew agreed solemnly. "He meant no more disrespect than usual, m'lord."

Gavin took hold of Peter's chin. "And 'twas the ale, I suppose, that led you into my chamber?"

The three shook their heads in denial.

"Nay, m'lord," Peter responded.

" 'Twas the ale that took the painting." Gavin glared into the man's perplexed face. "Do not try to deny it, Peter. It had to be you!"

"And you, Edmund," the laird said, rising from the burly man's chest and taking a step toward the tall, red-haired warrior. Edmund retreated at once, and Peter quickly clambered to his feet. "Too bad you didn't choke on my dinner. Though, now that I think more on it, you probably fed it to the dogs."

The man's denials were loud and pained, but Gavin waved him off, turning to Andrew, who stood by, looking totally bewildered.

"And you, too, Andrew. No doubt encouraged by these two in your first foray into crime against me."

"Nay, m'lord," the big man countered. "I—"

Gavin interrupted in frustration. "You couldn't even think of anything vicious . . . like your cronies here . . . so you hung my wet clothes by the hearth. I know you, Andrew. Is that not what happened? Well, for your efforts, the damn things now smell like singed sheep, I'll have you know."

As Gavin took a breath, Edmund quickly tried to get a word in. "M'lord, I swear on the grave of my dead mother that we had nothing to do with—"

"Nay, nothing, m'lord," Peter chirped in. " 'Tis true, we had more than our share of ale, but last night we—all three of us—slept right here in the Hall."

"You know the light sleeper that I am, m'lord," Andrew added. "If Peter had been up to no good, I would have been awake and at his throat—"

"Oh, so 'tis I who am the troublemaker, you say?" Peter now turned angrily on Andrew.

"Aye, you are," Andrew replied simply. "And you know it."

As the two men squared off, Gavin was suddenly aware that the rest of the men, including Allan the steward, had been moving cautiously closer, forming a crowd around them.

Before another word could be spoken, though, the sound of shouting drew everyone's attention to the entrance of the Great Hall. Gavin stepped forward as one of the young stablehands pushed breathlessly through the crowd. The young man's frightened eyes scanned the crowd, and upon finding both Gavin and Allan, his ashen face suddenly reflected his uncertainty over whom he should address.

"What is the matter, David?" Allan was the first to speak. "You look as if you've seen a ghost."

" 'Tis back . . . exactly where 'twas 'afore!"

The Hall was silent as David's wild eyes scanned the crowd. "Not since I was a bairn have I believed 'em. All them tales the womenfolk tell . . . of hauntings. I never believed 'em." He bobbed his head slowly. " 'Til now. Gibby says her cooking pots rattle at nights, that things are being took. Molly swears to hearing the walls cry and moan!"

"That's enough, lad. Such nonsense is for fools and—"

"Nay, Allan." Gavin raised his hand, silencing the steward's sharp rebuke. Glancing at the stablehand's startled face, the new laird gentled his voice. "What is back, David?"

"Why, the painting, m'lord," he answered shakily. "The one of Mistress Joanna!"

Gavin glared threateningly at his three warriors standing beside him. But all of them looked as baffled as the young worker.

"We took down the rest of the study floor, m'lord," Allan put in. "There is no way to get up there."

The young man again bobbed his head. "Aye, 'twas an eerie thing to walk in there and see her face looking down at us from so high." David unconsciously made the sign of the cross. "Whoever put it back there had no needs for legs, m'lord. Being so high, he must have just flew—"

"I think we'll take a look at the work of this ghost, David," Gavin commanded, nodding to the man to lead the way. Allan and the entire crowd followed behind.

As they entered the chamber beneath the study, David pointed to the painting hanging once again above the hearth. The floor had been pulled down completely now, and at first glance, it *did* appear as though one would have to fly up there. There was, however, one narrow edge of a beam, hardly visible from the floor below, running along the wall from the hearth, but away from the secret panel in the corner. It couldn't be more than two or three fingers wide, Gavin thought, dismissing it as a possibility. There was no way that he could see for anyone to get from the secret passageway to the hearth. Gavin shook his head.

"Did you bar the panel?" the laird asked, his gaze falling on Allan.

"Aye, m'lord. I did just as you bid me."

"Who slept the night in here?"

Three of his own men answered affirmatively.

"And you saw nothing?"

"Nay," one replied as the others shook their heads.

Well, he thought, so much for the possibility of anyone using a ladder to climb the wall.

Gavin let his eyes travel over the faces of his own men and those of Ironcross Castle. They all depended upon him now. The confused expressions, the low murmuring undercurrent of fear assured him that the culprit of this trick was not standing amongst them. And that included his three warriors.

"Well lads, if the worst this ghost can do is steal and rehang pictures, then 'tis a harmless fellow, to be sure." Gavin's words brought a smile and some encouraging nods from the men. "Through with all the work to be done in here, he might have busied himself a bit more productively."

"He's probably a gentleman," Peter said under his breath, loud enough for all to hear.

Gavin's laughter matched the response of the crowd

and dispelled the eeriness that had gripped them all just moments earlier. As the throng broke up, with most heading off to their day's tasks, Gavin turned to Edmund. "Get ladders and whatever else you need and bring the damned thing down."

"After we take the painting down, m'lord, where do you want it?" Edmund asked. "Shall we pack it for its journey?"

Gavin paused for a moment before answering and stared musingly at the smiling face on the wall. The honorable thing would be to send the portrait off to its rightful owner. But this bit of mischief from last night only added to his desire to hold on to the painting. Just for a short time.

"Take it back to my room," he ordered, walking away. "Put it where it was before."

"Shouldn't we have someone guard the painting, m'lord?" Edmund called after him. "To stop it from being stolen again?"

"Why?" Gavin asked, pausing and turning to look at the three. "Now that we know how far that painting can walk, I have no worries about it. Besides, with Andrew riding to Elgin, I should be able to keep my eye on two of you."

Chapter 6

Not a sheep. Not a shaggy red cow. Not a soul.

Gavin, riding alone toward the abbey, spurred his charger to the summit of the rocky, heather-covered hill. The last of the mists had burned off hours earlier, and only a few solitary wisps of white marred a brilliant azure sky. But the land that met the new laird's gaze was as empty as the vault of heaven.

To his right the waters of the loch curved away to the west. Beyond the line of peaks in the distance, Gavin knew that the Spey River flowed to the sea. And rising above the Spey, perhaps only a day or two away, sat Benmore Castle, home of the Macpherson clan. Twisting his body around, Gavin looked back over the ground he had traveled.

Above the hills, he could see Ironcross Castle, rugged and proud on its high ground overlooking the loch. It would be a good holding, he decided, once he rebuilt the south wing. And once he had dispelled the old beliefs in its curse.

The black-haired giant turned his gaze to the north. Drifting in the sky over the next hill, he could see a hawk circling and hanging in the occasional breeze. As he watched, the predator suddenly plummeted toward the ground, disappearing behind a jagged crest. To the north, the Earl of Athol was Gavin's nearest neighbor. Gavin had seen him on a number of occasions. He was a relative of the king . . . and an odd man, this John Stewart.

Shrugging off his thoughts of Athol, the warrior chief turned his attention back in the direction of the abbey.

The place lay in a small valley leading up from the loch. Not far, Andrew had told him.

At the bottom of this hill, beside a grove of tall trees, Gavin spotted a handful of huts huddled together. Turning his steed down the slope, the new laird was disappointed to find the dwellings deserted. He had hoped to find farm folk on this trip to the abbey, but so far he had found nothing on his lands but jagged outcroppings of rock and the broad empty waters of Loch Moray.

As Gavin reached the crest of the next hill, he brought his charger to a halt. At the bottom of the slope, beside a broad meandering creek, lay the ruined abbey. Stretching out from what had once been the front gates, a cluster of twenty or thirty cottages formed a thriving little village. On this side of the brook, an orchard of fruit trees ran in neat rows up the hillside, and shaggy red cattle grazed in a small herd in the pastureland. On the other side of the valley, he could see good-sized flocks of new-shorn sheep. Standing tall in his stirrups, Gavin let his eyes take in the fields of grain and other crops stretching up along the small, brisk-running stream.

And he saw men and women working diligently on the land.

The happy shrieks of children drew the laird's gaze back to the huts, and the edges of Gavin's mouth turned up in a smile as he watched a dozen small, barefooted urchins running in playful pursuit of a dog. Allan had mentioned that Joanna had a fondness for the abbey. He could now see why. For the first time since arriving, Gavin was faced with life.

"You see? They haven't all gone into Athol's service," the laird said aloud, patting the thick, muscular neck of his steed. "Well, what do you say we pay these folks a visit?"

As he rode down through the groves of trees that lined the steep hillside, Gavin considered what might have drawn these people to the ruined abbey. Certainly this valley was no better suited to farming or grazing than the land around the loch. He would need to entice them back, somehow, though perhaps they would be more than willing to come, were they to see that the laird of Ironcross was not about to fall before some curse.

He would give them time. After all, these lands were as much a part of his domain as those surrounding the castle. It was just the distance that he wished he could do away with. Having the bustling activity of a working clan around him—that was what he missed.

Breaking out of the trees into one of the upper pastures, Gavin reined in his mount with alarm.

Not a man, woman, or child remained to be seen in either field, pasture, or village. Where he had seen workers bending to their tasks, there now lay discarded farm tools. Alert to possible trouble, the warrior urged his stallion ahead slowly. Whatever had startled this community, Gavin could see no sign of it. As he approached the village, he glanced around at the freshly worked gardens, the baskets of vegetables abandoned in the flight. Before leaving Ironcross Castle, Gavin had strapped the scabbard of his broadsword to his back, and he reached over his shoulder now to loosen the weapon.

The little road that led up to the ruined abbey was eerily silent until, with a growl and a frightened bark, an agitated dog rushed at Gavin's horse from one of the first cottages. The lone animal was the only sign of the group of children who had been chasing him so playfully only moments past. Without stopping, Gavin spoke sharply to the cur, and as horse and rider continued on, the animal retired to the hut he had defended with such valor.

Rather than stopping at one of the hovels and searching out the peasants who lived there, the laird decided to ride straight on to the abbey. Whether they were hiding in the huts or had fled into the trees beyond the orchards, Gavin was certain that their eyes were upon him. He could feel their presence, and he could feel their fear. It was he they were hiding from, and the alarm his arrival in the village had caused disturbed him greatly. He tried to think back over everything that Andrew had said of his visit here. *An odd lack of farm folk.* Obviously, they had responded to his man in the same way

that they had responded to him. They had simply
vanished.

Beyond what had been the gates of the abbey, Gavin
could see the ruined walls of the kirk. While much of
the stone from the abbey walls had apparently been used
to construct the village cottages, the kirk's walls rose
high above the rest. There was no roof on the building,
though, and it had clearly gone unused for ages. A circle
of stone huts, ruder than the thatched cottages of the
village, sat to one side of the church, and as Gavin rode
past the first one, he spotted the old woman.

She sat on a stone, feeding twigs into a fire. Yellow
flames licked the bottom of a small cooking pot. Gavin
dismounted, tossing the reins of his horse over the
branch of a scrub oak, and approached her, watching
keenly as she never once lifted her head or acknowledged him in any way.

"Good day to you," Gavin called out pleasantly.

Finally, as she continued to work, the old woman's
gray eyes lifted slowly and fixed critically on his face.
The Lowlander returned her appraising gaze with one
of his own. She wore a veil of white, but a cross on a
leather thong about her neck was the only indication of
religious vocation. Her direct stare told him that she had
no fear of him, though beyond that, a guarded expression hid any hint of what emotions lay beneath.

He came to a stop before her fire and crouched down
across from her. "Your face is the first cheerful one I
have come across since leaving Ironcross this morning."

The arching of one thin eyebrow and a narrowing gaze
made him retract his words.

"Very well," he said. "Yours is the *only* face I have
come across since leaving this morning."

She lowered her eyes, seemingly directing her whole
attention to preparing the fire.

"Are you Mater?" he asked bluntly.

"I am." Her voice was strong, confident.

"I am Gavin Kerr," he returned. "I come from—"

"I know who you are, laird," she interrupted, lifting
her gray eyes again to his face. The piercing quality ema-

nating from their depths gave Gavin the impression that she knew more than just his identity.

He realized immediately that this was no woman for idle small talk. He also knew that she was not one to be questioned. There was something quite different about Mater, and he knew in his gut that it would be difficult to win her over. And it was true that he *wanted* to win her over. She was the first soul outside of Ironcross that he'd crossed paths with, but as the religious leader of the region, right now it was very important to Gavin that she accept his lairdship. From all he'd gathered from those at the castle, it was clear that the way to winning the trust of his folk was through Mater.

Mater's attention was focused on her task. As she stirred the contents of the kettle, the picture of Joanna MacInnes flashed into Gavin's head. It was so strange that he couldn't shake her free of his mind. This morning, before departing Ironcross Castle, he'd followed his impulse and gone back to his room simply to look again at her portrait. It was there where Edmund had returned it, upon the hearth.

Gavin was certain now that none of his men had taken the painting. He knew that the three warriors would have taken more pleasure in gloating over their daring move than in actually stealing the portrait out of his chamber. But the whole thing still puzzled him. It was so strange to have someone go to the trouble of stealing that painting and putting it back where it had always been. The act served no purpose.

Gavin shook his head and tried to tear his eyes away from the fire.

"She would come here, you know, and do exactly as you have done."

Mater's words pierced Gavin's thoughts like a bolt of lightning. His eyes snapped up and stared into her gray eyes. "Who?" he asked unsteadily.

Mater's eyes drifted toward the direction in which he'd come. "All alone, she would come to us, riding down the hill. She would get down from her mare and walk to this fire and sit so silently before it. Just as you are doing now."

How could she know this? he wondered. How could she bring up Joanna's name when he'd just been thinking of her. As far as Mater knew, he had never known the young woman. Despite what his heart kept trying to tell him, he never had so much as met her. He gazed across the fire at the old woman. One who can read thoughts, Gavin knew, can be a powerful friend . . . or an even more powerful foe.

"Your soul is tormented, laird," she added. "But hers was troubled as deeply as yours."

Gavin's face darkened and his eyes narrowed. As far as her words about him, the warrior knew his features reflected the grimness that he carried within him. But what she said about Joanna alarmed him. That portrait was a picture of youth and happiness and hope.

"Were you her confidante?" he asked. "Her advisor?"

"To her, I was Mater."

Her simple declaration was powerful, but he wasn't convinced. "A household of servants tell me she was happy," he stressed. "And yet—"

"Those who knew her well are dead."

"And you are the last living person who can tell me more about her?"

"Nay, not the last one," she said enigmatically, shaking her head. "But there was a time when she would escape Ironcross and take refuge here. Aye, many a time we would spend a few hours here by this fire . . . here in the abbey."

Gavin's eyes drifted to the woman's hands as she stirred the contents of the now-simmering kettle. "What was the reason for her misery?"

She didn't answer his question, but instead picked up a wooden bowl.

"How could a woman of her age be plagued with sorrow as deep as—" Gavin cut his own words short.

"As deep as your own?" she finished. "Nay, laird. How could a *man* in your place and position be so tortured as *she*!"

She dipped the wooden bowl into the kettle. Stretching her two hands across the fire, she offered him the steaming potion. Gavin took it.

"How?" The warrior chief looked her in the eye, and then, surprised at his own openness, heard himself say plainly, "Grief!"

She picked up the wooden spoon and continued to stir again. Gavin brought the bowl to his lips.

"A man who conceals his grief," she said, "will find no remedy for it."

Gavin paused. "I do not conceal it. I simply wonder if there is a remedy for it."

"You haven't been searching for one."

"Perhaps no remedy exists."

"What happens if I were to tell you that I have the answer?"

He just stared.

"Would you believe me?"

"This is foolishness!"

"You *don't* believe me!"

"I'm not here to discuss my grief." His tone was curt even to his own ear, but unexpectedly, he saw Mater's eyes soften with understanding.

"Learn to weep, laird, and you will learn to laugh again."

Looking at her, it occurred to him that she spoke as if she'd known him for years. And despite what he liked to admit, he knew that he did indeed conceal his grief beneath his fierce exterior. Gavin stared at her more closely. From the time he was a lad, he had never wept. He recalled once wondering if, once started, he would ever be able to stop.

He looked down at the bowl in his hands, and his thoughts returned to Joanna and her pain.

"For whom did she grieve?" he asked gruffly.

"The answers to your questions about Joanna MacInnes await you at your keep."

He shook his head. "All who knew her closely—the ones who could answer any questions about her—they are all dead. You said so yourself."

Gavin watched the spark again come back into her eyes as Mater looked at him straight in the eye. He waited for her to say more, but she didn't. Feeling the weight of the bowl in his hands, he brought it to his lips. The brew was soothing and warm as it went down.

A moment passed as Mater watched his face. Gavin returned her gaze and then finished the broth, as a curious frown creased the brow of the woman.

"Not all!" she answered then. "They are not *all* dead!"

Staring at her from behind the lowered rim of the bowl, Gavin waited, hoping to learn more. But the old woman was clearly done with their chat. He watched her as she raised herself to her feet and picked up a satchel that lay on the ground. Gavin sensed that he was being dismissed, but he had no desire to leave. So he pushed himself to his feet as well, and fell in step beside her.

For the next couple of hours, Gavin walked with her as she wandered through the sun-warmed hillsides surrounding the valley. Something about the way the sunlight fell on the river, on the rocks and the grass—something in the time they shared—reminded him of days he had spent as a lad in the hills around Jedburgh Abbey in the Borders. He didn't press her to tell him more, and she seemed to tolerate his presence. He helped whenever she allowed him to—pulling a stubborn root, holding her satchel when she would relinquish it. But when they eventually reached the fields where Gavin—from the top of the hill—had seen villagers working the land, the new laird bent down and took up in his hand a cast-off hoe.

"Why are they hiding?"

"They do not trust you," she said. "They are afraid!"

"But why?"

She turned her gray eyes up to his face. He could feel the sun on his back. But she never squinted or raised a hand to shield her eyes against the light. "What makes you so trusting?"

There was a sharp edge to her voice, and Gavin frowned at her, trying to understand what her question had to do with the overwhelming fear that could drive an entire village into hiding at the sight of one man.

"I *decide* where to place my trust," Gavin answered.

"You accepted the broth out of my hands and drank it unquestioningly."

"I would not pass an offering of hospitality," he argued.

"I could have poisoned you!"

"Aye. You could have, at that. But I trusted you."

"You did not know me."

"Still, I trust you."

"Why?" she almost hissed, frustration becoming apparent in her wrinkled features.

"Because I have done nothing to incur your ill will. Because I wanted us to be at peace. You did not run away and hide like the rest of them. You stayed out and faced me. For all that you knew, I might have come to harm you. But you trusted me, so I trusted you."

" 'Twas not trust, you fool," she snapped. "I have no fear of any violence that you or any other man might bring down upon me. At my age, I have no fear of death."

"Nor do I!" he said coolly.

She bit back her next words, and they stared at one another in silence. Gavin spoke again.

"I have come to the Highlands in peace. I am here to be laird, and I want the trust of you and these people."

"They fear you. They hate you."

Her harsh words were a blow, but Gavin shrugged them off. "I have done nothing to deserve their hate."

"Perhaps, laird. But the ones before you *have*!"

Gavin stared for a moment. There was so much that he needed to learn about these people—about Ironcross Castle and its past. His words were clipped when he spoke again. "I cannot change what is past. I can only control the present. I can only work for the future well-being of all who live on these lands."

"Ha! You think you can control the present?" She lifted a finger and pressed it against his chest. "You cannot force us to hear you. Nay, laird. You will have to bear the price of your predecessors' guilt. 'Tis too late to—"

"Nay, Mater." He cut her short, wrapping his giant hand around her bony fingers. He knew how easy it would be to crush them in his grip, and he could see in her face that she knew it too. But he just held the hand—gently—and let the flesh of his palm warm the coldness of her old bones. "Nay, Mater. I will earn their respect and trust. I will earn yours."

"Aye. So you can betray us."

"I do not betray a trust," Gavin growled. "That I vow!"

Chapter 7

The sun dropped from sight behind the high walls of Ironcross Castle as Gavin descended the last hill into the gorge, and it was fairly dark by the time he reached the jumbled slabs of rock that leaned against one another beside the path. The rocks looked nearly white in the gathering gloom; there were a dozen of the strange formations in the gorge, looking like an army of hideous monsters in the twilight.

He had never expected to be returning so late. But when he'd started for the abbey in the morning, he had never even hoped to learn so much in just one day.

Mater was certainly a fascinating woman. She had a kind of gruff charm about her that Gavin found quite engaging. Sometimes, the honest way that she spoke had been both heart-wrenching and enlightening. But as the afternoon had worn on, she had also spoken in what had the appearance of riddles. He was certain, though, that the words were intended to give him some clues about the origin of the curse that everyone believed hung over Ironcross Castle. After what he had heard today, Gavin knew that most of the truth that he was in search of lay in the combined histories of the abbey and the past lairds of Ironcross, both. What it was, however, she would not tell him.

In spite of her obstinacy in that, though, before the day had ended and Gavin had taken his leave, he was certain that he had somewhat effected a change in Mater. Though she clearly had no goodwill for the past lairds—and in spite of her open declaration that she would not trust him—she had become almost agreeable as the day went on. And before the end of the day,

Gavin had even spotted a few workers returning to the fields. Very few, he recalled, but today he had at least made a start.

Gavin's thoughts were drawn back to the present by the tossing of his steed's head as the trail narrowed. He patted him on the neck to calm him.

"Aye, Paris," the laird said aloud, "I can see the castle as well. We are nearly home, big fellow, and though those two dogs, Edmund and Peter, probably have eaten *my* supper, I am quite certain they've saved some oats for your—"

The boulder, large enough to crush Gavin's skull, grazed him on the shoulder with enough impact to unhorse the giant, sending him crashing into the rock wall beside the path.

Springing to his feet, Gavin whipped his broadsword from its scabbard and peered up at the rocky overhangs for his attacker. His startled charger had skittered off into the darkness, but the warrior knew he would not go far. The silence of the night was unbroken, and Gavin could see nothing.

His heart hammering in his chest, Gavin's mind suddenly flooded with those words of warning. *The curse! No laird of Ironcross Castle has died of old age for centuries.* The Lowlander shook his head, disgusted with himself. He was simply not going to allow nonsense to cloud his mind or rule his actions.

Moving cautiously across the path, Gavin knelt beside the boulder. One man could lift it—he was fairly certain of that. Two men could easily handle it, and perhaps aim it with some precision. One man, or perhaps even a woman, could roll it from a ledge. Gavin could feel blood running down the side of his face where he had struck the rock wall, and he flexed the muscles in his shoulder.

Quietly, Gavin sheathed his broadsword and drew his dirk. Holding the dagger in his teeth, he quickly crossed to the base of the mound of rocks and began to climb. This mound rose fairly high above the floor of the gorge, and there were a number of places that the boulder could have fallen from.

The night was still, but for the sound of Paris stamping

and snorting with impatience a few yards down the path. Gavin climbed carefully, but there was no movement above. And there was no one to be found. Though it was dark, not a shadow moved anywhere, and Gavin began to wonder if perhaps the rock had indeed fallen without human assistance.

On one of the ledges of the rocky formation, the warrior chief stopped and looked about him. The walls of Ironcross Castle loomed up high and black, and the laird could see a sentinel lighting torches as he made his way along the parapet. Above him the stars were like diamonds on the black velvet sky. There was no point in going up any further, he decided. Not without a torch.

Shaking his head, Gavin sheathed his dirk and started down. At the bottom, he whistled for Paris, and the huge animal trotted over. With a grunt of pain, the warrior swung up into the saddle and nudged the horse around toward the castle.

"Home, big fellow," the laird commanded, adding, "and if in the future you see any more ghosts, you can be certain I will be paying you closer heed."

Joanna froze at the creaking of the great oak door.

Standing in the center of underground crypt, the young woman looked around in terror. Never in the past had Mater and her cult entered the castle on any night other than the night of a full moon. At least, not on any night that she was aware of. Why were they coming tonight? The one night Joanna had chosen to finalize her plan for justice.

Panic swept through her at the heavy metallic clack of the door's ancient lock. She knew she needed to hide, and she silently flew across the stone floor toward the shadowy recess beside the altarlike table. The oil lamp that sat on the table, burning eternally, flickered with the threat of exposing her.

The sound of footsteps echoed down the tunnel as Joanna threw herself into the dark refuge. Pressing up against the wall, she held her breath as the steps paused at the entry to the crypt. One of the thick pillars obstructed her view of the door, but Joanna suddenly realized that the trespasser was alone. There was no talking, no hushed whispers—this was no cult gathering. She waited, but there was no sound. Whoever stood at the entrance was waiting, as well. If the intruder came in and searched, Joanna knew she would be found. She put her hand to the dirk in her belt.

After what seemed to be an eternity, whoever it was moved on down the tunnel.

Joanna waited a few more moments, but no one returned, and she let out a long sigh of relief. But then, an urgent sense of worry tugged at her senses. There was something terribly wrong. It had to be one of Mater's women who'd come, but why hadn't she come into the vault?

Joanna wracked her brain as she stepped into the crypt again. Why else would someone use that oaken door to enter the castle? These tunnels were never used as passageways by house servants, or by hungry peasants seeking shelter. Since the time Joanna had been hiding here, Mater and her evil followers had been the only intruders.

The young woman looked about, making certain she had left no clues to her presence there. Then she silently made her way out of the crypt. She wasn't finished with what she had come here to do, but there was still about a fortnight left to the next full moon. There was still time left to plan her final revenge.

Standing in the pitch-black of the tunnel, she listened for noises, but there was nothing. Once again, the stillness of the earth enveloped her. To her right the long, deep caverns and passages, burrowing beneath Ironcross, awaited her. To her left the oaken door. It was so close. It seemed to beckon to her in the darkness.

She went to it.

Joanna knew the huge iron key hung suspended from a spike driven into the stone wall, and hesitantly she felt for it. The ancient metal was cool on her fingertips, and she took it down, slipping it into the lock, and turning it.

Drawing a deep breath, Joanna opened the door and peered into the darkness behind her. There was nothing. No sound. No sign of life. Turning back to the open door, she stepped through and pushed cautiously along in the darkness. Soon the tunnel wall gave way to the stone walls of a small cave, and as the passage widened, a brush of cool, night breeze swept through her hair. Like some starving beggar who finally sits at the table, Joanna filled up her lungs with the fresh heather-scented air until she thought she might burst.

Suddenly, she was out from under the roof of the cave, and above her the stars sparkled with a brilliance like no time she could ever recall. The ability to breathe, to feel the cool breezes pulling gently at her clothes, at her hair—these were sensations Joanna thought she would never experience again. Like a prisoner chained in a deep pit, she had sentenced herself to confinement inside this castle. For more than six months, she had buried herself in what was—for her—the labyrinthine tomb near Ironcross. And it was a tomb from which there could be no escape. Her death could be the only end to this sentence.

She raised her hands high in the air, allowing the soft night air to wrap about her, to caress her body.

A low whistle, and then the sound of a horse floated upward to her, jerking her abruptly out of her reverie. Joanna peered down over the ledge.

It was he. The laird.

She was close enough to him to hear the huge man grunt with pain as he swung up onto the charger.

As she watched him ride off toward the castle, Joanna glanced back into the gloom of the tunnel, and then looked over the edge again at the trail below. As accustomed as her eyes were to the darkness, she could see clearly enough to realize what had happened. There was a boulder in the center of the path. Whoever had passed by the crypt had pushed the rock from this ledge.

Joanna gazed at the new laird as he disappeared into the night. He had once again escaped death.

But how much longer could he survive the evil of this keep? Joanna asked herself. Till the next full moon? If the man's luck could only last until then, she would set things right.

She would watch over him until then, she vowed. She had to.

Chapter 8

The laird's face was grim enough when he entered his chamber, but there was cold fury etched in it when he stormed out.

The two warriors had walked with their chieftain to his chamber, but they had barely even turned away from the door when he reappeared. The angry glare darkening Gavin Kerr's expression made Edmund and Peter both jump aside and follow him as he marched in the direction of the south wing.

"We were talking, m'lord," Peter puffed, trotting to keep up. "Edmund and I were, that is. And we were thinking that traveling around these Highlands unattended might not be the very best policy for such a man as yourself."

"Aye. For instance, that gash on the side of your head," Edmund put in. "If you had been knocked unconscious in those hills—"

"Riding by yourself, m'lord, as you were," Peter added.

"Aye. Well, we were thinking that, by now, you would have been prey to just about any wild four-legged creature that might be roaming about in the night."

"Not that gnawing on your tough old carcass would be any real treat for a beast, m'lord, but . . ." Peter swallowed his words at the threatening glare from his leader.

As the two exchanged smirking side glances, Gavin took a lit candle from a wall sconce and led them on in silence until they reached the corridors outside the South Hall. A great deal of debris had been piled in the courtyard, but more of it lay in piles within the south wing itself.

"What the devil!" Peter exclaimed, as they stepped into the nearly gutted hall.

Gavin preceded the other two into the center of the room and looked up at Joanna's picture hanging in the second level, above the earth. The same three warriors who had slept there the night before leaped up in alarm.

"Bring it down," he ordered sharply, gesturing to Edmund.

"M'lord, you saw me put it in your room this morning. By 'sblood, the men were working in here until nearly dark! 'Tis just that . . . how could—"

"Bring it down and take it back to my chamber," Gavin commanded, turning sharply on his two men.

Peter took a step back until his burly shoulders were flat against the doorjamb. "I swear on my mother's soul, m'lord. I never touched this . . . thing. 'Tis bewitched. It . . . it must be! I swear, m'lord, I was never once out of . . . out of Edmund's shadow while you were gone."

A frown still darkening his face, the laird pushed the candle into the sputtering warrior's hand and disappeared into the darkness of the corridor.

The two men left behind looked at each other in disbelief before raising their eyes in unison to the portrait.

"The first time, I admit, I found it to be humorous," Peter said quietly.

"Aye, we all did," Edmund replied. "Not anymore, though! Did you see the look in his eyes?"

"Aye."

The two men stare up at the painting in silence for a long moment.

"The poor bastard!" Peter said.

"Aye." Edmund returned. "Clever, though!"

"The master will catch him."

"And then—"

"His death won't come soon enough," Peter finished. "The poor bastard."

Just what he needed. Company.

His neighbor, the Earl of Athol, was to arrive the next day.

Absently rubbing his sore shoulder with one hand,

Gavin watched as Margaret, the mute younger sister of the steward, poured the last steaming kettle of water into the wooden tub. Nodding his thanks to the woman, the laird waited until the door of his chamber was closed before he began to shed his clothes.

Athol. Now Gavin was feeling the first pangs of doubt about lairdship in a Highland castle. To be hospitable to such men as Athol was a bit more of a challenge than he was accustomed to. And to welcome a damned Highlander into his keep! It had never been a secret at court that, aside from the Macphersons, Gavin Kerr despised the whole lot of them.

Fourteen years ago, on that bloody day at Flodden Field, King Jamie had lost his life in battle to the English because of these traitors. Admittedly, not all of them had been at fault. But enough of the Highland lairds had looked on—turning their heads and hanging back when they were most needed—that Scotland's chances had been doomed and her greatest king since the Bruce was cut down in his prime.

The warrior chief winced slightly as he pulled his shirt over his head. The sore shoulder was already stiffening up. Looking about the master's chambers and seeing what his fate had brought him, Gavin knew this was no time to dwell on the wounds of the past. And reason told him that he had enough to do here without adding a feud with a neighbor to the list of his troubles. So tomorrow he would put on his best show of manners and greet the scurvy dog Athol and his monkey-faced entourage. He was certainly capable of that much diplomacy.

As he tossed away the last of his clothes, Gavin's eyes rested on the portrait of Joanna MacInnes. Lowering himself into the tub, the warrior suddenly stopped and, stepping out of the warm water, crossed the room and returned with his broadsword. Easing himself in again, he laid the sword across the staves of the huge tube, and settled in for a comfortable soak. He had placed the painting above the hearth this time, and he gazed up at the beautiful features. He was not taking any chances of losing the picture again. And besides, it was so much more pleasant to think fanciful thoughts of her than it was to brood over arriving guests.

Daydreaming in a bath was one thing, but tomorrow there were so many things to be done. Things like questioning the priest about the history of the abbey. He needed to learn more about the past MacInnes lairds and their relationship with the Earl of Athol.

Gavin's eyes again studied the enigmatic smile of Joanna MacInnes. He wanted to find out more about the young woman . . . and the hidden sorrows Mater had referred to.

And in the meantime, he would catch the tricky bastard who kept stealing his prize.

Honestly, there wasn't a shred of modesty in the man.

Frowning at him from across the room, Joanna decided that he could also probably sleep on a row of spikes. She stood still and watched as he sighed in his sleep, shifted a bit, and settled again. The giant *had* to be uncomfortable, his chin on his massive chest, his muscular arms folded and resting on the flat of the sword-blade lying across the tub. Joanna tried to ignore the laird's bare knees and legs sticking out of the water and, instead, focused on his face. The wet hair smoothed back from his brow. The eyes closed in a scowling but still extremely handsome face.

She spotted some fresh droplets of blood on the side of his head. She wondered if these were from his mishap in the gorge.

Controlling an urge to move closer and inspect the wound, she decided that he certainly didn't seem to be in pain.

He shifted again, and one long arm moved, tumbling outward over the staves of the tub as he turned his shoulders slightly. The Lord forgive her, she thought, she could make a habit out of coming here every night and watching him sleep. And she was certain she could get away with it, too. The giant slept like the dead.

Tonight, after peeking into the bedchamber, Joanna had waited for quite a while in the passageway, assuming that the man would eventually finish with his bath and retire. When he hadn't, she had even gone down into the kitchens and found some supper. And here he was, still in the tub, fast asleep.

She had made some noises before entering the chamber—scratching at the woven mat on the floor, tapping on the wood panel—but to her delight, the Lowlander had continued to slumber peacefully on in what must be, by now, very cold water. So she had ventured in.

Laying the painting down carefully, Joanna kept her eyes glued to his face and slowly knelt beside the tub. His long arm dangled limply over the side, and she placed his dagger on the rush mat—a breath away from his knuckles.

He had clearly thought himself smart enough to outwit her. And he almost had. If it hadn't been for her quickness, she would have been caught, for when she had reached up for the portrait, Joanna was shocked when the dagger, tip down, had plunged downward toward her face. The villain had propped the weapon on top of the frame, knowing it would be a hazard, or at least an alarm.

It had been a miracle that she was able to catch the dagger in the palm of her hand without dropping the painting. It was almost ironic to think that the dressings she wore to hide her hideous scars had kept her hands from being further damaged. At least they had kept her from capture.

Joanna raised herself to her feet, trying not to let her gaze dwell on the rest of him. She turned away, knowing that she was getting far too impetuous. This game of coming back to his room to take the portrait was far too daring. But she knew it was something else as well. It was but an excuse she was using to look in on him. To be close to him. She had to be losing her mind, she decided.

She started toward the panel. She absolutely couldn't allow herself to get attached. She couldn't. And she certainly couldn't afford to be caught. Glancing one last time in his direction, watching the rise and fall of the drying mat of hair on his broad chest, a sudden concern swept over Joanna:

The water that he was slumbering in *had* to be ice cold by now. Whatever would happen if he caught a chill? Who would take care of him if he were to come down with a fever? He would be a much easier target to destroy then.

With that thought in mind, Joanna stepped back into the passageway. Holding the painting in her hand, she slammed the panel shut. As she fled through the darkness, the sounds of his curses, vividly descriptive and loud, brought a smile to her lips.

The fact that a hush fell over the crowd in the Great Hall when he entered was no surprise to Gavin Kerr. The buzz of conversation as warriors and castle workers bent over their morning meal ceased instantly, and more than a few began to rise before quickly sitting down again. Many of the gathered throng likely thought him mad and, as for the rest, he was certain that they were too afraid to bring any attention to themselves.

He had certainly created a disturbance in the middle of the night. Dressed in nothing other than his kilt, Gavin had marched noisily through the Great Hall, out into the courtyard and into the South Hall. Sure enough, he realized—along with two dozen followers—the knave had beaten him down there and hung up his prize. Gavin had hoisted a ladder onto his shoulder, climbed to the hearth, and brought down the picture himself. Without a word to the gaping onlookers, he had stalked angrily back to his chamber with the painting under his arm.

This scoundrel had courage, Gavin had to give him that. To think that this thief was so bold that he didn't even see a need to steal in silence! The scurvy knave had been so brazen that he had even slammed the damn panel on his way out!

Gavin couldn't help himself, but he was starting to like the blackguard!

As he crossed the room, he swore to himself that he'd catch the bastard next time. He must be a lightfooted creature, though, to be able to steal into a chamber where Gavin was sleeping. After all, he'd always prided himself on being a very light sleeper.

The Lowlander's frown deepened as he reached the table where Edmund and Peter were hunched over their morning meal. From the smirks the two rogues wore on their faces, it was obvious they were in a very good humor. And Gavin knew at whose expense they were so cheerful. Gavin sat himself down beside them.

Well, he could fix that, he decided.

"Well met, lads!" the laird growled in greeting. "A fine morning, I see."

"Aye, m'lord," Peter replied, brown bread stuffed in his cheeks.

A serving boy rushed over and placed a heaping bowl before the laird. Looking down, Gavin frowned at the thick mush before glancing over at Peter's dish of cheese, cold mutton, and bread. It didn't matter where they went, the thickset warrior had a way of getting better food than the rest of them.

"We've things to do today," the Lowlander announced, looking up into the faces of his two men, "before our neighbors arrive."

"We've given instructions to the warriors manning the walls and stationed those protecting the—"

"This castle has been unprotected for six months. If Athol had seriously wanted it . . ." Gavin shook his head. "Nay, you two have other duties this morning."

The two sat forward attentively. "Peter, after you've filled that barrel-shaped carcass of yours, I want you to go and fetch Molly, the woman who sees to the house. The two of you can decide which rooms will be suitable for lodging Athol and his entourage."

"Molly? But, m'lord," Peter protested. "You do not really want me traipsing after that old woman? Surely . . . I mean, surely she can do that herself? And besides, I'm certain, m'lord, that Allan—"

"You *will* go and help her with this, Peter!" Gavin growled. "And that is not all I want you to do this morning. After you are finished with Molly, you'll go and see Gibby, the cook, and go over with her—item by item— the meal she is preparing for supper."

Peter was staring at him in shock. "But, m'lord, the men say she hates having anyone meddling in her kitchen affairs. She's already boxed the ears of Lank Donald, our fletcher. I am telling you, she is a she-devil. I would sooner face Torquemada's ghost than her!"

Gavin ignored his man's protests as he poked at the contents of his bowl. "Just seeing the difference between what you and I have been served this morning, I would have to say that you have already found a safe haven in her kitchen." The laird reached and took a chunk of brown bread from Peter's trencher. "Just continue to use your charms, and I am sure you will be just fine."

Gavin then turned to the smirking Edmund. "And you, Red—"

The warrior's face grew immediately serious. "Aye, m'lord."

"You are to find the steward and start going through the tunnels beneath this keep. You will start from my chamber. See if you can make out a way to the upper floors of the south wing."

"But, m'lord, I heard Allan swear to you that he cannot remember the way around those tunnels. He claims no one has used them for years."

"Well, he's wrong." Gavin took a bite out of the bread and stared at the mush sticking hard to his spoon. Just looking at the thick mixture took his appetite away. Glancing up, he caught his two warriors watching his reaction to his food. One of these days he would ask Peter privately about the methods the warrior used to get half-decent food.

"But if he refuses to remember?"

"Bully him if need be." Gavin pushed the dish away abruptly. "That's why I am sending you with him. Bring wick lamps. Drag him every step, if that is the only way. Do whatever you need to do. But find the damn passage between my room and the south wing. I want you to show me the way later."

Gavin's strict command left no room for the two men to argue. The Lowlander came to his feet.

"But, m'lord. In case of trouble . . ." Peter stared at the direction of the kitchens. "I mean if someone were to . . . if a situation should arise—"

"Where could we find you, m'lord?" Edmund put in.

"In case hell breaks loose here," Peter finished.

"I will be with the priest."

She'd never battled an ailment such as this before.

Pulling the shutter open slightly, Joanna peered out and watched the laird stroll across the courtyard.

She knew the danger of discovery was great. Just a floor below her, a dozen men were hard at work on the burned wing. But somehow, none of that had mattered as she'd given in to her overwhelming desire to see him. So, climbing through the passageways to the tower chamber, she had taken her place by the window of her former refuge and waited.

He was so breathtakingly strong, and something stirred within her as she watched him turn and address a few men who approached him. At the laird's side, the dog Max gazed up at his new master with the same look of awe that Joanna suddenly sensed in herself.

Stifling a laugh, the young woman thought of how mortified she would be if he were to see her in her hiding place by the window, her tail end wagging and her tongue hanging out.

The sound of voices from the workers below drew Joanna back to the reality of her position, and she reluctantly backed away and headed toward the panel.

Indeed, this was a sickness, she scolded herself. But all the same, it was one of the few things that could bring a smile to her lips.

Chapter 9

The rising gusts of wind swirling around them in the kirkyard made the diminutive priest look frail against the power of nature. The small plot of ground that Father William had been turning with the sharp stick appeared black against the pale gray of the south wing.

"The Earl of Athol was here at Ironcross the night of the fire."

Gavin stared in surprise.

"How was it that the earl escaped the blaze while the rest perished?"

"He wasn't staying in the south wing with the rest of them. Before the fire, guests were usually lodged in the Old Keep, even those of noble blood. Athol was given the chambers you now occupy, m'lord."

Gavin's mind instantly flooded with an image of the hidden passage that he knew linked that bedchamber with the south wing. When he looked back into the priest's face, the man's eyes flickered away.

"Tell me about the night of the fire."

The chaplain paused, turning his face into the wind. "There was an evil that hung over the keep that night," he said, raising one hand and pointing out over the loch. "The full moon was cold, bright. By the saints, the castle dogs kept howling like the devil himself had taken possession of them. And then there was . . ." The man paused again and looked straight into Gavin's eyes. "Then there was the matter of the master!"

"What about your master?"

"For all the years I had known Sir John MacInnes, I always knew him to be a mild-tempered man. He was a strong man—when such action was called for—but not a violent one. He was never one to raise his hand in rashness or in anger. I never saw him beat a servant, even. There were times, m'lord, when I wondered if he were capable of rage." The priest shook his head. "Until that night!"

Gavin waited impatiently for the chaplain to continue, but the man's eyes and attention seemed to be straying.

A movement by the arched passageway that led to the courtyard drew Gavin's eye. Margaret, the mute serving woman, stared at them for a moment, then turned and disappeared. Gavin looked back at the priest.

"What happened that night . . . exactly?"

Father William shook himself out of his reverie and turned to face the laird.

"Let us go and sit out of this wind," he said, leading the warrior chief to a stone bench by the bluffs on the other side of the kirk.

Waving off the offer to sit, Gavin stood with his boot up on the low wall, and gazed out along the shoreline of the loch, past the line of the hills, toward the valley where the old abbey lay tucked away.

"What happened that night?" he repeated without looking back at the priest.

" 'Twas a fearful night. A night when God's face was turned from us," Father William began. "When the brawl broke out between Sir John and the earl, the air was foul with ill will. They had been arguing for two hours or more, starting over supper and continuing on without abatement. There were many harsh words passed between the two. If it were not for the presence of the ladies, I believe we would have had blood shed there in the Great Hall." The priest's eyes looked across the kirkyard. "Mistress Joanna took the quarrel quite to heart. I mean, being there at table with the two men arguing over her. She was a haughty and proud lass. Far too good for this cursed place. Though a woman, she knew her value far exceeded any piece of land, and she was not to be bartered for. All of us at the lower tables, we all felt sorry for her—sitting there with her eyes lowered, her fair skin turning more shades of scarlet . . ."

Father William leaned down and plucked a clover from the grass.

Gavin watched as the little man ground the clover into a pulpy mass between his nervous fingers.

"And then the words between the two men became even more violent. Sir John finally lost his temper with the earl, and the warriors in the Hall began to separate into companies. Those of us who remained crowded into the corners, certain that blood would flow.

"Suddenly, Mistress Joanna got up and stepped down from the dais. The two men stopped and looked at her, and she let them have a piece of her mind. When she turned and stormed out of the Great Hall, 'twas as silent as a tomb. And after her daughter left—before anyone could say a word—Lady Anne, the laird's wife, spoke out and eventually got the men to calm themselves and retire."

Gavin stared at the priest impatiently. "You have not told me why they were arguing. Why should Athol be arguing about the daughter?"

The cleric removed a set of prayer beads from his belt. Running the smooth wooden beads between his fingers, he looked back at the laird. "I do not know how 'tis in the Borders, m'lord, but in the Highlands, land, power, and the clan's good name stand above all calls for reason."

Gavin thought back over the age-old feuding that went on in the lands around Ferniehurst, his keep far to the south. " 'Tis no different in the Borders, but that is no answer."

The priest nodded grimly. "For over four generations, perhaps more, the earls of Athol have been trying to extend their lands southward from Balvenie Castle. I think it may be they have always wanted Ironcross Castle and Loch Moray. Word has it that in the old days, they tried to take Ironcross a good few times by force, but could never succeed. Then, when Duncan MacInnes was given the holding, the fighting stopped."

"So Duncan was the first of the MacInnes clan to be laird of Ironcross?"

"Aye," the priest answered. "The same that holds for

you, held for them. They were given Ironcross by the
king after the last of the Murray chiefs had died off or
moved on to other holdings . . . for fear of the curse."
William frowned up at the new laird. "You see, they all
knew about the curse, but most never believed in it until
it was too late for them."

Gavin knew the man's words were also aimed at him.

"You say that after Duncan MacInnes took over this
holding, the feuding with the Stewarts of Athol ceased.
From what I know of Highlanders, I find it hard to believe they would give up so easily on what they wanted
for so long."

"Aye, 'tis true what you say, m'lord. But you see, the
Murrays of Ironcross and the Stewarts of Athol have
been sworn enemies since the days of Noah. Duncan
MacInnes came here from Argyll, so there was no bad
blood to begin with. And from the first, I understand
that Duncan always made it understood to the earls of
Athol that one day the two families could join through
a marriage of some sort!" The priest shook his head.
"But Duncan was blessed with sons, so no match could
be made. Until—"

"Joanna!"

"Aye." The man nodded. "I believe that was the
earl's thinking."

"But not the thinking of John MacInnes," Gavin
added. Bit by bit, things were becoming much clearer.
"And Joanna was betrothed to James Gordon instead
of Athol."

"Aye, as you say! And that was the reason for the
earl's visit to Ironcross that night. News of the match
had just reached him."

"No pleasant surprise in that, I should think."

"Nay, m'lord," the priest returned solemnly. "The earl
clearly assumed that she . . . well, she being the last of
this MacInnes line and heir to the holding, was rightfully his."

"So the father defended the daughter's choice of husband, and the two men fell out with one another."

"The daughter's choice?" The priest shook his head
adamantly. "James Gordon was no choice of the lass's,

so far as I know. 'Twas Sir John himself who had arranged for Joanna to marry the man. But being who she was, the lass was willing to please her father. I suppose, in power and fortune, Gordon was at least as fine a match as Athol, in spite of his title. But that wasn't all!"

"What else?" Gavin asked shortly.

"Sir John wanted her away from this place. I believe he was the only one of the MacInnes lairds who truly believed in and dreaded the Ironcross curse—not so much out of fear for himself, but for what it might bring on his daughter and on any bairns she might bring into this wretched world. And James Gordon has his own kin to the north. Sir John knew that the man would have no interest in moving into Ironcross Castle. He wanted her farther away from here than Balvenie Castle, the Earl of Athol's holding."

Gavin turned and looked into the face of the priest. "And this was the reason for his argument with Athol!"

"All I know of it." The priest stood up and tucked his prayer beads into his belt. "If that is all you wanted from me . . ."

Gavin nodded and watched as Father William started across the kirkyard. As he moved out of the protective shelter of the chapel wall, the wind swept the clerical robes against his thin frame.

The warrior chief, too, straightened and crossed the graveyard toward the arched passageway that joined the Old Keep with the south wing, separating the little church from the courtyard. Allan and the others he had spoken with had never so much as hinted that the fire in the south wing had been anything more than an accident. After all, accidents seemed to happen with great frequency here at Ironcross Castle. Perhaps a candle too close to a tapestry, or a flaming ember falling into the rushes on the floor.

But what if the truth lay not in such thinking?

The sounds of shouting and then horses came from the courtyard. Gavin looked up. John Stewart, the Earl of Athol, laird of Balvenie Castle, had arrived.

Chapter 10

The stillness, taut and charged with hostility, hung suspended in the air over the warriors in the Great Hall. The threat of violence lurked in every corner, and the few audible murmurs poisoned the air with low, menacing growls. On the walls, armed hunters and dying animals glared down from tapestries amid the mounted heads of deer and elk and boar.

And at the head table, the two leaders seemed to be making no serious attempt to dispel the gloom or to ease the tension.

Gavin Kerr stared thoughtfully at the crystal goblet in his hand. The wine, red and potent, glowed in the light of the fire in the great hearth. It was difficult for him to ignore the seed of suspicion that the priest had planted in his mind. From the time he'd greeted the Earl of Athol and his men, a coldness had taken control of him, driving his actions. Gavin knew he was not very proficient at hiding his feelings, and he was certain that the tall, lean Highlander had read the distrust in his face. Now, sitting at the long table with the haughty, silent man, he wondered if John Stewart was indeed responsible for the deaths that had taken place here last fall. Athol had reasons for desiring revenge, and he had the opportunity.

The Lowlander eyed the men crowding the hall. Tonight, before everyone had seated themselves at supper, Gavin had drawn his steward, Allan, aside, and had questioned him again about that dreadful night. The steward had told him that when the fire was out—when it was clear that no survivors existed—the Earl of Athol and his men had immediately left Ironcross Castle. Nay,

Allan told him, they had not bothered to stay so long as to bury the dead. What would drive a man to flee such a catastrophe, Gavin wondered. If not the demons of guilt, then . . . what?

Gavin knew some of Athol's warriors. There were some very fine fighters among the Stewart company. Indeed, too many hands rested on the hilts of swords in the flashing light of hearth and torch. The warriors from both sides were watching them carefully, taking their signals from the two leaders. Edmund had seated himself with his men by the door to the courtyard, and Gavin could see Peter amidst his fighters.

Gavin knew the value of his own men, and he knew they could win a fight against Athol's company. But it would be a bloody victory, and for what? This was no time or place to settle the crimes of the past. Besides, he reminded himself, he had no proof . . . yet. He still needed to give the man the benefit of the doubt. After all, the Earl of Athol carried the blood of the royal family in his veins. John Stewart had been cousin to James IV—the king whom Gavin had honored above all men. Spilling John Stewart's blood would require irrefutable proofs of guilt.

He turned to the nobleman sitting at his side. Athol's hair had been adorned with thin braids that mingled with the rest of the long, dark red locks that he wore down his back. A bit of a dandy, Gavin thought, eyeing the jewel-encrusted broach that held his tartan of red and green in place. He would not make the mistake of underestimating the man, though. He had seen Athol wield a sword at a number of tournaments, and his speed was lethal.

Gavin forced himself to speak. "We have begun work on the south wing."

Athol lifted his goblet of wine and drained it. "I knew your Border men were renowned for their prowess in battle." His face had the faintest trace of mirth in it. "I did not know they were builders as well."

"My lads would tear down and rebuild the gates of hell if I commanded it." Gavin stared out at the tense fighters who were watching them with the eyes of hawks.

He lightened his tone perceptibly and looked back at his guest. "I have already sent a man to Elgin to fetch the needed carpenters and stonemasons. I plan to rebuild that wing as it once was."

"You waste no time."

"From what I understand, when you are laird of this keep, time is a precious commodity."

"Time is precious for all of us," Athol replied vaguely, before turning his gaze again on the Lowlander. "But tell me, Gavin Kerr. Do you believe in the curse of Ironcross?"

Gavin filled up his guest's cup and then did the same for himself. "You have lived in this region for all of your life. What do *you* believe?"

The Highlander paused thoughtfully as he brought the wine to his lips. Then he let his gaze range over the Hall before returning to his host. "What I believe matters naught. But it appears that history is on the side of believing."

"Then you believe in these curses and ghosts and the violent death that goes with being laird of this keep!"

"Perhaps I do."

Gavin took a long moment before continuing. "Then why did you press your claim to be the laird of this holding? Do you not value your life?"

A sudden flush darkened Athol's expression.

" 'Tis no secret," Gavin continued, motioning for a serving lad to bring more wine. "You and Sir John made no attempt to hide your feelings on the night he died. As I hear it, this Great Hall was filled with onlookers, as 'tis now." Calmly, he paused as he refilled both of their cups. "But why should you want it so badly, and then leave it the next morning—barren, unprotected, and ripe for the taking?"

"You push the bounds of a new . . . friendship."

"Do I?"

"Aye. 'Tis none of your business what went on between the MacInnes lairds and the Stewarts of Athol, and I owe you no explanations for anything I do. But I will tell you this—my claim was fair."

Gavin returned the man's steady gaze for a long moment. "Perhaps that is so . . . friend."

Athol hesitated and then reached for the goblet. Several of the visiting warriors were restlessly stirring in their seats—as were Gavin's men—but no weapons had yet been drawn.

Athol's look at Gavin told him that his neighbor was also very aware of the nearness of a confrontation. After taking another drink, the earl spoke again, clearly trying to keep his voice calm "How . . . how much progress have you made in that wing?"

Gavin paused a moment and then nodded, acknowledging Athol's effort to diffuse the potential violence between their men. "You can see for yourself." He rose from the table. "Come with me, and I'll show you."

From the commotion in the kitchens, she had known the keep was overflowing with guests—and she knew who the visitor was. But Joanna still had a ghostly reputation to maintain.

It had been a difficult day for her, though, and one without sleep. The cursed laird had his man and Allan exploring the passages for most of the day. After she had returned from the tower chamber, she had kept an eye on them, trailing them as they made it as far as the subterranean tunnels, but not so close that they had any idea she was there. Oddly enough, Allan did not seem to be very familiar with the passages, and so the two hadn't been able to go very far. They never even came close to the south wing. But Joanna was becoming quite weary now. Real ghosts, she supposed, don't need much rest.

But at last the deed was done, and Joanna smiled as she closed the panel beside the hearth in what had been the study. The passage entry where she had nearly been caught by the new laird was of no use to her now—with the floor all torn away and the panel nailed shut—but another small panel on the opposite side of the hearth was close enough for her to continue plaguing the man.

So after everyone had settled down to their supper in

the Great Hall, she had crept back to the laird's room, taken her portrait once again, and brought it back here.

Once, long ago, Joanna had prided herself on her strength and perseverance. Admittedly, she had even been a bit mischievous as a lass.

It was good to have a chance to be human again.

Gavin glared at the smiling image.

It took great restraint on his part not to curse out loud at the sight of the portrait hanging yet again on that blasted wall. Drawing in his breath deeply, he scowled at Edmund, who stood at his elbow gaping dumbly at the picture.

Tearing his eyes from the painting, the laird tried to pretend that nothing was amiss. Gavin stepped into the open area and continued with the explanation of the renovations he had planned.

"As you can see, we are still in process of pulling down those walls. My thought is to rebuild, using a style that I have seen in my travels." Gavin hesitated, noticing that his guest had not followed him into the room. Athol remained standing in the entryway, his eyes focused on Joanna's portrait. As the Lowlander looked into the earl's face, he sensed something far different than what he had expected to find there. For Gavin saw no guilt, and his jaws clenched tightly in response.

There was longing in Athol's eyes as the man gazed on the portrait.

Gavin turned away, fighting off the insane possessiveness that he could feel flooding through him. And it *was* insanity, he knew. He wanted to shrug off this intruder, climb the ladder, and carry the picture back to his chamber. As he had done before. As he would do again.

Athol broke the awkward silence, and his voice was husky, almost reverent. "I didn't know anything survived the fire."

"*She* did," Gavin put in shortly.

"Why have you left her there?"

"To oversee the work!"

Athol's eyes darted to Gavin. A glimmer of wry amusement flickered in their depths. "I see that the madness that runs rampant in these hills has affected you as well. I would pay a fine price for that painting if you could bear to part with her."

"She is not for sale," Gavin said shortly, ready to usher his guest out of the chamber. Edmund and a few men stood in the corridor beyond Athol.

The earl was not ready to budge from where he stood. He almost smiled at Gavin's response. "Perhaps this is not a good time to discuss the matter."

"There will *never* be a good time to discuss it."

Athol didn't seem convinced. Still rooted to the spot, he again looked longingly at Joanna's portrait. "I knew the grandmother well. She was quite attached to the lass."

"Aye. What of it?"

"I was wondering if you were going to honor her wish?"

"What do you know of Lady MacInnes's wishes?"

"I know she wants the painting for herself. She sent word to me last winter after the fire. She wanted me to ride down here and see if . . . if Joanna's portrait had survived the blaze."

"But you did not come back."

Athol stared at him. "Nay. I did not come back."

"Why?" Gavin pressed. "What was in this destruction that you could not bring yourself to look on? They say 'tis hard to return to a place where one feels . . ." The warrior chief paused, pretending to search for the right word.

"Once again you are meddling in my business!"

Gavin gestured to the chamber behind him. "I see the destruction in a keep that now belongs to me. 'Tis my business to learn the truth."

"This truth that you are after has nothing to do with me. What went on between John MacInnes and me that night was the same quarrel we had been having for some time. That night, though, so many were present."

"And that night, disaster followed."

"A disaster that had nothing to do with our disagreement."

"There are others who feel differently."

"They can all burn in hell," the earl exploded. "As far as I am concerned, they are nothing but a pack of cowardly dogs. If you look closer . . . laird . . . you will see that each one of them . . . well, you will see that there is more here beneath the surface than meets the eye. And far more reason for murder in some than you will find in any debate between the MacInneses and me."

Gavin looked at Athol's flushed face and saw it best to let the matter drop, for now. "Whatever happened, 'twas a waste of life, was it not?"

The Earl of Athol stared at his host for a long moment. "Aye, Gavin Kerr. A great waste."

Joanna awoke with a start.

Tucked away in a passage beneath the Great Hall, the young woman listened carefully. She must have dozed off, crouching next to the wall, but she was unsure what had awakened her.

Quietly, she stood up. As she moved confidently through the darkness, she considered how much bolder she had become of late. She knew that they had returned the painting to the laird's bedchamber just before he had retired, and as she reached that level, a thrill coursed through her. Aye, she thought, she would steal the thing again and no one would catch her!

But as Joanna closed a sliding panel behind her, a chill ran up her spine and she thought, suddenly, how fragile a looking-glass image can be. Someone had been through this passage, and not long before her. The smell of oil from a wick lamp was heavy in the enclosed space.

Pressing her back against the wall, the young woman stood motionless and considered her next move. The laird—rightfully so—was becoming irritated with her mischief. No doubt that was why he had sent his men to probe the passages earlier in the day. She peered through the darkness down the passage. She was only a few dozen steps from the laird's chamber. Could he be setting a trap for her? Could he himself be waiting to discover her? To her shock, waves of fear mingled with an insane sense of excitement and—though she denied even the thought of it—anticipation. She had been alone too long, she thought, biting at her lip.

She shook her head, becoming angry with herself for such silly, fanciful notions about the handsome laird. True, the man apparently seemed smitten with her portrait. But how would he react if he were ever faced with her in the flesh?

Perhaps it would be best if she were to give up her mischief for the night and let the poor soul rest in peace. She must not take foolish risks, she thought, scolding herself silently. With that thought in mind, Joanna turned and started away down the stairs.

But before she had gone even a step, the smell of death penetrated her senses.

She bolted forward through the darkness, following the trace of smoke.

Her heart pounded. Her eyes teared. Her hands shook.

Could it be that she had failed him as well?

Chapter 11

The sky threatened to smother him, for there was no air in the gray fog.

It didn't matter if it were night or day; he knew where he was. The rain was pouring down, and the dismal pall that surrounded him was thick and black with smoke from the heavy guns the English had used to pound their ranks to tattered heaps of broken bone and bleeding flesh.

He could taste his own blood in his mouth, the burning heat on his face.

Gavin tried to raise his head out of the mud. The smoke from the cannons enshrouded him, blinding him, but he knew he was back at Flodden Field, lying in the muck, with the dying and the dead. Around him, a river of blood was pushing down the hillside, gathering up souls in its relentless current. Closing his eyes, he laid his head back down and waited for the flood to claim him.

His time had come. At last, his end was here.

The small hands, shoving hard at his shoulder, forced him out of his slumber. As his eyes opened a crack, Gavin attempted to focus on the tumultuous scene of battle. But it had all disappeared, and he recognized his bedchamber. The wall of flames that surrounded his bed was not another dream. He awoke with a start.

The spiritlike creature was tugging ferociously at a burning bedcurtain by his feet. With disbelieving eyes, Gavin watched as one of her hands swept back her wild golden mane from the leaping tongues of fire, as the other continued to fight furiously with the blazing material. Seemingly without fear, she reached through the flames and struck hard at his feet with a small bandaged fist.

"Awaken! Rouse yourself, for God's sake!"

Her voice was no more than a desperate whisper. Gavin shook his head to try to clear it. His chest constricted, and he coughed, unable to take in a clear breath. The smoke was heavy and the fiery blaze was spreading to the top of the canopied bed.

The woman turned sharply at the sound of his cough. He watched in sudden horror as the flames caught at the hem of her skirts, spreading upward rapidly. Leaping from the bed, he grabbed at his cloak and wrapped it tightly around her, reaching down and smothering the flames on her dress with his hands. She struggled against him, pushing at his arms as she tried again to reach for the burning bedcurtains. The giant warrior held her back until he was certain that she was no longer on fire.

Then, shoving her behind him, Gavin himself moved to the burning bed. Ripping down the curtains, he yanked off the canopy and threw them all onto the stone hearth. Pulling the bedclothes from the mattress, he spread them over the burning rushes on the floor and trampled out the flames.

The heavy smoke hung like a black cloud in the room, mixing with the sickening smell of burnt cloth and making it almost impossible to breathe. They were both coughing now, and, looking behind him, Gavin saw the woman turning away and throwing off the covering he'd wrapped around her. In the dim light of the chamber, her golden hair reflected the flickering light from the hearth, but there was little else he could see. Crossing the room, the laird roughly pulled open the shutters of the narrow windows, shutters that had been open when he'd retired. The night air rushed in, and as he turned back to her, the sounds of banging and shouting came from the outside of his door.

"The door is barred . . . he must be asleep . . . break it down . . ."

Her panic was as apparent as it was immediate. Gavin saw her bolt for the open panel by his bed. Racing across the chamber, he grabbed her by the arm before she could disappear again. She struggled hard in his arms, but he was not about to let her escape.

"M'lord! Gavin!" Edmund's voice could be heard the loudest. "Break it down, I say. The fire is—"

"The fire is out! I'm coming," Gavin shouted back as he dragged her roughly toward the door. But as he reached out to lift off the bar, she twisted herself in his arms and their eyes met.

He stared for a moment, stunned and unable to speak.

"Joanna?" he whispered finally, unconsciously loosening his hold on her.

She stared back at him with blue eyes as dark and as deep as the sky at dawn. But then, realizing she was free, she made another dash for the wall panel.

The shock that had coursed through him was dispelled in an instant, and Gavin reacted with the speed of lightning at her attempt to escape. Catching her by the wrist, he swung her around.

"Not so fast, my bonny bugbear."

Again, the sound of his men's impatient pounding drew his attention toward the door. She planted her feet and held back as he dragged her across the chamber.

"*Coming!*" He shouted. "There is no need to rouse the entire household!"

"Please!" Her dark eyes pleaded. Desperation rang in her voice. "Do not let them find me here. In the name of heaven, let me go!"

"But you are alive," he returned, his eyes drinking in the pale, flawless skin of her face; the unruly mane of golden hair; the full, unsmiling lips. "How in the devil's name can you expect me to—"

"I cannot be *seen.*" She coughed, tugging anxiously to free her wrist. "You did not see me here. I do not exist!"

"You think me a fool? I am not letting you go—not until you explain what you have been doing for these many months."

"I'll . . . I'll come back! I promise, I'll come back and explain it all to you," she vowed, glancing toward the panel again and pulling in that direction. "I just cannot allow them to know that I still live."

"Who? *Who* cannot know that you are alive?"

"Can you reach the door, m'lord?" the shout came from the corridor.

"I beg you, don't let them find me! I . . ." She shook her head helplessly.

Gavin looked about the smoke-filled room. Lifting her struggling body, he carried her toward the door and dumped her unceremoniously on her feet beside the entry.

"Stay and do not move," he growled threateningly as he quickly unbarred the heavy door, swinging it open wide and trapping the startled young woman behind it.

The astounded expressions on the faces of the men gathered in the hall greeted him. The steward Allan was carrying a torch. "Aye. What is it?" Gavin barked.

"Well . . . the smoke, m'lord!" Edmund's eyes made a sweep of the room. "We smelled it, and then saw it coming from around your door."

Gavin scowled out at the group of warriors crowding around the entrance. The smoke drifting past their heads from behind him was beginning to abate somewhat. " 'Tis over, lads. All is well. I must have knocked a wick lamp over with my hand. The fire is out. Now be on your way. All of you."

None of them appeared ready to leave. They simply stood and stared at him, unwilling to return to the Great Hall if their leader needed them.

"Do you want a change of bedding, m'lord?" the steward asked.

Gavin glanced over his shoulder at the scorched bed and then back at Allan. "Nay, tomorrow will do well enough. There is no reason to awaken your sister or anyone else at this hour." He paused for a moment. "On second thought, I could use another wick lamp."

With a quick nod, the steward handed the torch to Edmund and disappeared down the hall. Gavin glanced at his warriors again. "What are you waiting for, lads? Back to your rest! Away with you!"

All but Edmund and Peter moved reluctantly down the corridor at their laird's command.

"Are you certain 'twas you who started the fire, m'lord?"

"Nay, I am not certain how the blasted thing started," Gavin answered. "But at this hour of the night, I am not about to raise hell looking for ghosts."

Peter stared at him with amazement. "Are you certain you are feeling well enough, m'lord? I mean, 'tis not like you to be so—"

"I said that I am fine, you scurvy baboon," Gavin answered, glowering as Allan arrived with the wick lamp. "And now I intend to go back to bed . . . and nay, I do not need either of you staying behind to tuck me in. Now, be off with you!"

Taking the lamp from the steward, the Lowlander slammed the door in the faces of the three who continued to stand gaping in the corridor as if the warrior chief had grown a second head.

Joanna pressed the palms of her bandaged hands against the panel of the wall behind her and waited, fighting to stay calm in the face of her rising anxiety.

As the door banged shut, she glanced briefly at him as the giant once again dropped the bar in place. Then, fixing her gaze on the ruined bedding piled high in the hearth, she refused to turn and look in his direction.

Conscious of his gaze on her, Joanna turned her eyes upward to her own portrait—the youthful, laughing expression mocking the woman standing in rags against the wall. How long it seemed since she had sat for that painting. How long it seemed since she had been that young woman. The portrait amused him, perhaps. But how would this man react now that he was faced with the scarred, ravaged woman Joanna had become? The truth was far uglier than that fantasy of color and oil.

She shot a quick glance at him. The Lowlander was leaning comfortably against the door, his muscular arms folded across his impossibly broad chest. In his hands, the wick lamp looked like a tiny toy. His dark eyes were roving over her. Well, he deserved that much, she thought. It isn't everyday someone meets the dead.

"I could not be certain you would still be standing here when I closed the door."

"You thought me a ghost? A goblin?" Her voice was

unsteady. "Some eldritch fiend that would steal off to hell when your back was to me?"

"I feared you were only a dream!"

It took incredible self-control not to turn and face him. "Some horrible nightmare, I would assume."

"Nay, not a nightmare. But a recurring dream."

Joanna quickly stole a look at his face. He seemed amused by her discomfort. "So, m'lord. You dream of being burned to cinders and rescued by spirits often?"

He shook his head. "Nay, not of burning. Now, of being rescued by spirits—that's quite another thing. What man wouldn't fancy being rescued by so bonny a phantom as the one standing before me now?"

Joanna couldn't help either the sudden fever that she felt burning her cheeks or the intense heat that was suddenly spreading through her.

"Ahh, you can blush!" he said quietly, nodding. "Apparitions do not have the blood for that, I believe." A smile played over the corners of his mouth. "I am Gavin Kerr, mistress."

There was not much that did not reach her ears. "The new laird. I know."

"But do you also know that, since becoming laird of Ironcross Castle, dreaming of you has become a habit of mine?"

Now she couldn't tear her eyes away from those dark mischievous eyes. She saw them lower and focus on her lips. She swallowed, stumbled, looking for the right words. "Must you . . . speak to me . . ."

"What, lass? Speak of dreaming?"

"Nay." She shook her head, daring herself and looking down to his bare chest. "Must you speak . . . You are . . . ah . . . you are undressed, m'lord. 'Tis a wee bit . . . well, disconcerting."

Holding the wick lamp out, Gavin straightened from the door and looked down at himself. "So I am."

She averted her eyes, trying to look at anything else but him.

Gavin blew out the wick lamp and placed it in a wall sconce beside the door. "But then," he continued, "the sight of my body surely can be of no consequence to you, considering the way you have been using my chamber nightly for your sport."

"Sport?"

"Aye, for nightly hunting! Entertaining! Why, it has served you well even as a dinner hall! Do you deny it, my wandering spirit?"

"What makes you think 'twas me?" she challenged, glancing at his face. The diminished light made her a bit more comfortable, but only until he took a step closer to her.

"Has it not been you?" he asked, his eyes looking into hers in a way that swept away all vestiges of tranquillity within her. She tried to look away again, but he reached out and took a hold of her chin, lifting it until their eyes once again locked. "Tell me, has it not been you who has, time after time, stolen her own portrait from under my nose." His touch made her burn hotter than the fires she'd faced earlier in rescuing him.

"Well?" he asked again, his thumb resting gently on her cheek.

She shrugged her shoulder in response. She was too shaken by his closeness and his touch to attempt a coherent response. His skin was red gold in the flickering embers of firelight, and Joanna's ability even to breathe had ceased.

As he dropped his hand and walked toward his bed, confusion wracked her brain. How could it be possible that an ache so much like disappointment plunged like a stake into her chest as he released her? She stared at him as he reached for his kilt on the floor by the great bed.

She couldn't help looking at his broad, naked back and hard, muscular buttocks. A tightness quickly gathered in her middle. He was incredibly tall and a powerfully built man. Marks from old wounds stood out white on his shoulders and arms, and she had seen a terrible jagged scar along his left ribs, just beneath his heart. But he was more stunningly perfect than any likeness of man she had ever seen in life or in paintings. She let her eyes travel down his lean, sinewy legs, watching the flex of muscles as he wrapped the kilt about his waist.

"I still cannot see the reason for your discomfort at my nakedness," he said without turning.

She jumped, startled at the feeling of being caught. As she stared, he unfastened his broadsword from a thick belt and dropped it on the bed before wrapping the brown leather strap around him.

Gavin turned and faced her. "I have lost track of how many times you have broken into this chamber, but you must have seen me in bed on numerous occasions. Is this not true?"

Embarrassed and angry with herself for being so bold, Joanna turned her face away, trying to cool the heat racing through her. "Once or twice," she whispered.

"And then, of course, there was the time when you came in here to steal the portrait while I was dozing in the tub. I believe I was less than modestly attired at that time as well."

"Hmm . . . I can only suppose that you were adequately attired for the situation, m'lord." She tried to hide her smile. "Not that I noticed!"

"And you expect me to believe that?" he replied, folding his arms over his chest. "That you didn't *notice*?"

"It matters little whether you do or not. But regarding the painting, I would hardly consider taking what is mine 'stealing.' "

"You consider that portrait yours?" The laird smiled mischievously as his eyes raked over her. "Have you forgotten, Mistress Joanna, that you have been dead for well over half a year, now?"

"You might find me as ugly as a corpse just risen from the grave, but I assure you, I am not dead."

"And I assure *you*, I would willingly die a thousand times over if I thought someone the likes of you would be keeping me company for all eternity."

Joanna gaped at him. His eyes radiated heat. His expressions were surely empty words of flattery, but the look in his face continued to disconcert her. His eyes were black and flashing as they now fixed boldly on her face. She struggled for a moment to find her voice—and her composure. "As . . . as I was saying . . . I can assure you, m'lord, I am flesh and blood . . . and alive."

"So I can see."

Joanna almost wished he would stop staring at her. Was he blind? She was certainly no goddess descending to him from the heavens. But then his reaction to her was so much like a dream. So many times she had wished to be whole again. To be a fraction of what she had once been.

"Why do you look at me this way?" she asked, returning his bold stare with one of her own.

"This way?" he asked with a half smile. "I have only begun to feed my curiosity, and I have far to go before 'tis satisfied. And as I can see, you have begun to do the same."

Joanna jerked her gaze away. He had a point, and she knew it. It was all too obvious that she herself had allowed her eyes to feast openly on him. And watching him dress in this fashion! But she had never before felt the liquid fire that was coursing now through her veins. Standing there, gazing into the embers of a dying fire, Joanna realized now that she had somewhere, long ago, given up the expectation of such feelings.

"Where were we, lass?"

The mere sound of his voice shook her out of her wild reverie, and a sudden panic took hold of her.

"I had better be on my way. 'Tis so late. Too late. You will sleep if I leave you be." She looked up at him, unable to tear her eyes away from his hard face as he approached her. "You must certainly be tired. I shan't take the painting again . . ."

Joanna couldn't continue. The words withered on her lips, her breath caught up short as he came to a stop only a half step away. All she could see was the span of his wide shoulders blocking her escape. She leaned her head back against the wall and stared up into his black eyes. A shiver coursed like a fever through her.

"You are not leaving."

" 'Tis late, and you—"

"Have not even started yet!"

This was a dangerous man, and she knew she should be frightened, but somehow she wasn't. "What do you mean by that? About not . . ."

The laird ignored her question, and she found his eyes slowly appraising her—from head to foot, and back again.

"What is it that you are after?" she asked hoarsely.

He paused for a long moment. "Answers."

"And that is all you . . .?" Joanna bit at her lip, embarrassment boiling beneath the skin of her face.

The laird's full lips lifted in a smile at her impulsive utterance, and he reached up and framed her face with his large hands. His hands were stunningly cool on her skin, and Joanna's eyes fixed on the dark curls that adorned the scarred musculature of his chest. A long moment passed, and suddenly she realized that she was wondering what it would be like to run her fingers through those curls, to feel them against her cheek.

"Well, lass. You've managed to read my mind. There are many questions that are nagging at me. But not one of them is interesting enough to break this spell you have cast on me."

"I am a ghost, m'lord, not a witch. There has been no spell cast here," she said softly as his fingers made a sensual journey of the planes of her face. He was driving her mad. Joanna reached up and took hold of his wrist. "Your own imagination is driving you to this. 'Tis simply a portrait that holds you."

"So bonny you are, Joanna MacInnes," he whispered. "So soft, just as I imagined you would be."

"You are mistaken. I am not she, m'lord. That beauty sits over your hearth. But she is gone. I carry the scars of—"

"Hush." He lowered his head and brushed his lips lightly over hers. Joanna's eyes flew open in shock, and she stared in awe as his lips hung a breath above hers. His dark, mysterious eyes drifted over her features, caressing her face. "You are beautiful . . . and real . . . and alive."

Then, as if in a dream, Joanna moved her hand from behind her and wrapped them around his neck. With a passion that blinded her, she lifted her lips to his.

Chapter 12

The flames, leaping up in the hearth behind him, made the earl's shadow stretch out like some fiend, ready to snuff out the very existence of the young man standing against the far wall.

"And you are certain that no one suspects you. Even now?"

"Aye, m'lord," David said quietly. "No one suspects me of anything. To all of them, I am just another stable lad. It runs in our blood—looking dim does—and my ma always said—"

The Earl of Athol raised a hand to silence his faithful young informer. He then started pacing the room, pulling thoughtfully at one ear as he strode before the fire. He stopped and looked back at the lad. "But back to what you just said. You are certain that he survived the fire unscathed."

"He did," David bobbed his head. "When all the men were gathered in the hallway right outside his door, I sneaked behind them and watched the laird open his door. He escaped the whole thing without a burn marking his skin. I mean, everyone in the keep talks about the man sleeping like a corpse, but somehow he must have managed to wake up in time to save his hide."

Sleeping like the dead is not truly wanting to be dead, Athol thought with a shake of his head. Gavin Kerr's death wish didn't run as deep as he'd been led to believe.

"It appears the man has some fight left in him yet!" Athol whispered, turning and staring into the flames.

*   *   *

Gavin's response to her own boldness left her utterly dazed.

Joanna's breath caught in her throat. The wrappings on her palms were suddenly soaked. Her mind and her thoughts were in shambles. She shivered in his tight embrace, and thrilled at the feverish heat that was spreading through her.

A hungry sound emitted from Gavin's throat as he deepened the kiss, crushing her closer to his hard, unyielding body. Intense longing swept over her. She could feel the heat of his bare chest burn and caress her. Then Joanna felt his tongue trace the edges of her lips, and she realized that he wanted her to open her mouth to him. Tentatively, she parted her lips, and Gavin's tongue surged inside.

Stunned by the intimacy of the kiss, Joanna trembled, her knees weakening. The world spun around her, and she gripped Gavin's shoulders very tightly, certain that she would fall if he were to release her.

But Gavin made no move to set her free. Instead, his bare arms tightened around her, pulling her so close that—through the haze of desire that was clouding her mind—she could feel the press of his manhood beneath the wool of his kilt. Vaguely, she knew she should be alarmed by the rising danger, but the aching of her breasts obliterated such thoughts of caution. More than anything right now, she wanted to feel her bare skin against his.

He shifted slightly, lifting her chin and running his fingers along the line of her jaw. She turned a bit in his arms, and his bare knee pressed against the inside of her thighs. She could feel the sinewy strength in his leg against hers. His hand caressed the skin of her throat, the top of her breast. Joanna took in a deep breath, her body rising to his touch. His fingers traced the wide neckline of her oversized dress and pulled it gently downward, exposing her flesh until her breast sprang free.

As his thumb circled her hardening nipple, Joanna gasped. Strange feelings flowed through her—wild, turbulent sensations—that were unlike anything she had ever known.

So this, at long last, was true passion. The thought emerged from the shadowy recesses of her mind, and a thrill of fiery excitement uncoiled within Joanna. She was alive—truly alive—and being given the chance to taste this fruit of heaven before reaching her life's end.

With a surge of rapturous delight, she tightened her arms around his neck, matching and returning the pressure of Gavin's demanding mouth.

"Joanna," he whispered against her lips, breaking off the kiss and moving his lips to her ear. "You *have* bewitched me." As he suckled her earlobe, his hand made a wider journey of her breast, kneading and caressing her firm flesh. Then, with a low groan, Gavin slid his hand around her hip and cupped her buttocks.

She felt him lift her body against him until she could feel his hardening arousal pressing against the juncture of her legs.

Joanna swayed in his arms, pleasure washing over her with each new sensation. The world around her was becoming fluid, dissolving with each passing heartbeat. This growing ecstasy—this sweet hunger that she felt in his embrace—it was now the ruling passion.

"I think the devil has possessed my soul," he said hoarsely into her ear. Pressing her against the wall, Gavin took hold of her wrists and brought them down to her sides. His voice was ragged with desire. "Tell me to stop, Joanna, before I carry you to my bed." His powerful hands gently cradled her face as he tipped her head back and stared into her eyes. "You *are* flesh and blood. And for too long I have looked at you, fancied you, dreamed of making love to you."

Joanna stared into his chiseled face, his black burning eyes. Desire, like dark pools of molten steel, filled them, and she could feel the power of his control, taut and strained, but ready to unleash his own needs.

"Then do with me what you desire," she heard herself whisper softly. Her body burned for him, for his touch. She knew only in the vaguest terms what to do, what to expect, but she also knew that she would die if he did not show her the rest of the way. His hands once again cradled her face.

"Make me yours . . . now . . ." she added with a whisper, turning her face and kissing the palm of his hand. "I have not much time left to me. Grant me this one wish."

It took only an instant for her words to sink in, and then the hands that had only a moment earlier gently caressed her, now inflicted pain as he took her by the shoulders in a viselike grip.

She stared at him in amazement. His eyes were cold fury, and his fingers felt as if they would crush the bones beneath her skin.

"What the devil are you talking about? What do you mean, you have not much time left?"

The spell was broken and everything crystallized before her eyes. The chamber that had been blurred and dreamlike in his tender embrace, suddenly became a mass of sharply defined lines and colors.

"Joanna," he said, shaking her hard and forcing her eyes to snap up to his. "Explain to me what you meant by those words."

This outburst of temper, as stunning in its suddenness as in its ferocity, left her shocked and unwilling to speak. Whatever had possessed her to say what she had, was gone from her now, and Joanna knew it would be unwise to reveal anything of her plans to him. She pulled up the neckline of her dress to cover herself, and tried to gather her wits.

She fixed her gaze on the lips that were now drawn tight. "To the world, I have been dead for months. Alone in these caverns, I have thought a great deal of death. In my mind's eye, I have seen myself die numerous times. I do not fear that end. We all must die someday—some of us sooner than others."

"Do not talk in riddles," he ordered harshly, still holding her tightly. "You were not speaking of one's destiny or of the heaven or hell that awaits us when our time in this life is through. You were speaking of yourself. What are you not telling me?"

She tried to laugh off his question. "You read so much

into so little! Well, m'lord, you're wrong," She made an attempt to shrug her way out of his grasp, but he wouldn't relinquish his hold on her. "Now let me go."

"I am demanding that you, Joanna MacInnes, tell me—"

"Nay," she broke in, her temper flaring as she thumped his broad chest hard with her fist. She might as well have hammered the walls of Ironcross Castle itself. "You have no right to demand anything of me."

"I am the laird of these lands now."

"Take Ironcross and be damned! That is nothing to me."

"You *will* answer my questions."

"I will not," she responded stubbornly, matching his glare, "Not until you calm yourself and tell me what cause *you* have for this anger."

Gavin stared at her for a moment, and from his look Joanna was certain he thought her daft.

"Well?" she probed, feeling the weight of his hands still on her shoulders.

"You are the one who started all of this. You are the one who wished to be hidden. And then, trying to bewitch me . . . so soft and willing in my arms."

Joanna felt her skin on fire at his words. She had indeed practically thrown herself into his arms.

"You may think yourself clever," he continued, easing his grip and once again running his hands more gently down her arms. "You may very well be quite clever for surviving as you have for all these months. But tonight that has all come to an end. I have discovered you. You are alive and—well, 'tis time you stepped out of the shadows and told me what drove you to such foolishness—"

"Foolishness?" she flared. He was humoring her, treating her like an idiot who has no ability to think for herself. "What do you know of any of this? I swear by the Virgin, the only foolishness that I have committed in all this time, was to come here and try to save your miserable life from those flames."

"You could very well have set the fire yourself."

Joanna's eyes flashed as if she had been slapped.

"Aye, you have been in and out of this chamber for days now. You yourself just told me that you are the only soul living in the caverns beneath this keep. Who else other than you would have access to—"

"Many, you simple-minded brute," she snapped. "These passageways can be reached from a dozen rooms in this keep."

"But no one—not even the steward—appears to know that they even exist."

"And only dolt of a laird will believe everything that he is told." She hit him on the chest again. "Release me."

"When I am done with you," he said arrogantly. "Are you telling me that these people—these servants—know the ways and yet will not admit to it?"

"I am telling you that these passageways are accessible even from outside of the castle . . . and that there are many who come and go without your knowledge." She paused. "And there are some who bring death to your very door."

"You mean other than you?"

"Other than me? You thankless knave!" She twisted her body in his arms. "You are hurting me!"

Gavin's eyes did not release her as he eased his grip on her shoulder. "Who? Who are these people that you talk of?" he asked.

"The same ones who, last fall, killed my parents, along with innocent, unsuspecting serving folk."

The sudden quiver in her voice made Gavin stare more deeply into her blue eyes. They were so dark in the dim light of the chamber, but they showed the anger and pain, their intense sadness that lay curled like a snake around her heart.

"You know who killed your parents?" he asked at last.

She nodded without hesitation. "Aye. I know."

"Then, why is it that you went into hiding? Why wait so long to bring justice down upon his head?"

The flicker of sorrow that he saw her quickly hide was betrayed by the crystal droplets that pooled along the lids of her eyes. Gavin watched her struggle to hold back the tears. The mere mention of her loss and she had turned from a lioness to a battered lamb right before his eyes.

"Why did you not come forward sooner, lass?" he asked gently.

"I tried, but I could not bring myself to." Joanna brought a hand up to her face to dash away at a tear that had escaped and lay like a diamond on her cheek. It was then, before she could hide it again, that Gavin caught hold of her bandaged hand.

To his great relief, she did not try to fight him this time. The warrior chief stared at the loosely bandaged hand in his grip. The strips of linens wrapped around the palm and fingers only managed to cover parts of the damaged flesh. Patches of red, scarred skin showed around the edge. Gently, he drew the other hand from behind her back and examined that one as well. Though the scars were healing quite well, he knew they must have been extremely painful for some time after the fire. He looked up and found Joanna's eyes locked on the picture hanging above his hearth.

"Now you know. I am not she." Her voice was a mere whisper. "The Joanna MacInnes that you see in that portrait perished like the rest in that fire."

What a blind fool he had been to not realize the pain and suffering she must have endured to survive. Since finding her alive tonight, he had not once voiced his sympathy over the loss of her family nor thought to ask if she herself had been hurt. Looking down again at the fingers that had now curled tensely in his palms, Gavin raised one of her fisted hands to his lips and placed a gentle kiss on the exposed, red skin.

She withdrew it at once. "Do not pity me, Gavin Kerr."

"There is no pity in what I do, lass."

"Then why did you do . . . what you—" Frustrated, she cut her words short and looked away.

"For the same reason that I kissed your lips, your face. For the same reason I will kiss the rest of you as well, if you give me the chance." He took a hold of her chin and brought her face around. It took great deal of control on his part to not bend down and kiss her again. Her eyes were dewy with the emotions battling within her,

her skin glowing in the flickering embers of the fire, her lips swollen from his kisses. But a hint of a smile sat at the corner of her mouth. She had heard his confession.

"Seeing your bandaged hand," he continued gently, "reminded me how thoughtless I have been."

She stared at him, a hint of bewilderment evident in her face.

"I ask you, Joanna. Tell me about your life here. How have you managed to live since . . . since the fire?"

She started warily. "That is not a tale for one night, m'lord. Especially this night. As you can see, the sky is growing lighter outside your windows, and dawn will be breaking quite soon. You must release me, for I . . . I am so tired, as you must be yourself."

Gavin gazed into her eyes, reluctant to let her go. If this were a matter of trust, he considered how tenuous the thread was between them.

"You expect me simply to let you disappear like a spirit of the night?"

She nodded.

"I fear that if I were to let you go, in an hour I would wonder if you were ever here at all."

"Would that be so terrible, m'lord?"

"Aye, lass."

The deep violet blue of her eyes glistened as Joanna stared into his face. At last, she nodded again.

"I give you my word that I will return to you. You have a guest to attend to, but I'll come back." She glanced around the chamber. "Perhaps then we can talk."

To let her go was a foolishness, he knew.

Her words broke into his thoughts. "You now know that I live. And as large and complicated as the caverns beneath this keep might seem, I am certain if I were not to honor my part of the bargain, you would be able to find me. But I will not break my word."

He continued to look at her. She could seduce even a saint with that husky and alluring voice of hers.

"How do I know that you'll be safe?"

Joanna tilted her head and peered at him, her face grave, but her look impatient. "Considering the . . . the accidents that have plagued you since arriving here, I should think *your* safety might be of greater concern to us at the present."

"Have you been getting enough to eat while you've been in hiding? Has anyone been helping you? Bringing you food? Clothes?"

"You did not hear me," she said quietly, the spark of anger again kindling in her eyes. "I told you *your life* is in danger!"

"Aye, I heard you, lass. But you must answer my questions if you expect me to let you go."

She paused for an instant while studying his stubborn expression. "I've been eating better meals since you and your men arrived. And nay, no one knows that I've even survived the fire. I am just one more ghost that wanders the halls and corridors of Ironcross Castle. So you see, there is no danger awaiting me outside of this chamber."

The sound of the servants of the keep in the corridor right outside of his room drew Gavin's attention, and he glanced at the open window. The first streaks of dawn were indeed beginning to brighten the eastern sky.

"I will come back," she whispered again. "I promise you, I will."

Gavin's eyes flew back to her bonny face. He couldn't keep her here. He knew that Molly and the other serving women would be turning this room upside down—as soon as he stepped out of it—cleaning up the damage caused by the fire. Of course, he thought, he could always force her into the open.

The image of John Stewart, Earl of Athol, staring longingly at Joanna's portrait, came immediately to Gavin's mind.

"You will come back tomorrow night . . . I mean, tonight," he commanded with a growl that sounded more like a threat than an invitation. "You will return immediately after everyone has retired."

She paused a moment, staring at him, her lips pursed. Then, obviously too tired to argue, she nodded her assent. "If you wish."

"I do," he muttered. He started to step aside to allow

her to pass, but then he paused. "What happens if I need to get hold of you before then?"

"But why should you?"

"In case . . . how should I know? I simply want to know!"

Gavin scowled, and then watched her eyes glance about the room as she tried to think of an answer. She could take all the time she wanted, as far as he was concerned. The fact that she was alive, standing before him, all seemed so unreal, somehow. He just wanted to stare at her, study her, to drink in the pleasures of this enchantress who made him feel once again like an abbey school lad.

Too soon, her eyes brightened and returned to his. "If you ever *need* to get hold of me, go and see the priest, Father William. Have him take you to the underground crypt."

"I have seen it."

Joanna peered at him uncertainly. "You have?"

"Aye, he took me through the chapel when I first arrived."

Her face cleared as she shook her head. "Nay. There is another crypt, with tombs far older than the one you have seen. This one lies deep in the ground—far beneath the castle walls. The chaplain will know of an outside entrance to the place. Get him to take you there." Joanna glanced nervously at the door as the sound of steps making their way down the corridor could be heard. She lowered her voice. "When you get there, just send the priest back the way he came, and then I'll come to you."

"But how will you know that I am there?"

She edged around him. "I am very much attuned to that room. Trust me. If you should need me, I will be there."

As much as he wanted to, Gavin did not try to stop her as she moved quickly toward the panel in the wall.

"One more thing before you go," he said, drawing her gaze. "Who set the fire that killed your parents, Joanna? You told me that you know the murderer."

Her eyes bored into him as she stood by the open section of the wall. Her voice carried the note of absolute conviction.

"Mater," she answered. "Mater killed them."

Chapter 13

Down the hill, by the edge of the thick grove of trees that ran the length of the glen, Allan was supervising the butchering of the buck and the two does they had taken. Leaning on his hunting lance and holding his steed's reins, Gavin looked on vacantly as the steward tossed scraps of the kill to the waiting dogs.

Joanna MacInnes had lost her mind. How could she not? he mused, thinking back on their meeting, and on her parting words prior to disappearing from his bedchamber as the dawn threatened.

It was certainly understandable that a young woman would be distraught and overwrought with grief after such a tragedy. But to live as she had been living for the past six months! The loss of her parents in such a fire—under such circumstances—could easily have tipped the balance of anyone's reason. That must be it, he thought. It certainly seemed likely, at least, when one considered that in the aftermath she had willingly chosen a hermit's life for herself, shunning all human contact, and then conjuring up some wild idea about that harmless old woman somehow committing a murder of such heinous proportions.

But she certainly did not look mad, he thought.

If he'd only taken more time this morning to question Joanna about her accusation, before she had simply stepped back into the passageway and vanished into the darkness.

And if it hadn't been for his scurvy blackguard of a guest, he would have gone after her. It was a blasted devilish thing to have company who intrude on you when you least want them about, Gavin thought, steadying his restless horse. The damned earl was planning to stay through the week, and short of openly insulting the arrogant bastard—and starting a neighborhood war—the Lowlander didn't quite know how to cut the other man's visit short.

But still though, before leaving for their hunt this morning, Gavin had taken a moment to question the priest about the underground crypts that Joanna had spoken of. Gavin had not blinked an eye when Father William's jaw dropped in surprise at his laird's knowledge of the subterranean vaults.

With only the slightest pressure, Gavin had gotten the cleric to talk, though the information the man had conveyed had been cursory, at best. The tombs there were hundreds of years old, the priest had told the warrior, though he himself had almost no knowledge of who was buried there. But when Gavin had then asked if he knew how to take him down there, the priest had reluctantly nodded and said that the old priest before him had showed him the way. Looking out over the wall into the gorge where Gavin had encountered the falling rock, Father William had said there was an outside entrance to the crypt, and that he was fairly certain he could find it still.

It might be all for nothing, Gavin thought, watching the hound Max carry off a good-sized chunk of meat. Still though, the laird was determined to seek out answers to those questions that had arisen in his mind as a result of Joanna's appearance. A restlessness washed over him at the thought of her coming back tonight. Forcing himself to ignore the stirring in his loins, he drove the end of his hunting lance into the fallow ground. Perhaps a man with functioning reason would not have trusted her to return, certain that she would use the opportunity to escape him. But not Gavin.

An unspoken vow of trust had passed between them, and it was a pact that had made Gavin believe that she would come back. And when she did return, he wanted to greet her with information of his own. He could not bring himself to believe that Mater was a murderer, and he needed to know what made her accuse the old woman. But if he wanted to argue with her over who her parents' killer might be, then he knew he had better know more of this keep's history than he knew now.

Looking up the glen, along the line of trees, Gavin could still see no sign of Athol. The earl and the rest of his hunting party had taken off after a number of does, and frankly, this suited Gavin perfectly. It seemed that every time he had looked at John Stewart this morning, a dark, seething anger had coursed through him. And though the warrior refused to admit that he might be jealous of the man, knowing that Athol obviously had some shared past with Joanna raised an ire in Gavin that he could neither deny nor shake off.

She was not a child. He knew that. Her open and fiery response to his kisses told Gavin of her passionate nature. But it also spoke of her past experience. And all morning, like some thorn, the thought of her life before pricked at him. If this scurvy blackguard Athol were not a guest at Ironcross Castle, if he were not forced to look so often upon the Highlander's damnably handsome face, then perhaps this thought would not be plaguing him so.

But it was, damn it!

Once again, Gavin drove his lance into the side of the brae, cursing himself for feeling this way. Never in the past had he cared a whit about a woman's past. Virginity was an overrated condition, so far as he was concerned. Why, though she was long dead now, Mary Boleyn— one of the finest women he had ever known—had been a mistress to a king and to heaven knows who else. His lips pressed into a thin line. So why must he feel this way about Joanna MacInnes?

Gavin stared darkly at his thick, scarred hands, wrapped around the lance. By the devil, man, he told himself, she stirs you to want her, but surely the draw can be nothing more than physical. No one knew better than Gavin himself how little the future could hold. This was lust, he reminded himself, nothing else. Whatever else was pushing at him could . . . well, could go to blazes.

With an effort, Gavin closed his mind to such thoughts

and turned his attention back to Allan. Dismounting from his horse, he started down the slope toward the older man, his thoughts once again on the underground crypts and what little the priest had been able to tell him.

As the laird approached the small group of men, the shaggy hound Max loped over. As Gavin slowed down, the beast jumped up and placed his large paws against Gavin's chest, stretching out his neck and licking the master's face.

Dropping the reins of his horse, Gavin grabbed the scruff on either side of the dog's face. Scratching behind the dog's ears, Gavin turned to the steward and caught his eye. "I thought these dogs were raised to be hunters," he said gruffly. "They're as gentle as lap dogs."

"Most are better trained. But this one somehow is a bit confused." Allan shook his head at the animal. "We should have beaten him more, I should think."

"Nonetheless, they performed well today." As the steward nodded in acknowledgment of the compliment, Gavin pushed the dog off his chest and turned to eye the piles of meat already dressed and ready to go. "Not even counting what Athol and his men might bring back, I should say we have had a successful day."

"Aye, m'lord. 'Twill all be put to good use."

Gavin bent down and picked up a stick, throwing it for the dog. As Max raced off after it, the laird turned and faced the steward. "What do you know of the crypts that lie beneath Ironcross Castle, Allan?"

The look of shock in the steward's face was quickly replaced with an expression of bewilderment.

"Well?" Gavin prodded, unwilling to give the other man a chance to recover from the suddenness of the question.

"How do you know about—?"

"Why is it that this is the first question everyone asks? It is so strange that I should know about the crypt? Is there something forbidden in my knowing what lies beneath my own keep?"

"Nay, m'lord." The steward shook his head quickly. "I meant no disrespect. 'Tis just . . . I mean . . . m'lord,

no one has talked of or gone down there for years . . .
that I can recall. I am just a bit taken aback that you
should have heard about it. I do not know that many
in the keep even know that there are crypts beneath
the castle.''

"Well, some know. And I assume a few even remember how to get down there." Gavin frowned. "Though I
continue to marvel that, the other day when I was asking
who knew their way about the passages, no one spoke
up. Not even you."

" 'Tis not what you think, m'lord." The steward again
shook his head. "We all mean to serve you. 'Tis just that
those crypts, being so old . . . well, no one has any reason
to go there anymore."

As the steward's voice trailed off, Gavin frowned. Perhaps in expecting his new serving folk to confide in him,
he was expecting too much. If he was not going to make
them fear him, then he had to gain their trust—and then
hope for their confidence. But then there was still the
question of that vault. There was too much being kept
secret from him.

"So who is buried in that crypt?"

The steward paused as he looked uncertainly from
Gavin to a prospect down to a glen to the west.

"Who is buried there, Allan?"

"Many," the older man said quietly. "The crypt you
are speaking of holds many tombs, m'lord. The old folks
used to say, 'tis not one spirit that hunts Ironcross Castle, but many."

An awkward silence fell between the two, and Gavin
became aware of the strong, gusty wind that was whipping up, startling the dogs and worrying the horses.
Gavin realized that he no longer had the steward's attention. The old man's gaze—his very soul—seemed distant,
withdrawn, in another world.

Gavin's mind drifted back to Joanna. She knew about
that crypt. Surely, the belief of these people in the spirits
that were haunting the castle and the passageways had
only helped keep her from being discovered.

But did she know anything of the origins of those who
were buried there? Turning and looking at the still dis-

tant expression in the steward's face, Gavin felt his impatience to know more growing stronger. Curses, spirits, long-forgotten crypts . . .

Gavin shook his head. As strange as the answer was that Joanna had given him to his question about the murder of her parents, she, too, clearly believed that there were human hands involved in these killings.

"Allan," Gavin barked, drawing the man's attention back to him. "These folk that you speak of—the ones lying in the crypt—who were they and where did they come from?"

The steward looked back, seemingly unwilling to offer any answer.

But Gavin was not about to give up. "And how long has it been that they have been buried there?"

Allan took another long pause, and Gavin took a step toward him, losing his grip on his rising temper. But then, responding to his laird's obvious impatience, the steward opened his mouth and spoke.

"The age of that vault goes back beyond the memory of anyone living. For certain, 'tis more than thrice my age. And as for the names of the dead, all I ever was told was that they are saints, m'lord. From the abbey."

"From the abbey?"

Allan met Gavin's questioning gaze. "Aye, m'lord. That's all I know for certain. Over the years, though, as the curse . . . as the accidents began to claim more and more of the lairds of Ironcross, peasants began to make up tales about the crypts and the powers of those buried there. As a lad, I remember them coming."

"You remember *who* coming?"

"Peasants, m'lord. Poor, ignorant folk. Leaving gifts in the vault to ward off the evil . . . and not just the evil of the curse. Like pilgrims they would come from all over the Highlands—MacKenzies and MacLeods, Campbells and MacIntyres. You'd think it was Jerusalem. But in those days, we had no laird who spent any time at Ironcross, so there was no one to pay any mind to people from the hills tramping around beneath the castle."

Allan looked out at the thin sliver of loch visible at the end of the glen.

"Go on," Gavin ordered, stirring the old steward from his reverie.

"That all ended when Sir Duncan MacInnes became master of Ironcross Castle. He ordered the common folk to stay away, and ordered a punishment for those who were found trespassing in the passages." Allan shrugged his broad, old shoulders and looked away again. "No one goes there anymore. That is why no one in the house would dare to go into the passages. No one has been down there in ages. That is why no one remembers."

"Why, Allan, would a laird of Ironcross bury someone from the abbey in the caverns beneath his own castle. Why not in the chapel yard? Why not in the churchyard at the abbey? Saints or no, burying them here makes no sense!"

"I . . . I don't know, m'lord."

Gavin's face clouded over at the steward's inability to satisfy his questions.

"How much do you think Mater knows of the history of those people?"

Allan stared at his master and then began to shake his head slowly "I don't—"

"You don't believe she knows?" Gavin glowered. "Or you don't think she will tell me?"

"She . . . it surely would not be wise—"

"Wise? To question Mater? Why, Allan?"

The steward hesitated, but then looked positively relieved at the sound of horses in the distance. Gavin turned and looked up the glen as Athol and his men broke out of the wood and rode along the edge of the trees. He could see a pair of does draped across the saddles of the earl's men.

Watching his guest approach, Gavin turned again to the steward. "It seemed we have taken more than we need. Prepare the earl's kill, and advise the men that on our way back we will be stopping at the abbey."

"The reason for this visit, m'lord," Allan asked hesitantly, his face showing his perplexity. "Do you intend to try to question Mater? About the crypt, I mean!"

"Aye." Gavin nodded, looking hard into the steward's

face. " 'Tis clear to me I'll not be getting much information from my own people . . . unless I care to cudgel it out of them. I'm thinking I can learn a great deal more speaking with the woman."

The steward showed no further willingness to speak, though concern was etched on his features. With a look of disgust, Gavin turned and mounted his horse. Of course, he thought, whether *she* is willing to tell me what she knows is a different matter entirely. Shaking his head, he nudged his steed down the steep hill where Athol and his men waited.

From the time Joanna had named Mater as the one responsible for the killings, Gavin had been looking for an excuse to visit the old woman before meeting with the lass again. There was something very unsettling about this whole thing. On his last visit to the abbey, Mater had spoken of Joanna as a frequent visitor. She had spoken of her as a friend. But Gavin also recalled how she had spoken in riddles when she had answered his questions about the young woman. Now, knowing that Joanna had been alive all along, the warrior chief couldn't help but wonder if the old abbess knew the truth as well. But then, how? And more importantly, why—unless she saw the woman light the fire with her own eyes—should Joanna MacInnes go from seeking out the old woman's company to calling her a murderer?

"So, you were able to run a few of them down," Gavin said, approaching his neighbor.

"Aye," the earl replied with a nod. "And we could have taken two more with little effort. With no one hunting here of late, you should have plenty of meat to stock the larders of Ironcross."

Gavin ran a hand down the side of Paris's neck. "Well, I've thought of a more worthy use for the meat that we've gathered today. We are stopping at the old abbey on the way back to Ironcross. I plan to drop off some of the meat our party killed. While we're there, I thought I might visit a few moments with the abbess, Mater."

Athol's silence drew Gavin's eyes to the Highlander's face. His expression had darkened visibly, and his gaze was directed past the glen—in the direction of the abbey.

"If you do not wish to accompany me there, we could meet back at the keep. My steward will accompany you and make certain you are comfortable." Gavin watched the changing shades of color in the earl's face.

"Aye," the earl said finally. "I have no desire to see the old woman or her sad pile of stones. I will meet you back at Ironcross."

As Gavin struggled to hide his satisfaction, Athol's sharp, gray eyes turned to the warrior's face. "Tell me," he said in a conversational tone. "Were you welcomed there . . . when you first visited them?"

"How would you know if I visited them before?"

Though the Highlander never averted his eyes, Gavin noted the changing hue in his face.

Athol's voice was steady when he responded. "I just assumed you had been there. The abbey ruins and the land around it have been the undisputed property of the Ironcross lairds for . . . the devil knows how long. I simply assumed you would have wanted to meet her right away."

After a pause, Gavin accepted the other man's reasoning. "As you say, I have been there before. She is an interesting woman. But to answer your question, they are not the most friendly lot, if I take your meaning correctly. But what makes you ask?"

The Highlander leaned forward on his horse, patting his steed's ebony colored neck. "Well, I do not know how much you have heard, but over the years quite a few of the peasants from your lands have moved onto mine. Some looking for work, others simply wanting the protection of a laird."

Gavin had been told that much by the priest and he nodded.

"The stories that these simple folk brought with them always led me to think that there was something very peculiar—perhaps even dangerous—about this abbey." Athol stared at his host. "And the old woman."

"What kind of stories?"

"Stories about . . ." Athol waved a hand at the direction of the glen. "About women being the ones there . . . strange and savage women . . . living and working the fields. And other stories about men being abducted from the lands around Ironcross and held as slaves on the abbey lands. Wild stories about using these men only for planting his seed in a wife. About them being drowned in the loch afterwards . . . or burned!"

"And you believed these tales?" Gavin asked incredulously.

"Of course not!" Athol shook his head. "I attributed it all to the excuses these men felt they needed for leaving behind the lands their families had worked from the time of Noah. But I suppose there is always anger in a man who sees women who can survive without him. My opinion changed, though, when I faced their hostility myself."

Gavin's attention was riveted to the earl now.

"That first summer Joanna came to Ironcross Castle, I was a frequent caller. She was no stranger to the High—"

"This was last summer, I assume." Gavin could hear the hostility in his own voice, and looked down the brook as Athol's gaze flashed toward him. Though this was certainly not the time, something in Gavin wanted to wring the man's neck.

"The summer before last," the earl said slowly. "The first summer that Ironcross became her home. I was a *constant* guest here. But she was sent back to court in the fall, only to return the following fall with news of her . . ." He stopped, his face as dark and as fierce as a winter storm.

Joanna had returned to Ironcross betrothed to James Gordon, Gavin knew. How could he forget, his own face hardening in anger. She was alive and still legally bound to him. The hostility that both men were feeling almost crackled in the air between them. In a moment, the visitor's face cleared a bit, and he continued with his story.

"Well, that is finished. But that first summer, I soon found that she was a constant visitor to the abbey. And any time I questioned her about the place, she showed such enthusiasm for the people and what they were doing there that one would have thought she had discovered a band of angels living among the rest of us mortals."

"And in her praises of the folk there, did she include the abbess Mater?" Gavin asked.

"Aye, her the most." The Highlander nodded. "That old woman was the source of all that was good at the abbey, so far as Joanna was concerned. She looked at Mater with awe for the old woman's spiritual influence over her flock of followers. She definitely admired and respected the woman."

Gavin tugged at his ear and looked off at the crest of the hill, working hard to stifle the questions that were gnawing at him. Then what happened? he wanted to know.

"As I said, for most of my years as the laird of Balvenie Castle, I had heard the stories about the abbey. But when . . . when I set out to woo Joanna directly, I decided I needed to know the truth about the place . . . and about Mater. So I accompanied her there."

"And did her description of the place—and of Mater—agree with what you saw?"

Athol's gray eyes fixed on Gavin's face. "With the exception of Mater, I never saw a soul. 'Twas quite odd, being the beginning of harvest time, but the crops just stood untended in the fields. No one was working the land at all. 'Twas the eeriest thing I think I ever saw. That first day, when we left, I asked Joanna about it, and she just said that my presence must have frightened the peasants off. Perhaps the next time, she said, they might be more accepting."

"Was it any different when you went back?"

Athol gave an empty laugh. "Nay, 'twas no different. But stubborn as I am, I thought I could force my will on a bunch of women. That is all I thought them to be. Frightened, faceless, invisible women! In the end I was the one who was made to feel invisible."

"Through all of this," Gavin asked, his face grave, "how did Mater treat you?"

"She tolerated my presence, I think, because of Joanna. But she never once spoke to me, or included me. I went perhaps a half dozen times—until Joanna asked me to stop. It had become very clear that my presence with her at the abbey was putting some kind of pressure on her relationship with those women. So, in the end, she chose them over me."

Gavin looked away from the Highlander's grim expression. There was much to sort through in his words. But one thing was immediately apparent—the force of the connection between Joanna and those women, including Mater, had been stronger than anything she'd felt for this man. It was clear Athol had thought himself a suitor—and one with a claim to her hand in marriage. But Joanna had rejected him, first by excluding him from her world and then by becoming betrothed to another.

Gavin looked again in the direction of the abbey. Though he had much to learn from Mater, the warrior chief suddenly knew that whatever information Joanna had to share, it was perhaps worth more than anything he could learn from Mater, Allan, Athol, or any of the rest of them.

Joanna alone appeared to hold the key of the past.

Chapter 14

He hadn't believed her.

Although she might have forgotten many of the manners of day-to-day court life, she would never forget how fine a weapon a look of scorn could be. It was clear to her now that Gavin Kerr regarded her revelation to him as daft. And it was crystal clear as well that he held the same opinion of her.

Indeed, she thought, she must be daft, because she was clearly smitten by the man. There was no denying it now, not after what had happened last night. Not after the way he'd kissed her, caressed her in his chamber. Not after the way she had felt in his embrace. Joanna knew now that Gavin Kerr had held the same fascination for her as her portrait had for him. And she had to admit—albeit reluctantly—that feelings for him had stirred long before she'd come face-to-face with him. Well, she *was* daft, after all. And in the same stubborn manner that he'd carried her picture back to his room time and time again, she too had been driven by some mad desire to look in upon him night after night. As difficult as it was to admit, she now knew the truth behind her midnight jaunts to his chamber. True, her visits had then only seemed to be a pleasurable thrill. But after meeting with him last night, she knew now that thrill could easily become a habit. And one to revel in at that.

But then, who was *he* to think her mad? She could picture him in her mind now, hardly listening to the truth—or anything else for that matter—if she were to say it. The thought of him standing by the door, the gray smoke from the fire still drifting about his magnificent body, flickering in her mind's eye, and she drew in a sharp breath.

Well damn him, she thought, forcing the vision—reluctantly—from her thoughts.

Joanna leaned down and tried to focus on her task, stabbing again at the hard earth beneath her fingers. She hadn't needed anyone for a long, long while, and she wasn't about to start asking for help now. Not when it concerned a fight *that was hers by right.*

"Damn!" she cursed aloud as the dagger slipped out of her hand. She listened for a moment, startled by the echoing reverberation of her voice.

Moving the flickering wick lamp back a bit, Joanna straightened and stretched her stiff joints—knees, back, shoulders, and fingers—before kneeling again on the crypt floor. Edging backward, the young woman resumed her digging, using the tip of the dagger to extend the channel she had been working on for weeks. She had to wash all thoughts of him out of her mind. She had to forget his stirring kisses, his roaming hands—touches that had made her feel like a woman. She had to focus her mind on one thing. Justice. This was why she was here. This was the reason she had endured these endless months of darkness and loneliness and pain. She had to proceed. She had to execute her plan.

After watching these women carrying out their rituals month in and month out, she had crept into the crypt when she knew she could search without fear of discovery. And she had found the way. Joanna had discovered the small channel that had been dug in a circle at the center of the vault. Over the channel they would build their pyre of branches and reeds. And around this circle, the woman gathered. All of them at the full moon.

At the end of the circle, beyond where Mater stood, there was a large container of oil. Joanna had watched repeatedly how at the fevered height of their orgy, the old woman would release the oil from the container into the channel.

She edged back again along her path. This was her plan, simple and just. She had simply added an extension to the channel. One that would bring the river of oil to

the door and block their only escape route. In the dim
light, they would not even know there was anything different. Not until the fire had already been touched to
the oil.

She could already feel the heat of the flames around
her. She had envisioned the scene so many times in her
mind. All of them still wild and unheedful in their
frenzy. Her, standing by the door, blocking their way,
the flames leaping at her back. For the rushes she would
have quickly pulled from behind the crypts closest to the
door, the ones she'd soaked in oil and hidden, would
now be ablaze. Their only exit would be a smoky in-
ferno. She'd feed the fire and watch them scream and
die. The same way she knew her own parents had died.
She would meet her own end in that room. But then,
this was her destiny.

If it was madness, Joanna thought, then so be it. What
other choices did she have? She was the one true heir
to Ironcross. She was the only one capable of handing
out justice to the she-devil.

He was a fool to think his reception would be any
different than the one they'd given him before. But still,
Gavin thought wryly, one could always hope.

Having left the few men who had come with him by
the river on the outskirts of the village, Gavin led the
mare carrying his offering of meat down the path toward
the ruined abbey gates. Just the same as last time, emptiness and silence were all that greeted him.

Gavin tethered his horse to a small shrub by the same
hut where he had seen Mater last. This time, however,
the dying embers of an old fire and an empty block of
stone beyond it were all he found. Still unaffected by
this lack of welcome, the Lowlander turned to the mare
and quickly unloaded the butchered venison. Bringing it
back to the fire, Gavin spread the hide of one of the
animals and laid the meat on it. As he worked, he was
very conscious of the weight of many eyes peering at
him from the darkness of the huts around him.

Moments later, after the laird had finished with this
portion of what he'd come here to do, he crouched down

beside the fire and started feeding kindling into the coals. Small flames leapt up, and, though the day was still warm, Gavin gradually added larger pieces of wood until he had a fairly large blaze. For all any of the onlookers would be able to tell, he looked as if he planned to spend the day. This, Gavin knew, would be somewhat bothersome to the folk who had hurriedly left their undone work in the fields. He knew the abbey had been feeding its people and eking out an existence, without any help from the Ironcross lairds, for a long while. He also knew that the growing season was short enough in the Highlands. Losing out on a day's work, he was quite sure, would be a high price for them to pay.

It took some time, but at last Mater's thin frame emerged from the hut. Her disapproving scowl at his relaxed position by her fire was a prize well worth waiting for. Gavin smiled in greeting and stood up. She glared back at him before casting a disdainful look in the direction of the meat.

"What brings you here?" Her tone was ice cold and impatient.

With a nod, he crouched down and began to feed the fire again—the same way she had done the last time he'd been here. "We finished a fine day of hunting, and I thought it appropriate to share the spoils."

"We have no need for acts of charity!"

"If that is so, Mater, then you must be the only religious leader this side of Jerusalem who feels that way."

The old woman stared at the laird in silence, and Gavin knew she was working hard to hold her tongue.

"Actually," he continued, " 'tis no charity. At least one of these does was probably taken on your lands. 'Twas only right that your people have a share of the meat."

She stood still, looking across the flames at Gavin's face. "You keep yourself and your men away from this abbey. We gladly forfeit all rights to any game you take. And we will not touch this meat."

"That, of course, is up to you, but you'll have to put up with a fearful stench as it rots here by your fire."

"Now, that is a feeble threat," she scolded. "But wast-

ing such quantities is sinful. Nay, laird, you have to take
it back."

"I will not," he answered determinedly. "And if you
continue with this foolishness, I will have my men bring
provisions for you on a daily basis. In fact, I may just
have them go back to Ironcross and return with the *rest*
of what we killed today."

She stared at him as if he was some hideous, savage
beast. Gavin came to his feet in one fluid motion and
smiled down on her. "But I must tell you that they have
had a hard day of riding. And once I drag them in here
after all that extra work, I do not believe it will be a
very easy task getting them back on their horses so soon.
I fear you may just end up with a wee bit more company
than you are accustomed to. But you needn't trouble
yourself—they will be happy enough sleeping out here
on what is sure to be a fine, clear night."

Her wrinkled complexion flushed and her eyes were
blazing coals. "Are you threatening me?" she asked, her
fury ready to burst forth.

"Nay, I am trying to befriend you."

Gavin watched as his simple statement caught her up
short in whatever she was about to say. A fleeting look
of confusion played across her wrinkled brow as the flash
of anger visibly diminished.

"I do not understand you, laird," she said at last.

"That *is* your own fault and none of mine."

She again resumed her effort to stare him down, but
Gavin had heard the distant alarums of victory, and he
was not about to back away now.

"What is it that you want from us?"

"Are you going to ask me that every time I come here
for a visit?"

"If I thought anything I might say could deter you
from persecuting us, I would pray for angels to repeat
those words each day over Ironcross Castle!"

"Well, you might consider praying for something more
useful, abbess," he answered. "Just accept the fact that
Ironcross has a laird who takes an interest in his people.
You must become accustomed to having me around. The
sooner you do, the more comfortable your people will

be and the less disrupted . . ." He gestured toward the empty fields. "The less disrupted everyone's life will be."

"You think 'tis just that simple!"

"*You* make it too difficult."

Mater's frustration hissed out in a loud breath as she turned on her heel and stormed toward the gate.

"Wait, Mater," he said, laying a huge hand on her bony arm. She paused, glaring at him. "You might tell your legions of angels that this meat should be taken out of the sun."

The old woman glanced at the meat for a moment, and then gave an almost imperceptible nod in the direction of the hut she had come out of. Without another word or even a look at the warrior chief, she strode— with Gavin on her heels—out the gate, following the ruined wall until the valley floor began to rise toward the fields above the village.

Before they had traveled an arrowshot from the abbey, the sun faded from view. As he glanced to the west, Gavin could see the black clouds of a storm advancing over the distant loch. He turned his attention back to the wizened old woman.

"How many times will it take for me to come to the abbey before your people begin to accept my presence here?"

"How many breaths remain in your body, laird?" she said harshly. "You cannot force yourself upon them."

"I do not intend to use force," Gavin said matter-of-factly. "But these are now my people as well, Mater, and I want you to understand that you cannot make me simply disappear."

She gave him a critical, sidelong glance. "I should not be so self-assured, if I were you. You are only a mortal creature—flesh and blood."

"Do you think that only men are mortal?"

She didn't answer him, but turned her attention back to eyeing the plants around them as they walked.

"What do you have against us, Mater?" Gavin continued after a slight pause. "Why is it that you welcome the visit of any woman, and yet you despise the company of all men?"

She ignored his question but came to a halt. Gavin watched as her gaze swept over the ground. As her eyes lit on some frail-looking white flowers at the base of a protruding boulder, she turned from him and headed toward her prize.

Once again, he'd been dismissed, Gavin knew. But he was far from ready to leave. He strolled after her, watching her carefully. "Mater, what do you know of the crypts and the vaults beneath Ironcross?"

The obvious stiffening of her shoulders did not go unnoticed by the Lowlander.

"Why is it, Mater, that those people of the abbey were buried beneath the castle and not here . . . where they belong?"

She slowly came to a stop.

"Why are they thought of as saints?"

She turned her face and Gavin watched her hard, unchanging profile as she looked down at the abbey below. She stood in stony silence.

"Is there a link between the deaths of those entombed in the crypt and the curse that has been plaguing Ironcross Castle?" he continued doggedly. "Why is it that no one even wants to speak of them anymore? What is the reason for such mystery, Mater?"

He moved around her until they were face-to-face. His tall frame and broad chest blocked her line of vision. She was forced to look up and meet his gaze.

"I will not give up until you answer at least some of my questions." He tried to keep the harshness out of his voice. "Who is it that is buried there, and why?"

Standing there, awaiting her answer, he became for the first time aware of the sharp wind that had come whistling up the open valley from the loch. The heather and the grasses were bending to the rush of air, and he shook back the black mane that was whipping about his face. The old woman simply stared at him, seemingly unaffected by the piercing gusts.

"Tell me, Mater. Tell me of their past."

Their eyes locked in a fierce battle of wills as the wind pummeled them.

"Women! They are women who are buried there,"

she said at last over the rising wind. "They are our ancestors, our saints, and our sisters. And you, laird . . . 'twould be wiser for you to cease asking your foolish questions and let their souls lie in peace. 'Twould be best for you to ride back down into the flatlands and never look back."

"And if I do not?" he challenged, trying to ignore the wind that was yanking at his tartan. "Would I then fall from a horse and crack my skull on a rock like Duncan MacInnes? Or would I drown in the loch like his son Alexander? Or perhaps I shall be poisoned like Thomas. But I suppose all of those are better deaths than being burned alive in a blaze that takes my family and innocent serving folk along with me."

He saw the smallest of quivers in the line of her jaw. "So what is it, Mater? If I do not bend to your will, will you order my death as well? Will you call on the powers of those women and wish me into my grave?"

"What do you know of bending to one's will? You . . . and those like you . . . know nothing of what 'tis like to bend . . . to suffer!"

Somewhere not far down the valley, a flash of lightning was followed by the crack of thunder. The storm was coming on fast. Gavin did not remove his piercing gaze from her hard gray eyes, even when he felt the first droplets of rain strike his face.

"I'll do what I must to protect my people," she said ominously. "And I'll use whatever power I can muster to crush the evil in men."

Without waiting for him to say more, the old woman turned and moved quickly past him and down the hill toward the abbey. She was halfway to the ruined walls before Gavin turned to watch her. Above her the sky had taken on strange, unsettling hues of gray and green, and the flashes of lightning were now followed immediately by crashes that seemed ready to split the firmament with their noise.

Gavin watched her march through the gate, and as she disappeared amid the stone huts, he was more certain than ever that Joanna's accusation of last night had to be false.

Mater's words echoed in his brain, and he considered all she had said. True, she would protect her people. But somehow Gavin knew in his gut that her solemn vow did not include murder.

Nay, he thought as the wind hammered against him, Mater was no murderer.

Chapter 15

Adding another log to the hearth, Gavin came to his feet and stared into the leaping flames. For the entire ride back from the abbey, he'd tried to recall everything he had learned from Lady MacInnes before leaving the Scottish court, since the old woman's recollection of events past was the only thing he felt certain he could rely on.

By Saint Andrew, from the time he stepped foot in Ironcross Castle, he had yet to hear a complete story from anyone—and that included Joanna. To Gavin, she was clearly too distraught from the tragedy she'd faced to relay anything that might be construed as rational or objective.

And what of Mater?

Leaning one arm on the carved mantel, Gavin pictured the old woman's razor-sharp look. She cut an impressive figure—no question about that—taking the approach that she had. And she was clever, for it was an art to talk so tough and to be effective without anything to back it up. To scare off an opponent with allusions to powers beyond those of the natural world. But that was her best possible defense, Gavin thought.

Still, though, there had been an attempt on his life. The acrid smell of drying wool wafted upward from his kilt, mixing with the lingering scent of burnt damask from the curtains that had hung from his bed. Someone had come into his room last night and had set his bed ablaze. Although he hadn't had time to think about it before now, Gavin was certain that this had not been the result of any accident. He had put out the wick lamp. There had been no candles left burning. The embers of the fire in his hearth were simply too far away for the mat of woven rushes to catch fire. Nay, it had been no accident.

And, Gavin decided, the intruder had been a person, not some demon invoked from the bowels of hell as Mater would like him to believe. Whoever had been here, the warrior felt with some certainty that he or she was living in his keep. No doubt it was someone who had witnessed Gavin's repeated contest for possession of Joanna's portrait, for the intruder had known him to be a sound sleeper. That was why the would-be killer had had enough courage to close the chamber's shutters before setting the bed ablaze, hoping his victim would die amid the thick, choking smoke.

The soft sound of a latch sliding and the quiet creak of the panel opening on its hinges erased in an instant the warrior chief's thoughtful scowl, chasing all unpleasant thoughts from his mind. Gavin straightened before the fire and looked hopefully in the direction of the secret door. As she stepped through and closed the panel door, Joanna's frame formed a shadowy silhouette on the wall from the light of the crackling fire.

She had come, just as he knew she would.

She hesitantly stepped further into the room and met his welcoming gaze. My God, he thought, she is beautiful. This time, not quite so dazed as he had been the first time they'd met, Gavin let his eyes study her face. She had been truthful when she'd said that she was no longer the woman in the portrait. A bit thinner in the face; paler in complexion; her eyes larger, wilder, and somewhat more intense; her lips fuller, her features all combined to make her even more stunning than the incredible beauty captured by the brush of oil over canvas.

Tonight she had pulled her golden hair back, and Gavin's eyes followed the one long, thick rope of a braid that draped over her shoulder, hanging down over her breast nearly to her waist. She still wore the same large old dress he'd seen her in the previous night. The dress seemed designed to hide all signs of her womanly curves, though it did indeed reach only to her calves. But, looking at the smooth, ivory skin above the square neckline,

Gavin felt the prickling warmth stir in his loins at the recollection that he had touched and caressed what was beneath the ill-fitting garment. Gavin glanced with a lusty appreciation at the sculpted beauty of the legs showing below the hem of the dress and above the tops of the soft, worn shoes that covered her feet. The singed marks around the hem reminded him of how close she'd come to getting hurt herself.

Suddenly he was startled from his reverie by the sight of her bandaged hands tugging at her skirts in an effort to cover her legs. As he glanced up with amusement at her actions, he was rewarded with a revealing view of the tops of her ample breasts above the neckline of the dress.

Her dark blue eyes flashed at him as she realized the futility of her actions, and she crossed her arms over her breasts.

"So you have come back."

"I told you I would."

His eyes again wandered lingeringly over her body.

"But I don't want you to assume . . ." she started quickly. "I mean, since I have come back tonight . . ."

Even her voice had the husky resonance of some rare, unworldly creature. She was like some fine angel sent to watch over the night dwellers of this dangerous and uncertain world, Gavin thought, waiting for her to continue.

Obviously frustrated, she let out a long breath and shifted her weight from one foot to the other. " 'Tis just what happened between us last night. I don't want you to think—"

"You don't want me to think that I owe my life to you!"

She nodded, and then shook her head. "Nay, that's not it at all."

Gavin continued unperturbed. "And you don't want me to think that I should expect you to watch over me."

She shook her head again. "I did not mean any of that. I meant—"

"Oh, so I *do* owe my life to you and you *will* watch over me and protect me," he teased.

Joanna looked at him through slitted eyes. She was quick to rile, Gavin recalled, thinking of their short encounter last night. He liked that in her.

"That was not what I was about to say. You are putting words in my mouth."

"Then why not tell me what exactly was on your tongue?" A bonny shade of pink had now settled on her cheeks.

"I was . . . I am trying, but you keep interrupting me."

Gavin started toward her. "I promise to not interrupt. Please continue." She was watching him suspiciously as he moved around her to the closed panel, coming close enough to her that his arm brushed softly against her shoulder.

Checking to see that the secret door was securely closed, Gavin turned and glanced at her slender shoulder and straight back. More than anything else right now, he just wanted to reach for her, turn her in his arms, and feel her lips beneath his. As if reading his mind, she looked quickly over her shoulder, giving him a withering scowl. He shot a smile at her in return before moving away from the panel.

"You were saying?" he asked, walking toward the small table that was spread with food. Gavin had used the ordeal of the previous night as an excuse for retiring to his chamber as the visiting bard had begun to sing what was sure to be a long tale of the ancient Celtic hero, Cuchulain. Gavin's guest, the Earl of Athol, had seemed to take no offense at his host's decision. Striding out of the Hall, Gavin had sent Peter in with a word to the cook to have some food sent up to his chamber.

And the cook had done as she was told, providing a formidable spread of meat, fish, breads, sweetmeats, and wine. But now, looking at the candles already half burnt in length, Gavin realized that had been hours ago. Joanna had taken her time in coming.

He glanced back at her and found her attention focused on the table filled with food. Lifting the covers off the dishes, he breathed in the aromatic scents of food that immediately filled the room.

"Since you no longer recall your earlier concerns,

would you do me the honor of joining me for a bit of supper?"

Joanna lifted her eyes slowly from the food and stared into his face. "You need not have gone to all this trouble just to question me. I have come back here of my own free will, and with the intention of telling you whatever you wish to know." The young woman hesitated. "Though I am certain you will not like nor believe some of what I have to say."

Gavin was not quite ready to engage her in an argument over Mater, so he stood behind a chair and waited. "But I did go to 'all this trouble,' and our supper is waiting. So why not join me?"

"And your questions?" she asked, gnawing her lip.

"Trust me, I shall not forget them."

"And . . ." She held her chin high. "And is there something else?"

He gazed at her with raised brows, shaking his head innocently.

"You know what I am speaking of. Beyond just the answers to your questions!"

"You mean in exchange for this food?"

She nodded, and a smile tugged at the corner of his mouth.

"Do you truly think me such a brute, Joanna?" He gave the table a reproachful glance. Then, he let his eyes travel the length of her appraisingly, noting how her body grew even more tense beneath his scrutiny. Suddenly, he shook his head determinedly. "Never!

"Now, if this were food from the kitchens of my cook at Ferniehurst Castle—or even a dish served at Ambrose and Elizabeth Macpherson's—"

As he'd hoped, at the mention of those names from her past, Joanna brightened immediately. "Do you know them?"

He stared at her, mesmerized by the radiance that emitted from her. This was the first time she had smiled since he had seen her, and suddenly she lit up the chamber.

"They happen to be my closest friends," he answered

finally. "In fact, I might say that they are the *only* friends I have."

"Then you must be quite difficult to get along with!" She frowned. "Are you?"

"Considering the fact that we've only recently met, I would be a great fool to answer such a question, would I not?" Gavin pulled the chair back and made a courteous bow, inviting her to sit. "Why not keep my company during this dinner and then decide for yourself about my . . . suitability as a companion."

She started across the room and then hesitated, studying him with a somewhat guarded expression. Then, at last resolving the issue that was holding her back, she nodded and closed the distance between them.

Gavin didn't realize that he had been holding his breath until she began to sit. Watching the soft, golden braid that now trailed down her back, the span of creamy skin showing above the neckline of her dress, the Lowlander openly admitted to himself that learning the truth about the past six months was not the only thing on his mind.

"I hope you are not planning on standing behind me while I eat!"

"I . . . well . . . I plan to do no such thing," he said as casually as he could, taking his own seat beside her. His knees brushed against her skirt, and he noticed how quickly she adjusted herself in her chair, moving it until a discreet distance existed between them. Then she turned her deep blue eyes back to his face. He flushed, suddenly feeling again like a lad at the abbey school, and the thought raced through him that a man could happily drown in the depths of those eyes.

"So you know the Macphersons?" Her question was punctuated by a growling noise from her stomach that had the sound of a charging boar.

As the color abruptly rose in her face, Gavin was reminded of the sight of wildflowers in an open field. A noisy open field, he thought wryly, but a bonny one, nonetheless.

"Aye, I have known the family for many years." He turned to the food and began to serve her. "Though I must admit that Ambrose was the one who introduced me to the rest of the family." Placing a heaping trencher before her, Gavin next reached for a pitcher and filled their cups with wine. She stared at the food but hesitated to start, so Gavin reached for a piece of bannock cake and tore it, handing her half. This was all the encouragement Joanna needed.

"And you?" he probed.

"I have only had the pleasure of getting to know Elizabeth and Ambrose." She paused and closed her eyes after she took the first bite. The expression of pure pleasure on her face made Gavin envy the food she ate. With the longing of a pauper, he watched her full lips pause as she savored each bit before taking the next. What he wouldn't give to have those lips against his.

By His Wounds, Gavin thought with a start, if he didn't say or do something to distract himself from this line of thinking, he would be hauling her on his lap in a moment.

"You . . ." He stumbled, searching for something to say. "You never met Alec Macpherson and his wife Fiona at court?"

She opened her eyes and glanced at him with some embarrassment. "I am sorry, what was it that you asked?"

"I said I . . . I wondered that you were not one of the legion of women at court who spent their time mooning over John Macpherson."

The severity of her scowl almost made him laugh. "This was not what you said! You said something about Ambrose's older brother and his wife!"

"So you did hear me! And yet you pretended to be lost on the moor somewhere."

"I was just testing your honesty," she replied casually, turning her attention back to the food before her. "And your temperament."

Gavin leaned back and watched her with amusement as she started again on the supper. "So I failed!"

"Aye, miserably," she answered, swallowing a mouthful. "But I'll disregard it this time and give you another chance."

He gave her a small bow of the head. "And I will take that chance!"

Joanna gave him a small smile as she took a sip of wine from her cup.

The warrior felt the hunger stirring within him, but he knew that food would offer no remedy for it. His eyes brushed over the soft lines of her throat. He could see the flicker of her pulse beneath the ivory skin. Clenching his jaws together, Gavin leaned back and crossed his arms over his massive chest, watching her as she continued to eat.

"So back to my question," he probed, reaching over and lifting his cup of wine. "About the Macphersons."

"Aye, I met Fiona and Alec, but only once, at Elizabeth's studio. And nay, I never mooned over John Macpherson. But then again, I never met him, and I know many who do think . . . highly of him." She raised a brow and looked seriously into his face. "Now that you mention it, I must say that Ambrose failed me in not introducing me to his younger brother, the good Lord of the Navy, when there was a chance. But if he had . . . and if he be anywhere near as handsome as his two older brothers . . ." Joanna gazed at him with the innocence of a lamb. "Who knows, perhaps I *might* have joined the moonstruck legions at his feet."

Gavin glared at her for a moment. "You have a devil in you, Joanna MacInnes."

"And you seem to bring it out in me."

"I asked a simple question."

"Aye, a question tainted with your mischief. You deserve worse than you received."

"Humph," he snorted. "To be told a Highlander, particularly one as ugly as John Macpherson—not that I do not feel a fondness for his family—well, to be told that the lout is *handsome*!" He looked at her with shock. "If you are implying that he is superior to—"

"You just have to learn to accept your flaws." She patted his arm gently with a bandaged hands. "But, being a Lowlander and a Border man, to boot, you surely must be accustomed to such comparisons."

Gavin growled at her, and Joanna quickly snatched her hand away.

"Well, perhaps I shouldn't be so harsh. I shall try, in the future, to be more gentle."

With a pitying look, she hid a smirk as she turned her attention back to her food.

She had a sense of humor. She had charm. And she had beauty. By His Wounds, Gavin thought, what had she been doing locked away in these vaults for the past six months? Add those qualities to the wealth she brought to a marriage, and she became the kind of woman that men fought over, so often to the death. Men with power and wealth of their own—men like Athol and Gordon. Perhaps men like himself, Gavin admitted grudgingly. But never before, he added quickly, had he ever had the inclination or the desire to pursue any woman.

Well, not for the purpose of marriage, he thought wryly, his eyes once again taking in her perfect features, her stunningly feminine form. But though Joanna brought out the deepest feelings of lust in him, already he felt that there was something more in this woman, this almost otherworldly creature whose very portrait had captivated him. He had only kissed her once, and yet some insatiable thirst had plagued him since, a whispering in his brain telling him over and over that he must have her. That he *would* have her. Not simply tonight or tomorrow, but for a time beyond the present—perhaps far beyond the here and now.

Joanna looked up for a moment, and he found himself again drowning in the violet blue of her eyes. For perhaps the first time in his life, Fortune had condescended to smile on him, in bringing Joanna into his life. Something deep inside him—something he had felt stirring from the moment he had first laid eyes on her portrait—was telling him that he had been brought to the Highlands for a purpose. Now more than ever, Gavin felt the certainty that he and Joanna had been brought together for a greater design than just bringing justice to those who had murdered her parents.

He took a deep breath and wondered if he should dare hope for such a blessing.

" 'Tis quite unusual," she said quietly, looking up and catching his eyes again. "I mean you from the Borders, being so friendly with a Highland clan!"

"Well, my ancestry is tainted with a wee bit of Ross blood from my mother's kin, so 'tis probably a weakness on my part." This time it was she who growled, a response that pleased him immensely. "But what you say is true," he continued, looking away. "I know 'tis rare indeed for a Lowlander to trust the wild, thieving blackguards that roam these hills. Exceptions do exist, though."

Gavin didn't need to look up to feel the daggers that were blazing from her eyes. He reached for the pitcher and filled his cup, swirling it in his hand. He noticed now that she was already finished with nearly everything he had served her. She must have gone without a solid meal for days, Gavin decided, perhaps weeks.

"Every now and then, you know, 'tis possible to find a fairly refined Highlander with whom a body might not be too embarrassed to be seen." He swallowed a mouthful of wine and looked at her. "But did I mention, 'tis rare?"

"Aye, you did." Without any ceremony, Joanna reached across the table and, picking up his untouched trencher, emptied the contents onto her own.

"I can see there is no reason for any pretense of refinement when you already think me a barbarian!"

"So you take my supper," he complained, placing his cup back on the table and leaning toward her menacingly. "You know we Lowlanders are not known to share."

Joanna shrugged her shoulders as she reached in front of him and snatched the piece of bannock cake that he'd left, as well. "But we Highlanders have been known to steal!"

With the speed of lightning, he caught her hand in his huge grip. They both glanced at the piece of bread still clutched in her fingers, then their eyes again met.

"And we Lowlanders are known to take back what is

ours." Slowly, Gavin started to haul her bandaged fist—
and the bread—toward his mouth. She tried to resist
him, but her weak struggle could have no more affect
against his overwhelming strength than a lamb might in
the clutches of a lion. Closer and closer her hand moved
to his mouth, until suddenly Joanna rose from her chair
and, leaning over quickly, she took the bread between
her teeth.

"Ah," she mumbled, her mouth full. "But we Highlanders are far too fast to get caught!"

Gavin fought back a smile, instead glaring at her
threateningly as she munched defiantly on the bread.

"Return it to me!" he growled in jest, letting go of
her hand and roughly taking hold of the braid at the
back of her neck.

Joanna shook her head as she fought his hold. "But
especially, we are too fast for you lazy Lowlanders!"

"You call me lazy?" He brought her face closer to his
own, as he relaxed his rough grip on her hair.

" 'Twould not be very smart for me to admit to that,
now would it, m'lord?" Her voice suddenly turned silken
in her defiance, her eyes smoldering with a glow of embers as she returned his gaze. All jesting disappeared in
an instant as something far stronger than mirth took
hold of the two of them.

Gavin could wait no longer before tasting her lips. As
he framed her face with his huge hands, his mouth
supped on her full lips. "I believe I can taste my dinner,"
he whispered wryly, drawing back a breath.

She gave him a soft smile in return. "Nay. But perhaps
they can send something up from the kitchens for you!"

"Think what you like," he replied, brushing his lips
against her. "But what I have in mind promises to be
far more delectable than anything that cook Gibby could
dream up."

Chapter 16

He thrust quick and hard as her hips ground tightly against his loins.

"Iris!" he cried out through clenched teeth, as bolts of fire shot through him and he poured his seed into the woman.

After a moment, Margaret's thin arms slipped around his slight frame as he lay exhausted atop her. And a moment later, when the man's tears started soaking the mute woman's shift, she ran her fingers soothingly over the rumpled linen of his shirt. As the weeping subsided, the man lifted his head and gazed down at the grave expression of the gaunt, almost fragile woman.

"Why do you do this, Margaret? Why do you allow me to do such things to you?"

Her reply could be only silence, and not even her eyes answered him. But her fingers continued to caress his face gently.

"I know 'tis a terrible thing for a man to use a woman like this. Lust is a killing thing, to be sure." He rolled off of her and onto his back, the back of his hand draping carelessly over his eyes. His voice had the low rasp of a knife on a stone. "And 'tis worse still, that I only see Iris's face when I lay with you. Our child planted deep in her womb is all I think of when I . . ."

Margaret sat up and pushed her shift down over her exposed thighs. Reaching for a blanket thrown to the side of the straw pallet, she gently tucked it over the man's naked sex.

"Always fussing over me," he muttered harshly. "Always kind and ready."

She let her fingers trail over the palm of his hand.

"And I am so undeserving of you, Margaret!" The man's hand lifted off his brow, and he looked deeply into the woman's dark brown eyes. "And you never hear or understand a word I say. You never will reveal the terrible secrets that . . ."

She watched him in silence, and he turned away.

"My Iris betrayed me, Margaret. She could not help herself. 'Twas her foul gypsy blood." A fresh tear worked itself out of the corner of his eye. The mute woman reached for it and touched it with the tip of her thumb. The drop spread wet and shining over her callused skin.

"I told her not to go to the laird," he continued gruffly, the rough edges of anger creeping into his voice. "I gave her my word that I would think of a way. That I would take care of her and our child. But she was impatient, my Iris was. In the end, the vixen set her mind to ruin me."

He jerked into a sitting position and reached for a ewer of ale sitting on the floor. Taking a deep swallow of the liquor, he glanced with distaste at Margaret's fingers gently stroking his arm. He pushed her hand away with a fierce, snarling sound, and then pulled his knees to his chest. He said nothing for a long moment, and the woman gazed intently at his face.

When he spoke again, his voice carried all the anguish of the damned. "She deserved to die that night, you know." He slumped back onto the bedding, covering his eyes with his arms. "There was no way for us, woman. I saw it clear as day then, and I see it now. She went to the laird, the vile sweet slut, and after that, there was no way to recover from the damage she caused."

He glanced at Margaret, a wild, tormenting misery in his eyes.

"She deserved to die, I tell you!" he cried. "And he, too! He would have taken it all from me! All! He deserved to die as well!"

The priest tore his eyes from the mute woman's face and stared up for a long time into the blackness of the ceiling.

After a while Margaret, nodding imperceptibly, placed

a kiss on the man's shoulder and lay her head on the bedding beside him.

Joanna opened her lips and felt a moan emanate from somewhere deep in her own throat as his tongue swept into the recesses of her mouth. Wrapping her arms tightly around his neck, she snuggled closer on his lap, where he had drawn her only a moment ago. Losing herself in the depth of their kiss, Joanna felt a warm, pulsing haze crowd all thoughts from her mind, and she gave in to it, unafraid as an insatiable desire suddenly blazed within her, setting her senses afire. There was nothing else that mattered now. No one else existed.

She so desperately wanted to feel him, to touch him, to taste that passion that had been so unattainable in her life. But she would not make the same mistake that she had before. She knew her end was near, but that was not something Gavin Kerr would accept lightly.

Angling her head and allowing him to deepen his kiss even further, Joanna swore that she would not allow him to stop. Not this time.

As if he could read her mind, he broke off the kiss, and she cursed herself for tempting fate. Her fingers kneaded the thick muscles of his shoulders and back, and threaded themselves into his soft, black mane as the warrior breathed deeply into her ear, crushing her body against his chest.

"Joanna," he growled against her hair. "Fire brought you to me, and from that first moment, flames have tormented my soul. I have been burning to touch you, to make love to you . . . to possess you." His hands raked fiercely at her back, lifting her and pressing her even closer to him. " 'Tis not like me to lose control of my desires. To feel so . . . obsessed!"

She raised her head and brushed his mouth with her lips, silencing him. "Are you certain 'tis not the Joanna MacInnes who sits above your hearth whom you intended to possess, and not me whom you desire?"

"Nay," he said intensely. "I want *you*. The bonny and formidable ghost who has been haunting my soul."

In his eyes, she saw the blazing passion that came

from within, and his desire tore away the last of her hesitancy. To hell with propriety. In his eyes, she was whole and beautiful, and the time had come for her to give in to the flame that would take them both to madness and to soaring passion.

"I am no ghost, Gavin Kerr." Joanna slid off his lap and moved brazenly between his legs. Amazed at her own boldness, she nonetheless undid the strip of the clothing that held the large dress gathered at her waist. "The time has come for you to see the rest of me."

His eyes burned into hers and she saw his jaw stiffen as she started pushing the large neckline of the dress first over one shoulder and then the next. "Joanna, this . . . this passion . . . you must know that I will have you and keep you forever."

"That you shall," she whispered, lowering the dress from her shoulders and down to her waist. "For as long as life allows."

Giving it one last tug, the dress pooled around her feet, and she stood in the thin fabric of her chemise before his scorching eyes.

Joanna shivered with excitement when he raised his hands to the cloth and ever so slightly traced the swells of her breasts. Her eyes followed the movement of his fingers, and she looked down and saw her nipples come to life beneath his touch. Then he ran his hands down her shoulders, slowly pushing down her chemise until it was only held by the tips of her breasts. She thought she would die of the anticipation that inflamed her. But then his hands moved down her arms, until they took hold of her hands. Suddenly aware of his intention, she stiffened.

"Don't." She tried to pull her scarred flesh out of his grip, but he held them tight and raised her hands against his heart.

"I'll have all of you, Joanna," he said hoarsely, leaning down and placing a kiss on the tips of her fingers. "As you are." He started unwrapping her hand. "I will possess all of you, lass."

She turned her face to the side, not wanting to witness the repulsion she was certain to find in his eyes when he was exposed to her hideous form. But he came to his feet and, trapping her bare hands against his chest, leaned down and captured her mouth.

Even had she wanted to, he wouldn't allow her to hold back. His lips demanded, his mouth took and yet made her melt from under the heat of his passion. When he pulled back again, she followed him with her lips, until once again she was faced with the sight of her hands on his heart. He then raised them before his eyes and kissed her palms, turning them over and continuing to caress with his lips, her healing flesh.

Joanna gave up her attempt at holding back the tears that were stealing down her cheeks. Looking at him, his head bent over her hands, she felt her stubborn heart soften, opening its ironbound gates with bittersweet joy as he silently glided in. She had wanted the tie between them to be only that of desire, of mindless passion. But with the touch of his lips, he had forced her to think again, to feel again. He was determined to possess her, she knew, but it was more than her body that he would be getting, for she was adding her soul, as well.

He raised his hands to the thick braid of her hair.

Awkwardly, but with a determination that reflected in his face, Gavin pulled loose the golden locks, combing it with his fingers until it rippled like a blanket over her breasts.

He paused. "Joanna, we have to speak of marriage. I cannot simply take you with no plans for the future." His voice was husky with emotion, but she pressed her fingers to his lips.

Silently, she slipped the chemise past her breasts, letting it drop to the floor. There was nothing now that separated her body from his gaze.

"You are so beautiful." He paused, his eyes a battleground of restraint and desire. "But I must settle your betrothal."

With a smile, she placed her fingers on his mouth again and traced his full lips.

"There is no betrothal," she responded with a faint smile.

"But there is."

"After you, there will be no other man. I am yours

alone. Please, Gavin," she continued, taking a step
toward him until her bare breasts rested against the linen
of his shirt. "I want you now. Please, let us not talk of
the future. Not now."

She caressed his face and Gavin's restraint slipped
away along with his composure. He put his hands over
hers, trapping them against his cheeks. She was vividly
aware of the strength in his fingers as they crushed her
own between them.

"God help me, Joanna," he said thickly. "All . . . all
I know is . . . now! But you must help me to think of—"

"Now is all I ask."

He held her captive in his arms, and his mouth descended on hers, crushing her lips with his bruising
passion.

A hot, liquid yearning began to flow deep within her,
rising from her very core and searing her flesh with its
heat. Wrapping her arms tightly around his neck, Joanna
felt Gavin's hands move down her bare back and cup
her buttocks, lifting her against him. She moaned at the
feel of his huge arousal pressing against her through the
soft wool of his kilt.

As he ended the kiss, she drew her breath to protest
until the touch of his lips on her ear transformed her
objection into a rapturous sigh. Her head fell back, and
she swayed slightly in his embrace.

"Joanna," he murmured, "my bewitching spirit." He
laid a trail of kisses from her jaw to the tender flesh of
her throat, his lips lingering on her fluttering pulse.

Suddenly overwhelmed by the need to feel his bare
skin against hers, Joanna slipped her hands inside his
shirt. True, she had seen him naked before, but the ac-
tual feel of his sinewy muscles beneath her fingers made
her thrill for more.

He lifted her off the ground, and Joanna instinctively
wrapped her legs around his waist. He groaned and
pulled his mouth away. "Joanna, I shall surely die if I
do not take you now."

She bit his ear before suckling it. "Then take me,
Gavin. Make me yours." She pressed her lips into the
hollow above his collarbone. Saltiness tingled on her

tongue as she ran her tongue along the bone to his shoulder where she nipped at the powerful flesh she found there. As his deep groan penetrated her brain, a glorious sense of wickedness swept through her as she felt him discard the last shreds of his control. With a few quick strides, he carried her to his bed and perched her on the edge.

The giant warrior hurriedly kicked off his boots, and her fingers pulled awkwardly at his belt. When he took over the task, tossing away the kilt and kneeling before her, her eyes focused momentarily on his huge manhood. Her breath caught in her chest. Joanna leaned forward and tore open the front of his shirt.

She had just touched the taut warmth of his muscular chest when Gavin pushed her back slightly, his mouth closing over her breast. Her mouth fell open with a gasp as he circled her hard, erect nipple with his tongue before tugging at it with his lips and teeth. She paused, paralyzed with excitement, and watched him through half lidded eyes until she could lie still no longer.

Engulfed by a rising fever that demanded release, Joanna pushed him back by the shoulders, yanking the shirt down over his massive arms. As he shrugged it off, she threw it aside with a sigh.

"I have wanted to do that from the first moment I walked in here tonight," she murmured, gazing into his fierce face, his smoldering eyes.

He buried one hand in the heavy silken spill of her hair, tugging it back, exposing the stretch of her neck. He ran his tongue and lips over the skin of her throat while his other hand cupped her breast, his thumb stroking the aroused nipple.

"And *I* wanted to drag you to this bed and bury myself in you from the moment you stepped through the panel door."

"Such wicked thoughts," she groaned as his hand slid down her stomach, over the downy mound, and between the folds of her womanhood. She shook from the vibration of her body's response. Her hips curled against his hand, and one leg lifted and wrapped itself around his waist and his naked buttocks.

Her blood pounded in her brain and the pulsing lights that had replaced the earlier haze now flashed, ablaze with a myriad of colors. Her body and skin caught fire, and she felt her breaths growing shorter as he continued to stroke the sensitive spot within her. Joanna threw back her head and moaned as he probed deeper and deeper into her intimate heat, and his mouth once again suckled one breast.

Sensation began to crowd out her consciousness. It was like gliding along on some fast-moving cloud, or running in a dream down some endless hill, feeling the excitement rising and never wanting it to end. But in a bright corner of her brain, Joanna knew that this could not go on forever. There was an urgency that told her that complete fulfillment was near at hand. But she didn't want it to finish. No matter how rapturous whatever lay beyond could be, she didn't want to cross that line—not without him.

Blindly, she reached out for him, her fingers groping down his body until she found the long, hard shaft. The skin was hot, and he throbbed to her touch. Her hand curled around him and slid the entire length until her thumb caressed the satiny crown.

"Nay, Joanna," he groaned tearing his mouth away from her breast. "Not yet."

But in spite of his voiced reluctance, the warrior hardly resisted as she brought the broad tip of his manhood to her moist folds and pressed herself against it.

"Now, Gavin," she whispered, the note of ardor evident in her voice as she gazed into his dark and passion glazed eyes. "Please, take me now."

Now driven with the urgency to have him inside of her, she moved with him as he centered himself over her and took hold of her hips.

"And will you be mine, Joanna? Will you forever belong to me?"

She nodded and drew his head down, kissing him with all the passion she had in her.

As he drove into her, Joanna stiffened at first, stunned by the tearing pain of his entry. She kept her eyelids pressed shut and bit her lip to keep from crying out as he ceased to move for what seemed like an eternity. But then, gradually, she felt his throbbing shaft begin to move, slowly at first, and then faster and faster, until her mind cast off all memory of pain, all memory of innocence, and the white hot lights of some blazing heaven opened up and consumed her.

Stepping away from the murky waters of the underground lake, the man held up the wick lamp and peered through the darkness of the cavern beneath Ironcross Castle. Something by a wall caught his sharp eye. Ducking his head as he moved beneath a rock overhang, the Earl of Athol crouched before the rough bed of straw, noticing the corner of a dark cloth peeking from beneath. Pushing away the straw, he uncovered the meager possessions the inhabitant had hidden there. A cloak besmirched with black grime and a rolled heap of rags. He picked the clothing up, scanning them for some telltale mark. Putting the wick lamp on the packed earth, he held the rags up before his eyes, recognizing that the shreds may once have been a woman's shift.

Casting the cloth aside, he turned to the small heap of sticks not too far away. Putting his hand over the still-warm ashes of the fire, he knew that the owner of these things had left here not long before.

Picking up the wick lamp, the earl looked about for other clues and turned his attention back to the straw. Shoving the clothing back under, he found a wooden bowl with the remains of some dry bread. An empty wooden cup.

Pushing himself up to his feet, Athol swept his long red hair back over his shoulder and peered around the cavern for anything else that he might learn of this poor, timid soul, the latest of the Ironcross 'ghosts.'

By the devil, since he was a lad—hell, since he was no more than a bairn—he had known his way around these caverns, racing through them with John MacInnes and the stable lads. Back then, the only ghosts haunting the castle had been he and his friends. He smiled in the darkness at the memory, but his face quickly grew serious. His man David had spoken of a spirit roaming the castle now, but Athol had been inclined not to believe him then. Now, glancing down at the belongings of some poor beggar, he was certain of it. No ghost he had ever heard of kept warm by a fire or helped himself to bread. What still perplexed the earl, though, was the behavior of a 'phantom' who seemed determined to keep returning Joanna's picture to the place where it had originally hung.

Having the new laird of Ironcross retire early tonight had been fine, so far as Athol was concerned. Finding the truth behind this 'ghost' was something that the earl knew he himself must do. He certainly couldn't rely on David.

Athol pushed at the ragged cloak with his foot. He wasn't about to allow some poor beggar to ruin his efforts.

Not when he was this close to succeeding.

Settling back on the down-stuffed pillows, Gavin took a deep breath and listened to the rain whipped by the wind against the walls of the keep. Occasionally, the low rumbling sound of thunder rolled across the loch, and the laird tried to yield to the warm sense of tranquillity that was seeping into his bones.

There was something wonderfully intimate about lying in his huge bed with Joanna curled up against his side. Just a moment ago, after their lovemaking, he'd levered himself up and repositioned her in the bed, lifting her into the center and covering her with the soft wool blanket. It had been then that he'd seen the proof of her innocence. When he had first entered her, he'd discovered he had been her first. And although he'd never considered a woman's virginity an important issue before, something of its dearness struck him now. He turned onto his side and gently brushed the dark golden hair from her damp brow.

"You were a virgin," he said simply.

She rolled onto her back, her gaze sliding away from his. "So I was."

He caught her chin and brought her eyes back to him. "But why didn't you tell me?"

She gently wrenched her chin loose. "You would have thought what you wished no matter what I told you!"

"Nay, Joanna, you cannot think that," Gavin argued gently, pulling her back to her side until she faced him. Her head rested against his arm, and he absently combed his fingers through her long tresses with his other hand. "That does not say much for my character, now, does it? I must be more depraved than I thought."

She shook her head. "We were talking of my virginity. And what does it matter now, anyway? What's done is done. But why must you scold me for giving you what was mine to give?"

" 'Tis not what *you* have done," he said, letting his hand rest lightly on her cheek. " 'Tis the way *I* behaved that is bothering me. I should have been . . . more gentle. I should had taken my time, but instead I just took you like you were a woman of the world—a woman familiar with—"

She placed a finger on his lips, "Did you enjoy our lovemaking?"

He stared at her for a moment, but then laughed, lifting her hand to his lips and placing a kiss on her palm. "Aye, Joanna. Immensely."

"And am I what you expected? I mean in my shape . . . my body? Am I too thin or too fat? Am I—?"

"You are just as I have dreamed you would be." He bent over her and brushed his lips against hers. "You *are* just perfect."

She pulled back. "Then it must be that I was inept in your arms!"

He shook his head. "Nay, Joanna. You were incredibly able."

She paused a moment before letting a smile break across her lips. "Then I believe I was successful in seducing you."

For the space of a dozen heartbeats, there was silence as he stared into her shining, violet-blue eyes. "Aye, you were successful in seducing me."

"And you think me wanton?"

"Nay . . . well, a wee bit wanton is a fine thing, to my thinking."

"Are you not shocked?"

"At what?" he asked, his eyebrows arching with amusement. "At you seducing me before I could seduce you?" He slid his hand down over her neck and collarbone, pushing at the blanket until his hand caressed the side of one breast. "I did have plans of my own, you know." Gavin ran his thumb gently across her nipple. It hardened like a pebble beneath his touch. He watched as Joanna closed her eyes for a fleeting moment and drew in her breath. "But now, considering how far we have come—certainly faster than I could have possibly hoped for—I will gladly admit that I approve of your method the best."

"Then we are done with your questioning?"

Gavin studied her expression. Her sparkling eyes held within them a devilish gleam, a playful expectancy. Her full lips, turned up at the corners, told of her mirth. Her hand stretched out against his chest, and began to move lower over the hard planes of his belly. He caught it just above his rising manhood.

"Only if you let me seduce you," he growled.

She freed her hand and slipped it around his waist. Scooting closer, she pressed the length of her body against him, and he felt his fully aroused member nestle between her thighs.

"You can try," she challenged. "But I warn you, I have plans of my own."

Chapter 17

Margaret's hands quivered as they tried to raise the latch of the door behind her. Her darting eyes followed her brother's impatient steps as he paced the small room. He came to a sudden halt.

"So you've decided to return to us at last."

She pressed her back hard against the door and looked down at the rushes on the floor.

"Where were you, Margaret?"

She wiped her wet palms on her skirts, but never raised her eyes.

"Where the *hell* have you been, Margaret?"

The vehemence in Allan's voice caused her to cringe. Hesitantly, she lifted her gaze and looked into his angry eyes.

"Vaw . . . cuh . . ."

"Nay. Molly was there, but she said she hadn't seen you."

She shook her head and repeated her broken words. "Vaw . . . cuh . . ."

"You would never lie to me, now, would you, sister?"

The violent shake of her head was instantly followed by the tearing of her eyes.

"One of the stable lads saw you go to the chapel."

Margaret crossed herself. "P . . . P . . ."

"Why do you redden so? Why, Margaret?" Allan's hands fisted at his sides. "Were you with that dwarfish pig of a priest?"

She shook her head again and then looked at the floor. "Vaw . . . vaw . . ."

Allan unclenched a big hand and laid it on her shoulder. "He is as bad as the devil himself, sister. Do you understand that?"

Margaret reached up and took hold of his hand..

"I don't want you to go near him. I don't want you to have anything to do with him. Do you understand?"

She nodded.

"We cannot allow anyone to cause us more pain. No one, Margaret. No one!"

Trembling, she nodded again.

Shoving another log to the crackling blaze, the warrior chief straightened up and turned, looking earnestly into Joanna's troubled face. She was sitting at the head of his bed, her knees drawn tightly to her chest. Her chin rested on the blanket she had gathered around her legs, and as he gazed at her eyes, he found them staring into a dark corner of the room. Even at this distance, he could see within them the flicker of troubled memories.

Moments before, she had been perfectly happy in his arms. As long as they were making love or talking of anything but the past, her spirit had been alive, enchanting, soaring.

But as soon as he'd started asking the questions that they both knew he must ask, she had withdrawn, the magic of the moment broken, dragged to earth, subdued.

Gavin picked up the ewer of wine and the two full cups from the table before heading back to the bed. She looked toward him and met his gaze.

"There is still so much I need to learn," Gavin said quietly.

"Where would you like me to start? Do you want me to tell all of the horrible details of that fire? Do you want to hear how I escaped that hellish death when my family did not?" Her voice was a mere whisper.

Placing the wine and the cups beside the bed, he sat down next to her and moved beneath the blanket. Her icy feet touched his leg, and he could feel her shiver as he wrapped his arm around her shoulder. Sitting back against the carved headboard, he pulled her close to his side. Immediately, she nestled her head under his chin.

It was a simple thing, this gesture of trust, but it wrapped his heart in a satisfying warmth.

"Why don't you start from the beginning." He brushed his lips against her hair. "I want to know everything."

"You mean the first summer I came to Ironcross Castle?"

"Nay," he responded, shaking his head. "Why not start even earlier. Tell me of your childhood."

She turned her face up to his. "Are you asking this simply to put me at ease?"

He looked down at the small smile that now graced her lips. He bowed his head and kissed them. Her lips were soft, supple, and they parted invitingly. But before he allowed himself to deepen the kiss and forget everything else, he pulled back with a deep sigh.

"Joanna, there is so much about you that I want to know. After all, you are the only woman I have ever asked to be my wife."

"Your wife. You mean you still . . .?"

Her words trailed off, but the frown that stole across her face, creasing her brow, told him quite clearly that she still had not yet come to grips with his proposal of marriage. But that was discussion for another time.

"Tell me," he encouraged. "As a wee lass, were you as serene and timid as you are now?"

She snorted scoffingly in response. "Serene and timid? Now those are words I do not recall ever hearing my mother or father use to describe me."

"Of course not! How could I forget? You were an only child!"

"Aye. And not only that, but the last of the MacInnes line."

"You must have been a hellion." He grinned. "I can see you now—headstrong, obstinate, and contrary. Was that it?"

Joanna nodded as she nestled her head back onto his shoulder. "My grandsire Duncan died before I was born and my two elder uncles, Alexander and Thomas, never showed any interest in marrying. So, anyway, the whole family just treated me as their own darling."

"So in addition to being ornery by nature, you were spoiled and pampered as well."

"Aye, and worse," she admitted. "My parents knew very little of what I did. They were perhaps a bit too consumed with one another, but they saw nothing wrong with giving me all that I sought. Between them and my two uncles' endless indulgences, I am certain I would have ended up ruined forever if it hadn't been for my grandmother's influence."

"She does have an air of authority."

"You know her?" Joanna asked with great surprise.

"Aye, she is a grand woman. I met her before leaving for the Highlands to claim Ironcross Castle." Gavin ran his hand caressingly up and down her bare arm. "She was the one who first introduced *you* to me, my little enchantress, though only through her wondrous descriptions."

"Is she well?" Joanna asked softly, taking his other hand in her own. "It must have been crushing for her to hear of the death of my father and . . . the rest of us!"

"When I left her, she seemed somewhat frail in body, though she has a spirit—and a mind—that more than make up for what she has lost with age." Gavin listened for a moment to the rain. "There was nothing that she said in my meeting with her that led me to believe she is ready to give up hope."

"Hope?" Joanna asked, looking up at him with puzzlement. "Do you think she suspects someone survived?"

Gavin frowned. "I am not certain if she dared even to wish for such a miracle. But the way she talked—the way she convinced me to come to the Highlands—all made me believe that she still hoped that, at the very least, justice would be meted out to the ones responsible."

Gavin caught the change in Joanna's expression. He saw her eyes shift and stare intently across the room. Something he'd just said had struck a chord in her troubled memory.

"Does my description of Lady MacInnes fit what you recall of her?" he asked.

She turned quickly and nodded with a half smile. "She

always was quite determined, once she set her mind to something. As I said before, it was her influence and constant reproaches that set me on the right path. Did she say anything to you, when you last met . . . about me, I mean? Or about this castle?"

"I thought I was the one asking the questions!"

"You are," she said softly, reaching up and smoothing the crease in his forehead with a gentle touch. "But after all I have learned in these months—I keep remembering certain things that she hinted to me in the years past. Looking back at it all—so much seems somehow related."

"She asked me to look for your portrait. To speak the truth, I believe that picture was the only thing that she ever hoped to recover from this castle."

She sat up straight in bed and turned to him. "Did she speak of anything else? Did she tell you about the disasters that have plagued our family?"

Gavin watched as her fingers fluttered nervously in his encompassing hands.

"She told me of the way that each of her sons died, and she said that the curse of Ironcross Castle lies not in the realm of ghosts and goblins. She spoke of the evil that haunts the place, but she said 'tis an evil that comes from the human heart."

"And she convinced you to seek the truth."

"Aye." He nodded. "I have my own lands and my own people in the Borders. I never intended Ironcross Castle to be my home for good. The Earl of Angus gave me these lands—and I can see that the people here need a laird now to look out for them—but I never would have come to the Highlands had it not been for your grandmother's visit."

"Are you sorry that you have come?" she asked quietly.

He looked deeply into her blue eyes and answered truthfully. "I am indebted to your grandmother forever. She has introduced to me the warmth of the sun." He brought her hand to his lips. "She introduced me to you."

Joanna quickly turned her face away, but not before

Gavin saw the tears that trickled down her flawless cheek. Reluctantly, he allowed her to withdraw her hand from his grasp, but he remained where he was, studying her beautiful profile and waiting for her to find her words.

In fact, he found his own throat dry, an unexpected emotion rising into his chest. His fingers ached to draw her back into his arms.

With an effort, Gavin tore his eyes from her and looked across the chamber at the fire. He simply could not allow himself to feel this way. All his life he had seen death claim those he felt the strongest ties to, and he had sworn to himself that he would never again make that mistake. He was a warrior chief, a laird. He had duties to others and no need for anyone to be so close. Gavin never wanted to love or be loved again.

But here she was, wreaking havoc on his heart.

True, he thought, he had offered her marriage. But the offer was based on what was right and honorable. Of course, Gavin mused, he had never experienced a physical attraction toward anyone that came even close to the lightning that fired his blood each time he so much as looked at her. But, in any case, the marriage he offered was suitable to their situations. She could not live like a hermit beneath his keep; their marriage would allow her to get back what was rightfully hers. After all, Ironcross Castle should be hers, in spite of the actions of the Lord Chancellor and the fact that Gavin now had taken possession of it.

But turning his gaze back to Joanna, he raised his hand to her silky skin and wiped away the glistening track of another tear.

All true, he thought. And all a lie.

"I still remember," she said, breaking the silence. "After the first summer that I spent here at Ironcross, I returned to court and to my grandmother, full of life and tales of how much I loved the Highlands. Loved this place." She dashed an escaping tear from her face with the back of her hand. "But her response was not at all what I expected. It stunned me with its vehemence." Joanna considered for a moment, her face reflecting the memory. "She raged at me, and I knew it somehow had to do with my feelings for the Highlands, but I couldn't understand the reason. My love for Ironcross and this country was nothing new; she herself had lived for some years among these people. I had never before seen her so fierce in her anger."

"And did she stay angry long? Did she ever explain the reasons for her behavior?"

Joanna's brow knitted at the question. "Not right away, but her anger quickly subsided when I drew back from her, defending myself and this place. Then, inexplicably, my grandmother became almost frightened. I had never seen her like that, either. She pleaded with me. Then, finally, she began to tell me the things that she would later tell you. About the deaths of my grandsire and my uncles. About how their deaths looked like accidents. But she called them murders."

"Lady MacInnes never went so far in what she told me, though her meaning was clear enough. But did she ever speak to you of proof? Did she accuse anyone specifically? Was it your grandmother who accused Mater?"

Joanna stared silently for a moment. Gavin could plainly see the struggle that she was going through.

"Joanna, when was it first that you suspected Mater?"

Her eyes snapped up to his, but she said nothing.

"Talk to me, Joanna," he pressed. "We're in this together."

"This is *my* battle. Not yours."

"Nay." He shook his head. "Perhaps that was so before I came up here. But, to the world, at least, I am laird of Ironcross Castle. And now, especially after tonight, 'tis very much my concern."

Her eyes flashed. "You have added no obligation because of tonight, but . . ." She raised a hand to silence his response. "You *should* be interested in this because of the fire in this room last night. That was no accident, you know. Someone was here. And they tried to kill you!" She looked down for a long moment at the redness of her hands. "You're correct. Your life is in danger and you *do* have the right to know."

"Fear of death has nothing to do with my desire to

learn the truth. But having you beside me—openly, alive, and safe—that is what is driving me now."

Her eyes were glowing when they focused on his. The affection Gavin saw in their depths made him draw in his breath. In the back of his mind came a pounding ache of grim memories of death, of those who had died, of those who had loved him.

"When was it that you first suspected Mater?" he demanded again, his voice sounding harsh to his own ears as he repeated the question. "From all I have heard from others, you and she were great friends before the fire."

"We were friends," she answered. "At one time, in fact, I was foolish enough to admire her. I defended her."

"Defended her against whom?"

"Against my grandmother."

"Did Lady MacInnes dislike her? Did she know Mater well?"

Joanna shook her head. "For all the years that the MacInnes men were lairds of these lands, I believe my grandmother spent very little time here. So I cannot imagine her ever having the chance to spend much time at the abbey—especially with Mater. But then, as I told you before, after that first summer—when I returned from the Highlands—it was my talk and praise of Mater that upset my grandmother the most."

"And it was then that you spoke in her behalf?"

"I did." She nodded. "And wrongly so. I know that now."

"But did your grandmother give you a reason for her feelings?"

Joanna nodded again slowly. "Aye, my grandmother hates Mater because she is the one responsible for all the deaths at Ironcross Castle. Is that not reason enough?"

"Aye," he said grimly. " 'Tis reason enough . . . if true. But what proof did she speak of?"

Joanna shook her head again. "She was quite unwilling to reveal anything specific. That was why I defended Mater so strenuously. But I was so naive," she said bitterly, running her hand absently over the blanket.

"Joanna, tell me what happened." He tried to sound encouraging. "Make me understand what you felt, what you saw."

"That fall, when I returned to Stirling, I was so full of dreams. During the summer, I'd had the chance to meet and work with Mater and with the women of the abbey. To me they had become the most incredible people alive. They were dedicated; they were good. I remember being so impressed by the strength of their will, by the amazing bond between them as they carried on in their efforts to help and protect their flock. So here, with that admiration well set in my mind, I went back to court and found my own grandmother calling the leader of these people 'the daughter of Satan himself'!" Joanna shook her head in frustration. "But whatever I said, no matter how much I pleaded, she simply refused to say any more."

She fisted one hand and pressed it into her palm. "I had been brought up not to believe in court gossip. I have never been one to participate in idle talk. And now, so far as I could see, the same woman who had taught me those values seemed to be expecting me to accept her words without question. She demanded that I stay away from Mater and the women she had gathered around her."

Gavin placed his hand on hers and drew her eyes up to his. "But when you came back to the Highlands the following fall—in spite of what she had told you—you still went back to the abbey."

"I did," she whispered. "And it hurts me now to admit that I decided to go against my grandmother's words."

"And then, something happened."

"Aye, something happened," she answered, her eyes taking on a faraway look. "In my last visit to the abbey, I accidentally happened to overhear a conversation about a gathering that was about to take place. A ritual of some sort for the women. My curiosity was aroused, and though I was not invited, I was determined to find out what I could."

Gavin noted the way her hands now clutched at the

blanket, so he reached over and took them in his own. She glanced up at him, almost startled by his attention.

"Where was this meeting, Joanna?"

"In the vault beneath the castle," she whispered hoarsely. "In the same room where the crypts lay."

Joanna shivered and Gavin himself felt a sudden chill sweep through the room. Looking in the direction of the hearth, he gazed for a moment at the fire. "So you went there?"

"I wanted to. You see, they were to meet that night. 'Twas a full moon. But it would not be so easy. Earlier in the day, a message had come from the castle that the Earl of Athol was due to arrive. I knew he would come, and I knew there would be harsh words between Athol and my father . . . on account of my betrothal. So there was no way I could excuse myself."

Gavin pulled up the blanket and covered her bare shoulder with it. "And this was the night of the fire."

"Aye. The same terrible night." Joanna nodded and shivered again. "I stayed as long as I could in the Great Hall. And as I had suspected, my father and Athol took up their argument. But to my dismay, they grew angrier than I had ever seen either of them. Finally, using their unwillingness to reason as an excuse, I fled back to my room and entered the passages. I wanted to get to the vault before the moon rose."

"How did you know your way around?" Gavin asked curiously.

"From Athol," she whispered. "The summer before, I had been able to talk him into showing me the tunnels and the caverns. He even took me as far as Hell's Gate."

" 'Tis a wonder that the laird of the neighboring lands might be so knowledgeable about the secrets of this keep!"

"Not so. The caverns are no secret. From what he told me, my own father had shown him the secret passageways when they were mere lads. Later, when my father had grown, Athol still spent many days roaming those passages, for there were many years, after my grandsire passed away, when neither of my uncles wanted to take their permanent seat as laird. Athol said those were the years when he and his friends would explore the caverns of Ironcross for the sheer adventure of it. Around that time, my father would occasionally return to the Highlands as well. From all I hear, at one time they were very close."

Joanna wrapped her hair around one hand, "Athol told me that everyone thought the castle a haunted place. 'Twas a true test of manhood for the young lads living nearby to cross the footbridge at Hell's Gate."

Gavin had to force his mind and attention back to the events of that fatal night. He wished to know more about Athol—and about this Hell's Gate—but that information would have to wait a bit.

"Tell me what happened next . . . the night of the fire . . . when you went into the tunnels."

" 'Twas easy to find the vault, but the place was silent as death itself." Joanna jumped suddenly as a gust of wind tore through the window, banging the wooden shutters hard against the walls. She clutched the blanket more tightly around her shoulders. "So I decided to stay and hide myself—and wait."

"And did they come?" Gavin asked.

The wind was whistling into the chamber, and the warrior looked irritably toward the open windows. Pushing back the covers, he strode across the chamber to close the shutters. Outside, it appeared that a tempest was brewing, and the rain that spattered against his naked skin was sharp and cold. With some effort, he pushed the shutters closed and latched them shut. Turning back to Joanna, he was amazed at how fragile and frightened she suddenly looked. He considered all the hardships she had endured during these months—the strength she must have worked so hard to garner simply to stay alive. And now, for the moment, all of it seemed to have drained completely out of her.

He reached the bed and, in a gesture that cut straight to his heart, Joanna gazed up and drew back the covers, opening her arms to him. Gavin gathered her tightly to his side. It was so easy to lose himself in her embrace. She was indeed an enchantress, robbing him of every shield, every barrier he had built up over the years. She laid her hand against his heart, touching him where he had thought surely he had constructed the greatest protection. He could see now how wrong he had been.

"They did come," she whispered quietly. "But not as the women I had come to know. They came as strangers—as a group of chanting, raving madwomen."

"Did they see you?"

She shook her head and laid her forehead against his chin. "Nay, I was so taken aback by their presence in that crypt—by the talk, by their evil prayers—that I found myself speechless, frozen where I hid."

She shivered again as Gavin ran a warm hand up and down her arm beneath the covers. Her skin was ice cold to his touch.

"What happened next, Joanna?"

" 'Twas some kind of ritual. The thing was as familiar to them as breathing the air is to you and me. I don't know if it was Christian or pagan or from the devil himself. But then, what came next will give me nightmares till the day I die!"

Gavin's head snapped around as the flames in the fireplace suddenly leapt up on the hearth. Between the wind and the blasted draft of the chimneys, he thought to himself, it was amazing the whole castle had not burned to the ground long ago.

" 'Twas the most upsetting part of all they did—up to that time." Joanna bit off her words. "As I watched, one of the women, with a shriek of some eldritch fiend, knelt by the pyre they had built in the center of the vault, and lit the brush. I can still hear the crackling roar, the rushes and the reeds and the sticks igniting. The blaze lighting up the entire crypt in an orgy of shadows and light. Then the women, like demons, breaking into some pagan dance, spinning and falling in a frenzy of moans and howls. 'Twas as if they ceased to be human! And Mater watched over them all."

Although he had never been a witness to such rituals, Gavin had heard, on occasion, of places in both the Highlands and in the western Borders where such strange gatherings occurred. Some said it was a part of the old religion. Most said nothing about it at all.

But this still offered no just cause for placing the guilt of the murders on Mater.

"And there was more," Joanna continued. "As these women carried on with their dancing and chanting, Mater began to preach to them, using words about lairds and the evils of such men and the curse and the traditions. From where I stood, hidden beyond a crypt, it took me no time at all to realize that she was talking about my father. She was calling down justice. Mater was calling on some 'power' to bring death . . . on him and on all who followed in his place."

Joanna reached and took hold of Gavin's hand tightly in hers. "As amazed as I was by what had gone before, 'twas nothing compared to that moment—to hearing those words. I mean, she was speaking of my father, John MacInnes! A peaceful man who had never willingly brought a jot of pain or hardship on any living soul. Why him?"

"What happened next, Joanna?"

"Finally, they all left the vault at last, still wild-eyed, possessed with the frenzy. I could not believe what I had seen. I sat huddled in that corner for I do not know how long. I suppose I was completely shaken, confused with what I had witnessed." She stared into the darkness of her memory. "Whatever 'twas that moved me—fear or betrayal—after a while I did stir. Aye, I found some courage and started back to my room, though I know now it must have been some time later."

Joanna was no longer shivering; she was openly shaking in his arms. Gavin lifted her from her place, drawing her gently into his lap, and he wrapped his arms protectively around her. Outside, a long, low rumble of thunder rolled across the loch.

"I was too late," she croaked over the noise. "By the time I reached the passages into the south wing, the smoke was thick and the heat unbearable. I was choking, but I climbed upward. There were flames leaping everywhere. And there were choked screams above the roar of the fire. I killed them! I waited too long in the crypt! I—"

She broke down. Gavin gathered her tightly against

his chest. Her tears ran in streams down her cheeks and onto his chest. The warrior's throat knotted tightly and he clenched his jaws. How well he knew the sorrow that she was feeling. How well he knew the anguish of losing those you loved. The doomed helplessness of surviving. The guilt of having failed.

They sat like that for a long while, until finally she drew in a long, irregular breath and continued.

"I was barely able to make it to the upper floors. I think I was about to faint, the air was so hot and smoky. I pushed at the panel of my own chamber, but the latch would not give. From the edges of the door, flames licked at my hands. My hands were burning . . . I could smell my own flesh. But I . . . I was stuck in the passage with my mother and father trapped inside. I tore myself away. I stumbled, as if in a nightmare, along the passages. I found a different panel. 'Twas the same there. Everywhere I went, 'twas the same. I could not get through. I remember finding my way into the passageway that I was certain led to my parents' bedchamber. I threw myself against the panel—screaming and using my hands to dig at the burning wood—pleading to be let in. But . . . but they must have all been dead by then. They were all dead. And I was condemned to live."

Gavin placed his hand on her quivering fingers and flattened them against his heart. "How could anyone stand the heat of the flames?"

She tucked her head beneath his chin. Her voice was cold, almost lifeless. "The flames were nothing compared to the anguish I have endured at being forced to live."

In his mind, Gavin traveled back to the muddy fields of Flodden. He too had been forced to witness the death of his kin—being too far away to help his two older brothers in battle. He too had been forced to endure the memory of being struck down, of lying helpless with the dying and the dead.

He, as well, had hoped to die. But a Highlander had come after him. Though injured himself, Ambrose Macpherson had lifted him onto his shoulder and had carried him through the rain for two days back to Scotland. Gavin glanced vacantly at the windows of the chamber.

Outside, the storm had continued to grow, and thunder crashed with a resounding echo.

He remembered the misery he'd inflicted on Ambrose during that time! From physical threats to the verbal abuse of the man's honor, Gavin had done his best to make it impossible for the Highlander to continue on. Like Joanna, Gavin had been forced to live.

But Ambrose's stubborn bravery knew no bounds. Physically restraining him from bringing himself more harm, the Highlander had talked only of hope. Of a chance for the future. Of a Scotland that would need him now more than ever. Ambrose Macpherson had shown him the courage and the strength that comes with compassion. And later, he had taught him that there could exist a friendship and a loyalty that rivaled the ties of kinship. This was what Joanna needed to feel now. It was her turn, Gavin thought, to pass on the lesson that his friend had once long ago bestowed on him.

"I think in the midst of it, I must have passed out." Joanna's voice brought Gavin back to the present. "In fact, I must have been confused, delirious even, when I first regained consciousness, since I don't recall anything of those moments at all. My first clear memories are from some time later, finding myself beside the underground loch beneath the castle. My hands were lying in the cold water, my burned flesh soaking and the pain surging through my whole body in horrible waves."

"Did you go back to the south wing?"

"I tried, but a fever took hold of me. And the pain searing through my hands nearly drove me mad. I think I may have lain there in the blackness of that cavern for hours . . . or days . . . time meant nothing. But then, after who knows how long, I found myself standing. I don't know what kept me upright. I was like some puppet held up by invisible strings. Somehow, I made my way through the tunnels to the burnt out wing, but they were all gone. The place was in ruins. The ashes were cold, and there was nothing else."

Hardly breathing, Joanna had grown rigid in his arms, and Gavin gently caressed her back. He could see the tears coursing down her face. It took a few moments, but eventually her shoulders began to lose their tenseness, and her breathing became more normal.

"You think this was the next day?"

She shrugged. "I had no sense of time. I remember 'twas growing dark, and there was not a single soul to be found." She looked away, drawing in a deep breath.

"What about the rest of the house, Joanna? The remaining servants who had not been in that wing. Surely you could have sought out one of them for help?"

Suddenly angry, she shook her head. "I would *never* have gone to them. How could I? They were as much a part of these killings as Mater herself!"

Gavin reached around and took hold of her chin, raising it until their eyes met. As he looked into her face, the chamber was suddenly illuminated once again with a flash of lightning. "What do you mean—?" The cracking crash of thunder that followed immediately broke his question in two. "What do you mean, they were part of it?"

"They were all there," Joanna answered, her eyes growing wild. "All the women of this house are a part of Mater's flock. I saw them in the crypt. You think I would not know them? They were all there. Gibby, the cook. Molly and those who serve her in the household. Even the mute, Margaret. They were all part of it. All of them . . . carrying the flames of death!"

"But you never actually saw them set fire to the south wing, did you?"

"I didn't have to," she responded angrily. "Don't you think what I saw was enough?"

"Nay, I do not think 'twas enough," Gavin answered honestly. "But that doesn't mean we should stop looking for proof of their guilt."

"But they are guilty."

"You say they are," he argued. "But you can be no more certain than your grandmother of Mater's guilt. And there is not a thing you can do to mete out justice to those women."

"That may be *your* perception of the truth." She looked steadily into his eyes. "But 'tis yours alone!"

Chapter 18

When he stepped into the Great Hall, Gavin stopped to look about him at the long rows of tables. Most of his own men and many of Athol's had already settled at the tables, lounging or eating their morning meal.

The Lowlander's eyes settled on Allan, who was sitting with Edmund and Peter at one of the tables. The older man's surly expression told him that the steward looked to be the target of Peter's wit this morning. In a lull between the storms last night, Gavin had asked Joanna about the steward. Why, he'd asked, had Joanna not chosen to seek out the older man's assistance, rather than going into hiding?

The answer had been all too obvious to Joanna. The mute woman Margaret was Allan's younger sister, and what chance did a feverish, grieving young woman have of being believed against the word of kin and fellow workers the steward had known his whole life.

Well, he was not about to blame her now for being suspicious. After all she had been through, she had earned the right. Gavin looked about for his guest, Athol.

Against his wishes, Joanna had this morning insisted on returning to the darkness of the caverns beneath the keep. No matter what he said, he knew he had not even come close to persuading her to stop hiding her existence from the household. He had even tried to get her just to stay in his bedchamber and bar the door.

Stubbornly, she had refused his offer, giving him only her word before leaving that she would return after nightfall. But now, as Gavin thought a bit anxiously about the all too involved Earl of Athol, he felt a stab of uneasiness. He should not have let her go. She herself had told him that Athol knew his ways around the caverns of this keep. What if the blackguard was, right now, traipsing through those tunnels himself?

Gavin whirled, ready to return to his chamber and find Joanna himself. She would listen to reason if he had to . . .

"I see you are as late a riser as I this morning."

Gavin lurched to a stop before the Highlander, narrowly avoiding barreling into the man. As he looked into the earl's face, he struggled to hide the look of relief that he was certain was stealing across his face.

"On second thought," Athol added, irony evident in his tone, "you look as though you have been up for some time. And what occupies the master of Ironcross Castle this fine morning? Chasing Joanna's portrait around the South Hall?"

"Are you mocking me?" Gavin growled menacingly, studying the man. "It seems to me that, for someone who has been in this keep less than two days, you know a great deal more about the affairs of Ironcross Castle than befits a guest!"

Athol shrugged his shoulders with a wry smile as he turned toward the Great Hall and its occupants. " 'Tis not too often that one hears a more amusing story than the one being told around this keep. Do *you* not think it amusing that a man of your reputation should lose his temper every time some servant moves a painting? Every kitchen lass and stableman is talking of it, though I believe they are a wee bit unsure of whether to laugh or to fear you all the more."

"That shows great wisdom on their part," Gavin growled, keeping his eyes on the tall man's profile. "You know, Athol, I would almost believe you learned of this in the manner you say, if you were one to charm a scullery maid or even hang about the stables. But having had the pleasure of experiencing your sour disposition for the past two days, I'd have to say 'tis unlikely you would be welcome in either place."

Seemingly ignoring the barb, John Stewart looked through the huge doors of the Great Hall before turning and giving Gavin a half smile. "So you have not yet rooted out the culprit, if I am not mistaken."

Gavin paused and contemplated his answer. Right before him stood a man who—jovial though he might be on the surface—could easily be the very person responsible for the murder of Joanna's parents. In spite of what Joanna had seen and heard, Athol was still as suspect, in Gavin's eyes, as the women of the abbey. And besides, the Highlander irritated the hell out of him.

Gavin turned and met the other man's gray eyes. "So far I have been at a disadvantage, since this thief knows of more ways than one to travel through the passages of this keep." He furrowed his brow in a frown. "And every attempt I have made to find a guide to take me through the caverns has met with blank stares and silence. One might think my new vassals are siding with the scurvy dog."

"To be sure, any number of the household servants should have no difficulty in taking you around." The Highlander returned Gavin's frown. "Allan, for one, has been living in this place from the time he was a wee bairn. His great-great grandsires probably hauled stones to build the place. Aye, if I were to point to one with a fair, strong memory, Allan would be my first choice."

"Well, he claims that he hasn't been anywhere near those tunnels for quite some time. But from what I hear," Gavin continued, "you yourself were raised in these hills. I understand you spent more than a few hours in this castle as a lad."

"And who would tell you that? You wouldn't have me believe *you* are one to be fooling with the lasses in the kitchen!"

"Believe what you like," Gavin growled. "But I am not one to have a neighbor so near as you without wanting to know what I can about him."

Athol looked steadily at him for a moment, and then nodded thoughtfully. "Aye," he agreed. "And letting your neighbor know where he stands seems to be your way as well."

Gavin grunted his assent.

"You are a bluff and honest man," the earl said earnestly. "A rare quality in a flatlander." His attention was drawn to a trencher of food being carried by a serving boy across the Great Hall. "I don't know if you have chewed up your daily measure of stray neighbors, but I need to put some food in this empty belly of mine."

"First tell me—are you quite familiar with the tunnels beneath this keep?"

The Highlander's expression was controlled as he considered his answer, but watching him, Gavin decided that the man's answer would very likely confirm his own suspicions. In fact, as he waited, Gavin became more and more certain that Athol would try to hide the truth.

"Aye, my good host. In fact, I would say that there are few people outside this household *more* familiar with those caverns than I!"

Gavin watched the Highlander cock an eyebrow at him before turning and striding toward the table—and the food—that awaited them. Quickly disguising his surprise at the man's open acknowledgment, the laird followed a step behind.

As they reached their places at the head table, Gavin motioned for the earl to be seated. "I will make you an offer. An exchange. I will not ask you how it happens that you should be an expert on the so-called 'secret' passages beneath this keep, and you will give me a lesson."

Athol tore a leg off of one of the roasted ducks that sat before them, before turning to answer. "There is no need to bargain. I will gladly show you around . . . and still tell you how 'tis that I have come to know so much."

Gavin looked skeptically at his guest's face. "Is that so?"

"Are you always so mistrustful, or is it only when you are dealing with a new neighbor?"

Gavin frowned and fingered the goblet on the table. "I believe I've always been considered a trusting man. But somehow that trait has taken leave of me since I've arrived at the Highlands."

Athol grunted and turned his attention back to his food.

"Now," Gavin continued, "would you have any idea why I should be so afflicted?"

"I only offered you a tour through your own keep," the Highlander said between mouthfuls. "I think you should call a priest to exorcise *those* demons."

"Ah, 'tis a relief to find out that the good Earl of Athol is not a master of all trades." A wry grin tugged at Gavin's lips as he drew out his dirk and stabbed a hunk of cheese from his own trencher.

"I said you *should* call a priest," Athol said slyly, reaching for his cup. "But if you would like me to pray over you, as well—"

"Never mind all that," he growled. "Are you willing to take me through the caverns?"

"Are you serious?"

"Is there any reason I shouldn't be?" The Lowlander did not relax the intensity of his gaze while the earl considered the question.

"Nay, I can think of no reason at all, now that you mention it!" Athol drained his cup. "And when is it that you would like this merry expedition to take place?"

"Today," Gavin said with conviction. "This morning. Finish your food, m'lord earl, and we can start."

One quick look at her meager possessions and Joanna felt her heart leap with alarm in her chest. She crouched low, her eyes peering into the darkness beyond the little circle of light around her. Someone had been here; there could be no mistaking the signs. Her cloak and the ragged shift no longer lay where she had left them, folded and tucked beneath her little nest of straw. Someone had looked them over and shoved them back under the makeshift bed, and Joanna's blood ran cold.

The cavern beyond the low overhang was silent and still. Getting down on her hands and knees—the lamp in hand—she peered at the surface of the ground leading out of the little hollow until she found the footprints of the intruder. Boots. A large man's boots.

Giving her cloak one quick shake, Joanna hastily threw it around her shoulders and tied it at her throat. Well, as far as finding out who had gone through her belongings, there was not much she could do about it now. But there was something that she was certain of. Whoever had been here would be back.

Picking up the flint and putting whatever else she could into the deep pockets of her cloak, Joanna turned and gave her temporary quarters one last look. Once again—and so soon, it seemed—her shelter was being taken from her.

Once again, she thought wearily, it was time to go deeper into the darkness of these caverns to find yet another place of safety. But first, she had to go to the crypt. With so few days left until the full moon, she still had much to do to be ready.

Joanna moved hurriedly along the edge of the loch, but as she went, she did not see the shadow that flitted along the far wall, following her.

Chapter 19

Gavin knew he must be out of his mind to be touring the tunnels and caverns beneath Ironcross without having warned Joanna first. But then, Athol's candid acknowledgment, and his surprising willingness to serve as guide, had compelled the warrior chief to hammer away while the metal glowed hot. He could not hold back from putting Athol to the test.

Gavin knew, of course, that he must be alert and make enough noise to warn Joanna of their approach. Before leaving his chamber this morning, he had at least forced her to tell him that she had fixed a secure place by the underground loch. And from all that she'd said to make him feel comfortable about letting her go, Gavin had gotten a better sense of the extent and the complexity of these caverns and the maze of tunnels. Furthermore, she had sworn to him that there was no way anyone could approach her without her being aware of it long before they should happen upon her.

Raising the torch he carried high in the air as he followed a step behind the Highlander, Gavin hoped that she had been telling him the truth.

Hours ago, after letting all of their people know of their intent, the two leaders had moved quickly through the kitchens, past the questioning faces of the cook and her helpers, and down the stone steps behind the great hearth. This, apparently, was the only way Athol knew into the caverns from the keep itself, or at least so he had claimed.

The tunnels were indeed as confusing and mazelike as both the steward and Joanna had described. Low and narrow passages opened suddenly into huge caverns, with the entry of the two men rousing a thousand sleeping bats that had been roosting far above the flaring torches. Underground streams suddenly appeared beside a dry passage, gurgling and splashing along smooth walls, only to branch off and then disappear just as suddenly. And as if the sharp turns and endless series of carved steps—some leading up blind passages—were not enough, it seemed that every few moments they were passing sealed doors of ironbound oak.

Gavin tried to mark in his memory distinguishing points that they were passing, but soon the rock patterns and the twisting passages all began to blend together in a blurry melange of stone and dampness. And though Athol kept up a running commentary on the crystal formations of a particular cavern or the bottomless quality of some fissure that they were traversing, there were times, Gavin thought, when even his guide had become confused. One of those times happened when Gavin had asked him to bring them beneath the south wing, for the purpose of finding the way up to the passageways leading to the South Hall. Gavin was quite curious about the path that Joanna had taken when she had repeatedly stolen her own portrait, but instead they ended up standing on a ledge beneath an overhang, watching the wind-driven rain sweep across the broad loch. Gavin knew immediately that the walls surrounding the south wing were high above them.

After a quick glance at the breathtaking view, as well as at the sharp drop of cliffs beyond the ledge, Gavin turned to find the Highlander's gaze on him.

"Since arriving at Ironcross Castle," Athol began, his gray eyes intent on Gavin's face, "has there been any time that you have thought your life might be in danger? I mean, have there been any attempts on your life?"

"What makes you ask such a thing?"

Athol frowned and turned his gaze out over the stormswept loch. "Somehow, I had gotten a sense that in dealing with you, I would do best to approach you bluntly, honestly. Quite unlike so many of the good nobles spread around the Lowland countryside, you struck me as one who wastes no words in his dealings with others."

Gavin nodded at the other man's obvious compliment. "Some think so. But what makes you think I have anything to fear in my own keep?"

"The fire in your chamber the other night," Athol returned. "You did not survive at Flodden Field, or in the service of the king abroad, just to perish in your own bedchamber from an act of carelessness." He then turned and looked sharply into Gavin's face. "I know you to be a man of strength and courage, but I am certain you are not a careless man."

"Nay," the warrior replied. "That I am not."

"And then, there is the matter of this castle's past. After the incident last fall, I am more convinced than ever that the danger that seems to be stalking Ironcross's lairds is more than just a hoax."

"So you believe that the fire that destroyed the south wing was started intentionally?"

Athol nodded and then raised a brow questioningly. "Aye, I do. Do you have any doubt of it?"

Gavin frowned, unwilling to reveal his thoughts at this time. At least, as long as he considered this Highlander a possible force behind the evil of that night.

"Go on," Gavin paused, looking keenly into his guide's face. "Was this something that you suspected from the moment that the tragedy struck down those unsuspecting souls, or is this a recent conclusion?"

"I like to be forthright in my actions and in my words, no matter how condemning they might seem."

"So you have said." Gavin nodded.

"I knew the moment I walked into what remained of that wing that someone intent on murder started that fire."

Gavin stroked his chin and leaned his back against the damp stone wall at the mouth of the cave. "What did you see that made you so certain?"

John Stewart stepped away from the ledge and leaned his back as well against the opposing wall. "Going through the charred rooms, I could see that the fire had started not in one place but many. Every panel into the

passageways—every panel that *I* knew about, anyway—
was scorched, while other parts of the same room were
hardly burned. I believe those fires were set deliberately
to keep those in the south wing from escaping." Athol's
brow was furrowed and he stared out at the loch as he
continued. "John MacInnes knew his way through these
caverns as well as anyone alive. 'Twas he who, so many
years ago, first brought me down here. Now, for him
and his family to die in that wing and not use the passages after finding the door to the Old Keep barred—"

"What do you mean, 'barred'?"

"The door that led to the corridor over the archway,"
Athol replied, surprised by Gavin's response. "The way
was barred!"

The new laird stared at the earl.

Athol nodded as he continued. "I was the one, in fact,
who removed the bar, but then by the time we opened
the door, the wing was ablaze and the smoke so thick
you could not enter. By the time sections of roof began
to give way, letting in the rain, charred bodies were all
that remained. If it hadn't been for the downpours that
continued into the next morning, I don't believe any of
the south wing would be standing today."

"Why did you leave Ironcross so soon, Athol? Since
you were so certain of foul play, why did you not stay
longer and find the ones responsible?"

Angrily, the Highlander slapped his hand against the
rock wall and turned to face the loch. "I was left with
little choice. The steward, Allan, treated me as if I were
the one guilty of the crime. Not even had they carried
the bodies out of the ruin, before he started talking
about sealing the place off and waiting for Lady MacInnes to come north. He would not even take inventory
of what was left."

"Was there a reason why the steward would have suspected you?"

"Nay!" Athol scoffed. "Other than the fact that John
and I had argued that night, there was naught to make
the man even think of me. By the devil, John MacInnes
was like an older brother to me! There was no bad blood
between us. But to think of these people suspecting

me—of all people! And any one of them could have done it with less feeling than slaughtering a sheep. There was certainly no affection in these people for their laird. In fact," Athol said as he paused and turned to Gavin, "in his own quiet way, John had started a buzzing in their nests. I do not know that there was a great deal of sadness at his death. There was certainly no surprise."

"So you left!" he said gruffly.

"What difference did it make? Indirectly, my honor was being called into question by the damned steward, and my temper was growing shorter each moment I remained. I considered seizing the castle and forcing all under my control, but decided that would be counterproductive at best—and make me look even more guilty, taken together with the argument between John and myself. I was left with no other choice but to leave."

"Still, believing these murders had been committed and knowing yourself to be the only one capable of bringing justice in the wake of it all, you left."

At the sound of Gavin's words and accusing tone, the earl's brow darkened. He straightened from where he stood and glared across the way. "I might have left Ironcross Castle, but I did not give up my search for the truth. Seeing how quickly these people had steeled themselves against me, I thought it best to give the killer a false sense of security."

"But just how were you to find out the truth when you sat a day's ride away in Balvenie Castle?" When Athol hesitated to answer, Gavin looked suspiciously at his guest. Of course, he thought. He had been blind not to think of it before now. "You left behind spies."

Athol nodded. "It seemed like a good plan . . . then."

"Well? Did they come back to you with any information of value?"

"Nay." Athol shook his head. "Originally, I was paying two men here. But one of them, the more cunning of the two, died shortly after I left. From what I could gather, the man's skull was crushed by a falling rock."

"A rock?"

"Aye. He was walking through the gorge to the south of the keep."

"What about the other one? Dead as well?"

"Nay, he is alive and well!" Athol said coolly. "But I do not know if 'twas the fear from finding his accomplice dead, but he has been little use to me for the past six months."

Gavin stood away from the wall and looked into the other man's face. "Who is your spy?"

"Before you think of how to punish the man," Athol said, turning and peering into the darkness of the cave, "you must remember that at the time when he accepted the task, there were no lairds sitting at Ironcross Castle. If not the brightest of lads, he is a good one, and—"

"I'll not punish him. I do not even question your arrangement with the lad," Gavin said with finality, stepping up to the Highlander. "Considering the aftermath of that fire, I believe you did right. I might have done the same, were I in your position."

Athol clapped Gavin on the back of the shoulder. "For a Lowlander, you are an extremely understanding man."

"Get your paw off my back," the laird growled. Upon seeing the look of relief on Athol's face as his guest withdrew his hand, Gavin repeated his earlier question. "Who is your man? I'll not injure the lad, but I must know who your spy is."

Athol considered for a moment and then, nodding meaningfully at the darkness of cave before them, turned and spoke the lad's name.

Chapter 20

Margaret's hands grabbed at her own throat, strangling the anguished cry that was trying to escape her, as she watched the long blade of the dirk arc viciously through the air and rip into David's back.

The stable lad's head twisted about in an unnatural way as he tried to look back at his attacker, but the sharp ledge of the chasm, only a step away, was all he would ever see.

Pressing her back rigidly against the ice-cold walls of the cave, Margaret watched in mute horror as cold, sure hands reached out and pushed David hard over the edge.

Margaret shut her eyes, trying to block out the vision of the flailing arms of the stable lad as he went over.

If only I were blind, she prayed, sobbing. *Oh Blessed Virgin, strike me blind.*

Margaret sank to the ground, her eyes closed, but she could not shut out the sickening sound of the young man's crunching fall deep into the bowels of the earth.

And sitting there, stunned and alone, she could not shut out the sight of the bloody dirk in the hand of one whom she loved.

In the hand of a killer.

"I want you to know you are a complete failure as a guide, Athol! In fact, I am beginning to think you are either a liar or a thickheaded oaf."

Flushing crimson, the earl glared menacingly over his shoulder at Gavin. "Simply because I cannot find one damn panel, you have to attack my character!"

"Aye!" Gavin pushed the man aside and moved in

next to him. The two of them stared at the open space of what was once John MacInnes's study. "There is no way anyone can come through this panel and make their way to the hearth. By Saint Andrew, I found *this* panel by myself the second day I was here! There must be another passage that opens up next to that chimney."

"Well, I know of no other," Athol growled.

"That's the first admission of ignorance you have made today. There may be hope for you yet."

"Nay, I take back what I said. There is no passage up there."

"You're wrong. There is," Gavin snapped. "This is your thickheadedness coming through again. You might as well just admit defeat."

"I'll not!" Athol turned angrily into the passageway they'd just left. "By His Bones, I swear I'll find the damned passage."

"Not today," the laird said wearily, following the other man through the darkness to a creaking old ladder. "There is something else that may be far more valuable. Something that might add useful facts to the fairly worthless information you have gathered so far."

"You are a miserable, gruff, ill-mannered dog of a villian . . . even for a Lowlander!"

"Aye. All of those things." Gavin slapped him hard on the back. "But an understanding one. You told me so yourself!"

Athol turned and glowered at him. "Which side of hell do you want me to take you to now?"

"Not hell, blackguard. The crypt!"

"In the kirkyard?"

"Nay! Och, you're a dungheaded fool. The one beneath this keep."

Athol frowned, suddenly putting aside all interest in their verbal sparring. "Why in the devil's name do you want to see that place?"

Gavin picked up the wick lamp that they'd hung on the wall and looked back at his guide. "How long has it been since you have been there?"

"By the devil, I've *never* gone there!" the Highlander blurted. "Even as young lads, we always were sure to stay clear of those vaults . . . and that part of the caverns."

"Are you telling me you are afraid of the place?"

The earl considered for a moment before answering. "What you don't understand, you stay away from. Even as lads, we had that much sense. We knew that vault had only women buried within it. Only women went there, and it has always had an air of . . . I don't know . . . unwelcome is the only way to express it.

Gavin frowned. "Has anything ever happened to a man for going in there? Or is all of this, again, just a part of this nonsense about the curse?"

Athol shook his head. "I don't know, Gavin. Although there were always tales of painful deaths suffered by those foolhardy enough to trespass, I myself never knew of anyone who tried." He shrugged his shoulders in acceptance. "The fact that John MacInnes would never go in there himself was reason enough for me to stay clear of the place."

"So then, my good lord earl, this day has been a complete waste?" Gavin challenged. "Now that you have failed to show me the way from my chamber to the south wing, you are telling me that you cannot even find your way to the crypts?"

"Nay, my wee, dainty bull. I *can* take you, nuisance though you are," Athol retorted in response.

"The same way that you took me to the panel beside the hearth?"

The Highlander glared threatening before turning and starting down the passageway. "All we need to do is head east . . . which would be this way. From what I remember, any one of these tunnels should take us in that direction."

"East!" Gavin muttered disgustedly as he fell in beside the man. "Well, at least when we reach Jerusalem, I'll knew we've gone too far."

To Joanna, the beat of her heart, hammering loudly and treacherously in her chest, seemed to echo through the crypt. Cursing the very sounds of her breaths, she crouched, hidden in the darkness behind one of the stone tombs.

Continuing her daily effort of digging at the trenches on the floor, she had been startled by the sound of a cough emanating from somewhere down the tunnel passages. Quickly, she had covered her work with straw and hidden herself behind the crypt, just as the intruder's footsteps could be heard at the vault's entrance.

In a moment the light of another wick lamp flickered and came to life. The source of this new light moved across the floor, the shadows of the great stone pillars making their way across the wall behind the hidden woman. Joanna heard the sound of the top being removed from the keg of oil. Whoever was here obviously had been given the charge of preparing the crypt for the upcoming meeting of the women. A hot flash of panic coursed through her at the thought that the woman's efforts might include some duty regarding the individual tombs. If it did, Joanna knew, she would be discovered.

"Ah, you are here at last."

Joanna froze, recognizing Mater's voice at once. When, from the vault's entrance, the sound of a low moan came in response, Joanna slowly crouched into a ball once again and listened.

"There are more reeds and brush that need to be brought in from outside that door. And why have you not brought down more oil? Why are you standing there?"

There was a pause, and silence filled the crypt. A silence so deep that it chilled her soul.

"What is it, Margaret?" The older woman's voice rose in pitch, as a sudden concern eclipsed her original tone of cold superiority. "Are you crying?"

Joanna wished she had the courage to move and peek out at them. But instead, pressing her head against the cold stones, she tried to focus on any sound the mute woman might make. She heard Mater's feet move across the floor toward the entrance.

"Why are you acting this way? Why do you move away from me?" Mater's voice was suddenly sharp, reproachful. "I only want to see if you are hurt!"

Knowing the two women were far enough away, Joanna summoned up her courage and edged to one side of the stone tomb until she could peer out around the corner of the crypt. Margaret stood next to the entrance, her back pressed against the wall, her pale face stained with tears and dirt. As Joanna watched Mater try to approach her again, the weeping woman's hands shot out and made a waving motion in the air, warding the older woman off.

"What is it, Margaret?" Mater entreated gently, pushing through the mute woman's hands before succeeding in enfolding Margaret's shaking shoulders in her embrace. "What has come over you, my sweet?"

Joanna watched in astonishment as Mater held the other in her arms. The two women stood together—one middle-aged, one older—and Margaret seemed to melt in the abbess's embrace. The serving woman continued to shake and she was beginning to sob audibly—a strangled, unnatural sound. Yet even as Joanna watched, Margaret visibly yielded to the comfort of Mater's soothing words and gentle hands.

For a lingering moment, the memory of another Mater came alive—the Mater whom Joanna had respected and trusted so long ago. The wise and ever protective Mater.

But behind the vision and the memory, Joanna could not erase the thought that this was the same Mater whose life served to ignite the flames of death.

"Did anyone hurt you, my love?"

Surprised, Joanna watched as the crying woman shook her head in response. How many in the castle thought Margaret was deaf as well as mute! Watching what was happening between the two women here, there was no question in Joanna's mind that Margaret could hear and understand perfectly well.

"It tears at my heart to see you suffer." Mater ran her gnarled fingers down the tear-stained face of the other. "My beloved sister."

Joanna held her breath, trying to comprehend the abbess's address of the mute woman.

"Och, what have I done to you?" Mater said softly as she continued to pat away the other woman's rolling tears. "Why is it that I've been able to walk away from my suffering, and yet you—with so many years having gone by—still must bear the agony of a useless tongue and tormented soul?"

Margaret shook her head in protest as she grabbed one of Mater's hands tightly in hers and brought it to her lips. After placing kisses on the wrinkled skin's back, she placed her wet cheek against it, like a child taking comfort in the strength of an adult.

Joanna edged back into her hiding place behind the tomb. Sitting there, she channeled her fingers through her hair and pressed her palms to her temples, trying to quell the sudden pounding in her head. How could it be that now, after so long, she suddenly felt such confusion? Why, so late in her plans, was she flooded with second thoughts? *Damn* Gavin for making her doubt what she had seen with her own eyes!

Leaning her head back against the cold stone, Joanna tried to force herself back, in her mind's eyes, to the charred wreckage of the south wing, to the smell of burned flesh, and the cloud of death suspended in the air. It was there. She could see it. Feel it. The sadness and anger tightened its grip on her heart. Her eyes flew open, and tears began to stream down her face. Nay, she thought adamantly. She would not doubt. She could not forget.

Behind her, the two women began to move about the chamber, and Joanna continued to listen to everything Mater said. In a short while their preparations were completed, and nothing more was revealed to the young woman.

Then, on their way out, Joanna heard Mater address Margaret one last time.

"Wait, sister. I want you to go back to the keep and get Allan. I will wait for you in the passages above Hell's Gate."

Margaret's questioning response appeared, to Joanna, to carry a note of muffled protest.

"Go, Margaret!" Mater ordered. "I believe 'tis time I reminded him again of his responsibility for caring for our precious younger sister."

At the sound of another barely audible protest, Joanna peered again around the side of the crypt, only to see Margaret's waving of hands at the older woman.

"You will do as you are told, Margaret," Mater scolded. "The three of us are all that are left. And though we are advancing in age, both Allan and I are quite capable of looking after our needs. But you . . ." Her voice cracked with the intensity of her feelings. "I am not returning to the abbey, not until such time as our brother gives me his word that he will do a better job. Well, if he will not look after you more carefully, he will have to answer to me!"

Mater is their sister, Joanna thought in amazement as she slid silently back into the shadows.

The dank smell of the grave was all he could breathe . . . and he found it remarkably disagreeable.

There was no way in hell, Gavin swore, that he would let her return to these tunnels. To think that he had been foolish enough to accept her reasoning without having witnessed for himself the dangers that lurked at every turn! True, she had survived for six months without him, but during that time she had been able to take refuge in that tower room in the south wing. She had told him that much herself, last night. But he, too drunk with the heat of their passion, from the excitement he felt in having her in his arms and at his side, had simply accepted her wishes.

Well, standing now by the edge of the deep chasm that Athol called Hell's Gate, Gavin was more than ever before certain that he'd been a careless fool to let her have her way.

The seemingly bottomless cleft stretched the length of the cavern, disappearing beneath a sheer rock wall at one end and continuing on into the darkness beyond their ledge at the other. In breadth, it was far too wide to allow any one man to jump, and the ledge across was higher by the height of two men, at least.

Gavin eyed the ancient rope bridge dubiously and, reaching out, tugged at one of the ropes that stretched across the chasm. Behind them, the ends of the ropes disappeared into a hand-hewn tunnel. Following them back, he found the iron rings that protruded from the rock wall and supported this end of the bridge. With a frown, he returned to the ledge. Lifting his torch, the warrior chief peered up at the stone slabs that had been placed at the edge of the opposite ledge. The ropes disappeared beyond, and the Lowlander guessed that the same means of anchoring the bridge existed there.

Looking over at Athol, Gavin found the Highlander studying the bridge as well. As he watched him, the red-haired nobleman kicked a loose rock into the abyss, and they both listened as it struck the sides of the chasm as it dropped. It never did hit bottom.

"Hell's Gate," Gavin muttered, shaking his head.

"Aye. Aptly named, I would say."

"Is this the only way to cross over, then?"

Athol shook his head, a mischievous grin creeping across his face. "Nay. There are other ways around, I believe . . . for the faint of heart." Looking away from the scowling giant, the Highlander continued. "I myself never took any of them, of course. I believe there is a natural bridge that crosses this beast, in an area of the caverns we haven't seen, yet. 'Tis down by an underground loch. A wee bit out of our way, but if you are feeling a mite queasy about the bridge—"

"I've already spent more time down here than I'd planned. This rope bridge seems sturdy enough to carry our weight. Try not to fall off, though. I don't want to be explaining this to your men."

The Highlander shrugged goodnaturedly as he gestured for Gavin to lead the way. "Remember, though, from here on my knowledge of these caves comes to an end."

"Not that your knowledge was reliable to start with," the Lowlander grumbled as he lifted the lamp and studied the way.

Athol snorted. "You're a thankless blackguard, Gavin Kerr!"

"And you . . ." Gavin said, stepping onto the wooden slats and bouncing lightly to test the bridge's strength against his weight. "You are an unhappy excuse for a guide, John Stewart!"

"This footbridge," the earl said, laying a hand on the laird's arm, "was built before the time of your grandfather—whoever that was. But even then it was meant to support calm walking—not any leaping about by baboons the size of you!" Pushing Gavin aside, he squeezed by and took the lead. "Say what you will, 'tis clear I have more sense than you and all your kin put together . . . and I am still the better man to guide you through these tunnels."

John Stewart started across the bridge, and Gavin followed. But when they were almost halfway across, the laird paused to look past the Highlander. Just over the top of the ledge, something caught his eyes. A movement.

Gavin raised his wick lamp higher as the rope on one side of the bridge gave way with a snap.

Chapter 21

The bridge fell away beneath their feet, caught momentarily, and then fell away again when the weight of the two warriors hit the remaining support ropes.

Gavin's lamp was gone, and as Athol fell past him, he reached out with one hand and grabbed at the man, catching him by the back of his belt. With his other hand, Gavin clung to the rope with a viselike grip and braced himself as they swung down into the blackness of Hell's Gate.

In less than an instant the two men smashed into the side of the chasm, and Gavin felt a sharp pain knife through his shoulder as he fought to keep his hold. They were hanging in total darkness, and he realized suddenly that the ropes on this side had held.

Cursing, he felt for the slats of the bridge with his feet as a groan came from the doubled-over body hanging limply beneath him. It was the only sound to break the terrible silence.

It took a long moment for Gavin to catch his breath, and Athol was growing unbearably heavy. This was the same damn shoulder he'd hurt when the rock had fallen on him in the gorge. He tried to ignore the pain. The warrior looked upward, but with both lamps gone, the blackness was as absolute as death.

The Highlander moaned in pain and twisted his body, knocking Gavin's foot from its step. The two men jerked downward, and Gavin felt as if his arm would tear from its socket. Bloody hell, he thought, grimacing and struggling to gain his foothold again. One more movement like that and they'd both be on their way to the devil.

The Highlander took several sharp breaths, and then Gavin felt the man using his hands to get a grip on the rope and the wooden treads. Gradually, the pressure on his belt hand diminished until the earl had a secure hold on the bridge.

"Are you strong enough to hold yourself?"

"Aye," came Athol's raspy reply from the darkness. "What the hell happened?"

Gavin again peered upward into the darkness above them. "Someone cut the rope at the far end. That was enough for the whole thing to give way."

"You saw them?"

"I saw a movement in the shadows, right before the damn thing snapped." Gavin slowly eased his deathgrip on Athol's belt. "Can you climb unaided?"

Gavin felt the earl hoist himself upward a bit. "Aye. I can do it."

"Are you badly hurt?"

"A bit groggy. I banged my head against the rocks."

"Well, that's your least vulnerable spot."

"I'm grateful for your concern," Athol snarled.

"Not at all. If you can climb, we'd best be moving."

There was no need for Gavin to say the words. Someone had tried to murder them on this bridge. And more than likely, that someone had by now surmised that they were not dead, but rather hanging suspended from one end from the bridge.

"I'm going to release my grip on your belt."

"Then you'd best bloody well do it!" Athol growled irritably. "In fact, I wish you would climb ahead of me. You're taking up most of this space now."

Gavin smiled grimly and started the hard climb in the dark, feeling with his feet as he went. "You said there are other ways around this chasm."

"There are." The Highlander's clipped tone was sounding stronger and clearer. "We might not have much time before he makes it around."

"Be quick, my friend," Gavin ordered. "Before that scurvy devil lays a blade to the ropes on this side!"

At the sound of the shout echoing through the tunnels, Joanna leapt up from her hiding place behind the stone tomb.

Gavin. She was certain of it.

Yanking a torch down from the sconce beside the crypt's entryway. Joanna hurriedly struck a flint and lifted the lit torch overhead. Hell's Gate, she thought, running down the tunnel toward the chasm. His shout had definitely come from that direction.

After Margaret and Mater had gone, she had continued to sit, numb from what she had heard. But the sound of Gavin's voice had abruptly shaken her out of her reverie.

But now, as she ran, Joanna felt a cold hand squeeze her heart, and she wondered how far from the tomb Mater had gone.

Perhaps it was the sudden draught of air, or a difference in the way the sound echoed back to him. Whatever it was, Gavin sensed that he was getting close to the ledge.

The cutting of the rope bridge and their subsequent fall had stripped away any remaining trace of suspicion in Gavin's mind regarding Athol. Whatever desires the Highlander harbored toward the lands of Ironcross Castle, Gavin no longer believed John Stewart was behind any of the violence aimed at its lairds. This attack on Gavin had been no accident, and had he not caught the earl by the belt, Athol would have unquestionably plunged to his death.

Suddenly, Athol grabbed at his boot, bringing Gavin to a halt. Peering down into the darkness below him, he was about to speak when he heard the running footsteps.

Listening carefully, he quickly realized that the sound of footsteps was coming from this side of the chasm.

Foolishly hopeful, he thought for an instant that this might be help. But that idea was soon shattered when he felt someone try to jerk the line and shake them loose.

Letting out a fierce cry, the Lowlander quickened his climb up the rope as the sound of a knife's blade cutting into the fibers of the cord turned his blood into fire.

She was nearing the black, bottomless pit they called Hell's Gate when she heard him again. A surge of joy propelled her forward. The tunnels that ran off this passage were dark and threatening, but she raced past them with hardly a thought of whom they might be hiding.

After a sharp bend the tunnel suddenly widened, and Joanna broke out onto the ledge that stretched a few feet in either direction beside the chasm. With a sharp intake of air, she stopped herself abruptly.

The footbridge was gone. Holding her torch aloft, Joanna peered downward across the divide. On the far side, only one of the ropes of the ancient footbridge could be seen disappearing into the darkness. As she tried to comprehend what had occurred, a shadow moved in the tunnel beyond and Joanna froze momentarily. The shadow moved again.

"Are you there?" she cried out in panic.

The sound of Gavin's voice calling up from the darkness of the chasm below the opposite ledge made the shadow retreat, this time in haste, down the tunnels beyond. Lifting the lamp higher in the air, Joanna stared for an instant. She could possibly run and, taking one of the longer, roundabout tunnels, reach the other side in time to give chase to the fleeing coward. But the thought of Gavin somewhere below forced her attention back to the bottomless pit.

Joanna knelt on the edge of the abyss and lowered the torch, straining to make out his shape in the blackness. There! She could see him moving up what remained of the footbridge dangling from the ledge across the divide.

But before she had a chance to say anything, the voice of another man shattered her momentary relief.

"Joanna!" the man called out, and she could not help but cringe at the disbelief and the delight in Athol's voice.

The old woman emerged breathlessly from the darkness of the tunnel, only to pull back abruptly at the sight of Joanna kneeling on the ledge across the divide.

So, Mater thought with satisfaction, at last the lass is done with her senseless game of hiding.

She backed away at the sound of the men climbing from the depths of the chasm. Then, nodding to herself, the abbess turned and glided silently through the caves.

Chapter 22

Gavin's gaze never wavered from Joanna's stunned expression across the way as he extended his hand down to pull the injured Highlander up onto the ledge.

Neither he nor Joanna had whispered a word since Athol had called out upon seeing her on the opposite ledge.

As the Highlander straightened up unsteadily and looked across the way at Joanna, Gavin saw a look of fear in her stance. She half turned. There was no question about her next move, the laird thought. She was ready to flee.

"Don't go," Gavin commanded.

She looked back at him in confusion.

"Are you Joanna MacInnes?" he called, trying to sound surprised in light of all that Athol had already said.

"Aye, that she is," the other man affirmed.

Glancing over at him, Gavin saw, from the light of Joanna's torch, the bloody gash on the Athol's brow. At that moment the Highlander's knees buckled, and he staggered backward a step. Gavin's hand shot out and grabbed him by the shoulder, yanking him away from the edge of the abyss.

"I did not drag you out of there just to have you stumble back in. Sit yourself."

"But what of Joanna—" he protested.

"Sit here and try not to let the blackguard who cut the ropes do the same to your throat," Gavin ordered. "If she will tell me the way to go, I will escort her back."

Athol shook his head in disagreement, only to have

his eyes glaze over from the movement. "Nay, I . . . I know the way. We could both go."

Joanna's voice echoed imperiously off the cavern walls. "John, you will stay where you are!"

Her order carried the greater weight. Athol put his weight heavily on one foot as he stared dazedly across the chasm.

"Stay, John," she commanded again. "I *will* come around. And you . . . you take the second fork to the right and follow that. I will meet you."

Athol gave a weak smile at the torch-wielding figure across the divide. "Quite a lass, that one."

"Aye," Gavin growled, helping the Highlander back to the rock wall of a cavern. "So it appears."

As Gavin stepped back, the earl drew his dirk from his belt and sat gingerly. The warrior chief eyed him doubtfully.

"I don't need any Lowlander playing wetnurse for me." Athol waved the blade of his dagger toward the tunnel. "Just move along. I'll try not to get too worried for you while you're off getting yourself lost."

With a wry smile, the laird turned and watched Joanna disappear beyond the ledge at the other side of the chasm.

Margaret wrapped her hands tightly around her middle and watched as the priest hastily gathered together his possessions. Unable to hold back the tears that were running freely down her face, she dashed at them every now and then with a shaking hand. His leather satchel sat open on the bed, and she hesitantly reached down and picked up his cowl. Bringing the wool garment to her face, she smelled it and ran the soft material over her wet cheeks. But then, glancing up at her, Father William snatched it roughly from her hands and threw it back into the bag.

He paused and stared for a long moment at the ornate silver cross that hung on the wall. Then, upending the satchel on the bed, the priest pawed through the meager contents, as if searching for something. With a frustrated oath, the little man stuffed the items back into the leather bag and then threw it with unexpected violence to the floor. His hands raking through his thinning hair, he stood, looking lost and distracted, beside the bed.

"I'll . . . I'll be back for you, Iris," he muttered, his eyes darting toward Margaret and then around the room. Walking the length of the chamber, he stopped and stared again at the cross. "You have my word that I'll be back for you. I'll not desert you and the bairn."

His look was wild, and she wondered if he had truly gone mad. His eyes almost glittered, like one drunk . . . or possessed with a devil's spirit.

No matter, Margaret thought. No matter at all.

She loved him. That he still called her by another woman's name, that he was running because of a wrong he'd done—it all meant nothing. But he had to take her with him, Margaret thought, a hot flush of panic coursing through her. She had to go with him.

Resolved on her actions, Margaret quickly drew the plaid from the bed, knotting two of the corners and slipping it over her head. Then, gathering the items that had spilled from the satchel, she lifted that onto her shoulder as well.

He needed her, Margaret assured herself, ignoring the desperation that lingered like the taste of iron in her mouth. He needed her more than he could ever admit to himself.

Moving slowly toward him, she reached for his hand and took it in her own. His eyes were truly wild now, darting to her face and away. He would never hurt her, she told herself.

She stood there, ready, and fought back her tears. Something within her was desperately seeking release. As if the soul within her was trying to speak to him, to scream the words of her heart. *I am coming with you— fear nothing. I will stay by you and care for you and love you, no matter what others might think or say or do!*

Tell me that you need me. Please, William, tell me that you want me!

"Well, Iris, you are coming, I see." His voice was barely a whisper, his tone hoarse and deadened, like a

man weary from lack of sleep. "This time you are coming with me."

Margaret nodded as she allowed relief and gratitude
to bury all sense of reason within her. Hiding her tears
of joy, she brought his hand up to her face and pressed
her trembling lips against it.

You understand, she wept. *You want me!*

Joanna dropped her torch on the packed earth and
ran into his arms, nestling her cheek against the soft
weave of his tartan. He was safe. He'd come so close to
disappearing into the depths of the abyss. He could have
been killed, taken from her forever! She shuddered violently in his arms, clutching him tightly.

Gavin's cheek pressed warmly against her hair. "Joanna, so far as Athol knows, we have never met." He
spoke hurriedly, his arms still not loosening his grip on
her body. "I will not have your reputation ruined
with—"

"My reputation be damned, Gavin. When I think of
what almost happened." She looked up into his dark
eyes, flashing in the torch light. His face descended, and
she parted her lips as his tongue swept hungrily into her
waiting mouth. In a moment far too short, though, he
broke off the kiss.

"Joanna," he growled, pressing his lips to her ear.
"You will come out into the open, but nothing has
changed between us, my love. We still—"

"What did you say?" she asked, pulling back and gazing into his intense eyes.

"We still belong to each other, Joanna. You *will* be
my wife."

My love. Such simple words. And yet, she knew he
was not about to repeat them. But that was fine, she
decided then. No doubt for the better. For what time
had they for such thoughts, for such terms of endear-
ment? What time had they for love?

"We will make our way around and take Athol back
up to the keep, and then—"

"But I cannot," she protested. "If I go with you, all
will be—"

"Joanna, Athol has seen you!" Gavin pressed. "If you think there is any way in hell I'll be able to convince him that you were just a delusion caused by a wee bump on his thick head . . ." The Lowlander shook his head. "Nay, lass. He would never believe such a thing. And that, of course, is assuming I would do such a thing!"

As soon as she drew a breath to argue, Gavin drew her hard against his chest. " 'Tis time you left these caverns and joined the living. The danger that lurks in this place is not simply directed at me. Whoever it was that was trying to cut that last of the rope, they saw you, Joanna. They will come after you."

Joanna shivered, settling willingly against his chest.

"I'll not leave you down here any longer, my sweet. You can argue all you want, but you're coming with me."

Gavin was right in his assumption that the killer hiding in the shadows across the way was indeed aware of her presence beneath the keep. Joanna's mind flashed back to Mater and Margaret in the crypt. Margaret had left the vault first, but even so, Mater would have had ample time to arrive at the bridge and cut the lines. But how would she have known of the two men's whereabouts, Joanna wondered? Perhaps she had simply seized the opportunity that Hell's Gate offered her.

Again, Gavin's concerns worked to disturb her thoughts. If, as she was inclined to believe, Mater had cut the ropes, then she knew of Joanna's presence in the caverns. If she did, she would not rest until she had finished what she had set out to do when she had lit the fires in the south wing months ago.

Joanna's mind raced. If that were the case, how could she follow through with her plans to avenge her parents' deaths? Nay, Gavin was correct. It would be best to return with him and rethink what must be done from the relative safety of the keep.

But there were problems with that as well.

"How would I explain where I've been?"

"You have no need. You owe no explanation to anyone," he answered. "In fact, let me take care of the details."

"But what are *you* going to say?"

"Only what needs to be said, lass," he said confidently. "I'll mention that you came upon the two of us hanging from a rope in the chasm and managed to save our lives. But as to your whereabouts prior to that moment, from what we can gather, you remember nothing after the fire."

She tried to find fault in what he had just said, but couldn't. Suddenly concerned with another thought, she looked into his eyes questioningly. "You'll not try to protect me by sending me back to court to my grandmother, now, would you? No matter what she says or demands or requests, I am to stay at Ironcross Castle with you."

A small smile tugged at the corner of his handsome mouth as he nodded his agreement. "But that is only on the condition that you promise to marry me as soon as I settle the business of your betrothal with Gordon."

She paused, struggling to ignore the sudden ache in her chest at the thought that she might not live through the next full moon, that dispensing justice to the women of the abbey would put a quick end to the possibility of such a life, a marriage, children of her own. Joanna drew in a deep breath.

But then, there was no reason for Gavin to know her thoughts. If things were different, if her life were her own, if she could be a women with dreams and plans like any other her age, then marrying Gavin Kerr would be a grand and exciting thing. Perhaps all she could ever wish for.

"Aye," she said brightly, hiding the sadness that was crushing the life from her. "I will marry you."

Chapter 23

The Earl of Athol's face, suddenly ashen, said it all. Gavin watched warily as the Highlander brought a shaky hand to his bandaged head. Seeing the man's bloodshot eyes snap at him with a look of contempt mixed with disbelief, Gavin questioned his own decision to break the news to his injured guest so soon.

He knew how taken John Stewart was with Joanna. Yesterday, behaving like some abbey schoolboy, Athol had never taken his eyes off of her—not from the moment they began working their way back up to the keep. Gavin was willing to ignore it then, but something he could not quite identify—something he had no wish to identify—had made Gavin anxious to put an immediate end to the Highlander's attentions to *his* future wife.

"You jest," Athol growled, finally finding his voice. "This talk of marrying Joanna—this is just your miserable sense of humor. Tell me that is all 'tis."

"Nay," Gavin put in determinedly, holding his ground. "I'm planning to marry Joanna MacInnes. 'Tis the right thing to do, all things considered."

Taking hold of the back of the chair he had flown out of a moment earlier, John Stewart's eyes flashed with anger. "You? Impossible! 'Tis bad enough she is already betrothed to that blackguard James Gordon."

"Never mind that! She *was* promised to him, but that was nearly a year ago. Everyone in Scotland thinks she is dead."

"But that makes no difference." Athol scowled and banged his hand on the chair. "Och, you've got the brain of a marmoset! She's still his, you fool!"

"She wishes to break off the agreement," Gavin corrected stubbornly. "I have already talked to her, Athol. She has consented to become my wife. So this morning, I sent my man Edmund to Gordon's place near Huntly with a letter."

"Wait!" Athol snapped. "You cannot possibly think she means it. By the devil, the woman has been underground for the last six months. She more than likely has yet to gather her wits about her."

"There is nothing wrong with her mind. You, on the other hand—"

"What is your hurry?" Athol snapped angrily, obviously frustrated. "You do not need her gold. As far as this castle is concerned, I know that the holding is nothing compared to all you have in the Borders. I don't even know why you came up here in the first place."

"They told me in Stirling that the weather here was unmatched anywhere in Scotland."

"Aye, that may be true enough."

Gavin eyed Athol, wondering for a moment that he had taken the jest seriously.

"But listen," John Stewart continued, "even if you only wanted the lands, thinking to become another one of the line of little-seen lairds of Ironcross, you have no need to marry her. Angus has already given you all of it, not that the holding will yield you much if you are not here to see to it. Look, man, when it comes down to it, the fact that Joanna is alive will make no difference if you want to keep the land!"

"What you say is true. 'Tis not for a title or fortune that I have asked for her hand. But all I can tell you is that—and Joanna and I both agree—'tis the right thing to do."

Athol stared open mouthed in disbelief. "That's it?" he spluttered finally. " 'Tis *right?*"

Gavin raised a hand. "Joanna has every wish to stay at Ironcross Castle and see that justice is brought to bear on the one—or the ones—responsible for her parents' deaths—"

"So you are forcing her to marry you in exchange for her wish to stay! This is madness on her part, and you are the lowest, base born, knavish, son of a—"

"Stop, dog, before you go too far! I tell you I'm forcing nothing!" This time Gavin was the one who was shouting, surprised that the unfairness of John Stewart's accusation had stung him so. "The desire to learn more about Joanna and her parents' fate was the main reason that drove me here in the first place. From the very beginning—before we ever met—there was something that drew me to her."

"Bah!" Athol scoffed, reinforcing his vocal expression of disbelief with a dismissive wave of his hands. "Now you expect me to believe you—a baboon in a stolen kilt—have come like a lover out of a French romance to save the lady in distress."

"I expect a blackhearted dog like you to believe nothing but the rope that finally hangs you!" The two men glared at one another for a moment before Gavin continued. "I don't know why I'm even telling you this, but I was . . . well, curious about her from the moment I first spoke with Lady MacInnes. And since I arrived at Ironcross Castle, everything about her has haunted me, day and night." Gavin looked directly into the other man's eyes. "Is it so difficult for you to understand that I . . . that I'm fond of her and she, as well, likes what she sees in me? Is it so—"

"Difficult?" Athol exploded. "By the devil, 'tis impossible! Aside from looking at you—which would be enough to frighten to death a flock of sheep—she hasn't had time to learn anything about you! Before yesterday, she hadn't even met you!" The Highlander eyed the laird suspiciously. "What have you been doing while I've been confined to this chamber?"

Gavin wished he had been able to spend time with her. But with all that had to be done, he and Joanna had actually seen very little of one another.

"I think you have intentionally drugged me with the potions that witch of a cook has been sending up." The Highlander waved a hand in the direction of the jars and pitchers sitting on a table beside the bed. "You did that so you could have your way with her."

"You are just angry because she prefers me to you," Gavin interrupted abruptly. "Why not accept the fact that Joanna has once again—and this time finally—decided on another? She does not want to wed *you*!"

Scowling darkly, Athol sank back in the chair and looked up into Gavin's face. "Is that what she told you?"

Gavin lowered his voice and looked steadily at the man. "You should speak to her yourself if you wish to understand her feelings. All I can say is that she refers to you as a valuable friend, one whom she would not care to lose. She has very few people left in this world, so don't be rash in your thinking about her."

The Earl of Athol stared, and as Gavin looked back, he could see the emotions flickering across the man's face.

"Aye," Athol said finally. "I *will* talk to Joanna, and I *will* question her motives. But in the meantime I need to know something more about you. Something that will assure me that you are indeed deserving of her hand."

"You are an arrogant, overreaching man, to be sure."

"Aye." Athol nodded, with a smile tugging at the corner of his mouth. "And all I know of you is that you are a gruff, warlike bear of a Lowlander with quick hands and a sure grip. But what does that have to do with making you a fit husband for the lass, or even a good laird?"

Feeling the tension slide smoothly from the space between them, Gavin dragged a chair from the wall and took a seat, as well. "Ah, so this was the cause of your argument with John MacInnes the night be died. You were questioning James Gordon's worthiness in having Joanna's hand?"

"Aye." Athol nodded, his face growing grim, and in his eyes, the weariness of one remembering a battle fought—and lost—long ago. "I have known her since she was a wee thing, no bigger than my two hands. I always thought her deserving of no less than the best man Scotland could offer."

"You are a greater fool than I thought, John Stewart, thinking that your place as a friend gives you the right to question her father's choice."

Sitting erect in his chair, Athol's eyes suddenly flashed

with indignation. "Aye, but here he was, giving his precious daughter to Gordon, the devil take him. A womanizer and a scoundrel at that! And for what? For the sole purpose of keeping her a few more miles from Ironcross Castle! What kind of thinking is that? To make a decision based on a fear of demons and old curses!"

"Considering how many kin John MacInnes lost in this keep, how can you blame the man?"

The skin on Athol's taut face flushed a ruddy shade. "That night, I called him a fool and told him how wrongheaded he was. Hours later, he lost his life and proved me the fool. He didn't want Joanna exposed to the evils that he believed surround this keep. But here we are today, and I cannot stop you from going against his wishes."

" 'Tis all different now."

"Is it?"

Gavin's face grew fierce. "Aye. Joanna has been exposed to the worst of whatever this place has to offer. In these months past, she has suffered and she has lived through it all. Even if John MacInnes were alive today, he would agree that Joanna today is a far different woman than she was that night. I tell you she is a woman whose heart is full of pain, and yet she still seeks to bring justice—and life—to this godforsaken castle."

"All the more reason, then, to get her out of here," Athol stressed. "Perhaps 'tis best for her to marry James Gordon after all, or at least to return to court and Lady MacInnes."

Gavin shook his head, his voice barely more than a low growl. "If you were in her position, is that what you would wish for yourself? To skulk away and leave those murders unavenged?"

"But she is a woman! By His Blood, she has already seen more pain and more—"

"Hold, Athol." Gavin broke in. "Be her friend and not her father. Joanna MacInnes is a great deal stronger than you might think. Think of what you and I went through yesterday. I wonder if either of us would have been able to survive in that maze of darkness for six months—as she did!"

"Curses or not, there is an evil that lurks in these walls. Death hangs over the place like a shroud!"

"Be it so, she and I will face that together," Gavin asserted confidently. "Six months ago, the words of a curse struck fear into the hearts of folks in these parts. But today I know it to be the foul work not of some demon, but of someone made of flesh and blood. One vulnerable enough to fear being discovered. One who needed the edge of a blade to send us nearly through the gates of hell."

Athol's deep frown told Gavin that the Highlander was considering everything that he'd just said. But in case he wasn't convinced, there was more that Gavin could tell him.

At about the same time that he'd sent Edmund off to meet with James Gordon, Gavin had also given Peter the mission of searching out the priest who had served as chaplain here before Father William. Gavin knew that the chances were slim of Peter finding the man still living, but if he could, Gavin was certain he could learn a great deal more about the history of the keep.

That was where the key to Ironcross Castle's secrets lay. The reason for these killings were rooted in the past. Perhaps as far back as the time of Duncan MacInnes, or even more distant than that. Perhaps in the time when the women buried in the vault still walked on this earth. Gavin certainly hoped the old priest would have the answers.

"I believe I will continue to enjoy your hospitality a while longer, laird."

"Is that a request, m'lord earl, or a statement?"

"Take it as you wish." Athol shrugged. "But with Joanna MacInnes living within these walls while you wait for a response from James Gordon, I see it as my duty to remain."

Gavin felt the hackles on his neck rise. "If that's the only reason—"

"Nay, 'tis hardly the only reason. Do not forget, that attempt was on my life as well as yours. I do not take kindly to such impertinence. I have as great a desire to find this blackguard as you do."

Gavin considered Athol's words for a moment before agreeing. "Aye, you may stay. But only so long as you keep your wily ways to yourself and that bruised and ugly face away from Joanna."

"Och!" the Highlander responded, feigning injury. "I thought sweet Joanna was unaffected by my charms."

"Aye." Gavin eyed the earl suspiciously.

"Well then, I will make no promises that I intend to break. And *you* have nothing to fear."

"I wish I could say the same for you," Gavin growled with a menacing look.

Chapter 24

Sitting in an elaborately carved chair by her bed, Joanna started abruptly as the beam of late afternoon sunlight that had been creeping unnoticed across the chamber, caressed her foot with its warm rays.

Why, she thought, must he stay away?

Standing and moving across the chamber, she stood with her back to the wall. Night would soon be falling, and Joanna was glad. It was painful to pretend that there was nothing amiss around her. Joanna knew she would inevitably have to leave this chamber that Gavin had his people hastily prepare for her. She knew she would have to go out and face the members of the household. But she hated the thought of it. Despised the false front she would have to put on before them.

Joanna moved restlessly about her bedchamber. They would ask her questions. They would smile and pretend to be solicitous. Running her fingers along the smooth edge of the damask bedcurtains, she cringed inwardly at the thought of the encounters. She knew she couldn't trust herself to look into the women's faces and still keep her fury in check.

Already, Joanna had caught a glimpse of Molly, the housekeeper. She, too, had been among the women of the crypt. How different she had looked that terrible night, dressed in white, chanting and moving with the rest. There had been no trace of that Molly when yesterday, she and two of the serving boys had brought into her room a chest of clothing that had been undamaged by the fire.

Joanna had remained seated, her face averted until

they had left the room. She sat for a long while after that, staring at the chest.

When Joanna opened the chest, she had found the dresses that had once belonged to her mother, and tears had followed. Tears of sadness. Tears of regret. Tears of anger.

But those tears were finished now. The young woman moved to the window and looked down at the dress that had once been her mother's. She smoothed her hands over the cloth the way she had seen her mother do it a thousand times. She straightened up and gazed out at the lengthening shadows.

And for the hundredth time today, Joanna told herself that she would bide her time for the present and await that moment of justice.

When the time came, Joanna was determined to follow through on her plan, but in the meantime she found herself longing more and more for time alone with Gavin. The happiness of that single night in his arms was firmly imprinted on her heart. And with so few days left, she simply could not content herself with this ache that seemed to gnaw at her very bones.

The night she had stepped into his arms and into his bed, she had done so knowing that she could no longer be bound by what others might think or say. This was her life to live. No one else would decide her path.

And she had said as much to the Earl of Athol in his visit to her chamber this afternoon. In response to his concern at her remaining at Ironcross Castle, at her "alleged" consent to marrying Gavin Kerr, she had spoken her mind—bluntly and freely—telling the Highlander that it was not his place to question her decisions if he wished to remain her friend. Though she had spoken from her heart, Joanna was nonetheless surprised that John Stewart had shown such goodwill, even relief, in accepting her wishes.

But with that done, Joanna still had the problem of luring Gavin into her room.

The young woman glided across the chamber to her bed. Her virtuous lover was determined, it seemed, to await the return of his messenger from James Gordon, so he could wed her first before taking her back into his bed. Well, as far as Joanna was concerned, by the time that happened, she could very well be dead and buried, and she had no intention of waiting that long. Each moment now was more precious than Gavin could possibly imagine.

As the sounds of night gradually descended on the Old Keep, Gavin strode out of the Great Hall, past sleeping warriors and servants, and into the corridors leading up to his chamber.

Moving along the dim corridors of the keep, Gavin considered the priest. Father William had been missing since this morning, so far as anyone could tell, but Gavin was not going to just sit back and hope that the strange little man would return. From what the new laird could see, the chaplain was not one to spend his time visiting sick crofters or doing anything else quite so noble. For the short time he'd known the cleric, Gavin hadn't once seen him venture out of the castle. The spiritual needs of anyone outside of these walls were obviously being met by Mater.

But the priest's absence had not been the only disappearance of the day. In talking to Athol, Gavin had learned that the earl's informer, the stablehand David, had also disappeared. The earl had openly admitted that, having found the meager provisions and bedding of some wayward peasant, he'd left David in the shadows of the underground loch to keep an eye on the spot. But now, a day later, there had been no word from the man.

And that hadn't been all of it. During supper, word had reached Gavin that Molly was upset since she had not been able to locate Margaret, the steward's sister, anywhere.

Three people missing. At this rate, Gavin thought grimly, in a fortnight or so there will be no need for a laird.

But then, the mute woman's disappearance perhaps would be the easiest to resolve, Gavin thought. In talking briefly with Joanna this morning, she had told him of the scene she'd witnessed in the vault the day before—the one in which she had learned of Margaret and Mater being sisters. More than likely, that was where Margaret had gone—to the abbey to be with her sister.

Gavin slowed down as he passed by Joanna's door. His warrior, who was leaning with his back against the wall, straightened up and nodded to him.

Tempted to relieve the man of his duty and send him on his way, Gavin paused, fighting the longing that was suddenly stabbing at him with every step he took.

Nay! Don't do it, he told himself. His reason told him that this distance he was forcing between Joanna and himself was needed. Until the message came back from James Gordon, until Gavin could claim her as his own, he was not about to jeopardize her reputation in public.

But his heart fought him every step of the way. He missed her, and he ached for her the way he had never ached for another woman in his life. Raking a hand through his black hair, Gavin forced the thought from his mind and trudged onward.

Reaching his chamber, he pushed open the heavy door and walked into the darkened chamber. This would be a long night, he thought with frustration. Between searching for a murderer and overseeing the massive reconstruction of the south wing, which was just beginning in earnest, Gavin had hoped that his mind would be preoccupied enough that he would not miss Joanna's company.

"You are a fool if you think that!" he muttered aloud, wearily making his way in the darkness to the window and yanking open the shutters.

The light of the half moon flooded the chamber with a blue-white glow, and Gavin turned around, gazing across the room at the portrait still sitting above his hearth. Looking into her smiling eyes, thoughts filtered through his mind of what life would be between the two of them once they were done with the cursed problems of the present.

The two of them, he thought, a smile creasing his face.

For the first time in his life, Gavin Kerr found himself dreaming of a future. Not since he was a lad had he allowed himself to look into the night sky and dream of what lay beyond the stars. But now, here he was, seeing the two of them in a vision as clear as a Highland loch, standing side by side in the years to come. Stunned, he allowed his thoughts to wander. He could see her now, her middle swelling with his child. He could see their daughters and sons around them. And again he could see them—the two of them—growing old.

Aye, he thought, how good it would be to live and to grow old beside the one you love.

The sudden tightness in his throat caught him unawares, and he leaned his head back against the wall beside the window and closed his eyes.

The movement of the panel in the wall opening beside his bed snapped him sharply out of his reverie. Alert to the possibility that this may very well be another attempt on his life, Gavin silently drew the gleaming blade of his dirk from its sheath . . . and then replaced it.

He didn't have to see her face to know that it was Joanna. Like an apparition she moved, gliding into his chamber with the same grace and ease that she had moved into his soul. With a smile, Gavin moved away from the wall, more than willing to offer her his heart as well.

"Gavin," she called softly, taking a couple of steps in his direction before coming to a halt in the moonlight pooling in the center of the room. "I heard your footsteps passing by my door. I had hoped . . . I wondered . . ."

She stopped, her hands nervously clutched before her. Gavin's heart swelled at the sight of her. He'd thought her breathtakingly beautiful, clad only in rags. But now, standing before him, a woman of substance, adorned with the finery appropriate to her station in life, she stunned him with her beauty.

"I . . ." he fumbled. "By . . . well, I thought . . ."

She smiled at him, and he forced himself to focus his attention. "Joanna, I put a guard outside your chamber and a latch on that panel door, thinking that you would stay put."

"And I would have, if you had not persisted in staying away."

"Oh?" he raised a brow and moved closer, drawing her hands into his. Holding her at arm's length, he let his eyes roam appreciatively from head to toe and back again. "I was there this morning."

"So were three of your men, working on the panel, and a serving girl seeing after my things. You were all there at the same time." She pulled one hand free and touched him on the shoulder. Gavin thought he did a good job at hiding the pain that shot through his body. "Is this the shoulder that struck the side of the chasm?"

He could not hold back any longer. Encircling her waist with a brawny arm, he drew her into his embrace, brushing his mouth against her parted lips.

"What shoulder?" he whispered.

"The one that John Stewart told me you injured!"

"John Stewart has a big mouth and *no* sense of discretion." Gavin deepened the kiss and felt Joanna rise against him, wrapping her arms tightly around his neck and pressing her body firmly against his. The hunger he constantly felt for her took charge. His fingers traced the firm flesh of her breasts before moving around to her buttocks and pressing her hard against his rising manhood. Her response, immediate and passionate, brought out a madness in him. A madness pricked with desire.

"This was my fear," he said hoarsely, breaking off the kiss and settling his lips onto the sweet, ivory skin of her neck. "Of being left alone with you and being unable to stop."

"Then don't stop," she said hoarsely, running her hands down his back, tracing his backside. Her fingers started to pull at his belt.

"I cannot risk having someone discover you here." His fingers were making short work of the laces on the back of her dress.

"No one will," she whispered as he tugged down at the neckline, freeing one of her breasts. "I have a guard . . ." He leaned down and took her nipple between his lips. ". . . Inside my door . . ." she managed to gasp, digging her fingers into his hair.

"He had better be outside," Gavin growled, pulling her dress down her body and sliding it over her hips.

He eyed the thin chemise that failed to hide her perfect form.

"Outside," she repeated. As she unfastened his belt and dropped it to the floor, Gavin kicked off his boots and helped her as Joanna pushed his shirt up over his head. Now it was her turn to eye him as she ran her hands over his chest, and he could see in her face the embers of desire. She glanced up at him and smiled. "I have a guard *outside* my door!"

"Even so," he continued, the conviction of his argument somewhat undermined by the fact that his fingers were gently peeling the chemise over her head. "We could be . . ." His breath caught in his throat as he cast the garment aside. "We could be caught!"

He had seen her like this before. But each time they met, it seemed, she grew more beautiful than the last. Taking her hands, Gavin gazed on the vision looking up at him. His eyes drank in the flawless and glowing skin.

"The latch on the panel in my room will keep me out."

"Keep you *in*," he corrected with a smile, lifting and kissing the palm of her hand. Then, placing her arm on his shoulder, he lifted her effortlessly and moved easily to the bed, laying her gently across it.

"Aye, keep me *in*," she repeated. She reached out over the side of the bed to where he stood and pulled at his kilt. The garment fell away, and her eyes roamed his body, broad and naked in the moonlight.

"Still," he said teasingly, letting his fingers travel lightly over the inside of her thighs. The way her eyes closed, the parted lips, the sharp intake of air, all spoke of her anticipation of what was to come. "We should think of answers in case—"

"I am here to see to your . . . your injuries," she said, quietly turning on her side and facing him at the edge of the bed. "You are hurt, and I am here to help you . . . heal."

"Heal?" he growled as her fingers traveled up his thigh toward his aroused manhood.

"Aye." She nodded. "You are in need of my gentle touch, my loving care." She smiled mischievously. "And this gives me a chance to practice what I learned the other night."

Gavin knew exactly what she was talking about. During their night together, she had been persistent in having him show her the ways of making love.

Raising herself to her knees, she first kissed his lips, then let her mouth travel down along his neck and collarbone, kissing his bruised shoulder with care. He watched her draw back and gaze with concern at the patch of black and yellow and blue that had formed beneath the skin.

Gavin let his fingers run through her hair, feeling the softness of it tumble over the back of his hand.

Lowering herself again onto the bed, Joanna's mouth brushed over the flat planes of his stomach, and her tongue swirled in the hollow in his naval. Gavin held his breath as she moved still lower in her journey.

Hesitantly, almost shyly, Joanna rubbed the warm crown of his thick shaft against her cheek. Then, growing bolder, she ran her lips along the length of it.

Gavin clenched his jaw, forcing himself to keep a tight rein on his control. Digging his fingers into her golden mane, he watched Joanna's lips part and move around his member, her tongue touching him, tasting him.

"By the . . ." He groaned as he watched her take him deep in her mouth. Sweat was beading on his brow as he struggled for control, and his eyes focused on her full lips as they threatened to draw out his essence.

One moment Gavin had a tenuous leash on his desire, the next moment he knew he was teetering out of control. Within him, passions surged, burning him, filling his chest with a tightness that constricted all breathing. His hands again grabbed her silken tresses, and he rolled her onto her back. Their eyes met, and even in the darkened room, he could see her own matching desire.

Dropping to his knees beside the bed, Gavin's mouth descended upon her still-parted lips. His tongue thrust deeply into her warmth, probing the soft, moist recesses of her mouth.

"You were saying something about a gentle touch?" he whispered raggedly against her lips before reaching down and taking hold of Joanna's legs. "About a loving touch?" He dragged her slowly around until her legs dangled over the edge of the billowy mattress. She began to lift herself up, but he met her halfway, taking her wrists and pushing them back, trapping them with one huge hand above her head. His mouth was rough as he took possession of hers again, and Joanna responded with a driving passion that equaled his own.

He tore his mouth from hers. " 'Tis time I ministered some medicine of my own." His ardor, though, threatened to engulf him as Joanna's leg raised and hooked around his thigh. He kissed the hollow of her throat and felt her body arch against him as his mouth suckled the hardened nipple. Joanna moaned softly as Gavin continued to caress the sensitive flesh with his tongue.

When his lips moved down the ivory softness of her belly, he could feel Joanna stop breathing. He parted her legs, then, and his tongue found the sweet, moist darkness and thrust inside.

Her hands freed, Joanna laced her fingers into his thick black locks. Without breaking off the intimacy, he lifted her buttocks, raising her up and thrusting his tongue ever more deeply into her pulsating recesses until she cried out, a breathless throaty cry of ecstasy and release.

Gavin took her into his arms and held her until her shudders subsided, and then, without a word, slid smoothly into her. Like two lost souls at last finding their joyous destiny, their bodies and souls molded together with a completeness that shocked them both. As they lay momentarily still, he felt her arms tighten around him, and for the first time in his life, he felt loved. When Gavin begin to move, Joanna went with him, the pulsing rhythms they each felt, rising undeniably within them.

And when at last they reached that climactic moment of rapture, it was the two of them together, body and soul, connected as one. Clinging to one another, each felt a destiny of loss, betrayal, and death melt away. Wrapped in one another's arms, each was suddenly aware of a life, a future—a love they could not deny.

Chapter 25

Gavin pushed back a lock of golden hair from her furrowed brow. Leaning on one elbow, he traced the outline of her face with a finger.

"You must try!" he encouraged again. "For once, try to put Mater out of your mind and think of others who might have had a reason to commit that crime."

"I still cannot understand your reluctance," she argued, rolling onto her side and facing him. "I tell you, even yesterday, she was there in the crypt. She was headed toward the keep. She very well could have been the one who cut the rope to that footbridge."

"Perhaps she did. But let us assume that she was not the one."

"Why do you continually defend her? You put no faith in me," she said, hurt evident in her voice. "Has she not already done enough harm? How many more have to die before you are convinced?"

Gavin gently wiped away the tear starting down her cheek. " 'Tis not a case of having no faith, but until such time as we can find some proof of her guilt, we simply cannot ignore other possibilities."

"I need no more proof." Joanna's eyes flared. "No one else needs to die! If you were down there in that vault—if you were witness to the frenzy of their hatred—you would not be questioning—"

"Aye, what you say is true!" Gavin interrupted. " 'Tis easy to become blinded by what we *think* we see. We think one is guilty and then let the real murderer pass by undetected." As she opened her mouth to argue, he brushed his thumb gently against her lips. "I've been doing just that for the past few days. I was so certain of Athol's guilt, that—"

"Athol?" she said with great surprise. "He would never . . . he could never—"

"I know that now," Gavin nodded. "But before yesterday, before finding his life in as much danger as my own, I could not ignore what was possible. I saw him as a man with both reason and the means to murder. And I, perhaps, wanted him to be the guilty one."

"Then he is fortunate you did him no harm."

"Aye. That he is," Gavin answered. Framing her face with one large hand, the laird looked deep into her violet-blue eyes. "I simply do not want to make the same mistake twice. I am not trying to act as protector to Mater and her women, but I am only trying to learn the truth about any others who may have been involved. From the first moment I arrived at Ironcross, not a single person has willingly spoken the truth. Everyone says only what must be said and no more. Secrecy enshrouds this place like the morning mists."

"But this is all the influence of Mater."

"Perhaps," he agreed. "But I think there is something more. Something that goes deeper than the will of one woman." Gavin reached and pulled a blanket high on her shoulder.

"You are talking about the curse."

"Did you ever ask anyone about the crypt?" he asked. His gaze flickered toward the open window as an unseasonably chilly breeze blew through, raising the goose-flesh on his skin. "Did you ever ask why those women were buried beneath this keep?"

"I tried to ask once or twice, but I never received a complete answer. They are saints who died. I never learned how or why."

"But I think that the truth lies with those old bones," he whispered. "I believe if we were to discover the secret of that crypt, we might find the origin of the Ironcross curse."

"And the murders!"

"Perhaps." He nodded. "The curse seems to go back many years, 'tis true, but we know very little of what happened before your family came here. We need to remember that, though those tombs have been sitting there for many years, the deaths of your family and the attempts on my life are fairly recent."

Joanna's face was troubled as she placed her hand on top of his. "But that is all the more reason to believe in the evil behind those rituals."

He shook his head. "Or perhaps all the more reason to consider that someone might simply want to use that as a shield. We cannot know for certain until we understand the history of those dead women." He clasped her hand tightly in his. " 'Tis up to you and me, Joanna. Between us, we will avenge the crimes that have been committed. But we must keep an open mind and consider every possibility, however remote it might seem to be."

Her expression softened, and Gavin sensed that though she was not persuaded, she was at least willing to trust in him.

She didn't have to speak the words; he knew how she felt about him. So unlike him, whose feelings lay hidden beneath layers of thick, battle-scarred skin, she wore hers in the open. She showed her affection, her love, her trust.

Just then, he fought back the urge to tell her how much he loved her. He wanted to, but he couldn't. A voice inside his head kept reminding him that it was not time. He couldn't speak the truth. He couldn't reveal his soul, not until such time as he could honestly say that he had slain his own demons . . . his own curses.

"There is another," she whispered softly, bringing him out of his troubled reflection. "In the days preceding the death of my parents, my father had harsh words with the priest."

"Father William? I have spoken at length with the man, questioning him on the past. The dog never once hinted at any disagreement with your father."

"He wouldn't," Joanna continued. "My father's death saved him from ruin. And Iris's death gave him a second chance at life."

"Iris?" Gavin repeated, recalling the name.

"Father William might wear the cowl of a priest, but we all found out the cloak he wears."

Her voice trailed off, but Gavin remained silent, waiting for her to continue.

"Iris was one of my mother's maids. A wild, red-haired creature who took great joy in the attention that she received from the townsmen while my parents were at court. She was one of very few young women in my mother's company, and Ironcross Castle was just too secluded for her. In fact, before my last visit here, she asked my mother if she could be sent back with me and become part of my grandmother's household in Stirling."

"But because of the fire, she never got the chance."

"Nay, she never got the chance. But even if that fire had never happened, she would not have gone to Stirling." Joanna looked gravely into Gavin's face. "The same week that I arrived in the Highlands, I heard from my mother that Iris was with child."

"Let me guess. No man willingly stepped forward to take responsibility for his actions."

She shook her head.

"And she would not name the father?"

"At first, she wouldn't. Not until my mother told Iris that she was sending her to the abbey until she gave birth to the bairn."

"Under Mater's care?"

"Aye." Joanna nodded. "I cannot blame my mother now, although at the time I thought she was being harsh for not letting the poor creature stay at Ironcross Castle, close to the people she knew. But my mother never fared well amid crisis. She always preferred to live her life quietly, undisturbed."

"But this Iris did finally name the man?"

"She did," Joanna answered. "She named Father William as the one responsible for getting her with child."

Somehow, hearing Joanna's revelation came as no great surprise. There had been something about the priest from the very first that had nagged at him. Gavin's mind returned to the time he'd spent with Father William in the small kirkyard. The attachment he'd shown to one of the newer graves along the wall. The priest

had even mentioned her name. All of that now rose
fresh in his mind.

"And did he accept responsibility for the lass?"

"My father was the one who confronted him, and the
priest did not dare deny anything that had been said.
Father threatened him with ruin. From what my mother
told me, he gave the priest a week to gather his things
and leave Ironcross Castle for good."

"John MacInnes was indeed a gentle man," Gavin said
quietly. "I have known many a laird who would have
brought down a much harsher punishment for such con-
duct. Even if the blackguard were a priest."

Joanna shook her head sadly. "There was no chance
of Iris ever having a future with the man. So I suppose,
other than sending him away, there was very little else
for my father to do. Although," she said as an after-
thought, "as inadequate a punishment that it seems to
you now, Father William was outraged with being dis-
charged so 'recklessly,' as he put it."

"So after the fire, with no one in a position of authority, no one to punish the man's villainy, the priest just
stayed put. And all along, you also knew that he had
remained."

She shrugged her shoulders. "Iris and the unborn
bairn were dead, and I had other matters to concern
me."

Gavin's eyes bore into hers and she frowned.

"Nay," she said in answer to his unspoken question.
"He is too weak—too cowardly a creature ever to commit a crime of such magnitude."

"He was about to lose everything he had," Gavin
argued.

She stubbornly shook her head, rolled onto her back,
and stared at the blackened ceiling. "Hurting my
father . . . nay, 'tis too far-fetched, too unbelievable
when you think of the man. But even if we consider it,
killing half a household, and the woman he loved along
with them—"

"Bedded, Joanna," he corrected. "The priest may
have bedded her, but we have no idea of what feelings,
if any, he harbored for the lass. As far as we know, he

may have bedded every other serving woman in this keep."

Joanna's beautiful face turned suddenly on the pillow, and the look in her eyes went straight to his heart. His tone had been harsh and the vulnerability of their situation was clearly reflected in her face. He gently framed her face in his palm as he lifted himself on his elbow.

"You are the only woman in my life, Joanna," he said thickly. "Not in my past nor in the future has there been, or could there ever be, one so well matched to my heart and soul."

She ran a hand down the side of his face before speaking out softly. "I love you, Gavin. And I want you always to remember how I feel for you now."

"Now?" he teased gently, fighting back the words that he knew she wanted to hear. "And are you planning to hate me tomorrow?"

She pressed the heel of her hand onto his sore shoulder and rolled him onto his back. Moving quickly on top of him, she gazed down into his eyes with a playfully warlike look.

"Well, you have me in your power, lass. I can see I will have to do anything you ask." He eyed the swells of her breasts pressing on his chest. His hands slid over her lower back and cupped her firm buttocks, shifting her slightly as his hardening member nestled tightly between her legs. "Anything," he growled.

"Perhaps we should speak to the priest," she said absently, sliding her body over his and eliciting a groan. She pressed her lips to the hollow of his throat, then raised her head abruptly. "Not that I think the man guilty of the killings. But still, 'tis only proper making him understand that we are aware of his past. That he might still need to own up to his responsibility for his past."

Gavin's mind tried to follow her words, but his body was quickly taking control. The way she lifted herself off his chest, her swollen nipples waiting, beckoning to his lips. Rolling her roughly onto her back, he moved on top of her and took both of her breasts in his large palms and ran his thumbs over them.

"I want to . . . be with you." She arched her back as his lips descended, biting and tugging at one nipple. "I want . . . to be there . . . when you question him."

"Fair enough," he breathed, lifting his head and smiling mischievously into her flushed face before eyeing the next breast. "Once I find him."

"Is he missing?" she said softly, hooking her feet behind his thighs. Her hand slipped between their bodies, and Gavin groaned again deep in his throat as he felt it close around his manhood.

"Since yesterday." He bent his head and laved her other breast before taking it sharply into his mouth. When he pulled back, the sight of her arched neck, the passionate clouding in her eyes, all brought a satisfied smile to his face. "For some reason, Joanna, just looking at you makes me lose all interest in the cur."

A devilish smile tugged at her full lips as she drew his arousal to her moist opening. "So he has been missing since we came up from the caverns."

"The two could be related."

She lifted her knees and wiggled beneath him. She was teasing him, and he mustered all his control to hold back. He probed the entry lightly. He was in control.

"But what I'm trying to understand . . ." Gavin found himself speaking through clenched teeth. He could hold out longer. He was in control. ". . . that . . . I was . . . He was . . ."

The warrior chief breathed in sharply as her hands kneaded his lower back, pulling him, coaxing him to drive into her. Sweat was beading on his brow. Control. He attempted to finish his thought. He was . . .

Gavin gazed into her face and Joanna's tongue slipped along her parted lips.

"He was . . ." Gavin began again, but his mind had gone blank.

"You think . . . ?" Joanna stopped, her gasp turning into a moan as Gavin drove deeply into her.

Control be damned, he thought, feeling her tighten around his throbbing manhood.

"He ran," Gavin started in a ragged voice.

Struggling against the wild urge to draw back and

drive into her, again and again, he wrapped his hands around her and rolled them together on the bed until she was astride him. As she lifted her head, her silken hair draped like a golden blanket to one side.

"Nice view from up here," she murmured.

"You are a Highland lass, to be sure," he growled.

Her mouth descended onto his, and he kissed her—deeply, thoroughly. She drew back, breathless, and Gavin felt his breath catch in his throat as her hips ground into him.

"I have already sent my men out . . . in search of him." Gavin took hold of her hips and lifted, causing her to glide the full length of his member, his tongue finding her nipple at the top of the stroke. Her gasp of pleasure only encouraged him to repeat the action. "We should . . . find him . . ." He couldn't finish, as she took charge, riding him.

Her body arched at the moment of her release, and Gavin felt her tighten like a sheath around him. As she cried out in ecstasy, the last vestiges of his control exploded in a fireball of passion. There was no holding back—there was only the need to pour his seed into her.

"Joanna!" he called out, rolling her onto the bed beneath him. As she clung to him, a few fierce strokes completed the task, leaving them both panting and spent.

They lay there side by side for a long while, wrapped in one another's arms, the night soft and sweet around them. She was the first one to speak, and her eyes sparkled as they looked into his.

"I think there are quite a few *more* members of the household that we need to discuss. 'Tis our responsibility, Gavin."

With a rumbling laugh, Gavin rolled her onto her back. "True enough, Joanna. And I suppose there is no better time to begin than now!"

Chapter 26

He had to go down there.

He had heard it in her words last night. Joanna had her own plans regarding the dispensing of justice to the women she held responsible for her parents' death. And Gavin was certain it involved that underground crypt.

With the priest still gone and Athol not completely recovered from his injuries, the laird knew that he had to rely on his own memory and find his way back to Hell's Gate.

Padding through the underground passages, Gavin felt certain he would find the crypt. He would find it as surely as he would eventually find his way through the secrets of Ironcross Castle's past. And he was driven to find the truth—the only truth that Joanna continued to hold back from him. The truth she felt the need to die for.

Well, she would not die. He would not let her.

Half an hour later, Gavin held his torch before him and peered into the vaulted chamber of the crypt.

He had a deathgrip on her hand.

Joanna once again tried to work herself out of his grasp, but his grip on her only tightened. This was it, she thought decisively. No further. The Old Keep was as far as she intended to go. If he gave her half a chance, she would escape. Back to the safety of her chamber.

Gavin's reproachful glare told her that she had no chance.

Joanna glared back at him defiantly. It was bad enough that he was forcing her to take her meals in the

Great Hall, a host of curious eyes watching her every move, her every mouthful; now he was going to physically drag her out into the brilliant sunshine of the late spring morning. He was a monster.

She was still resolved to go through with her plan at the next full moon, and knowing that held her back. Death was looking her in the face, and Joanna knew it would hurt her to engage in any more of life's little pleasures.

The memories were quite vivid. Strolling in the sun. Feeling the whip of the wind against your cheek. Breathing fresh, heather-scented air. Aye, she thought. She had her memories. They would suffice.

Gavin yanked once again on her hand, and Joanna turned and glowered at him. How could he be so damnably persistent? He was ruining everything she had planned. She had hardly had a moment alone to herself. She still needed to return to the vault and make certain her original plans remained undisturbed. But Gavin seemed determined not to give her a chance to do so.

Of course, the way she had been spending her nights caused her no complaints, Joanna thought wickedly. She continued to go to him and join him in his bed. But her days! If she weren't answering Athol's endless queries, Gavin had her involved with the renovation of the south wing. Should we have a door here? What about bringing a glazier up from Edinburgh to put in windows? What about the fireplaces? The questions went on and on.

"For someone who is so conscious about not bringing attention to herself, you have certainly managed to draw a crowd."

She turned and looked in the direction that he indicated. By the door leading to the Great Hall, a nosy gaggle of servants and soldiers were all peering curiously after her.

"If you would stop being so stubborn, and simply let me choose my time—"

He shook his head with a smile. "You have had your chance, lass, and done nothing about it." He tugged again on her hand, and his face took on a menacing edge. "Come with me, Joanna, before I *carry* you outside. Though I'm really looking forward to giving them a sight to remember."

"You wouldn't dare!"

He cocked an eyebrow and took a step toward her. There was no question in her mind that he would make good on his threat.

"You're an oaf!" she cried, tearing her hand out of his grip as she swept by him and out the door.

The courtyard bustled with the noise and activity of builders, warriors, stablemen, and others—all engaged in their crafts—and Joanna stopped abruptly on the top step leading down from the great door of the Old Keep. The pleasure she felt at that moment was as astounding as it was immediate.

The velvet hand of the sun touched her skin, wrapping her in its warmth. Closing her eyes and remaining on the step, Joanna filled her lungs with the smells of the day. Gavin's large hand caressed the small of her back, and her eyes opened to the sight of his handsome face. He towered over her.

"This is only the start, lass," he said in a low voice.

Taking her again by the hand, he started down the steps. By the stables, she could see two saddled horses.

"Where are you taking me?"

"I thought a bit of a ride would be pleasant." He accepted a traveling cloak from a waiting serving woman and wrapped it around Joanna's shoulders. This gesture of concern brought a smile to her lips.

Letting her eyes roam the courtyard as they crossed to the stables, Joanna took in everything. This was all so different, she thought. Yesterday, one of Gavin's men, a giant warrior by the name of Andrew, had returned from Elgin with a crew of stonemasons, carpenters, and other craftsmen, as well as a boisterous legion of apprentices. Since then, the noise and activity in the castle had doubled. She paused for a moment, watching two young men hoisting a load of slate to the roof.

As much as she had tried, it was difficult for Joanna to close her mind to the excitement that surrounded her. Gavin had continued to talk about the future of Iron-cross and about their lives together as husband and wife.

She had remained fairly silent, steadfast in her insistence on living only for the present.

When they reached the horses, Gavin lifted her effortlessly into her saddle. Joanna looked about her. "What did you have to do to John Stewart to keep him from joining us?"

"I had him gagged and thrown into one of the new pits we are digging in the kirkyard. Easy, Paris," he said, steadying his own huge horse.

"Is the good earl wearing on you?"

"I am a patient man, but the winsome creature is overstaying his welcome." He swatted her horse on the flank, and they both started off toward the open gate. "In fact, if he is not over this feigned injury of his by the end of the week, I will strap his damned carcass onto his horse and let his men drag him back to Balvenie Castle!"

The image of the tall, haughty Highlander being manhandled by Gavin brought a smile to her lips. Turning, she found his eyes on her.

"He thinks he is playing chaperon to us," he growled as they rode out into the open. Down the hill, the roofs of small, nearly deserted village could be seen, but Gavin turned his horse to the right, along base of the castle wall. "And I am tired of having him question every moment we spend in each other's company."

She giggled.

"What are you laughing at?"

"I wonder how he would feel about our midnight visits, if he were to learn of them."

A slow smile tugged at his lips as his gaze lowered lingeringly on her breasts. A shiver of excitement prickled her skin.

"To hell with what he thinks. I am looking forward to the time when we can have *midday* visits!"

Joanna looked away as the molten heat that was streaming through her body surged into her cheeks.

"By week's end, at the latest, we should have all of our answers," he said with a note of certainty. "By then, Edmund should be back with a word from James Gordon. Also, I expect Peter to return with some news of the old priest."

And the end of this week would also bring the full moon, she thought silently, feeling the fire inside her suddenly turn to ice.

"Your message to your grandmother should have arrived by now as well."

She turned and looked at him.

"Do you think she'll make the trip north for our wedding?"

"I don't know," she whispered softly. It would be so easy to fall under his spell, Joanna thought, sadness suddenly clutching at her heart. With a shake of her head, she pushed aside the dreary thoughts.

"You did tell her that as soon as we get an answer from James Gordon, we intend to wed."

She nodded. There had been no reason to say anything different, though a pang of regret had struck her after the messenger had ridden out.

Her grandmother was about to receive a message saying that her long-dead granddaughter was alive. But the old woman would learn a week later that Joanna had perished in a fire in the crypt. It would have been so much easier not to contact her at all. But Gavin had insisted, and this far into her plans, Joanna could not risk raising his suspicions.

"Any news of Father William?" she asked, to change the subject.

"Nay." He shook his head. "But I am certain we will find him. With no horses and so few who would want to shelter the man, 'tis just a matter of time before he returns."

"Returns?" she asked hesitantly.

"Of course. I want to ask him a few questions."

"And you think . . . ?" Joanna shifted in her saddle. "Do you still suspect him of setting the fire?"

Gavin looked into her face. "Well, it appears he ran as soon as news of your survival became known."

"But he could have simply been afraid that you've heard about Iris!"

"Aye. But in any case, we'll find him, and my guess is that he'll be on his way *back* to Ironcross Castle when we do."

"Why do you say that?"

"Because Father William is not a fool, and I have spread the word that he needs to clear his name of any involvement with the fire. His life will be forfeit if we catch him in hiding."

"But 'tis the bishop he must answer to."

"I'll take care of that."

"But he's innocent," Joanna said emphatically, adding, "of the fire, at least."

"Then he has nothing to fear, and he'll return of his own accord. Come on, let's see if that little mare is as lively as she looks. I'll race you to that stone jutting from the next hill."

Before answering, Joanna fixed her gaze on something in the distance. Whirling in his saddle, Gavin turned to look at what had caught her eye, and when he did, Joanna flicked the mare's reins with a loud whoop and dashed off up the hill, leaving him grinning in her wake.

Chapter 27

The mute woman's eyes were blood red with despair. For days now, fear had robbed her of all sleep, all rest. She twisted the rough wool of her skirt between her thin fingers, and her body remained rigid as she peered past the stiff red skin that served as a door, covering the only opening in the hut's walls.

On the other side of the muddy pool of water beyond the entryway, her brother Allan stood glaring down at the diminutive priest. When her brother had come striding over the hill, William had rushed out to meet him on the path, rather than have him discover Margaret inside.

Margaret continued to watch nervously from the hut. The steward's face was a storm cloud of pent-up fury, and his eyes shot lightning bolts at the little man as he waited for an answer.

The priest's sister, a bent woman, wrinkled and old before her time, moved wearily from the piles of new-shorn fleece that she had stacked in the corner of the tiny hovel. Clinging to her skirts, two ragged urchins stared wide-eyed, hiding their faces when Margaret glanced down at them.

Turning her attention back to William and her brother, Margaret realized that Allan had not once so much as glanced at the hut, and suddenly it occurred to her that he must not know she was there.

The mute woman's eyes again searched the empty path beyond the two men. She so desperately hoped that the woman's husband would come back from the fields.

Glancing again in William's direction, Margaret saw him shake his head at the steward. Allan addressed the little priest angrily, though his words were unaudible at this distance. Still getting no positive response from the cleric, the steward glanced suspiciously toward the hovel, and a flash of panic raced through the mute woman.

Turning to William's sister, Margaret took the hands of the two children and drew them quickly to her side. Looking desperately at the woman, Margaret motioned pleadingly toward the door.

She had wanted the peasant woman to go outside and do whatever needed to be done to break into the tension of the encounter between the two men, but instead, the older woman pulled the two children out of her grasp, pushing them with one quick motion through the skin door and toward the muddy pool of water.

Margaret watched as Allan glared at the children for a moment, and then relief washed over her as he turned on his heel and strode back up the path toward the ridge.

Joanna had been entranced by the story of his life and had been lulled by the lilt of his voice. But all that came to an abrupt halt as soon as they came to the crest of the last hill.

She jerked the rein of her horse in an attempt to bring the animal to a sudden stop. But the mare, objecting to the abruptness of the command, reared up. It took great effort to keep her place in saddle as Gavin's huge hands grabbed for the horse's bridle.

"What did you do that for? You could have killed yourself!"

"Where do you think you are taking me?" she asked angrily, letting her eyes dart from the huts in the valley back to his face.

"We are going to the abbey."

"I can see that! But for what reason?"

"To meet with Mater."

"Why?" she spat out, her anger rising. "What right have you to do such a thing? I thought we were out for a ride. You tricked me. You lied!"

"Nay, I didn't lie," he argued. "And with all the times you must have traveled this route, I simply thought you knew where we were going."

"Well, you were wrong. I wasn't paying attention, and you did your best to distract me."

Gavin's voice was gruff. "Joanna, this is important."

"Nay," she protested, trying unsuccessfully to yank the horse's head free. "I had no intention of coming here. You cannot force me to go down into that valley. I'm going back."

"Joanna." Still holding her mare's bridle with one hand, Gavin reached over and grabbed her hand roughly in his, forcing her attention. "You said you wanted to be involved in discovering the truth of your parents' death."

"I do. I am."

"How?" he pressed. "By hiding in the darkness of some underground cave, or by locking yourself within the walls of that keep?"

"I do not need to come here to learn anything more about these women. This abbey is a lie, and no one knows that better than I." She glared angrily at him. "I know the truth. I've been a witness to their wretched evil. All I need to wait for now is the day of justice, and that day is coming."

"Just listen to yourself, Joanna." He pulled his horse sharply to her side until their knees touched—their two animals stamped restlessly. "If I were to follow your way of thinking, Athol's blood would already be spilled. The priest would be a dead man. Mater and her flock would all be hung, and my steward would have been drawn and quartered for negligence to his duty, if not disloyalty. How is that for justice?"

Joanna shivered as she looked into his hard, angry eyes. His quiet fury was more unnerving than if he had threatened her with a point of a sword. She had never seen him like this, and for the first time, she sensed how extremely dangerous Gavin Kerr could be.

"I cannot go through with what you want me to do."

"Do you think Mater guilty?"

"I do!" She spoke without hesitation.

"Is she an enemy?"

"The fiercest of foes."

"Do you want to see justice served?"

"I do."

"Then face her," he ordered. "She is much more than the shell of old skin and bone that we see. 'Tis her will, her spirit, that is the source of her power. You cannot defeat her without weakening that spirit first. And that will be no easy task."

For a long moment she stared at him, too stunned by his words to respond.

"You are the last MacInnes left," he challenged. "If it were your father or any of the men in your family still alive, have you thought what *they* would be doing now?"

She forced herself to speak. "Don't press me to do this, Gavin! I cannot."

"Why?" he scolded. "Because you're a woman? Joanna, you have more spirit in you than I have found in many a warrior. Remember, you are the rightful heir to Ironcross Castle. And the same way that you want to be present when I meet with the priest, or when I question any other man who might be involved in these murders, you have to be here when I talk with Mater."

She started to tremble as the truth of his words began to sink in.

"If you think Mater guilty of that vicious crime, then 'tis your right and responsibility to be standing beside me when I question her." His voice gentled as his hands wrapped more tightly around hers. "I am not asking you to walk into this battle unarmed. The last thing I want is for any harm to come to you. I will be there with you, Joanna. But Mater *must* see the two of us as one. 'Tis essential for her to understand that we will not perish or disappear in an instant, simply because she wishes it."

Joanna tore her hands out of his grasp. In her heart she felt like a coward. All her long thought-out plans had been no more than a coward's way of meting out justice. It had all seemed so courageous to her in the darkness and solitude of the caverns, but here in the bright sunlight, faced with Gavin's words, Joanna felt a strong sense of guilt and inadequacy gnawing at her heart.

"Face her, Joanna. Do not be afraid."

"I am not afraid. 'Twas not fear that kept me alive these past six months. 'Twas my will to see justice done."

"Then come with me and face her, love," he encouraged. "Prove to her—and to yourself—that you *are* alive and that you *will* survive. Show her that there is nothing that she can do that will deter you from doing what is right!"

Margaret remained kneeling on the stony ground, holding tightly to the hem of the priest's cloak. She was oblivious to the rounded eyes of the two young and dirty faces of the children looking on. She had no interest in the expression of disapproval on the peasant woman's face. She was even indifferent to the kick that the priest gave her in the side in an attempt to wrench himself free.

"I am going back to that castle now," he shouted angrily. "And you can go to hell, for all I care."

She sobbed loudly, reaching up and getting a better grip on his cloak.

"Let me go, woman," he pulled. "Take your devilish claws off me."

"You cannot leave her here with us," the peasant woman screeched, suddenly concerned. "I'll have no dumb wench living in this hovel with us. You take her back to those you took her from. You hear me, William?"

The man gave Margaret another sharp kick to her side. She doubled over, unable to breathe, but still she managed to hold on to the rough wool.

"Just throw her out into the road," William called over his shoulder to his sister. "She is not your concern. Her brother will find her . . . or some night animal . . . it does not matter which."

Margaret looked up into the priest's cold, gray eyes and shook her head in anguish. Her mouth opened and closed like some tortured animal.

Don't go, she screamed inwardly. *Please, don't go back.*

"Help me with this foul creature," the man shouted at his sister.

Margaret reached out and tried to get hold of his legs, but something heavy struck her in the back of the head.

As bright yellow and orange flashes blotted out all vision, she felt the strength in her arms and fingers disappear. Her last conscious sensation was that of being dragged by the feet across the dirt floor of the hut.

Chapter 28

Gavin knew he had taken a great chance in bringing her here.

Of course, it was not so much Joanna's safety that concerned him as it was Mater's treatment of her.

He was not blind, and he was not a fool. In the past few days, since Joanna had stepped out of the darkness of the tunnels and into the daily life of Ironcross Castle, Gavin had seen the haunted expression in her violet-blue eyes. Rather than reveling in the joys and the comforts of the life she had been accustomed to prior to the fire, Joanna had been doing her best to remain secluded.

But he wouldn't let her, if he could help it, for he had been to the crypt. It had not taken long to discover what she was planning to do.

Gavin looked to his side and admired her strength. Though only moments ago she had fought him for bringing her here, the determined and noble look that she now wore told him that she was ready for whatever challenge awaited them. Her eyes met his.

"You've never seen them in the past like this, have you?" she asked.

Gavin looked out across the fields. For the first time, the laird found farm folk working the land. They were approaching the village, and a dog was racing toward them, barking and announcing their presence. But with few faces lifted with interest, and no one ran away and hid as they had done in times past.

"Nay." He shook his head, amazed. "But *you* have."

"Aye, when I came here alone."

Gavin's eyes drifted to a group of children chasing after the dog. These were the first young ones he'd seen this close since arriving at Ironcross and its lands. " 'Tis amazing to me that they haven't run off."

Joanna looked at him steadily. "Obviously, they've accepted you as the laird . . . and as one they do not find threatening."

He shook his head. "This is all for you, Joanna. 'Tis their way of welcoming you back from the dead. Back to the flock."

"I never was one of them," she whispered angrily, her violet-blue eyes flashing.

"In rank and position, that's true."

She flushed crimson. "I didn't mean it that way."

"You might have severed your connections with them when you joined the dead in the caverns beneath Ironcross, but from all that I can see, you are certainly accepted here."

Joanna looked away, and Gavin followed the direction of her gaze. Muddy children were running barefoot through the puddles.

"They do not look so vicious from this distance."

She scowled, but remained silent.

"They must train their children early on to hide the evil they carry in their hearts. Ah, the filthy murderers!"

Joanna whirled on him. "I never said they *all* were capable of such viciousness. There are many good folk here!"

He raised a brow and looked at her critically. "I would never have guessed that from hearing you talk."

Her eyes narrowed to dark blue slits. "I'm here, am I not? You might give up this endless taunting."

"I might, Joanna. But honestly, that is a lifelong pleasure that I am looking forward to indulging in." His face creased with a wry smile. "And in more ways than one."

"Villain!" she whispered, trying to retain a frown. "I hardly think it wise to talk so boldly this long before we are wed. A woman's mind might change."

He quickly reached out and grabbed hold of one of her hands, squeezing it tight before bringing it to his lips. Her embarrassment at his open display of affection was evident in the rosy tint that colored her fair skin.

"I believe you *do* intend to marry me, lass."

She turned a deeper shade of red as he placed another lingering kiss on her palm.

"Aye," she croaked as she jerked her hand out of his grasp. "I have said that I will."

Gavin took a deep and satisfied breath. Unable to tear his eyes away from her face, he rode beside her as they entered the village, and Gavin relished the thought of her being his, for today and for tomorrow and forever. The group of children were peeking at them wide eyed from the corner of one of the cottages, and the laird winked, sending them scurrying out of sight.

"You have quite a way with wee ones," Joanna remarked wryly.

He turned and smiled. " 'Tis a gift."

They would get past this—of that he was certain. And then they would have many days ahead of them, days when it would be just the two of them. Or perhaps three, he thought suddenly. As Joanna's eyes scanned the ruins of the abbey, Gavin's gaze slowly fell to her waist. Could it be that she already carried his child, he wondered? They'd been reckless in their passion, but Gavin knew he would not have done anything differently. Even now, he felt the stirring in his loins.

Clearing his head quickly, he vowed silently that they would marry as soon as Edmund returned from James Gordon.

One look from the old woman and Joanna felt a wind whirl through her, whipping her insides into a frothy sea of confused emotion.

Joanna did not look away from Mater's gray eyes. When she had seen the abbess standing quietly by her fire, looking as if she were waiting for them, Joanna had been certain that in the old woman's eyes she would find guilt, anger, death. But instead, all she found was sorrow, as ancient and gnarled as the some of the pines standing dwarfed and alone on the western hillsides. Something in Mater's look went straight through Joanna's shield of righteous anger, through her armor of justice. The sorrow in Mater's eyes went straight to her heart.

Unconsciously, Joanna handed her rein to Gavin and

let him tie the mare next to his horse. And as he reached up and took her by the waist, lowering her to the ground, not even once was she able to tear her eyes away from the old woman's gaze.

Her body moved of its own accord, making its way around Gavin. But halfway to the fire, Joanna came to an abrupt stop. A voice in her head had begun screaming, and her heart ached with an anguish that threatened to tear her in two.

"You have come." Mater's voice shook slightly as she extended one thin hand in invitation. "At last, you've decided to come back to us."

A tremor tore through Joanna's body, and her knees were beginning to buckle beneath her weight. She felt it then, his large hand, pressing reassuringly into the small of her back. But then, gently, he was pushing her toward the elder woman. Confused, she looked up into his dark eyes and saw the strength, the confidence, the love.

" 'Tis the two of us," he whispered softly. "You and I."

His words filled her with strength, and Joanna turned her eyes back to Mater. This time, though, it was the older woman who took the steps and closed the distance between them.

Gavin's voice was gruff, but Joanna could hear the wryness in his tone. "Did my visits in the past cause the farm folk to lose so much time in the fields that they can no longer afford to hide?"

"Do not laud yourself too highly for your cleverness, laird." Mater scolded, never lifting her eyes from Joanna's face. "This is simply our way of commending you for bringing her back to us, to her people."

"She would not be here if she hadn't given her consent."

"I know," Mater said softly as she reached out and took Joanna's hands in her own. "She is a woman and has a will much stronger than any living man."

As much as she wanted to, Joanna couldn't bring herself to jerk her hands free of the abbess's grasp. Instead, she watched in silence as Mater turned her scarred palms upward and stared at the blotches of red skin as if she had known that they would be there.

"They have healed well," the old woman said encouragingly. "Keep them open to the air, and the rest of the scarring will disappear as well."

Joanna stared at her in stunned amazement, but Mater ignored her surprised look and turned, drawing her in the direction of the fire.

"How did you know that her hands were burned?"

Gavin's question to Mater didn't cause the old woman even a moment's hesitation.

"Before this moment, Gavin Kerr was the only living being who knew of my burned hands." Joanna couldn't keep a quiver of anger out of her voice. She stood waiting as the abbess sat by the fire.

"Sit down, Joanna," the old woman offered, waving to the block of stone beside her.

"I need an answer."

"Aye, and I will answer. Sit down."

Joanna glanced at Gavin, who nodded slightly and then sat across from them.

As she seated herself, she watched Mater's gray eyes lift to her face. "The laird was not the *only* one to know of your burns."

Joanna waited, but the old woman didn't offer more. Growing agitated, she glanced in Gavin's direction, but he not only seemed unaffected by Mater's words, he changed the subject entirely.

"Contrary to what I have been assuming," he said, "I learned this morning that your sister was not staying with you during these past two days."

"My sister?" Mater's brow raised in challenge.

"Aye. Margaret, your younger sister," Gavin nodded matter-of-factly. "And your brother, Allan, asked my leave last night to go in search of her, himself."

There was a moment of hesitation in Mater's expression, and her eyes never left off their close scrutiny of Gavin's hardened face. "I'm surprised that you know of my family connections."

"And I am not the only one who knows," he answered casually.

The sudden flicker in her glare did not go unnoticed by Joanna. This was clearly a sensitive area for Mater. Just the mention of Margaret's name had illuminated a crack in the armor. A breach in the wall.

"When was the last time you saw your sister?"

"Are you questioning me, laird?"

"Do you care that she is lost?"

Mater's back straightened in anger. " 'Tis your responsibility as the laird to keep her safe."

"And I intend to—once I find her. Unless you know of a reason why she would not care to be found."

"There is no such reason," she answered quickly. "She has no place to go. Nowhere to hide. She has no means of taking care of herself."

"The last time she was seen, she was very upset." Joanna's statement drew both Gavin's and Mater's eyes to her face. He'd said it was the two of them. Having had time to gather her nerves, Joanna was now prepared to be part of this talk—as Gavin had wanted. "Can you think of any reason for her to be upset?"

Mater's gaze sat heavily on her face, but Joanna did not flinch. She would need to display all of her strength in her dealings with this woman.

"Nay, I don't know of a reason for her distress." Mater's voice sounded suddenly thinner, older than it had ever been.

Gavin's tone, in comparison, was hard and his question blunt. "Do you think she and the priest might have had something between them?"

His question brought a flush of indignation into the old woman's face. "Never!"

"There are those in the castle who've seen her pay him frequent visits."

Joanna herself bristled at Gavin's insinuation. She looked into Mater's face and found it stone hard.

" 'Tis fairly certain that she left with the priest, Mater," Gavin continued. "And though he is a man of the cloth, that old dwarf seems to have had his way with more than one woman in that keep."

There was a note of cruelty in Gavin's tone, and before now, Joanna would not have believed him capable of it. But when she glanced again in Mater's direction, she saw that the abbess's composure was on the verge of crumbling.

"I have to admit that her age will work to her advantage."

"Stop it, Gavin," Joanna ordered.

"This time," he rumbled on, "he'll not have to worry about getting her with child."

"Gavin!"

"At least there will be no immediate cause for deserting her!"

"I said stop!" Joanna reached down and took hold of the old woman's hand. She hadn't missed the tears welling up in the abbess's gray eyes. "I see no reason for such callous brutality."

"Nay, lass?" he asked, his black eyes boring into her own. "Is that so?"

Suddenly, it dawned on her what he had done. In the space of a few moments, he had torn down the stone facade that Mater hid behind. And in so doing he had awakened a compassion for the old woman that Joanna thought had died long ago.

Angry with him and angry with herself, Joanna tore her eyes away from his face and looked down to the gnarled little hand that was entwined with her own.

"When was the last time you saw your sister?" Gavin asked, this time more gently.

Joanna felt Mater's hands tighten around hers as the old woman looked up at Gavin. "Last week, laird, the same day that she was seen last by others."

"And you do not know why she was upset?"

"She had been crying," Mater said wearily. "Something Margaret rarely does. But then, with her tongue tied as 'tis, there was only so much that she could tell me."

Though Joanna was focused on the words that were being spoken, a growing realization was stealing over her, and it shocked her. She could feel the coldness that had crept into the abbess's hand. She could feel every callus, every pulse of the old woman's blood. But also, for the first time in her life, she felt as if *she* were providing the strength. Like Mater, the source of power for the women around her, she, Joanna MacInnes, was acting as the giver, the provider of some force of will that she knew Mater desperately needed right now.

"We have been searching for the priest since he disappeared," Gavin said quietly. "The few peasants who admit to seeing Father William all tell of a thin woman keeping the cleric's company. That woman can only have been Margaret."

"What do you intend to do?" Mater asked coldly, an edge creeping back into her voice. "She *is* your responsibility."

"We are doing what we can. I have sent my men in all directions looking, but last night Allan told me of a cottage to the north where a sister of the priest once lived."

"Did Allan go there by himself—alone?"

Joanna and Gavin both looked into the older woman's pale complexion.

"A few of my men went along, though they may have separated to search the hills if they thought it necessary. Why?"

"Because if he finds Margaret with that no-good priest, there is no telling what he will do." Mater paused a moment as she gazed in the direction of the sky to the north. "He and I both have spent most of our lives being very protective of Margaret. Perhaps Allan even more so than I."

"Your brother knows I want the priest back alive. There are questions to be answered. He'll not harm the man."

Joanna looked to Gavin's face, trying to see if he really believed what he'd just said, but his expression again gave nothing away. So she turned to Mater. "You do not think he would hurt Margaret?"

The old woman's eyes jerked to her face.

"Never!" she said vehemently.

Chapter 29

Wait, she cried out in her mind.

Margaret stumbled down the hillside as the priest's dark form disappeared over the crest of the next rocky hill.

Wait for me, she prayed, lifting her feet in the struggle to keep pace.

A goshawk circled above the next ridge, but it was just a dark blur to her. Her head was still spinning, and the scream in her chest came out as a strangled moan.

Wait! Wait for me!

She had not said a word since they left the abbey, but he was not truly surprised. As short as their visit had been, Gavin was certain that Joanna had been deeply affected by this encounter with Mater. And there was no question in his mind that the old woman had been touched as well.

They had already gone over the crest of the hill, leaving the valley and the abbey behind them. Groves of trees and heather-crowned hills stretched away to the broad loch, and Gavin decided it was as good a time as any to draw her out of her silence.

He turned to Joanna. "Do you still think her guilty?"

She reluctantly tore her gaze from their path and glanced in his direction. Her eyes reflected her indecision.

"Do you still believe that Mater and her people were the ones that started the fire in the south wing?"

Her gaze followed the line of hills as if there were nothing disturbing in what he'd just asked. But he could see the deep blush that covered her fair skin.

"Do you still believe them to be cold-blooded murderers?" He paused a moment, then raised a questioning brow as he continued. "Was the compassion you showed that old woman no more than some artifice?"

"You are taking advantage of me!" she exploded suddenly, bringing her horse to a halt. "First you force me, against my will, to go to the abbey, then you use your rough and callous ways to break the will of that old woman. Who would not feel sorry for the abuse she took from you? And now this!"

He quickly brought his horse around until it moved right next to hers. "'And now what, Joanna?" he asked, leaning in her direction. "You do not want to hear your own conscience crying out for fairness? You do not want to hear the truth when your heart tries to speak it? Why not accept it, Joanna? You are no longer certain of her guilt! Why not put your stubbornness aside and start looking at all that we know? Treat each fact as we see it, uncolored by what we *want* to believe?"

"I do not *want* to believe her guilty!" she said angrily. "I hate you, Gavin Kerr."

"Nay, that's a lie. You love me. You told me yourself."

"That was before I knew of this barbarous streak that runs in your blood."

"Not true," he reached and grabbed one of her hands tightly within his grasp. She tried to pull it back, but he held it tight and then started to bring it slowly to his lips. "You like my roughness. You like my honesty." He turned her hand and placed his lips on her pulse. "I know that I am gruff, and that my actions are not always what you expect."

"You have a way of trifling with my mind," she cut in with a shaking voice. "I cannot allow a moment of—"

He ran the tip of his tongue along the delicate skin of her wrist. "You cannot *what*, Joanna?"

"You have a way of making me forget things."

"Do I?" he asked slowly. "I just asked a simple question."

"But you . . ."

Her words died on her lips as Gavin gently tugged at

her hand and brought her face closer to his. "What about me?" His mouth hovered over hers. " 'Tis you who robs me of my sense."

He lowered his mouth and took her lips in a searing kiss. She lifted one hand around his neck and encouraged him on.

"You see?" he pulled back slightly. "And you complain about me! I tell you, Joanna, we cannot do this anytime you decide you don't want to answer my questions."

"Nay?" she asked seductively, brushing her lips against his.

"Hell!" As the word left his mouth, Gavin grasped her by the waist, lifted her gently from her horse, and placed her in his lap.

Her words were soft and alluring. "You *are* a barbarian. But is this *not* a fine way to resolve an argument?"

His lips once again found hers and his tongue delved into her mouth. He drew back slightly. "We never argue."

"Aye," she breathed, smiling. "We fight!"

"Nay," he scoffed, running his hand along her thigh. "We disagree."

" 'Tis true," she answered, gasping and burying her lips in the crook of his neck. She rolled her head slightly and looked up at him. "And every time you feel the scale tip in my favor, you try to make love to me. And no matter what you say, Gavin Kerr, 'tis my senses that seem to steal away!"

With no attempt at being gentle, the warrior reached around and positioned her buttocks more snugly against his swelling manhood.

"I think, lass, that you are the most wild and passionate creature I've ever known."

"Wanton, you mean?" Joanna's words turned into a soft moan as his fingers found her nipple through the soft wool of her dress.

Gavin looked around him and found a high protected spot beneath a huge jutting rock. Spurring his steed up the hill, he scanned the open countryside. In the distance, the loch shimmered in the sunlight.

"When it comes to you, Joanna," he laughed, "I am the wanton one. And I think you're well aware of my weakness." As he reined in his horse by the base of the rock, Gavin tightened his grip on her and nipped at her earlobe. Laughing when she yelped, he lowered her from the horse and leaped off after her. Wordlessly, the two of them climbed around the boulder to a grassy space overlooking the loch, and there he pushed her with mock seriousness against the weathered face of the stone.

As his mouth took possession, his tongue delving deeply into soft recesses, Joanna's hands encircled him, and she rubbed her hips seductively against his groin.

"You can't win this argument," she said breathlessly as he broke off the kiss.

"What argument is that?" Gavin eyed the tie on her cloak and then reached up and tugged it loose.

"You cannot make me change my mind just by taking me to the abbey."

Jerking her cloak from her shoulders, he tossed it to the ground and lifted her breasts in his large palms, mouthing first one and then the other through the dress. She pressed her head back against the rock and threaded her fingers into his hair.

"Take me, Gavin. Make love to me."

Reaching behind her, he nimbly undid the laces of her dress.

"Not until you give me your word that you will think through our visit." He tugged hard at the neckline of her dress, smiling with satisfaction as one of her breasts spilled over the top. Taking the nipple between his finger and thumb, he paused, letting his mouth hover over the waiting prize. "Let go of your obstinacy, lass. Listen to your heart."

"Never," she moaned as his mouth descended and suckled her flesh. "I cannot forget the past."

He lifted her skirts to her waist and fitted one leg between her thighs. She wrapped her arms tightly around his neck and shoulders and let herself ride on the muscled hardness of his limb.

"I do not ask you to forget." His fingers found their

way to her naked buttocks, pressing her tighter against his groin. "All I ask is that you consider. She very well might not be the one responsible." As she shook her head in denial, he moved one hand between them and slid two fingers deeply into the moist cleft between her legs. As he stroked, Joanna's breaths started coming in ragged gasps. As she rose higher and higher, he continued to hold her tightly to him, teasing, stroking, watching her writhe blissfully in his arms.

"By the saints, take me, Gavin."

"Give Mater a chance, Joanna," he said hoarsely. He knew he couldn't hold back much longer. "Push aside your own guilt, and open your mind."

"I . . . I . . . there is . . . oh . . . guilt!"

He looked deeply into her dark, blue eyes, clouded over now with passion.

"Aye, Joanna," he growled. "You *do* carry a guilt. 'Tis the curse of the living. I know it because 'tis the same as I have carried nearly every day of my life."

He watched her closely as her release caused her to twist and arch in his arms. She cried aloud before wrapping herself tightly around his frame. As her shudders of pleasure began to subside, he continued to speak.

"I swear to you, I know how you feel. I have lived through the same kind of hurt since I was just a lad." As she rested her head in the crook of his neck, she listened, her hands slowly wandering over his linen shirt, and downward to the bulging manhood evident beneath his kilt. This time it was Gavin who found himself growing short on breath and his whisper grew hoarse as she ran her hand the length of him through the wool. "Just give her a chance . . . give *me* a chance."

Joanna lifted the front of his kilt and touched his bare skin.

"Don't," he ordered. "Not until you give me your word."

She pulled back slightly and looked into his eyes. "I'll try."

He lifted her off the ground, and she wrapped her legs around his waist.

"But that is all I can say for now. Just that I will try."

Gavin grunted, guiding his manhood into her. Rocking in his arms, she took in his full length and cried out at the sensation.

"Aye, Joanna," he panted, lifting her and driving into her with powerful strokes.

Chapter 30

The wailing cry reverberated through the rock-edged hills, startling the horses and piercing the souls of the listeners.

Joanna tightened her hold on the reins and looked up with alarm at the sheer cliff rising above their heads. The descending sun was casting long, irregular shadows, and the stark contrast of brilliant light and deep shadow only served to bury much of the terrain before them in an impenetrable darkness.

"What in hell . . . ?" Gavin growled.

The cry came again. The sound was not distinctly human, but it was a sound Joanna had heard before.

"If I were a superstitious man, I'd say 'tis the wail of a banshee."

Joanna held out a hand to shield her eyes from the light as she peered up again at the hills. Before them lay the last hill they would have to climb before dropping down into the gorge beneath the castle wall.

" 'Tis no unearthly creature, Gavin."

The wail cut through the air again, this time followed by a long, heart-wrenching moan.

" 'Tis this way," Gavin said, quickly spurring his horse up the next rise. "The sound is coming from beyond the brae."

Joanna followed his lead, her quick little mare closing the distance between them. As they galloped over the crest of the hill, she felt a knot grow tightly in her throat. It wasn't the fear of the unknown that had her heart thrumming, but the fact that the desperate wail had been a woman's cry. One of Mater's women, she feared.

The shadowy hillside was followed by a bright stretch of meadow dotted with rocks. There they saw her.

She was seated halfway down the hill in a stony patch of dirt. Her back was to them. Her moaning now filled the air, loud and distinct. As Joanna and Gavin moved closer, the dark body which the woman was huddled over came into view.

Gavin's hand shot up, motioning her to stay back, but Joanna could no more stay away from the pitiful creature than she could pull down the great iron cross hanging above the doorway of the Old Keep. But as they reached the pair, she felt the bile rise up in her throat.

Before the crying woman lay the still and bloodied figure of the priest. His head, nearly severed from its body, lay in Margaret's lap.

The mute woman, totally unaware of anything else around her, grieved with a ferocity that Joanna had never seen in anyone before. Gavin dismounted and approached the body slowly from the side. Still, Margaret did not look up. She never stopped the slow rocking of her body—the keening moan that chilled Joanna's bones. The woman's dress was covered with blood, and Joanna could see the streaks of dark crimson staining her face.

And then Joanna watched as Margaret's fingers dipped into the blood at the dead man's throat, smearing it on her cheeks.

"He is dead, Margaret," Gavin said quietly but firmly, crouching beside the body.

Joanna slowly dismounted and approached the woman. Margaret's eyes were focused on the bloody, mutilated neck of the priest. The young woman turned her attention to the grieving woman, unable to do anything for the dead cleric.

"This did not happen too long ago," Gavin said, looking at the savage cut. "His body is still warm."

Standing up, he looked in every direction, and Joanna followed his gaze. There was no one in sight anywhere, though the line of hills and the rocky terrain was well suited to hiding.

"We passed this way this morning, and we saw no sign

of these two." Joanna crouched and ran a gentle hand over Margaret's back. The mute woman never looked at her or even acknowledged their presence. "Who do you think could have done this? To cut him like this in—"

The rest of her sentence caught in her throat. There on Margaret's lap, the hilt of a bloodied dirk mingled with the priest's stringy hair. Glancing at the priest's belt, Joanna saw an empty scabbard, and as her eyes shot up and caught Gavin's, she saw from the hardening glare on his face that he too had seen the weapon.

"She wouldn't . . ." Joanna whispered adamantly, shaking her head at him.

Quickly, Gavin reached down and lifted the dagger from the woman's skirt, wiping its bloody haft and blade on the cloak of the priest. Joanna's eyes followed his as they moved from the gleaming blade edge to the man's throat. His eyes were accusing when they shifted to Margaret—to her face and crimson-stained hands—before studying the dirk again.

A sudden fury flamed up in her as Gavin continued to look on in silence. She glanced quickly at Margaret's face. No change. She still acted as if there were no one else around—dipping her fingers into the blood, smearing it onto the skin of her cheeks. Margaret could not have done this, Joanna thought, but she was sure to die for it. And it was the laird who would dispense such justice.

"Look at her, Gavin," Joanna urged. "Listen to her cries. She wouldn't mourn him . . . she wouldn't suffer like this if she killed him."

"We will have to take them back to the castle." He turned and whistled for his horse.

Joanna felt a sense of panic wash over her. She remembered Mater's words, about the mute woman's helplessness. There was no one here to look after her. There would be no one, not even her own brother, perhaps, who would believe in her innocence. Putting her arms more tightly around Margaret's shoulders, Joanna tried to shake the woman out of her trance. But there was nothing that she did that made a difference.

Nothing until Gavin tried to wrap the priest in his own cloak.

Right before their eyes, Margaret went wild. Clawing at the dark cloak, she uttered senseless sounds, wailing and tearing at Gavin's hands, throwing herself on the murdered priest's body in a frenzied and lunatic display of misery and loss.

Gavin motioned to Joanna to hold her back, but the young woman couldn't hold back her own tears. She struggled to keep Margaret away as he wrapped the corpse.

Margaret's struggles subsided, and now she just lay her bloody and grief-stricken face against the young woman's shoulder. Joanna absently stroked the thin woman's back, but there was no response. She had withdrawn into some dark space within herself, lost once more to all activity around her.

Joanna looked up at Gavin. He was busily tying the body of the priest on top of his horse. The grim expression on his face told her all she needed to know.

What would come next was clear. Margaret would be found guilty of killing the priest. A sense of horror seized her even more strongly when she realized that Gavin might even think her guilty of killing the others. Joanna herself had told him that Margaret had been one of the women present in the crypt. And in his mind, if she was capable of doing this killing, then she was capable as well of doing away with the others. Margaret *had* been one of them, but Joanna now knew that she was Mater's own sister, and something in that gave Joanna pause. Though her own response puzzled her, something in that fact seemed to excuse, rather than condemn.

The older woman clutched at Joanna's shoulder and began to sob silently.

"I know you didn't do this," Joanna murmured softly against the woman's head. "I know, Margaret."

She watched Gavin as he headed back in their direction, and Joanna looked into his face, hoping to see some sign of compassion for the broken creature in her arms. But there was none.

"We're ready to head back. You will ride your mare—"

"What about her?"

"She can walk."

"She cannot," Joanna said shortly. "She does not even know where she is, or who we are. Gavin, she's not moved out of my arms since you took his body away. You cannot expect her—"

"She *will* walk," he said, taking Joanna by the elbow and jerking her abruptly to her feet. Like a heap of rags, Margaret fell to the ground at their feet. "Now, I do not plan to stand here all day arguing. So get back to your horse. I want to be back in the castle before nightfall."

Joanna stared into his dark, cold eyes in disbelief. She'd never seen him this unfeeling, and suddenly the impact of Margaret's doom hit her full force.

"What are you planning to do with her?" she asked quietly. "After . . . after we get back to Ironcross Castle."

"We're not discussing that now." He turned to go after her mare.

She quickly placed a hand on his elbow, trying to force him to turn and face her again. "Gavin, speak to me. I cannot allow you punish this poor woman. I do not believe there is any way she could have done something so . . . so horrible."

"Well, she *could* have, and she *has*."

"Nay, you're wrong!" Joanna matched his glare. "Having a knife in her lap does not make her the killer. She could have come upon the body and picked up the weapon. Or she could have witnessed the killing. Look at her, for God's sake! She is amazed . . . stunned!" She let out a quick and frustrated breath before continuing. "There is no reason for her to kill the priest, when—"

"She would have known about Iris. She would have known that the priest got the lass with child, only to shrug off his responsibility. 'Tis clear what's happened here. Margaret went off with him. She thought that he was going to leave her, as well. That is plenty reason enough for her to kill him." Gavin looked steadily into Joanna's eyes and then held up his bloody hands for her to see. "And she did kill him."

"I cannot believe it," Joanna said stubbornly, looking

down at the weeping woman at her feet. "No one this distracted could be a murderer. How can you be so blind?"

"Blind?" he said through clenched teeth, grabbing her by the arms and shaking her roughly as he yanked her away from Margaret. "Does this not bring something else to your mind? You stand here and proclaim this pitiful creature innocent, even after finding her with the murder weapon in her lap, even with the man's blood covering her! None of this is enough to convince you that she is guilty of this murder! And yet, on the other hand, you hold Mater responsible for that fire, while all you witnessed was some ritual."

" 'Twas much more that!"

"Was it? Did you see something more damning than what we've found here? Did you see Mater set that wing on fire? Did you ever see her anywhere near that south wing?"

"I didn't have to see her there!" she shouted angrily. "If I had listened to my grandmother's warnings—"

"Nothing different would have happened," he said adamantly. "Because whatever her reasons were for speaking those words about Mater, they had nothing to do with what took place here last fall."

"But that's not true. I saw them—"

"Where, Joanna? You saw them in the crypt. Listen to me. 'Tis time *you* faced the truth!"

She shook her head, trying to fight off the tears that were starting to sting her eyes.

"There were things that your grandmother never told you, Joanna."

"I know that," she answered harshly.

"Things having to do with why Lady MacInnes never stayed here in the Highlands and why she made her home in Stirling. Things that might explain why she hated Mater."

A calmness suddenly descended on Joanna. A clarity that startled her. She stared at him, wondering now what it was that he had not told her.

"Your grandsire, Duncan, had a . . . a taste for women." He placed his hands firmly on her shoulders.

"He had a reputation for taking mistresses. They say he never could pass by a bonny face, no matter who the lass was."

"How do you know this?"

"Some from Athol," he answered quietly. "But it only confirmed information I gathered about your family before coming to Ironcross Castle." He eased his hard grip on her. "Lady MacInnes left the Highlands because she was sick of watching the line of women making their way to and from Duncan's bed. Word is that early on she decided to spend as little time as possible with him."

"But what does this have to do with her hatred of Mater?" she asked, almost too afraid to hear the answer.

"I cannot say with any certainty," he answered. "But she too was a young woman once. I think it may not be too wild to suppose that your grandfather could have had eyes for her."

"But she has been at the abbey for as long as anyone remembers."

"For as long as *you* remember," he corrected. "And keep in mind, *you* were the one who discovered she is a sister to Allan and this miserable woman."

Joanna looked down at the sobbing creature at her feet. Margaret had gathered her knees to her chest, her expression that of one totally lost to the world.

"She could very well have lived at Ironcross when Duncan was laird," Gavin continued. "Is it not likely that is how your grandmother knew her?"

Joanna's head pounded, her thoughts and her feelings a muddle of contradictions. She wished she could have some time just to wade through this flood of information.

She stared at Gavin. "How are we ever going to learn any more of Mater's past unless she is willing to tell us herself?"

Gavin looked thoughtfully at the mute woman before answering. "Well, we may have just found a way."

Chapter 31

James Gordon was already married. Not that it seemed to matter!

Foolishly, Joanna had thought that Gavin would be exhilarated with the news, but he hadn't even come to see her since his warrior Edmund had returned with the message from the Earl of Huntly, early this morning.

Thinking Joanna lost in the fire, the good earl's nephew had since been betrothed and wed to a well-placed lass that Joanna knew from her time at court. To Joanna, this news was of little consequence, since she had already given herself, body and soul, to Gavin Kerr. But even before Gavin had come to Ironcross, she had never felt any sense of belonging to the handsome young Highlander. After all, she had only met him a handful of times, every one of those visits in the company of her family.

But still, she had thought that the response would have elicited some enthusiasm on the part of Gavin, for he was the one who had pushed so hard to resolve the issue of her former betrothal.

Enthusiasm, she thought. Ha! Nothing! At least James Gordon had had enough decency to write a letter to her—a letter filled with explanation and apology. But Gavin had not even deigned to come and see her.

Seeing no purpose in dwelling in self-inflicted misery, Joanna sat up in her bed and drew back the damask curtains. Feeling a pang of hunger, she knew that she herself would not be sleeping for hours yet. Her body was still telling her that this was the time to rise and go scavenging for food. Pushing herself to her feet and reaching for her clothes, Joanna decided to check on Margaret one more time before trying to sleep.

There had been no reason to put the mute woman in chains. It was evident to all that Margaret herself had erected iron bars that imprisoned her more effectively than anything man could construct.

She had remained in a continuous trancelike state for the past two days. Unable to recognize anyone or anything around her, Margaret had simply remained in one of the small chambers off of a narrow corridor leading from the kitchens, and after the initial curiosity had worn off, none of her fellow servants had shown any interest in her or in her well-being.

Stepping into the corridor from her room, the young woman faced the guard who seemed to always be by her door. The Lowlander appeared surprised to see her.

"The laird thought you might already have retired for the night, m'lady. He left a message for me to give you in the morning."

"A message?"

"Well, m'lady, you probably heard that Peter came for the laird this morning."

"Peter?" she asked, trying to remember the name.

"Aye, he was searching the villages south of here for some sign of a priest who was here . . . before this one that was murdered."

"Oh! Aye . . . Peter!" Joanna blurted out, recollecting.

"Well, the laird wanted me to tell you that Peter has found the old priest. He's in a spital house for lepers. He said there was no way for Peter to drag the old man all the way here. And since the priest wouldn't answer any questions of a Lowlander—"

"What happened?" she asked impatiently, watching the man's frown darken.

"Well," the warrior scratched the back of his neck. "The laird and the Earl of Athol decided to ride back with Peter and question the man themselves."

"Are you telling me they are gone?"

"They are, m'lady. But—"

"He told me he would take me with him." He had implied as much when they had gone to the abbey. She'd wanted to be present when he questioned anyone who knew anything.

"He said to convey his apologies. He hoped to be back tomorrow or the next day. And he also wanted me to tell you not to be . . . well, too angry with him . . . but he was not going to take you visiting any lepers!"

She gaped with disbelief at the Lowlander, coloring brightly and feeling like a shrew. Nonetheless, she forced a smile and nodded, turning down the corridor.

Coward, she thought, turning and heading for the kitchen. Gavin Kerr was no more than a coward. Too afraid to face her for fear of her seeing through him. Too afraid of her seeing his lack of joy over the news from James Gordon.

Joanna was still fuming when she reached the door that led to Margaret's small room. Even here, Gavin had put a couple of his men at either end of the corridor. Not to keep the mute woman from escaping, of course, since Gavin knew that her room, like so many others, had panels that led to the secret passages of the tunnels. The men, she knew, were to serve as a deterrent to others in the household from paying unwanted—or un-friendly—visits.

Acknowledging the nod of one of the men, Joanna silently pulled the door open and stepped into the dimly lit chamber. Just where she had left her, Margaret lay curled in a small heap on the straw pallet in the corner. As she stepped into the room and closed the door quietly behind her, she saw the woman's eyes open and stare in her direction. Even this was no different than how she had behaved before. Still, the emptiness of her gaze opened up to Joanna a vision of unfathomable depths of despair.

Knowing that Margaret could hear and understand despite her inability to speak, Joanna had been hoping to draw her out of this death trance. Each time she'd come to visit, she had talked to her. But she had yet to get any reaction from the mute woman.

"I could not sleep," Joanna whispered gently. "And I was a bit hungry as well." She took the couple of short steps and reached the side of the bed. Crouching before the straw, she spotted beside the wall a full bowl of broth and a wooden cup half filled with some clear liquid. It filled her with a sense of relief that at least the cook Gibby had finally taken pity on this pour soul and sent up some food.

Placing her hand gently on Margaret's tightened fist, Joanna appraised the older woman's ghostly face. "I spent too many months down there alone, Margaret. The one thing I prefer—now that I can walk among the living—is having someone's company when I eat."

This was a lie, of course, but right now the truth about herself was hardly important.

Joanna's eyes again came to rest on Margaret's distracted face. Other than the very few spoonfuls that she'd been able to force-feed the woman in the past couple of days, Joanna knew that Margaret had not eaten at all.

Putting a hand behind Margaret's head and adjusting her own position until the woman's head was cradled in the crook of her arm, Joanna picked up the broth and brought it to the dry, cracked lips.

"I don't know where you are, Margaret," she said gently. "But as long as your body is still among the living, we need to feed you some of this broth."

She poured a small amount of the liquid down her throat. The mute woman sputtered, made a choking sound, and then closed her eyes before clamping her mouth shut and turning her face away.

"She did the same thing to me."

Joanna almost leaped out of her skin at the sound of the voice behind her. But she didn't have to turn to know who it was.

The sound of Mater's shuffling feet moved in behind her. Rather than putting Margaret's head back on the mattress, though, Joanna held the woman tightly to her chest. Frozen, she found herself wondering whom it was she was trying to protect, herself or Margaret.

"I tried to feed her, too. But she seems to have lost the will to live."

Joanna felt Mater's cloak brush against her shoulder as the abbess stood over them. There followed an eerie silence while Joanna gently laid Margaret back down on the mattress and ran a gentle hand over her graying hair.

"I didn't think any of the people here would care for her to live."

The thickness of the old woman's voice drew Joanna's eyes upward until she looked into her face. Hidden in the shadows of the hood of her cloak, Mater's eyes were the only things that she could see. She shivered at their brightness.

"Surely . . ." she stopped and cleared her throat, desperately wanting to hide the fear in her voice. "Surely, Allan would care."

"That I cannot tell you." Mater crouched stiffly beside her. "He was quite disturbed at her running away the way she did. I don't know that he has had time to think it through so far as to realize that she needs our help."

Joanna just nodded silently and stared at the bowl of broth. Reaching out self-consciously, she repositioned the dish. No matter how hard she tried, the idea of being alone in this room with the old woman made Joanna's blood run cold. It was sheer foolishness, she knew, especially when she considered that for so many months she had lived fearlessly, a disembodied spirit, in the tunnels beneath Ironcross. But now, again among the living . . . Joanna shuddered, feeling Mater's bony hand rest on her knee.

"What is wrong, Joanna?"

"Wrong?" The sound that came out was barely a hoarse croak. She cleared her throat. "Nothing! There is nothing wrong!"

"Why do you fear me so?"

She had to do it. As important as her next breath was for her body, being able to face this woman was suddenly as important as her very soul. She slowly turned her face and looked into Mater's gray eyes. "What makes you think I am afraid?"

"You've been to the crypt!"

Joanna felt her face burning with heat. She didn't dare break eye contact with the old woman; that would be an admission to guilt. It would be an act of cowardice. But then, there was no way she could reasonably deny having been there. She had left plenty of proof for any-one who might look closely enough.

"You don't have to hide when you come to us there."

Joanna opened her mouth, but she had lost her voice. Looking into her face, all she saw were Mater's large eyes in a halo of darkness. She felt herself beginning to shiver uncontrollably.

"You are one of us," Mater said thickly. "In fact, you are more than welcome to join us in two nights. 'Tis time you learned."

The full moon, Joanna screamed inwardly. She was inviting her to be part of their fiendish ceremony at the full moon.

" 'Tis only what you do not understand that causes your fear. I want you to come. It will make you realize the purpose behind all that we stand for. Behind all that we are."

Joanna fought to gather her courage as she looked into the abbess's luminescent eyes. "Why not explain it to me now?"

"I will not do it justice. And, in truth, 'tis not my position to relay the centuries-old tales of our ancestors without our sisters."

"You are their mistress."

"I'm a guide, sister. Nothing more than a humble escort."

"And what did you do?" Joanna asked, drawing in a tremulous breath. "What has given you the right to such a position?"

There was a sudden wavering in Mater's gaze.

"There must have been a reason for you to leave your kin at Ironcross Castle and take your place leading the women at the abbey."

For the first time, Joanna thought that she could see the wrinkled shadows of her face coming to view from beneath her hood.

"For me to be . . . to feel like one of you, I need to trust you," Joanna said quietly. "Trust *you*, Mater."

Mater's eyes came to her face. "There are many in our flock who do not ask the truth and yet follow us in this journey." She slowly put a bony hand on top of

Joanna's. The incredible heat in her touch made Joanna start, but she forced herself to keep her hand where it was.

"But *you,* lass," Mater continued. "You are one who does not easily bestow her trust."

"Not twice, Mater."

"And have I done anything to cause you to distrust me?"

Joanna looked steadily into the older woman's eyes but did not answer her. Instead, she repeated her earlier question. "Why did these women pick you to become their guide?"

Mater lifted her chin slightly as she answered. "Because I have shared, in some ways, in the fate of our predecessors."

"Shared?" Joanna repeated hesitantly. "I have been told those crypts have been there for centuries."

"Aye, 'tis true. But we still share their suffering to this day, Joanna. Some of us . . . too many of us . . . share in their pain."

"What kind of pain?"

"The pain . . . the pain that comes of man's lust, of his abuse and rape and murder."

Joanna twisted around sharply and looked into Mater's face.

"They . . . they were raped and murdered? Is that how those women died? And you?"

A silence fell between them. Mater hesitated, and Joanna felt a rush of air on her face. She glanced quickly at the door, but it was closed, and she turned back to the abbess.

"What happened to you?" she repeated.

"I was raped by . . . a man." Mater's voice was pained. "I was chosen to guide our flock because, in the abbey women's eyes, I endured the same torment. My body, too, had been defiled."

Joanna suddenly felt unable to speak. A tight knot had grown in her throat, and Gavin's earlier words slowly started racing through her mind. Words of her grandfather's infidelity to the woman whom he had wed.

"Who . . . ?" she managed to get out. "Who was responsible?" She couldn't finish. Instead, searchingly, she looked into Mater's still, inscrutable face.

The older woman looked away. " 'Tis not for you to dwell on the past. 'Tis not *your* guilt to carry."

" 'Twas Duncan, wasn't it?" Joanna felt as if the name would choke her. " 'Twas my grandsire who raped you."

Mater's eyes slowly turned and focused on her own. The sudden vulnerability that Joanna saw in their depths told her more of a tortured past than the woman's words could ever convey.

"This is not your guilt to carry, Joanna!" Mater's voice rasped in the dim light. "You must push it from you."

"I cannot!" She desperately entwined her burn-scarred fingers with the gnarled bones of the older woman's hand. "Make me understand. I am tired of this confusion. I need to see the past so that I can face the present."

"I can teach you the history of those tombs."

"Nay! I want to learn *your* past. *Your* connection with the blood that flows through my body."

"I tell you 'tis not *your* guilt to bear," Mater argued.

"But do you not see that it must be mine to bear? It always will be until I know the truth."

Mater shook her head.

"Mater, help me," Joanna pleaded. "Without knowing, I have been taught to hate. Without realizing, I have put a blindfold over my own eyes! Let me see! 'Tis my right, Mater!"

The old abbess took another moment to gaze into Joanna's eyes before looking away into the darkness. "What more do you want to know? 'Twas he. Your grandsire, Duncan."

"He took you against your will?"

"He took me as he was used to taking any woman whom he saw and fancied."

"But there is a difference. Others, perhaps, were willing."

"He never understood the difference," Mater said

softly. "As far as Duncan MacInnes was concerned, he had a right to the bodies of all who lived on his lands."

Joanna stared, nausea gripping her middle, sickened at the thought that the very blood she felt pounding in her temples was the same blood that had flowed in the veins of such a monster.

"He took you against your will, and then he threw you out?"

Mater didn't meet her gaze but looked away instead into the darkness.

"Tell me the truth, Mater," Joanna's voice shook with desperation, with the need to know and to understand. "What happened to you?"

The old woman's eyes snapped back to hers. "I ran away! In my struggles to fight him off, I had been beaten. I was torn and bloody. After he left me, I could not stay any longer at Ironcross. I would not live with the fear that at any time he might decide to do the same thing to me again. So I ran away." Mater let out a shaky breath. "That night, I left the only place I had ever lived, and crawled into the hills. The full moon shone down on me and I wept with despair. In truth, I almost hoped that some wild animal might find me and relieve me of my shame. But 'twas not to be. The Lord had other plans for me. The women of the abbey found me. They took me into their care."

Mater's eyes took on a faraway look as they stared into an empty corner of the room. "They were compassionate and strong, those women. They never asked any questions. They just accepted me as I was."

"So that is how you stayed and became one of them. Became their leader."

"You know, Joanna, I think I would have believed my life blessed if that were all I have to tell." Mater's gaze returned to fix on Joanna's face. "But there is more. I did not know it then, but I was with child. Duncan's child."

Joanna took one of Mater's thin hands and held it tightly between her own. "What happened to that child?"

"I . . ." The old woman's voice was choked, and it

was a long moment before she spoke. "Foolish as I was, I thought that the bairn might be better off raised as Duncan's own. Though a bastard, the bairn would live a better life at Ironcross than in the ruins of the abbey among poor women who could barely manage to feed themselves."

"So you went back."

"Aye. I went back. And I will die again every time I think of it."

There were tears now, and Joanna saw them coursing down the wrinkled face.

"If I had thought the first time was a penance for my past sins, this time was the punishment for even living. When Duncan heard I had returned, that I was in the kitchens, he came to me and dragged me into the scullery. Aye, right out there—with the others looking on! I begged, I cried, I pleaded with him. It all meant nothing to him. He raped me again, and more brutally than before. And what is worse, I remember—even as I lay sprawled beneath him, thinking my flesh had been torn asunder—I remember thinking, fool that I was . . . that perhaps there was a way to make some peace with him . . . for the bairn. When he was done with me, I told him that I was carrying his child."

Mater raised a shaky hand and stabbed away the tears that hung on her sharp, bony chin.

"Duncan laughed. It was a vile, drunken, disbelieving laugh, and he told me that he would take care of it. And then he left me there." She let out a mirthless laugh. "I never even had a chance to gather myself together. I looked up and saw your grandmother standing by the door. Aye, that was Duncan's way of taking care of it. He'd gone to his wife and told her to see to it."

"Did she help you?" Joanna asked, choking on her question.

"Help me? Aye, she helped me. Lady MacInnes was young, and did not yet know Duncan the way she would someday. She called me a whore." Mater held Joanna's hands tightly in her own. "She called for one of Duncan's men. He dragged me out the front entrance to the

Great Hall and threw me down the steps into the courtyard.''

"Nay," Joanna whispered raggedly, unable to hold back her tears. "It cannot be so."

"Aye. 'Tis the truth. Every word."

"I know of my grandmother's hatred for you. 'Tis then that it all started?"

Mater nodded. "Aye, she has always blamed me. Seeing me there and knowing it was not the first time, since I carried his child."

"Still, for her to carry her hatred for so many years."

"A woman does not forget." Mater paused and her eyes took an unnatural brightness. "But 'twas what I said later, when I was thrown out, that she holds against me. I fell down the stone steps and landed on my belly in a bloody heap beneath the great iron cross that hangs above that door. I could feel the warmth of the rushing blood against my legs, the pain, and I knew that already I'd lost my child. But then I looked up at the moon, and when I saw the iron cross, I remembered the tales of the women who were buried in the vault. The ones that the women of the abbey still venerated. Everything came together in my mind then. I was a victim, just like them. I was lying sprawled in my own blood, as they had in theirs.''

Mater's hands squeezed Joanna's hard. She was sure that the old woman did not even know that she was hurting her.

"I cursed her then. The wind came up, strong and fresh, and I cursed your grandmother. I should not have done it, but 'twas she who stood above me."

"She had hurt you."

"Nay. 'Twas Duncan who hurt me. Only he. As the years have passed, I have never held a grudge against your grandmother. She was hurt as well. He used her, too—I know that—and tortured her like any other woman.''

Joanna stared, tears streaming from her eyes, her heart ripped from her chest.

"I cried out to God against their lust and their brutality. I shrieked the curse of Ironcross Castle. The wind whipped at those who looked upon me, and I brought back that curse with my cries. I invoked the Power. 'Twas then that she started hating me. 'Twas then that she began fearing me."

Margaret stirred slightly, but settled again on the straw bedding.

" 'Twas then that I became Mater."

Chapter 32

As the first rays of morning sun were breaking across the sky, Joanna wrapped herself in her cloak and stepped into the darkness of the passages behind the panel door in her chamber.

She needed to go to the vault. She had to see it again.

In the past, she'd treated the crypt as a place of evil. To Joanna, it had been the unhallowed ground of fiends and their rituals. But now Joanna understood it to be a place of goodness, a sanctuary, a temple from which the women drew sustenance as well as peace.

She needed to go there and experience that herself, look at it with a new eye, feel it with an open heart. And she needed to go there to undo all she had prepared. After hearing the abbess's story, a story in which her own grandfather had played the most horrible part, Joanna simply could no longer see herself as Mater's judge and executioner.

Their talk last night had ended with Joanna asking about the ritual. Mater had explained it as the prayers that their sisters offered to keep away the violence and the lust of the lairds. Prayers! That's all she had said. But Joanna did not believe prayers were capable of killing people.

Not that Duncan had not deserved to die after all the misery he'd caused so many women. But what could explain the other deaths—of his sons, and Joanna's mother, and the servants who had perished as well?

Perhaps what Gavin had said before had been true. The power of the curse was at work, but perhaps the human hand controlling that power was not Mater after all.

Making her way through the darkness of the tunnels, Joanna desperately hoped it was so. Indeed, since their talk together last night, Joanna had decided that no MacInnes would bring any more harm to the old woman.

Mater had suffered enough.

The moon rested atop the crenellated ramparts of the Old Keep as they rode into the courtyard. Leaving his steed with the stablemen, Gavin stared at the giant iron cross, gleaming in the torchlight over the door of the Old Keep.

They wanted women. They were warriors. They deserved them . . . or so they thought.

Wild eyed and drunk, they rode out—you know the look, laird, the old leper priest had said—*and across the gorge their lust-crazed shouts rang to the skies. The moon, full as a nine-month bride, lit their way. The men, drunken, possessed, riding across hills and into the valley of the virgins.*

When the church roof at the abbey blazed up, the flames scorched the very sky. The light from the fire could be seen from Elgin to Aberdour.

Binding the women, they dragged them out and tossed them like deer across the saddles of their waiting steeds. A few of the villagers and the chaplain of the abbey protested, and the warriors cut them down like dogs. And so they rode back, bloody and hot with killing and lust. Back they came to their laird, full of themselves, boasting, cruel.

Tossing aside his great drinking horn, the laird stood on the steps of his keep, smiling like some pagan king, his feet spread and his huge fists on his hips. Above him, the great iron cross shone brightly on the wall of his new keep, and a great fire burned in the courtyard before him. The women were wild, thrashing against their bonds and crying out as, one after another, the warriors dumped them from the backs of the horses into the dust.

A virgin. Aye, a virgin. How long had it been, the laird thought, the throaty bark of his laugh cutting through the night. Ah, a virgin to bury himself in? That's what he'd sent them after!

Strip them all, he commanded. I shall have my choice

of them. That one! Nay, that one! By the devil, I shall have all of them!

There in the courtyard, beneath the full moon and the cross of our faith, they stole the maidenheads of the innocent saints of that abbey.

'Twas a horrible night, a night of evil that this laird wrought.

And then the women cried out, cursing him. Torn and bloodied, but still proud and strong, they spat in the dirt of that courtyard and cursed. Invoking the power of God, the power of the cross, the power of the moon and the earth herself, they cursed him and all who followed him, unrepentant.

The laird had them struck down. His men beat and kicked them. Before that iron cross, they inflicted again and again their foul lusts upon those guiltless women.

But then, when he thought they were finally broken, the laird heard the women's voices rise. Louder and louder they moaned and wailed until their laments drowned out the foul laughter of those monsters. The voices rose higher and higher until they touched the moon, and that white glowing orb turned crimson with shame.

They all stared, those warriors. Then someone shouted, The cross! The laird looked on it, the once-shining iron now red with innocent blood. Spitting in the dirt, he drew his sword. He would show them. The bloodlust gleamed in his wild eyes. He raised his sword over the first woman. He would hack her body into a thousand pieces and burn her in that fire. Then he would do the same to all of them. He was laird of Ironcross Castle. He would not be cowed by these witches' tricks.

But before his sword could descend, the wind came. As the women's voices continued to wail, the wind grew wild, sweeping across the loch and blasting the walls of the castle. Never before had anyone seen such power.

The laird staggered and fell, and the warriors backed away. They watched as the gust swirled about the women, watched as their bodies writhed as if possessed, watched as the sparks of the bonfire swept around them, watched as one by one, the women dropped lifeless to the ground.

Then, as quick as it came, the wind died, leaving behind only the bodies of the women.

Without a sword riving them in two, without a dagger cutting their throats, all from the abbey were dead. And with them the laird—his neck broken, his unseeing eyes staring up at the full moon.

*No one knows who took the bodies and buried them in the vault beneath the keep—*Have you seen the crypt, laird? *the priest had asked.* It does not truly matter who put them there. However it was they came to rest there, the Highland women knew where they lay, and they began to appear. Every full moon, every year, they would come.

They would come. And they would remember!

Gavin stared at the red stain that covered the giant cross above the door. How much was legend and how much truth, the ancient priest had shrugged, was anyone's guess. But the lairdship of Ironcross Castle passed on to other, ill-fated men, and eventually it came to Duncan MacInnes.

The old leper priest had looked hard at Athol and then at Gavin. He knew more of Duncan that he cared to recall, he'd said. And he remembered the laird's death.

Gavin crossed the courtyard and ducked through the arched passageway into the kirkyard. Past the graves of former lairds, past the unmarked remains of countless others, he stepped into the little church.

He stood there for a long while as thoughts of dead innocents flooded through his mind. Thoughts of the women of the abbey, of those who had died so senselessly in the fire. Thoughts of his own family.

For the first time in his life, Gavin allowed his grief to spill out of him. Kneeling before the wooden cross in the darkened chapel of Ironcross Castle, he wept.

He was standing there when she opened her eyes. The moon was streaming in, bathing her bedchamber in a bluish glow. Gavin had come to her.

And it was obvious what he had in mind.

Shamelessly, she let her eyes take in every bit of his glorious and naked body as he approached the bed.

His voice, a low growl, started her body tingling with anticipation. "I was waiting for you in my chamber, but you did not come." With one hand he grasped the blankets and cast them roughly aside.

She thrilled at the way his eyes traveled the length of her body. It was as if her thin shift could prove no barrier to his scorching gaze. "I wondered if perhaps you had no wish to see me. You went off . . . without saying a word . . . I didn't know you were back."

Gavin lowered himself beside her. One of his hands reached out and touched the neckline of her shift, running his fingers lightly over her skin, sliding downward over the smooth linen. She bit her lip, gasping with pleasure as his fingers gently squeezed her hardening nipple.

"I am here to apologize for that."

"Oh, is that what you are here for?" Joanna's gaze flickered over the fully aroused manhood pressing against her thigh.

Gavin smiled, following her eyes. "Aye. The old priest . . . well, Peter's concern that he was at death's door forced my hand. He was the only one, I thought, who would tell us the truth about Ironcross Castle and its past."

"And did you learn—?"

"Later," he ordered, pulling at the single tie at the neckline of her shift. Then, with a mischievous look, he slid the thin material down her body. Joanna moved slightly, and Gavin quickly tossed the garment to the side. "I haven't been forgiven, yet."

"But I—"

"Nay, lass. We will have plenty of time to talk about the priest after you have granted me your pardon."

Joanna shivered at the gleam in his eyes. "I—"

"I wronged you, and I deserve to suffer the penance of your choosing," he continued with mock-seriousness, draping a leg over her belly. "I must make amends. Force me to work hard, Joanna. I will sweat for your mercy."

His one hand slowly traced the curve of her breast.

"I am no expert . . . oh." She gasped as his mouth settled on her nipple. "I am no expert in methods of punishing a man like you. And besides, in seeking forgiveness, I have always believed we were given tongues for a reason." She stopped as Gavin raised burning eyes to her face.

"You are right, my love," he said huskily. Flicking his tongue over her nipple, he slowly moved down along her belly, the tip of his tongue scorching her skin as he went. When he reached the mound of curls, he raised his head. "But as far as methods, perhaps I can help."

"You had better," she said thickly, already consumed by the whirlwind of colors and light that were firing through her brain.

"Lie still, and do exactly as I tell you. That will be my greatest punishment."

She looked into his dark, clouded eyes and saw the glints of humor. She didn't know how far this game would go, but if she had her way—and she *would* have her way—the impending torture would be sweet, exquisite . . . and mutual.

"Spread your knees," he ordered.

Although she had given herself to him many times in these past days, her face still flushed with heat. But looking at his surly expression, Joanna knew she had no choice. So, slowly, with a pleasure she knew approached wantonness, she opened herself to him.

"I am twisting in pain," he said hoarsely, dipping his head and tasting her.

She almost came off the bed.

"Now, you will have to lie still if you want me truly to suffer."

She lay back against the sheets, struggling to do as he'd ordered.

Gavin's head dipped again, his tongue stroking the sensitive spot. Joanna moaned with pleasure.

"Lift your hips," he encouraged. "Tell me you want more from me, my love."

She arched her back and lifted her hips, grinding her soft mound against his devouring mouth. Teetering on the edge of the sheer madness of release, she whispered, "More."

He moved his hands beneath her, cupping her buttocks and delving even more deeply with his tongue, and she felt the physical world unravel.

Joanna cried out, and as violent shudders rolled through her, she let the waves of pleasure carry her with their power.

When she opened her eyes, he had moved up on her body and was looking at her in a way she had never seen. There was a pleased smile on his full lips, but there was also an expression of tenderness and love in those black eyes.

"So I'm forgiven?" he asked with a note of arrogance, placing slow, tantalizing kisses on her eyelids, her cheeks, her throat.

Joanna didn't answer, but instead lifted her hand and framed the hard lines of his chiseled face. She was his, and he was hers, forever. Finally, she could dare herself to dream. Finally, all of her preparations of the past months undone, she could set her mind to live and to let live.

Slowly raising her head off the bed, she kissed his lips and placed her hands firmly against his shoulders as he moved between her legs, readying himself to enter her.

"Not yet. I am not done punishing you."

With a slow and devilish smile, he eyed her breasts, but before he could do anything more, she forced him onto his back.

"As a sinner, lass, I may be too far gone to withstand any lengthy penance you have in mind," he whispered.

She ignored his complaint and moved over him, letting her breasts brush sensuously against the hair on his chest. With excruciating slowness, she kissed his lips and explored his mouth with her tongue. His body was tense, every muscle knotted and taut. When his hands began to slide over her back and buttocks, pulling her against his throbbing manhood, she pushed him away and moved down his body.

"Nay, Joanna, this is . . . I . . . I cannot take much more of this."

She smiled and peeked up at him, letting her tongue circle his navel before moving still lower. She felt his whole body tense under her touch, and listened with pleasure as he gasped when she ran her tongue slowly over the entire length of his fully aroused shaft.

"Now spread your knees, my love," she whispered.

A deep rumble of laughter in his chest brought a smile to her lips. Delighted, she dipped her head and took him into her mouth.

"Joanna!"

She raised her head and glanced up at him. "Now lift your hips!" she ordered, again bringing another surge of laughter to his rigid body.

Taking him again into her mouth, she suckled hard on his manhood.

He sat up so fast that she didn't have a chance to move. Taking her face and hair in his hands, Gavin drew her to him and crushed his mouth to hers. Too consumed in the demanding thrusts of his tongue, she could hardly complain as he lay back down with her atop him, his engorged member pressing against her so intimately.

"Wait!" he growled, tearing his mouth away. "Am I forgiven?"

She lifted herself slightly and slowly took him into her body. "You are, my *love*. But you have a lifetime of penance ahead of you."

Their eyes met and the humor dissolved into the air, as something gentle and deep passed between them.

"I love you, Gavin."

"I don't want to lose you."

"You never will. I am yours, forever."

"But you should know, I have ghosts from my past. They haunt me."

"We'll drive them away," she whispered, moving with deliberate slowness. "The same way that we've driven out mine."

He gripped her buttocks tightly, and she knew he had to be pressing the limits of his control.

"Have we slain yours?" he growled through clenched teeth.

"We have," she answered. "You helped me to open my eyes."

"I want you, Joanna."

"You have me. I am yours."

"Forever."

"I'll always be with you."

"But I am afraid," he said huskily. "I am afraid of losing you."

"There is no need to fear," she answered. "Open your eyes, Gavin, and see me. Open you heart, and you will keep me always."

"I need you, Joanna."

She tried to blink away the tears in her eyes. "Say it again, Gavin."

"I want you . . ." He started to thrust slowly into her. "I need you."

"Say it, Gavin," she commanded, feeling him deep within her.

"I love you."

Chapter 33

Curled in each other's arms in Joanna's bed, Gavin had spoken first, telling her of the ancient priest, so close to death, his flesh and his eyesight destroyed by leprosy, and yet still so proud and disdainful of the Lowlanders. Gavin told her that if Athol had not been present, he doubted the priest would have deigned to relate the horrible origins of the Ironcross curse. And when he was finished, Joanna told him what she'd learned from Mater about the abbess's terrifying experience with Duncan.

"Aye, the old priest knew of Duncan's rape of Mater. But I don't think he knew that she'd been with child." He pushed a strand of hair off Joanna's brow and thought back over the old man's words. "The first time that Mater disappeared, everyone thought that she'd just decided to leave and join the women of the abbey. But when she came back a while later, the whole castle witnessed her misery. They all heard her cries of anguish when she was raped and thrown into the courtyard."

"Holy Mother," she whispered, rolling onto her back and staring at the canopy above them. "Cleanse this blood that runs in my veins."

"Stop it, Joanna," he ordered, turning her to face him. "Duncan took his foul nature with him into his grave. The old priest swore that, for all their flaws, Duncan's sons were always kind to the people of Ironcross Castle."

He tipped her chin up until he could meet her gaze. "And there was something else that the priest said about Mater. Something she apparently did not tell you."

Joanna looked steadily into his eyes.

"When Mater came back to Ironcross the last time, Margaret and Allan were with her in the kitchens."

"You cannot mean those two witnessed their sister's rape?"

"Aye. They did," he answered quietly. "Allan was just a lad. Margaret, the youngest of the three, was barely more than a bairn, perhaps three or four."

"How could he do such a thing? How could he be such a monster?"

Gavin gathered her tightly to him. "The priest said that Margaret never spoke a word again after that night."

"You mean, she could speak before?"

"The priest says that she did, that she was no different than any of the other children running about the castle. But after that day, after they found her huddled and crying against the wall in the kitchens, they never heard her speak again."

"This explains a great deal," Joanna murmured.

"What do you mean?"

"The day I overheard the two of them in the vault, Mater asked Margaret why it was that she had been able to walk away from her suffering, when Margaret must still be tormented after so many years." Joanna looked up into Gavin's eyes. "This was what she meant. She was referring to Margaret's witnessing of Duncan's cruelty!"

Gavin nodded. "Aye. That makes sense."

"And what about Allan?" she asked. "How could he grow up and become the steward to Duncan and to his sons? To see such a crime must have crushed him!"

"The priest told us that the boy vanished the very same night. Some thought that perhaps Mater had taken him with her and left Margaret behind. But then, about a fortnight later the lad came back, noticeably thinner but seemingly resigned to what he'd witnessed."

Joanna placed her chin on Gavin's chest and looked thoughtfully in direction of the panel. "Did the priest mention where Allan had gone?"

"Nay. Why?"

"Down in the caverns, by the underground loch." Her eyes returned to his. "There are drawings on the walls.

They could have been done by a child. I just wondered—"

"And you think Allan took refuge in the caverns?"

"He surely knew the way," she argued. "If he had
escaped to the abbey and to Mater, she never would
have allowed him to return."

Gavin nodded. "Would you take me there?"

"To the loch?"

"Aye." He nodded, throwing off the covers and climbing from the bed. He picked up his kilt and wrapped it
around him.

"Now? In the middle of the night?"

"Why not, love?" He turned and offered her a hand
out of bed. "You think I have forgotten? I *know* this is
your customary hour for prowling about and stealing
things!"

The damp smell of the earth filled Gavin's senses as
Joanna led him into the large cavern beside the underground loch. He followed her gaze to a small pile of
bedding half hidden beneath a low overhang, and his
brow immediately furrowed.

"You lived like this? On this wet and cold ground for
so many months? You could have died, and no one
would have—"

"I did not die," she interrupted, taking him by the
hand and drawing him toward the walls on the opposite
side of the cavern. "And for most of the time since the
fire, I lived in relative comfort high in the tower, in the
south wing. If it hadn't been for you driving me out of
there, and—"

"Hold, lass. Now you're making me feel guilty."

"As you should," she quipped, holding her torch
above her head as they reached the farthest wall. "Here
are the marks," she said, her voice dropping to a
whisper.

Raising his own torch high, Gavin stared at the rough
images. Judging from their simplicity and their height on
the wall, one could easily think they had been done by
a child. And they were exactly as Joanna had described
them. A cross and, beneath it, the prone sticklike figure

of a woman. And not far away, another stick figure clutching a head by the hair and, in the other hand, a large knife or sword. Gavin brought the torch closer and leaned down to take a better look. At the swordbearer's feet there was another image—something that seemed to be faded with the passage of time.

" 'Tis a cup," Joanna said quietly.

"It seems to be catching the blood," he responded.

Gavin noticed Joanna's shiver as she moved closer to his side. "From the severed head," she finished. Suddenly she pointed to the cup. "Look!"

Gavin turned. From the cup a thin line of marks stretched along the wall of the cavern, as if someone had struck the wall at intervals as he had walked. The marks disappeared into the darkness at the very back of the cavern. Taking Joanna by the hand, he began to move along the markings.

"I never noticed these before. But then, I never looked this closely."

"They had to be there all along," he told her over his shoulder. "They are as faded as the rest of the marks."

The cavern roof sloped downward quickly, and in a moment Gavin was walking with his head ducked. A narrow fissure in the side wall came into view, and as they stepped into the tunnel, the laird turned to Joanna.

"Is this another way of getting back to the keep?"

"I don't know." She hesitated. "Nay. We're going in the direction of the vault."

The passage was higher here, and Gavin straightened up. As they continued, he could feel the growing reluctance in Joanna as he pulled her along by the hand.

They broke around another bend and she came to a stop. "We cannot go on."

"Why, Joanna? This is no different than any other time you have roamed these caverns by yourself."

"But 'tis," she pleaded. "You're with me, and I have a terrible feeling that something will go wrong."

"I'll take you up to—"

"Don't!" she ordered. " 'Tis *your* life that I am worrying about. 'Tis *you* whom I want away from that vault."

"Joanna, we have come this far, and I am not going to turn around and forget about this—unless you're too afraid to continue." He knew he was baiting her. "If you would prefer, I'll take you back up to the keep. I am certain I can make my way back down here and find where this tunnel leads."

"You are not taking me back to the keep," she said stubbornly, her eyes flashing as she marched past him.

Loosening his dirk in its sheath, Gavin smiled wryly and quickly caught up to her, once again taking hold of her hand.

"I want you to know that I have already been to the crypt."

Her surprise was evident in the way she pulled back and tried to stop. But he tugged on her hand and continued. "I found my way back there." He turned and smiled into her face. "And nay, despite what everyone says, I did not vanish nor die a horrible death the moment I stepped into that sacred chamber."

"You . . ." She cleared her throat. "Was there . . . anything—"

"I discovered your work, Joanna. Or what I thought must have been your doing. The rushes? The trenches on the floor covered with straw? Do you think Mater would not have seen that?"

"Is that why you were so brutal with me on the day we went to the abbey?"

Gavin stopped and, grabbing her tightly around the waist, he drew her slender body to his. "I don't think making love on the side of a mountain is—"

"I didn't mean that," she said quickly. "I . . . before that . . . You are a rogue, Gavin Kerr."

"And are you still considering going through with it?"

She shook her head. "Nay, I cannot! I have already undone all of that. After hearing the truth of Mater and my grandsire, I just cannot imagine bringing any more harm to her. Guilty or not guilty, I just could not go through with it."

He stopped and kissed her mouth with a passion so fierce it left her breathless.

"I love you, Joanna," he whispered. "But I must tell

you now that if we find that Mater is the murderer, we will bring her to justice, no matter what she has suffered."

Joanna stared back at him. "Then I'll pray that she is not guilty."

Chapter 34

When Gavin pulled open the heavy oak door, the stench that greeted them brought bile to Joanna's throat.

Revolted, she stood at the entrance as he stepped into the chamber. The room smelled of dead and rotted flesh. Not far from her foot lay the headless corpse of a sheep. Staying where she was, Joanna shot a glance at Gavin.

He looked back at her. "To think you spent the winter in the tower room when, all the time, you could have been here!"

"Stay where you are, Gavin," she said shakily, staring past him.

The floor at the far end of the room seemed to be moving. Gavin turned and raised his torch high in the air, and she saw him flinch and back up a step at the sight.

Joanna moved beside him, and looked up into his face. He was as pale as the full moon. "What is it?"

"Rats," he whispered through clenched teeth. She watched him draw out his dagger. "I hate rats!"

"You walk happily into a slaughterhouse, but you are afraid of a wee bit of a thing like a rat?"

" 'Tis not one wee bit of a thing. Look, there must be hundreds of them! And I am *not* afraid," he said threateningly. "I *hate* them!"

"Same thing," she murmured teasingly, lowering her torch and waving it, sending the vermin skittering into cracks and along the walls.

He growled at her.

Joanna surveyed with disgust the piles of rotting animal corpses. Chickens, sheep, dogs, what looked like a cow. "What . . . what is this place?"

"A butchery, I should think. But from all the old meat rotting on these bones, I do not believe this killing was done to feed any hungry mouths."

"I've no desire to stay here, Gavin," she said, panic prickling down her back.

"Nay," he agreed. "Nor do I."

Joanna turned back toward the heavy oak door. "But why would someone would use a room like this so far beneath the ground for butchering? Why . . . ?" The words withered on her lips.

"What is it, Joanna?"

"The cup!" She pointed at the ornate cup sitting on a small wooden table. "This is the cup!"

"What cup?" he asked taking a step at her direction but then pausing as a rat ran across the floor in front of him.

"This is the cup that I have seen Mater use every full moon."

He reached down and picked up the ornate piece, looking at it in the light of his torch.

"During their ceremony, Mater pours some liquid from this cup into the fire."

Gavin turned and gazed inside the empty cup. "Blood."

"They use this chamber for killing." She stepped back and glanced down the tunnel into the darkness before turning back to him. "We are not too far from the crypt. All the times I have passed this way, I never knew of this room. I never smelled these rotting animals."

"Well, I, for one, am happy that they use only animals," Gavin said, looking with curiosity at the bones and huge pile of assorted cadavers. "I have heard stories of some of the old religions that used other sacrifices as part of their ritual."

A cold breeze suddenly sent a chill down Joanna's back. She shivered uncomfortably and glanced back over her shoulder.

"Please, Gavin, put the cup back," she pleaded. "Let us leave this horrible place."

"Afraid?"

"I am not letting you taunt me," she whispered urgently, taking him by the arm. "We've seen too much already for one night. Let's be on our way, tomorrow is soon enough!"

"Aye, it certainly is!" He placed the cup back on the stone bench and straightened. "Tomorrow is the full moon."

"The full moon," she repeated numbly. "Mater has asked me to join them at their gathering."

Gavin took hold of her hand and started to lead her from the room.

"You have nothing to say about that? You're not objecting? You're not asking me to stay away?"

"Nay, I think you should go. In fact, I'll be there myself to keep an eye on you."

"You?" She looked at him incredulously. "There is no way you can be there and go unnoticed."

"You watched them for months," he said calmly. "Surely a wee bit of a thing like myself could manage to remain hidden for *one* night."

The warm caress of the breeze on her cold face awoke the mute woman.

Margaret opened her eyes and stared into the darkness of the windowless room. Throwing off the blanket that covered her, she sat up on the bedding and let the air swirl about her.

It was the full moon, she remembered, coming slowly to her feet. It was the time of the cleansing, and there was so much to do.

With her hands outstretched, she moved along the wall to the panel door and opened it wide. She took a deep breath and stepped into the passageway. She needed no light. She simply followed the wind.

It was the full moon, and there was so much to do.

The sun was already sinking in the western sky when Joanna woke up with a start from her restless sleep. Sitting up groggily, she gazed at the long shards of golden sunlight stretching across her bed and tried to remember where she was.

A sudden panic struck her as the realization sank in

that she must have fallen asleep. She looked at the windows, and realized that she had slept the entire afternoon away. When she lay down, she'd only intended to rest for a few moments.

As Joanna sat there, her dreams began to come back to her. All during her sleep, the images of what they'd seen beneath the castle had played in her mind. Slaughtered animals, a cup full of blood, dark walls closing in on them, with no way of escape.

Suddenly, remembering the reason for her worry, Joanna pushed the covers off of her and quickly came to her feet.

Tonight was the night of the full moon.

She wasn't certain if Gavin had truly meant to hide and witness the gathering of women. But if so, she needed to talk him out of it. The idea of him being down there amongst those who thought every man was an instrument of evil made her stomach queasy.

She had to protect him. Despite all his strength, he was no match for the power of their belief.

Quickly dressing, Joanna opened the door and, giving a nod to the warrior outside, started for the Great Hall. The growling of her stomach reminded her that she had eaten nothing since last night. Knowing that it was a long time until supper, she turned her steps toward the kitchens instead.

The shaggy hound Max greeted her in the corridor by the door of the kitchen. After giving his head an affectionate pat, Joanna stepped into the warm kitchen.

"Out! Out, you filthy cur!"

Joanna stopped dead in her tracks as the heavyset cook, Gibby, rushed toward her, wielding a huge wooden spoon like a broadsword.

"I—" the young woman began.

"Pardon, m'lady," Gibby said, forging past her. "Out, you thieving, good-for-nothing charmer."

With his tail tucked between his legs, Max scurried back toward the doorway and out of the cook's reach.

"Aye, you'd best stay away from me, you lazy—" Gibby turned back to the young woman, her face still red and her voice gruff. "Welcome, mistress. Are you needing something?"

"I know 'tis late," Joanna began, feeling suddenly as timid as the dog in the face of this woman who ran her kitchens with the same show of authority as Gavin ran his men. "But I had hoped—"

"Come and sit on this bench here," Gibby ordered abruptly, waving to a seat beside the large worktable. Turning a sharp eye to the kitchen staff, she barked, "Back to your work, you lazy imps, or there'll be no supper for any of you!"

Joanna did as she was told.

" 'Tis like having a troop of fairy folk working for you," the cook grumped as she moved to the side of the huge hearth and drew a platter of food covered with a linen cloth from a warming niche. Bringing it back to Joanna, she placed it before the young woman. "I knew you would be starved, mistress."

Joanna stared at the wonderful selection of bread and meat. The sweet aroma of the food filled her with contentment. "Gibby, this is far more than I ever could eat."

"Just do your best," the woman said with a wave of her hand, taking a seat on a solid stool beside the cooking fire. In front of her sat a bucketful of greens, and she continued her work preparing the supper. "We have to make sure we put some more meat back on your bones. Evan, turn that spit! If that side of beef burns . . . You are too thin, mistress. Och, by the saints! Mary, fetch a pitcher of wine for Mistress Joanna, and be quick about it!"

Joanna just smiled in return. For all the shouting, the boy turning the meat over the open fire did not appear overly concerned with her threats, and Joanna even noticed that several of the girls were exchanging covert looks of amusement at the cook's shouting. Starting on her food, Joanna realized that even before the terrible fire, she had never spent much time in this woman's company. Although rough in her manners, she could sense that the cook must have a gentle heart beneath.

Her trencher was nearly empty before the portly woman spoke again.

" 'Tis mighty decent of you to take care of Margaret the way you have been."

Joanna looked up into Gibby's round face. "I am . . . I was just surprised that the rest of the household was doing nothing for her."

"With her killing the priest, and with the new laird being so angry . . ." The heavyset cook looked down at the greens in her hand. "We just didn't think 'twas right to go against his wishes."

"There is something that you should know about your laird." As Gibby glanced up, Joanna looked her directly in the eyes. "He is much different from any of those who have gone before. And I am talking about my own kin as well. Gavin Kerr is a very good and compassionate man. He is one who truly believes in taking care of his people and in doing whatever needs to be done to guard them against harm."

"Your own father, mistress—"

"He was a good man, Gibby, but he had no interest in being laird. He led too peaceful a life to be bothered with the problems of running a castle and its lands. In truth, if my father had been the one who discovered Margaret with a knife in her hand and the chaplain dead, he would have had her hung that day and been done with it. But look what Gavin Kerr has done. He waits until she comes to her senses." Joanna pushed the empty trencher away. "And with Mater. I am certain 'tis obvious to all of you how much he respects Mater. Now my father, the best MacInnes laird of any of them, thought her mad and never even once bothered to ride over to the abbey or to look after them."

The cook's sudden pensiveness told Joanna that she had struck a chord. Well, she thought, it was about time these people started appreciating their new laird.

Coming to her feet, she smiled and nodded gratefully toward the food. "Thank you, Gibby. 'Twas very nice of you to save a plate for me."

As she turned toward the door, the quiet words of the

cook froze her steps. "Word has it that you'll be joining us tonight."

Joanna turned slowly and faced the woman. "Mater asked me to come. So I thought . . . I thought I might."

"That will truly make Mater happy, mistress. Of the whole year, tonight is the most special."

"Special?" She swallowed. "Why, Gibby?"

"This is the anniversary, mistress!" the cook replied in a hushed voice. "The night of cleansing! But I cannot say more. I don't want to spoil the night. You'll see for yourself."

With a slow nod, Joanna turned and left the kitchens. Whatever was planned for this night, she was certain it was something she'd not witnessed before.

And as much as Gavin hated rats, Joanna MacInnes hated surprises.

Chapter 35

The chamber whirled around his head, but Gavin forced his eyes open, staggered to his feet once more, and crashed into the wall by the window.

They've poisoned me.

The thought burned through the haze of fever, and Gavin realized that he was on the floor again. A cold sweat soaked his skin, and the light in his bedchamber was growing dimmer.

I'll not die until I get to Joanna!

Gavin felt the pain rip through his belly, and shoot like lightning into his brain.

I must warn her. I cannot let them kill me yet!

Half an hour earlier standing in the small kirkyard, Gavin had felt the first cramps grip his insides like a claw. Moving away from the men working on the MacInnes tombs, he had escaped to his chamber. The food he'd taken in the Great Hall! He hadn't eaten from the same platter as Athol and the rest, he remembered. Gavin had arrived late for the noon meal, and someone had placed a trencher of food before him. Too occupied with his talk with Athol, he hadn't even looked back.

Gavin opened his eyes, unsure whether night was falling or he was growing blind. He was not even certain how long he had been on the floor this time, and he attempted to wipe away the sweat that was stinging his eyes. But his arms were limp, lacking the coordination for even so simple a task.

The pain in his belly seemed to be lessening, and he managed to push himself erect on legs that wobbled like a newborn foal's. He squinted at the door. It seemed a hundred miles off.

Just then, he heard the panel door in his wall open, and turned his face toward the sound of footsteps.

"Joanna," he whispered weakly, trying to keep his head up.

His words froze in his mouth and his hand moved by reflex toward the dirk at his belt. Gavin's fingers, though, could not grip the haft of the dagger.

He peered into the gray eyes that approached. In those cruel eyes, Gavin saw hatred. In them, he saw death.

"He was in the kirkyard earlier, m'lady! I can tell him you're looking for him."

Joanna whispered her words of gratitude to Andrew and watched the giant Lowlander go out into the courtyard. Through the open doors she could see the torches were being lit, and she considered running after Andrew. Be patient, she told herself. Gavin was sure to come back in soon.

Clasping her cold hands behind her, she turned and strode into the Great Hall. Stopping by the entryway, she looked about uneasily and almost leaped out of her skin when Max put his wet nose into the palm of her hand.

An unsettling sense of imminent doom seemed to hang in the air. Nay, don't be foolish, she thought. He is outside checking on the construction. His own men had seen him. What place could be more safe, she argued silently, patting the dog on the head and starting to pace the hall.

Realizing that she was beginning to attract curious glances from the servants preparing for the evening meal, Joanna turned her steps toward the kitchen. She would pay Margaret a visit while she was waiting. She hadn't looked in on the ailing woman all day.

In a few moments, she reached the door of the small chamber and, holding up the wick lamp she carried, found the same guard on duty. With a quick nod that she hoped would not give away her agitation, she reached for the latch.

Instinctively, Joanna looked first in the direction of

the panel when she entered. She had no intention of being surprised by the presence of Mater again. But there was no one there, and the panel of the wall was closed. Shutting the door behind her, she turned to Margaret.

The straw bedding in the corner of the small chamber was empty.

Startled, she scanned the room. The bowl of broth and the cup lay untouched where she had left them last night. The woman's meager possessions, brought here on Joanna's directions, sat undisturbed in a corner.

Joanna turned and opened the door. Without so much as a glance at the warrior, she closed the door again and hurried down the corridor. Moving quickly through the kitchen into the Great Hall, she knew there were only two possibilities—Margaret had left of her own will, or Mater had taken her.

Either way, Gavin must know.

In the Great Hall she broke into a run, ignoring those beginning to gather there. In a moment she was down the steps and heading for the kirkyard.

The air was cool, but Joanna didn't feel it as she hurried across the courtyard and into the arched passageway. In the kirkyard, she spotted a few men still working by the light of a torch, but as she got closer, she could see Gavin was not among them.

She couldn't slow her pounding heart, nor could she calm her agitated state as she approached the men.

"Have you seen the laird?" she called out the group.

Suddenly, she stopped. On the grass behind the men, Joanna could see the large stone slab that had covered her parents and the poor soul that had been thought to be her. As every hand paused and the men stared with surprise at her, Joanna looked down into the open grave at the enshrouded bodies of her beloved family.

Stunned by the unexpected sight, she stepped back, and an older worker moved between her and the grave.

His voice was kindly. "You are looking for the laird, mistress?"

Feelings of grief that Joanna had thought were behind her suddenly welled up in her chest, and the young woman could not speak for a long moment as she fought to control her feelings. Forcing herself to focus on what she had come to do, she looked up at the man and nodded.

"He has not been here since late this afternoon."

"Not here?" she repeated, dumbfounded.

"He was standing where you are, telling us what to do and then he turned pale, mistress, like someone who's had a wee bit too much ale. He went off that way, mistress."

When Joanna turned to look at the Old Keep, where the man's hand was pointing, out of the corner of her eye she caught sight of the moon rising behind the hills across the gorge. The pale white orb was full and threatening.

Wordlessly, she turned and broke into a run, back through the arched passageway and across the courtyard. Fear clutched at her insides as she glanced up at the bloody iron cross, and up the steps into the Old Keep she flew. At the open doorway she barreled into the chest of the Earl of Athol, bouncing backward and nearly falling down the steps. The Highlander's hands reached out and grabbed onto her hand, steadying her.

"What is it, Joanna? You look like the devil's at your heels!"

She found herself fighting back tears, and cursed herself inwardly for her weakness.

"Have you seen Gavin?" she managed to get out.

"I thought he told you."

"Told me what?" she asked shortly.

Athol glanced behind him, making certain that no one was within earshot. His gray eyes then focused on her face. "He was going to the crypt, to witness the gathering of the women."

"You mean he already left?" She struck the giant Highlander in the chest with her fist, eliciting a startled look from him. "Of all people, *you* should know how dangerous those passages can be. How could you let him go alone? What kind of friend are you?"

"Who says I'm his friend? That bullheaded Lowlander is no more a—"

"Hold your tongue, John," she said shortly. "I know you."

As Joanna tried to go around him, Athol's large hand descended on her shoulder, stopping her in her tracks.

"Trust him, Joanna," he said calmly. "He has all of this planned."

"But how can he?" she snapped. "He is by himself down there."

Unwilling to tarry any longer, she pushed at the tall man's hand and moved quickly around him. She had to get down to the crypt and try to get Gavin out of there before Mater and the women arrived. Perhaps she still had time, Joanna prayed, running for the kitchen and the passageway behind the huge hearth.

Perhaps it was not too late.

Gavin found his eyes starting to clear as he stared at the reflection of the candle against the ornate cup.

What a fool he'd been, to wish for death for so many years. And now, here he was, a future of love and life seemingly within his grasp, only to have the threads of his life suddenly pulled taut against the cutting blade of misfortune.

Gavin twisted his hands, feeling the leather cords cut deeper into his wrists. His ankles were still bound with the short but stout cord that had allowed him to walk, or rather stumble, down from his chamber. He looked about the little room. The stench of the place was horrible, and he glanced at the decayed carcasses.

What do you know? he thought with disgust as a small gray creature appeared on the pile. Food for rats, after all.

His captor had left him only a short time ago, leaving the door ajar. He wouldn't get far with his ankles hobbled, that was for sure. Well, if he could make it as far as the chasm, perhaps falling into Hell's Gate would be preferable to having his throat cut. Gavin glanced at the cup that would catch his blood. The metal gleamed in the light of the candle. The candle!

Gavin hauled himself across the floor as quickly as he could. Though the distance was only a few feet, his head was spinning from the exertion. Reaching the candle, he lay back on the hardpacked dirt, lifting his feet and carefully stretching the cord over the tiny flame.

"Burn, you bastard," he cursed.

Out of the corner of his eye, he saw two more rats appear by the dead animals, looking at him with curiosity and moving cautiously toward him.

"Burn, you scurvy—"

But the cord had barely begun to smoke when the door swung wide, sending the rats scurrying for safety.

"Well, laird, I see I cannot leave you alone for a moment."

Gavin glared at the figure in the open doorway.

"Are you ready to meet your fate?" Athol asked breezily, stepping into the chamber.

Chapter 36

Mater stood in the center of the crypt and beckoned. Her heart in her throat, Joanna stared into the cold room at the few women who were moving about.

"You've decided to join us early," Mater said, holding a hand out to her.

"I . . . I thought it might be best . . . if I were to witness the entire ceremony." As inconspicuously as possible, Joanna glanced about the vault, looking for some sign of Gavin. But the deep shadows offered plenty of hiding places beyond the tombs. He could be anywhere, and in any case, it was too late to do anything about it now.

Mater turned to Molly. "As long as our sister is here, why not give her something to do?"

The housekeeper turned shyly toward her. Joanna knew that even in their little community, the fact that she was the daughter of the last laird created an uncomfortable gap between their positions. To make her feel more at ease, the young woman moved forward and reached for the bundle of rushes in the older woman's arms.

"Perhaps I could do this?" Joanna offered.

Molly nodded and handed her the bundle. Turning to the other two abbey women who were working silently, Joanna followed their lead in the preparations. But whenever she could, she peered into the shadows, searching for Gavin. She knew there was not a thing she could say if she were to find him hiding in this chamber. But somehow she hoped that seeing him might ease the hammering of her heart, the gnawing worry that was eating at her soul.

But he wasn't here. As the women continued to work in silence, she realized that he simply wasn't in the vault.

"Do you think Margaret will be able to perform her duties or shall I—"

"Of course she will!"

Molly's question and Mater's sharp response immediately drew Joanna's attention.

She moved toward the two older women. "I went by Margaret's room before coming down here. I could find no sign of her there."

The abbess turned and met Joanna's direct gaze. "No matter what her troubles might be, Margaret knows that she is the bearer of the cup. She will perform her duties. My guess is that she is already by the loch preparing for that portion of tonight's ceremony."

"By the loch?" Joanna asked in confusion.

Mater turned to Molly and gave her a small nod. "Why don't you tell the lass? She is better off knowing ahead of time, so that she can more fully appreciate the ritual."

Joanna felt the vault tip and start to spin as she turned her gaze on the housekeeper.

The thin woman straightened up to her full height as she began. "Once a year, at this full moon—the same night that our sainted sisters' souls were called to heaven—we begin our monthly remembrance with a special ritual at the loch."

"Why . . . why at the loch?"

"We go there to witness the killing," Molly said simply. "Other months Margaret brings us the filled cup here, but on this one night of the year, she waits at the loch and goes through the ceremony with the rest of us."

Joanna thought for a moment that her heart would burst from her chest. She remembered the image of Margaret sitting with the dagger and the slashed throat of the priest in her lap. She could no longer hear all of what the other woman said.

Where could Gavin be? Holy Mother, Joanna screamed inwardly, let it not be what she thought.

". . . anointing the brows with the fresh blood . . . 'tis a cleansing . . ."

Wild eyed, Joanna stared at Molly. What was it that she'd just heard her say? Dropping the rushes in her hand to the floor, she started for the door. But the firm grip of a hand on her arm jerked her to a stop.

"Do you hear them? They are here!"

Mater's bony fingers dug into her flesh, but the old abbess's voice seemed to be coming from far away.

"This is no time for you to leave, sister. We are about to begin."

Joanna felt a knot tighten in her throat. "But—"

"All will be well, child. All will be well!"

"Stop your damnable chattering and come loosen my hands."

"What would you have done if I hadn't decided to come down here ahead of time?" Athol leaned a shoulder casually against the door frame and looked on.

"I would have had my throat cut." Gavin twisted his hands behind him. "But when I met St. Peter, I would have demanded to be sent back so that I could torture your miserable carcass. Hurry, you indolent sloth of a dog; we've little time."

Athol straightened in the doorway. "We have time. I could hear the women gathering in the vault. Honestly, you're fortunate I saw the candle through the crack in the door. But where is . . ." He glanced at the dead animals with distaste. "Where is Joanna?"

"Loosen my hands," the laird demanded. "I am not going to let this . . . Athol!"

Gavin's shout was not quick enough to alert the Highlander. The hilt of the dirk struck John Stewart hard behind the ear, and without a sound he crumpled in the doorway.

Through the darkness they moved. The sputtering hiss of candles and the shuffle of feet on dirt and stone were the only sounds that broke the deadly silence of the cavern.

Clutching the burning candle in two hands, Joanna felt her tears coursing freely down her face as she looked at the back of Mater's head and moved with the rest toward the underground loch. The women had "honored" her in giving her the place behind the abbess, but as she walked, she could feel the eyes of the rest of the white-robed flock burning into her back, checking her every move.

She had no choice but to go along. She was outnumbered and could not fight her way free of them, so she decided to put on her best face and pretend to be both willing and interested—at least until they reached the loch. The only hope that was sustaining her now lay in what Molly had said about the women witnessing the killing. If what she feared were indeed true, perhaps Gavin was at least still unharmed.

Joanna felt with one hand for the small dagger at her belt beneath the white robe they had given her. She would die before she allowed any of them to hurt him.

She smelled the damp, cool air of the loch. They were quite close now. As she followed Mater into the cavern, Joanna scanned the area quickly in search of Gavin, but there was no sign of him there.

By the edge of the water, though, on the slab where she had noticed the dark stains, a small fire crackled by a wooden table. Beside it stood Margaret, garbed all in white, as silent and still as the dead.

She glanced along the water's edge to the far side of the cavern. There was no sign of the straw bedding or her meager belongings. A shudder raced through her at the thought that she had once taken refuge in this place, even walked upon this altar of evil.

The women formed a half circle around Margaret, and Joanna watched Mater move to the center beside her sister. Silence fell over the group, and Mater raised her thin hands in the air.

"Sisters!" she called. "For the souls of our dead sisters, we invoke the Power."

"Mater!" the women's voices proclaimed in response. "We invoke the Power."

No sooner had the echo of the words died when a swirling wind swept across the waters of the loch. Joanna felt every hair on her body stand on end as she looked about her in astonishment, the rushing air pulling at her robe.

"Sisters! For ourselves, in memory of their pain, we invoke the Power."

"Mater! We invoke the Power."

This was not like anything she'd witnessed before. The wind pushed at her. There was something in here with them—a force, a power beyond anything she could explain. Joanna stared as every one of the women raised their hands in the air, swaying and allowing the swirling breeze to caress their bodies. She felt the gentlest touch of a hand on her own face. Startled, she turned toward it. But there was nothing but the air. Full, charged, and warm as a summer night.

"They are here, sisters. They are with us," Mater chanted.

Stunned, Joanna watched as Margaret picked up a candle and moved quietly toward the passage leading to the slaughter chamber.

She was going to bring him here, Joanna screamed inwardly, a shaky hand clutching for her dagger.

Mater and the other women began to chant again, and Joanna's eyes scanned the faces of the gathering. They were all in a trance, swaying and calling as the air continued to swirl around them. She looked at Mater's face. The woman's gray eyes shone with the brightness of a hundred candles. She had the Power. She *was* the Power.

Joanna looked down at the rock slab, at the stains in front of Mater's feet. The red stain . . . the blood.

She started shaking her head. "Don't," she whispered. "Let me be wrong. Let it not be."

No one heard her. The air was whipping about them now with rapidly increasing violence. The sounds of the chanting were now blocked by the shrieking wind. She brought her hands to her ears, trying to keep out the sound. This was not real, Joanna told herself. There was no Power!

The shrieking cries pierced her brain; she could not keep them out. She shut her eyes, only to see things— the courtyard, the summer moon. There before the bleeding iron cross, the flames leaping up behind them, the innocent women of the abbey. The brutality of men. She cried out, and the vision was replaced with another. Duncan's face. Mater's.

A scream louder than the rest tore through the vision, and Joanna pressed her hands tighter against her ears. "No more!" she cried. "No more!"

Suddenly, a deadly silence fell over the group. Joanna opened her eyes slowly, certain that all eyes would be upon her. Amazingly, the gazes were not directed at her, at all, and she followed their stares to the darkness of the opening into which Margaret had disappeared. The air was dead and still.

Another scream cut through the semidarkness. A woman's scream. But it wasn't her own voice, Joanna realized. And this was no shriek of the wind.

With a wailing cry, she appeared. Lurching out of the opening of the passage like some wounded animal, Margaret staggered into view, wild and weeping.

"Ma . . . ki . . . Ma . . . ki . . . va!" The woman babbled incoherently as she cried and ran toward Mater. The candle was gone, and in its place, Joanna could see, Margaret held a long dagger.

"Where is he?" Joanna cried out, pushing forward. "What have you done with him?"

Hands clutched at her, grabbing her by the wrists and arms, and Joanna writhed to free herself as Margaret went down to her knees, started shaking her head and trying to speak.

"Ma . . . ki . . . va . . . ki . . . Wi . . . ki . . . la . . ."

"What are you saying, Margaret?" Mater asked, moving forward and raising her up. "Where is Allan?"

Chapter 37

Joanna watched Gavin being pushed into the light. His face, hard with anger, lacked its normal color, and his huge frame tottered unsteadily on legs that she could see were bound at the ankles.

With a cry, she leaped forward to run to him, but the hands of half a dozen women held her firmly in place.

Behind Gavin, Allan stepped from the tunnel and stopped short. The steward's face was hidden beneath the sloping roof of the cave, but the point of the gleaming dagger that he held to Gavin's back spoke clearly of his intent.

"What is the meaning of this?" Mater's voice, cold as mountain snow, chilled the very air in the cavern.

" 'Tis the full moon, sister. 'Tis the day to remember."

This was not the same man that Joanna had known. Something was wrong. It was in his voice, his eyes. Joanna felt a cold fear wash down her back, and she pulled at those who held her.

Mater took one step in her direction without ever taking her eyes from the Allan's face. "Why have you brought the laird here?"

Dropping his torch on the ground, Allan laid the blade of the dirk against Gavin's face and then shoved him with his other hand toward the rock slab by the loch. Joanna bit at her lip as a thin line on Gavin's cheek opened and blood began to run down his face and drip off his chin. Gavin turned and glared fearlessly at the man.

Mater's voice cut through the air with an edge as sharp as Allan's blade. "I asked you why you have brought this man here."

"He is the laird. 'Tis his blood that we will sacrifice."

Joanna tore a hand free, and she shook her head. The man was mad. Allan's face was a mask of fury, and she knew that he meant to do Gavin harm.

"Our saints never intended for us to shed human blood. 'Twas never our intention to bring more violence into this world."

"Ha!" Allan shoved Gavin closer. "Whatever their intentions were—or yours—it makes no difference. Violence begets violence, and the vengeance of God will fall on the sinner, to the seventh generation—"

"Nay, brother!" Matter argued. "This is wrong! 'Tis the *remembrance* of their sacrifice that brings us back here. 'Tis the power of the saints that we invoke, and their protection that we seek. There is no vengeance in forgiveness, Allan. You must release the laird. We will not go against the will of our long-dead sisters."

"No matter how strong your hatred?" he shouted. "I know what lies in your heart."

"You know nothing."

"I know the evil that blackens the hearts of these men, and still you think I can let him go?"

"Aye, Allan! You will let him go." Mater answered emphatically. "No matter *what* life has brought us—suffering or pain—it does not matter. We will not defile the memory of our sisters."

"Defile? Perhaps you have forgotten what that word means," he rasped, shoving Gavin into the circle of women and onto the slab of stone. He stared at Mater, and she looked back, unflinching. "But I have not forgotten *you*, used and thrown like a dog into the night. I have not forgotten how I watched you bleed your unborn bairn into the dirt beneath the iron cross."

Allan reached out and grabbed Margaret by the shoulder, bringing her roughly to his side. The mute woman's knees buckled, and she crumpled onto the rock.

"And look at her," Allan pointed at the woman at their feet. "*This* is our sister. A whore! But still our sister. And what of her? She has not spoken since that night, but she has not forgotten . . . and neither have I!"

The echoes of his voice had died away in the cavern before Mater spoke again.

"That was so long ago. That injury was done to me, and—"

"*He* is the cause of the injury!" Allan's bloodless face turned to Gavin. " 'Twas he who has caused us pain."

"Nay, Allan. 'Twas Duncan. And he is long dead."

"I know Duncan is dead, sister." He continued to stare at Gavin. "I killed him. I had to wait many years, but I killed him. As I killed his sons. Aye, they have all died for the sins they committed against our sisters. But none died as I had wanted them to. Only the priest died as he deserved! Too much secrecy, too much concern about what the whole world should know."

"Allan, you don't know what you are saying!"

"I know what I am saying," he shouted. "You think I am mad?"

"Allan—"

"Do you think 'tis easy to carry a secret in your heart for your whole life?"

"A secret?"

"Aye, 'tis I who carry the curse of Ironcross. 'Twas our great-great grandsire who was steward to the laird that summer night." His eyes were wild. "*He* killed the first laird. And his son and his grandson and his, in turn, have kept the curse alive. Aye, sister. We are the curse!"

Whirling around, Allan kicked Gavin's legs from under him and yanked the laird's head back, exposing his throat.

"I am the curse of Ironcross, sister. I am the hand of God. Now give me the cup and the dagger, and we will wash clean, once again, the sins of Ironcross Castle. Get me the cup, Margaret!"

Gavin jerked his head out of the steward's grip as Margaret struck at Allan. With the speed of lightning, the dagger in her hand flashed through the air, stabbing Allan in the chest. "Ki . . . Wi . . . Ki . . . yu . . . Wi . . . ki . . . ki . . ."

Stunned by the attack, the steward stared at the blade and hilt of the knife protruding from his breast, and then at his sister, still crying out in broken words and weeping as she backed haltingly away from him.

Gavin's move was quick. Dropping to his side, he swept the steward's feet with his own bound legs, and Allan dropped like a stone to the slab. Gavin was on him before the man could move, using his shoulder to drive the dagger deep into his heart.

As the laird kept his full weight on the man, the only sounds in the cavern were the last gurgling breaths of the steward, and the soft, whispered echo of a gentling wind.

Joanna shook off the hands holding her and dashed to his side. Ripping the dagger from her belt, she cut away the ropes binding his ankles and wrists. Gavin moved off the dead steward, but never even had a chance to get to his feet before Joanna threw herself into his arms.

"I thought I was going to lose you," she sobbed, unable to hold anything back. "I was sure that this was the end."

His arms pressed her fiercely against his chest. "I love you, Joanna." He rocked her in his arms. " 'Tis finished now."

His voice was still strained, and she quickly pulled away, checking him for signs of injury. His face was pale, but before she could open her mouth to voice her concern, he silenced it with a kiss. And there, in the silence of the cavern, the two clung to each other, savoring that simple act of love.

A moment later, Joanna helped Gavin to his feet. Aside from the cut on his face, he didn't seem to be wounded, but he still appeared to be weak. He wouldn't allow her to fuss over him, though, and together they made their way to Mater.

The group of women had moved off the stone slab, and the old abbess stood at the center of them, her arm around Margaret. As the group separated, letting Joanna and Gavin enter their midst, the young woman saw Mater's eyes lift and meet the laird's gaze.

"You know that we had nothing to do with this."

"I know," Gavin replied. "Your brother, it appears, had a ritual of his own."

"As children, we were told of the Ironcross curse," Mater started. "We learned the tales of the women. The stories of their deaths, and of the deaths of the lairds as well. But there was never anything said of our father or grandsires being in any way responsible for any of it." The old woman shook her head emphatically. "They were the stewards, 'tis true. But I cannot believe they were killers."

"I believe you." Gavin nodded. "After Duncan's treatment of you, it must have been easy for Allan to imagine the past as he wished it."

Margaret's head now rested on Mater's shoulder, and the old woman supported her weight, running a gentle hand through the weeping woman's hair. "I should have seen it, though, in the past. All those deaths . . . all the supposed accidents. And it wasn't only the lairds. Now so much makes sense. Whoever offended him, or challenged him, they all seemed to just vanish. I should have known."

" 'Twas Allan who frightened the priest into running away." Gavin nodded. "And he killed Father William when he found them returning to Ironcross."

Margaret's head lifted slowly and her eyes teared again as they gazed into Mater's. "Al . . . ki . . . Wi." She nodded.

"In Allan's mind, his sisters were as sacred as the saints." Mater looked down at the frail woman in her arms. " 'Tis the reason why he never allowed Margaret to wed when she was much younger. The killing of the priest had more to do with William touching her than anything else. In Allan's thinking, I suppose, that was a crime punishable only by death."

"H . . . ki . . . va . . ."

"He killed David as well," Gavin repeated, looking carefully at Margaret. "Athol had the stablehand watch this loch when he saw Joanna's possessions scattered about, but no one ever saw the young man again." He nodded toward the mute woman. "But it seems Margaret may have witnessed the killing."

The mute woman nodded slowly before returning her head to her sister's shoulder.

"On that full moon, the night when your parents were lost in the fire," Mater said as her eyes rested on Joanna, "that was the first time I sensed something gravely wrong in my brother. He was restless, and yet jubilant, and for no reason that we could see. 'Twas his behavior before the gathering that caused me to go back to talk to him afterwards. But by the time I came up into the passageways beneath the castle, the south wing was already ablaze."

"I suppose I was traveling the same paths as you," Joanna whispered, staring at Mater. "But I must have fainted in the passages of the south wing."

"The smoke was thick enough to kill."

Joanna and Gavin stared at her.

"'Twas you, Mater!" Joanna whispered. "You were the one who saved me from the fire. That was how you knew of my burned hands."

Mater paused a moment and then smiled grimly. "Aye, Joanna. I brought you down here with the hope that you would be safe. I went back to the Old Keep, but I couldn't find Allan. Everyone else seemed to be doing what they could to put out the fire, so I came back to you. But by the time I returned with the others to the loch, you were gone. Then, when you did not come to me, when you decided to keep your existence secret, I feared that you suspected us. I knew that I must leave you to find the truth for yourself."

"I could have died in those passages. But you saved my life, even after all Duncan did to you. All of this comes from the cruelty of my kin." Joanna pressed. "If it were not for the terrible sin against you, and Allan seeing it—"

"Nay," Mater interrupted. "My brother would have found another reason. 'Tis all so much clearer now, my dear. Even as a child, before ever witnessing Duncan's act, he was far too consumed with the past. 'Tis a family trait, it seems," The old woman gazed over at the still body on the slab. "His actions, his ways should have warned us long ago. While we were happy to sacrifice a cock pheasant at the full moon, he wanted to kill a dozen sheep. Now I know that he really wanted to be the high priest—like in the old religion—the slayer who draws blood."

Joanna gazed at the dead steward, his own blood seeping onto the rock slab.

"We were blind to it." Mater looked away.

"What do you want done with him?" Gavin asked, holding Joanna tightly to his side.

"He is . . . he was my brother, and I will grieve for him. I will pray for his soul. But I cannot forget that his actions have forever stained the pure memory of our sisters. He almost destroyed all we have strived for so long to remember . . . the promise of the healing Power."

Joanna felt the pressure of Gavin's hand and looked up and gazed into his dark eyes. The message was silent, and she agreed.

The young woman left his side and moved to Mater.

"Mater," she whispered, quietly drawing the old woman's gaze up to her own. "Word of Allan's actions, his ties to the women of the abbey, need never leave this place. You have done far too much for far too long to let one man's fall tear open the bond that unites so many." Joanna linked her hands gently with the gnarled bones of Mater. "Why not leave him with us? We will bury him in the kirkyard and take care of all that needs to be done here."

It was a long moment before Mater nodded her consent. "Will you come and see us?" she asked, looking deeply into Joanna's eyes.

"I will, and I'll bring my husband with me."

Mater's eyes sparkled as they glanced approvingly to the giant Lowlander. "Aye, you'll bring him to us. And we shall welcome him as our laird."

As the old woman and her sister turned to leave, Joanna stepped back beside Gavin, taking his hands in hers. In a single line the rest of the women followed their leader out of the cavern loch. The cook Gibby, however, moved out of her place and paused before the two.

"I should have known that Allan was up to no good when he came himself and fetched your platter this noon."

"And all along I thought it was your cooking that laid me so low."

The large woman blushed crimson.

Gavin smiled. "I thought it had to be something like that. But whatever he added to my food wasn't meant to kill me, since I am already starting to feel my insides."

The woman nodded in approval. "Get well, laird, and I'll cook you a meal that you will never forget."

"Aye, I'll hold you to that," he said as she joined the end of the line of women.

Joanna watched them until they all filed out, and she and Gavin were all that remained.

"I could kill you, Gavin Kerr, with my own two hands," Joanna exploded the moment they were alone. "Of all the stubbornness! I never witnessed anyone more obstinate than you. Damn it, you are not even a High- lander. What did you think you were doing, coming down here all alone?"

"Alone? Och, by the devil!" Gavin grabbed her hand tightly in his own and began pulling her in the direction that Allan had brought him in.

"Where are you taking me?" she asked, grabbing the torch that the steward had dropped. "And what are you going to do with that dead body?"

"I'm certain my three best warriors would be de- lighted to come down later and carry him up for a proper burial. But for now, my love, we cannot tarry here."

Joanna began to run to keep up with his lengthening strides. As they hurried through the passageways, she pulled on his hand, slowing him a bit. "Gavin, did you suspect Allan?"

"Aye, from the first time he took me into the south wing and made sure I went into the chamber with the bad floor. He placed some things of value, some books, where I couldn't help but see them. He wasn't the only one I suspected, but I soon saw that he was always ab- sent when an attempt was made on my life. Then, after the bridge was cut at Hell's Gate, I knew it couldn't be Athol, and I knew that whoever it was had to be strong enough to nearly shake us off those ropes."

"Then why didn't you stop him?"

"There was too much that I didn't know. Too many questions were still unanswered. I couldn't even be sure if Allan was acting alone, or as an accomplice to Mater and her women."

Joanna pulled on his arm, slowing him further.

"Then I am glad that you waited," she said innocently. "It would have been horrible to hold them responsible for a crime they didn't commit." She smiled and then shook her head. "Honestly, to think how much damage we could have done together, if we had been in agreement as well as being wrong."

Gavin nodded with a grim smile. "Aye. There wouldn't be a soul left alive at Ironcross Castle. We would have killed them all."

Joanna shuddered with exaggerated horror, and looked into the darkness ahead of them. "So where are you taking me?"

"You'll find out soon enough."

Grabbing her hand, the Lowlander hurried on. In just a few moments, though, as they neared the slaughter chamber, her steps began to falter.

"What else is there, Gavin, that you haven't told me yet? Please don't tell me that there are more dead bodies waiting for us."

He gave her a quick grin as they turned the last corner. "I wouldn't be that hopeful, my love. That would really be far too much to ask."

The sprawled figure of the Highlander lying motionless by the door to the chamber brought a gasp to Joanna's lips. "Is he dead?"

"If I were only that lucky," Gavin teased, motioning for her to bring the light closer as he rolled the Highlander gently onto his back. "Nay, he's not dead. John Stewart has too thick a skull to die from such a gentle tap to the head."

"Gentle . . . tap?" Athol groaned, his eyelids fluttering

before staying open. "My head has been split in two, and—"

"You blackguard!" Gavin scolded, taking a closer look at the gash to the side of the man's head. The blood had already started to harden at the cut, and a large, handsome lump was forming around it. "This whole time, while Joanna and I were saving the Highlands from the devil incarnate, you were up here taking a nap! What happened to watching my back?"

"Is there . . . och, stop the room from going around, will you?" Athol squinted at the two of them. "Is there something wrong with your back?"

"You were supposed to be down here in case of trouble?" Gavin prompted.

"Trouble? What trouble?" the Highlander asked, forcing one eye to open wider. "Is there trouble?"

Gavin looked up into Joanna's face and smiled. "My prayers have been answered at last. I believe, with this last blow, the good earl has indeed become an idiot, my love."

"Injured or not, you villainous dog, I won't have any Lowlander calling me '*my love*,'" Athol tried to shout before wincing and finishing with a whisper. "By His Wounds, I've a reputation to consider, you know!"

Epilogue

June 1528

A gentle breeze played against the pillars of the new abbey church as a silence fell over the gathering of women.

The light of the full moon poured in through the high windows on the side of the altar and blessed the three people and the bairn in a soft, bluish glow.

Feeling the reassuring touch of her husband's hand on her shoulder, Joanna reached out and placed their sleeping son into the outstretched hands of Mater. The abbess's gray eyes shone with affection as they looked down in the round face of the slumbering bairn.

This morning Joanna and Gavin had watched their child christened in the font of the chapel at Ironcross Castle. To their great delight, even Lady MacInnes had made the long trek northward. Though frail with advancing age, Joanna's grandmother had put aside her fears and her bitter memories of the past, and had accepted Elizabeth and Ambrose Macpherson's offer to accompany her on this trip. More than anything in the world, she had wanted to be here with her granddaughter and witness the baptism of her great-grandson.

And tonight, Joanna and Gavin had brought their son into the midst of their people for this second blessing. The new church had risen out of the ashes of the old with the aid of the Ironcross laird and his wife. These were now Gavin Kerr's people, and it would be a place of peace for the women of the abbey, as well as for all the rest who were returning to the lands and villages surrounding Ironcross Castle.

Tearing her eyes away from her son's cherubic face, Joanna looked up and caught her husband gazing lovingly on her. Her heart swelled with all that she felt for him. He'd brought her back from a life without a future, and warmed her with the rays of the sun. She knew that the flames of love burned within him. He cherished her beyond all others. And he had made her believe in the power of living.

"Sisters . . . and brothers!" Mater cried out, bringing Joanna out of her reverie.

"For the blessing of this child, we invoke the Power!"

The congregation answered in unison. "Mater! We invoke the Power!"

"For the healing peace this son of ours will bring to our land, we invoke the Power!"

As the warm breeze wafted in through the open door, Gavin and Joanna turned their gaze to the sleeping bairn in Mater's arms.

"We invoke the Power!"

Author's Note

Unlike our past works, in which we have tried to combine the history and politics of the sixteenth century with stories of love and passion, *Flame* is something a bit different. This novel represents our effort to bring our readers a dark and richly romantic tale, but one with a feel of Scotland's ancient, haunted castles—places with names like Fyvie, Cawdor, and Lochidorb.

There are curses that transcend time. There are ghosts who linger through the centuries.

And we are happy to admit that this book was written in response to the many letters we received after introducing Gavin Kerr in *Heart of Gold*. For those kind souls among you who wrote to us and asked for Gavin's story, thank you. We certainly hope you have not been disappointed.

We love to hear from our readers. You can contact us at:

May McGoldrick
P.O. Box 511
Sellersville, PA 18960
e-mail: mcgoldmay@aol.com
http: //www.romanceweb.com/mcgoldrick/index.html

SUSAN KING